SPELLBOOK

of the

LOST

and

FOUND

Moïra Fowley-Doyle is half French, half Irish and lives in Dublin with her husband, two young daughters and one old cat. Moïra's French half likes red wine and dark books in which everybody dies. Her Irish half likes tea and happy endings.

Moïra spent several years at university studying vampires in young adult fiction before concentrating on writing young adult fiction with no vampires in it whatsoever. She wrote her first novel at the age of eight, when she was told that if she wrote a story about spiders she wouldn't be afraid of them any more. Moïra is still afraid of spiders, but has never stopped writing stories.

Moïra's first novel, *The Accident Season*, was shortlisted for the Waterstones Children's Book Prize and received widespread critical acclaim.

For Alan

Prologue

That night, everybody lost something.

Not everybody noticed.

It was a Saturday night on the cusp of summer and the air smelled like hot wood and burning rubber, like alcohol and spit, like sweat and tears. It was warm because of the bonfire in the middle of the field, and because of the stolen beers, the wine coolers bought with older siblings' IDs, the vodka filched from step-parents' drinks cabinets. There was the hint of a strange sound, that some thought might have been a trapped dog howling, but most decided was just in their imagination.

Some kept drinking, thinking this was just another night spent in a field at the edge of town, close to that invisible line where suburbs become countryside.

Some noticed without really understanding what they'd

Olive

Sunday 7th May

Lost: Silver, star-shaped hair clip; jacket (light green, rip in one sleeve); flat silver shoe (right, scuffed at the toes)

Daylight is only just touching the tips of the trees when the bonfire goes out. I am leaning against a bale of hay upon which someone I don't know is sleeping.

I roll my head over to look for Rose, who I was sure was sitting, legs splayed, on the ground beside me. The grass is mostly muck at this point, beaten down by many pairs of shoes and feet. My own feet – bare, the nails painted a shiny metallic green that doesn't show up in the morning darkness – are dirty. So is the rest of me.

Rose isn't here. I call out for her but nobody answers. Not that I expect she'll be able to; sometime in the night she lost her voice from shouting over the music, from singing along to really bad songs and from all the crying.

Getting ready to go out last night, Rose told me, 'Our plan for the evening is to get excessively drunk and then cry.' She swiped her lashes with another layer of mascara, which seemed fairly unwise, given the aforementioned plan.

'Can we make the crying optional?' I said. 'My eyeliner's really good right now.' It had taken me twenty minutes, six cotton buds and five tissues to get it even.

'Absolutely not.'

I sneaked a look at my best friend's reflection. She blinked to dry her mascara. It gave her a deceptively innocent air.

'I don't know why you want to go to this thing in the first place,' I said.

This thing was the town's summer party. It's held in May every year. Until midnight it's filled with sugar-hyper children stuffed dangerously full of badly barbecued burgers threatening to throw up on the bouncy castle. Their parents bop self-consciously to decades-old pop music blaring from rented speakers while the teenagers – our classmates – sneak off to nearby fields to drink.

'I told you why I want to go,' Rose said. 'I plan to get excessively drunk.'

'And then cry,' I reminded her.

'And then cry.'

'Well, you know what they say,' I said to the back of her head. 'Be careful what you wish for.'

We slept in the field, which seemed like a good idea at the time. There is a growing chill despite the slowly rising sun and I don't know if it means that a storm is coming or just that I've been in the same position for far too long. I'm beginning to lose all feeling in my right shoulder, the one propped on the prickly pile of hay.

When I look down, on one bare and dirty arm I see the words: *If you don't get lost, you'll never be found.* They're blurry because my eyes are blurry; it takes five blinks for me to make them out. They run from shoulder to wrist and seem to be written in my own wobbly handwriting, although I don't remember writing them. When I lick a finger and rub at an *n*, it doesn't smudge.

For about as long as we've been friends, Rose and I have written what we refer to as our mottos on each other's arms. When we were younger, they were things like *You are beautiful* or *Carpe diem.* These days they're in-jokes or particularly poignant quotes. We both got detention for a week last year because of our matching block capitals reading *DO NO HARM BUT TAKE NO SHIT.* I must have written this one during the party, although when or why, I have no idea.

My head feels fuzzy. With a wince and a sigh, I drag myself out of the last dregs of drunkenness and shakily stand up.

I take stock: I am missing a shoe (the other is half buried in the muck beside me) and my jacket. My dress is covered in grass stains and smells distinctly of vodka. I have the beginnings of an epic headache forming and I seem to have lost my best friend.

'Rose!' I call. 'Rose?'

The boy on the hay bale twitches in his sleep.

'Hey,' I say to him loudly. I poke his shoulder when he doesn't wake up. 'Hey!'

The boy opens one eye and grunts. He has dirty blond hair, a stubbly chin and an eyebrow piercing. I vaguely remember dancing with him last night. He squints at me.

'Olivia?' he says hesitantly.

'Olive.' I have absolutely no idea what his name is. 'Have you seen my friend?'

'Roisín?' he says in the tone of someone who isn't sure he's saying the right thing.

'Rose.'

'Olive,' he says, sitting up slowly. 'Rose.'

'Yes,' I say impatiently. He's clearly still very drunk. 'Yes, Rose, have you seen her?'

'She was crying?'

I pick up my shoe and shove it on my foot, figuring that one shoe is still better than none. 'I know. That was our plan for the evening. Did you see where she went?'

'Your plan?'

6

I scan the field for any sight of her. There's a blue denim jacket crumpled up on the ground not far away. I take it because I'm beginning to feel very cold.

Pale blue light spills over the trees and into the field. My phone is dead so I don't know what time it is, but it's probably close to 6 a.m.

I start to make my way towards the road. The boy on the hay bale calls out to me. 'Can I've another kiss before you go?'

I look back at him and make a face. *Another* kiss? 'Not a chance.'

'See you around?'

I shake my head and walk away quickly. Most of my memories of last night seem to have disappeared with Rose.

I make my way around the field, scanning the faces of the sleepers (trying to keep my eyes averted from the ones who clearly aren't sleeping). It doesn't take long; she isn't here. I glance behind me and see that the boy on the hay bale appears to have disappeared, probably slumped on the grass. I am the only person standing.

I turn round in a circle, taking in the stone wall and the tangle of bushes surrounding the field, the fence near the empty road on the other side, the small line of trees separating this field from the next one.

There's someone there, almost hidden between two spindly pines, staring at me.

It's a boy. He's wearing a flat cap and an old, holey jumper that might be green or black – it's hard to tell in the shadows. He has a lot of brown, curly hair under that awful hat and is wearing thick, black-framed glasses. He has a hundred freckles on his skin and a guitar slung over his back. He looks like a cross between a farmer and a teenage Victorian chimney sweep. He is unmistakably beautiful.

Before I have time to break his gaze, he turns and walks away and I lose him between the trees.

I look down at myself, at my dirty dress and borrowed denim jacket, at my one bare foot and my grass-stained legs. I could be Cinderella, if Cinderella was a short, chubby, hung-over seventeen-year-old with smudged make-up and tangled hair. And, while I'm very glad that I don't have a dead father and an evil stepmother, I'm not entirely sure how I'm going to explain my current state to my parents when I get home. I try in vain to smooth the creases out of my dress and reach into the bird's nest of my hair to pin it back with the silver, star-shaped hair clip I tied it up with yesterday, but either my tangles have eaten it or I lost it sometime in the night.

My bike is where I left it, chained to the fence by the side of the road, but it takes me several tries to unlock it because my hands don't seem to want to work properly and my brain feels increasingly like it's trying to turn itself inside out. When I clamber on, my bare foot sticks uncomfortably to the pedal.

I pass a grand total of three cars and one tractor on the road into town. The clouds above me are getting very grey, almost as if the dawn has changed its mind and wants to revert back to night. My dress blows up in the breeze, but there's no one around to see so I keep both hands on the handlebars and try to ride steadily. Under the sleeve of my borrowed denim jacket I can see the tail end of the sentence written there: *you'll never be found*.

It comes back to me in a flash. Rose in my bedroom last night, staring at her reflection in my vanity mirror while pouring generous measures of Tesco Value vodka into a bottle of Diet Coke.

She said, 'If you don't get lost, you'll never be found.'

We'd drunk a fair amount of the vodka already and her words were slightly slurred.

'At this rate,' I said to her, 'the only thing we'll lose tonight is the contents of our stomachs.'

My prediction was accurate: another flash of memory has me bent over a hay bale, throwing up some unholy mixture of slightly Diet-Coke-flavoured vodka and the barbecued hot dogs that we all ate on sticks, posing for pictures, holding the phallic meat like rude children. My stomach lurches at the thought and I have to pull over to the side of the road to retch again.

If you don't get lost, you'll never be found.

I cling to the low stone wall by the side of the road like a lifeboat, and sigh. Without warning, it begins to rain.

Fat drops fall on the mess of my hair, darken my jacket, hit the dry roadside like cartoon tears. *Splat.* I have to blink them out of my eyelashes. I sigh again and drag my bike from the ditch.

I cycle home through pounding rain and with a pounding headache. Maybe it's that I drank too much and remember too little about last night. Maybe it's that Rose left without me. Maybe it's what the blond-haired boy said about another kiss. Maybe it's the beautiful boy I saw at the edge of the field, looking like he'd lost something. But I feel like I might have lost something myself, and I have no idea what it is.

Laurel

Sunday 7th May

Found: Old red leather-bound notebook,
thin and worn, secured by a black elastic band;
ripped-up pages out of three lost diaries

We went to the party because our diaries went missing.

Holly's disappeared first. Then Ash's. I only thought to
look for mine when five pages torn from Holly's showed
up in Trina McEown's hands on Monday morning. And if
there's one place you don't want to find your diary it's in
Trina McEown's hands.

You'd think at our age we'd be too old for gossip and
giggling. But Trina stood up on a desk in the middle of
the classroom as we were packing away after maths and
read excerpts to the class. She only stopped when Ash

got on the desk with her, red curls flying, and punched her so hard her nose bled.

We tried to explain, me and Holly, that a bloody nose is nothing compared to your every secret haemorrhaging like a torn artery, spoken in somebody else's voice, but Mr Murphy despises both metaphors and emotions, so Ash was suspended and Trina was excused from homework for the day.

That's when it started.

We sat in Holly's bedroom and I stroked her hair while she cried and Ash inspected her bruised knuckles. She wears them now like a badge of pride.

'I don't see why you care so much, Holly,' Ash said. '*I* wouldn't, if it were me.'

I stroked and stroked Holly's hair, long and blonde, blonde and long and soft under my fingers like my whispered *hush*. I wanted to say, 'It's OK,' but it wasn't, not really. There are things you tell a diary that nobody else should know. Not your best friends. Not your favourite sister. Not a classroom full of staring eyes and leering, open mouths.

'They pretend they never think those kinds of things themselves,' Ash said scornfully. 'Like they never have sex dreams. Like they don't have bodies that bloat and bleed. Like they never question the world around them or their own sanity.'

Holly cried so hard her quilt was soaked with it, salt water in every seam.

'I'll bet half the girls in that classroom masturbate. And all of the boys.' Ash snorted. 'They're just a bunch of repressed hypocrites.'

Holly sobbed into her hands and rivers ran between her palms. Tears dripped from the bed on to the floor. *Pat, pat, pat* into the carpet.

'Everybody's parents fight. Everybody lies. No one knows what they're doing in this bloody life.' Ash clenched her fists.

I whispered, '*Hush, hush*.' The carpet was sodden with Holly's tears. The force of her crying raised the bed and set it bobbing. The bedroom became a little lake. Folders full of school notes, pencils and hair clips, books and tissues and childhood bears floated in it. I held her hair so as not to fall in. Blonde and long, long and blonde and beaded with salty tears.

'I'd punch her again if I could,' Ash said. 'I will. Next time I see her nasty face. I'll break her fucking nose next time.'

'Hush,' I said to Holly. 'You'll do no such thing,' I said to Ash. 'If you get expelled, it's just the two of us against the rest of them.' Together we are a three-headed dog, facing an army of hundreds of staring eyes and leering, open mouths. Without Ash, we've lost our fangs. 'It's hard enough in school already.'

Ash had the courtesy to look abashed. She leaned back on her elbows on Holly's bed and said, 'Then you'll have to hold me back at the party on Saturday, because with a few beers in me who knows what I'll do.'

'I don't want to go to the party, Laurel,' Holly said to me in a whisper. 'I don't want to go anywhere they'll be.'

'They're everywhere, I'm afraid,' I said softly, plaiting her hair, threading the tears into the braids like pearls. 'In a place like this, there's nowhere to hide.'

'So we won't hide,' Ash said loudly, and she stood up on the bed, her school shoes scuffing the quilt. She stamped and said, 'We won't fucking hide. Who cares? We'll go to the party like everybody else, Cinderella; we'll be the belles of the fucking ball.'

The town summer party is hardly a ball. It's more of an embarrassment. But there is always precious little supervision and often unattended coolers filled with beer. The adults either turn a blind eye or they don't even notice.

Holly's tears slowed to a trickle.

'Think about it,' I said. Holly had until Saturday to decide. 'We'll be right there with you.'

I didn't say that the reason I wanted to go was very similar to Ash's. I didn't want to punch Trina; don't get me wrong. But I did want to know how she got Holly's diary. I wanted to know what she'd done with the pages she hadn't torn out. And if she didn't give them back, well, maybe I could do with a bruised knuckle or two.

*

That night I tore my room apart. I called Ash around eleven. 'My diary's missing, too,' I said.

She was silent for a moment. 'I haven't been able to find mine since the weekend,' she said.

In our three separate houses, we confronted our parents, we yelled at our siblings, but nobody confessed. I still can't quite imagine Trina McEown or any of her cronies somehow sneaking into our houses and taking our things, but I don't see how there could be another explanation. We only know that our diaries have disappeared and pages of Holly's turned up in hostile hands, that Trina and her friends, or somebody else, have read the missing pages, have torn out entire weeks of our lives to keep like butterflies pinned to a wall somewhere.

I want to know where.

Then we found the spellbook. It was like it'd been waiting for us. Like it knew we'd need it.

I say we found it, but really it was Holly. We were on our way to the lake after school on Friday. Ash, still suspended, joined us outside town and we walked past her house, to where the forest gets thick and dark. It was warm – hot, even – but something in the air felt like rain. On either side of the road there were scraggly trees, tumbledown walls with gaps in the stone like missing teeth, green fields turning yellow under this unlikely heat.

We swung our jumpers like skipping ropes, holding the ends of the sleeves and jumping over the body, singing mindless children's songs. Ash rolled her T-shirt up to make a bikini top and Holly and I quickly followed suit, unbuttoning the bottom of our school shirts and tying the ends in a knot under our breasts. Our bellies white as the undersides of fish, blinding in the sunshine they hadn't seen since last summer. We imagined what the teachers would say if they saw us now, bare-bellied and skipping with our ugly school jumpers, knee socks peeled off and stuffed in our school bags.

Holly was more cheerful that afternoon. With Ash at our side, we were a three-headed dog once again. We walked so close together our hair started to tangle. Brown, blonde and red.

Holly wanted to climb trees. She's always seemed a little younger than me and Ash, even though we're all the same age. Maybe the skipping made her think of childhood. Or maybe she was trying to become a kid again, to exorcize words spoken aloud about period cramps and fighting parents, about positioning the spray of the shower head just so between her legs.

We stopped at the giant oak tree in the fork in the road. We tucked our school skirts into our knickers and clambered from branch to branch, scratching our arms and legs and leaving sap stains on our bellies. Ash is arguably the bravest of us, but Holly climbed the highest. That's where she found the spellbook: caught between two branches like it'd been left there by a bird.

She called out, 'Laurel! Ash!' and dropped it down to us: a small, slim notebook, red and leather-bound, secured by an elastic band. Holly came down and we sat beneath the branches to read it. The first page said only *SPELLBOOK OF THE LOST AND FOUND*, like a title.

You can't not read on with a title like that.

We didn't recognize the handwriting, but Holly said she thought it looked familiar. On every other page were prayers to St Anthony, suggestions of offerings to the goddess Mnemosyne, a map to the River Lethe: findings and forgettings. Stuck to the blank pages in between were things that made the spellbook creak at the seams. Prayer cards and sweet wrappers with strange symbols on them. Foreign coins. Pressed leaves and strips of bark covered in straight cuts like ogham stones. Or scars.

The spell was on the very first page: a calling for the lost to be found.

We wanted our diaries found. So Holly suggested we try it.

At first it was like a recipe: gathering moss and branches, raiding our cupboards for olive oil, slipping saints medals out of our nanas' wallets, rooting through the Christmas boxes in the attic, looking for silver string. It was silly and secret and made us feel like kids making mud pies. None of us took it seriously, not even Holly.

By Saturday we had all the ingredients except for the waters of Lethe.

Ash was frustrated. 'What does that even *mean*?'

'We learned about it in Classics,' Holly told her. 'Remember? The Lethe is one of the five rivers in the Greek underworld.'

'So we're unlikely to find any of its waters in Balmallen, County Mayo,' I said.

But then we found some of Mags's poteen, a canister accidentally left at the back door of Maguire's pub (although Ash, reading this now over my shoulder, would like me to note that Mags rarely does things by accident; Ash sees conspiracies between the trees).

'We can use this instead,' Holly breathed, showing us the spell again. 'See? It says poteen can be used as a substitute. It's got to be hand distilled – which Mags's stuff is – and, if anyone infuses her poteen with ancient magic, it's Mags.'

So we took some of Mags's poteen to the town summer party. We sneaked away from the crowds and slipped into the woods. We cut our fingers and drank the burning alcohol and wrote out our losses on the branches of trees.

And that's when the weirdness started.

Moss became fur became dead animals on the floor of the forest. The trees became the spaces between the trees. We three held hands and made noises that weren't words, but that Holly said later were a calling. A calling for the lost to be found.

We came to in the morning, beside the giant oak at the fork in the road, each of us with scraped knees and bloody noses, tied together with silver string.

And, all around us, our missing diary pages covered the ground like a blanket of snow. In the field in the distance, the bonfire was still burning.

Calling for the Lost to be Found

You will need:

A charm or talisman. (A medal or Mass card of St Anthony or St Jude, a dowsing rod, a crystal pendulum or an arrow-shaped hagstone will work best.)

A glass bottle filled with the waters of Lethe, the underground river in Hades that makes the drinker forget. (Poteen is an acceptable substitute. Must be hand-distilled in a pot still and infused with ancient magic.)

A length of silver string.

Red ink.

Olive oil.

A handful of rowan berries.

A hazel branch.

A vine of ivy.

As many rose thorns as you have losses.

Moss gathered from under an oak tree.

Human blood.

To *cast the calling:*
Gather fresh moss from under an oak tree.
Soak it in olive oil and crushed rowan berries.
Anoint it with human blood.

Snap a hazel branch in two and form an equal cross.
Bind the bloodmoss to the centre X with an ivy vine.

Tie one end of a length of silver string tight around it.
Fix the cross to the branch of a tree.

Write your losses in red ink on the branches around it.
Pin each word in place with a rose thorn.
Wind the string round each thorn.

At the opposite end of the string, attach your talisman.
Let neither the cross nor the talisman touch the ground.

Wait for a sign.
If the lights go out, you will know the lost are listening.
If you hear dogs barking, you will know the lost have heard your call.
If you hear the howling, you will know the lost have answered.

Be careful what you bargain with:
Every lost thing requires a sacrifice –
A new loss for every called thing found.

What will you let go of?
What can you not afford to lose?
Consider carefully before you cast the calling:
It may not be for you to choose.

Be careful what you wish for:
Not all lost things should be found.

Olive

Sunday 7th May

*Lost: Parents' trust
(not for the first time)*

My parents are early risers. Every morning the smell of fresh coffee sneaks into my dreams before my dad's voice booms through the house. He throws open the doors to our bedrooms and stands on the landing, loudly reciting whatever his favourite poem is that week.

When I walk in the kitchen door, grass-stained and hung over, he is three stanzas into 'The Stolen Child' by W. B. Yeats. My mum is sitting at the table, reading the paper. She raises her eyebrows as I come in. The clock above the kitchen door tells me it's ten past seven. And yet I'd dared to hope that this one morning they'd sleep in.

'*In pools among the rushes / That scarce could bathe a star, / We seek for slumbering trout / And whispering in their ears / Give them unquiet dreams,*' intones my dad's voice.

'I always thought this one was kind of depressing,' I say.

My mum sips her coffee. 'Aren't they all?'

I pull my borrowed jacket tight around me to hide the state of my dress. I hope I smell of the strawberry bubblegum I found in one of its pockets, but in reality I probably just stink of vodka.

'So, on a scale of one to that time Rose threw up in your car after a party, how in trouble am I?'

My mum folds over the paper to the next page. 'We're rapidly approaching Rose-vomit territory,' she tells me.

'Right.'

My dad appears in the doorway from the hall. His voice gets progressively more ominous as he approaches. '*For he comes, the human child, / To the waters and the wild / With a faery, hand in hand, / For the world's more full of weeping than he can understand.* So. I see that you're home in one piece, albeit a relatively ragged piece,' he says. 'And by ragged I mean tired, dirty, drunk and grounded.'

I abandon any pretence and slump into a chair. 'Not drunk,' I mumble. 'Hung over.'

'Oh, well, in that case forget I said anything; please go about your day.'

I drop my head between my folded arms on the kitchen table. I turned my hearing aid off sometime during the party because the speakers kept making it scream tinnily in my deaf ear. With my good ear against the table and silence in the other, every sound is strangely magnified: my dad's heavy footsteps across to the stove; my siblings clattering down the stairs; my mum's coffee cup clinking quietly against her plate as she raises it to her lips; my own breath rasping between my teeth.

There's a thud on the table in front of me. 'This'll help,' comes my dad's loud voice. I raise my head and see a giant mug of black coffee. 'Freshly *grounded*, get it?' says Dad. He chuckles to himself.

My sister Emily bursts through the door as I take the first tentative sip. She stares at me.

'Whoa,' she says. 'You look like shit.'

'Emily!' Mum says sharply.

'Sorry, Mum. Olive, you look like defecation.'

Dad hides a laugh behind his beard. Mum's mouth twitches. 'Slightly better,' she says. Then she trains her eyes on me and there's something to the slant of the lines around them that makes me wonder if I'm in even more trouble than I thought.

My brother Max materializes bleary-eyed in the doorway as I plug my phone into the tangle of chargers on the counter beside the fridge. He has pillow creases on his cheek and is dragging Bunny, his tattered teddy, by one ear.

'Can I have a biscuit?' Max asks Mum. He's five. He always wants a biscuit. Cornflakes (a dog) sticks out his tongue beside him. He also always wants a biscuit. Is there much difference between a dog and a five-year-old boy?

'You can't have biscuits for breakfast,' says Emily, who slowly backs away from the cupboard she was about to open, obviously also looking for biscuits herself. Emily is thirteen, skinny as a snake and twice as mean. She probably shares half her DNA with some form of reptile.

Coco Pops (a dog) watches her with adoration. Weetabix (also a dog) snuffles around under the table for crumbs. The cat, Bacon, scratches at the back door.

With my battery five per cent recharged, I call Rose. There's no answer. I suppose there must be an equation to calculate the probability of Rose's hangover being mine to the power of N, given that she seemed so much drunker than me last night, but I doubt these things can be measured. Either way I'm sure she's sleeping it off somewhere. This isn't the first time I've had to cycle home alone. Still, I'd feel a lot better if she'd replied. I don't leave a voicemail because Rose never listens to them. I message her to call me instead.

I'm about to get up and take my coffee into my room when Mum looks at me.

'Did you meet a boy?' she asks me suddenly, folding the paper over to another page with feigned nonchalance. Emily, sensing that I'm about to be told off, perks up and listens in.

'In my life?' I say. An image of the curly-haired, freckled boy I saw this morning between the trees flashes into my mind. Old flat cap and guitar slung over his back. He must have been someone's cousin, or a friend from out of town. I didn't recognize him, and he was far too beautiful to be from around here.

'Last night,' she clarifies.

'Unsurprisingly, the town summer festivities were a mixed-sex event,' I say to the ceiling. 'As you will recall. There were quite a few boys there.'

Emily snorts.

'I'm a boy,' Max pipes up from the other side of the table.

'You're an alien,' Emily retorts.

'If I'm an alien, you have to be an alien, too,' says Max. 'That's how brothers and sisters work.'

'So you didn't meet a boy?' My mum's repetition of the query brings her would-be casual tone into question.

'Why?' Emily asks.

'Mind your own business,' I hiss at her. 'May I please be excused?' I take my mug of coffee and stand up on slightly wobbly legs.

'You're confined to the house and garden for the week, apart from school,' my dad reminds me. I nod and turn to go.

'He's trouble,' my mum says. She says it very softly, almost in a whisper, but I hear her clearly even over the noise of my family and the dogs. Nobody else seems to hear her at all. 'He's lost a lot and so will you.' Her eyes are far away. Her eyes are not her eyes. She looks at me and it's like someone else is looking through her. 'Stay away from him,' she says, 'or you'll lose everything.'

Then she turns to make breakfast as if nothing has happened, as if she was never talking to me. The newspaper flutters to the floor.

Hazel

Sunday 7th May

Lost: Jacket (denim, missing third button);
some bits of broken teacup

Mags comes into the pub at twelve. We open at half past. I've set the whole place out already: the stools off the tables, the counters wiped down, the glasses polished, the trap unlocked for Cian and the boys to roll next week's kegs into the basement.

The windows are open just a crack, and I can still smell the bonfire smoke from last night's party. It's faded now, just this vague taste of ash on the air. Makes you wonder what it was they were burning.

I left when the flames were almost as high as the

random boy who placed a tiny square of paper on my tongue and tried to follow it with his own.

'I don't kiss boys,' I told him, and I walked home alone.

It was a long night of dreams and visions, but this morning is clearer, tinny and thirsty.

Ivy and Rowan still weren't home when I left for work.

'Well,' Mags says, and she flicks on the lights. They hardly brighten the dim room. 'You're here early.'

An ancient brown Labrador wanders in after her and settles heavily in her usual spot in front of the fireplace. She's the latest of Mags's long line of dogs who run away or get knocked over or have to be put down every few years. When one goes, she gets another. They're always big and they're always brown and she always gives them the same name: Lucky. Mags likes irony.

I shrug and blow on the paper in front of me. The latest Lucky yawns. Mags comes over to look at what I've drawn. She says she hates that I get charcoal all over the tables, complains that it gets in the air and sticks in her lungs, but she smokes two packs of cigarettes a day so I don't listen.

Mags lugs a big tin canister on to the bench beside me. The stuff inside sloshes. 'Why do you never draw people?' she asks, flipping through my sketchbook. A silver shoe, scuffed at the toes. A metal hip flask. The clock on the pub mantelpiece. A big, rusty key. 'People are more interesting than things.'

'Says you.'

'Yes, says me.' She flicks a line through the charcoal dust on the table. 'You could draw me, regal beauty that I am.' I try not to snort. Mags is about five hundred years old and built like a wiry-haired beer keg. She may be regal, but she's no beauty. 'You could draw Cian or Alicja,' she continues, ignoring my look.

I smudge the charcoal into shadows. Cian's the cook and Alicja serves drinks with me. They're pretty much the only people I know in this town. Runaways aren't social types.

'You could draw your brother or Ivy.' I can feel my cheeks reddening, but the room's dim enough to hide my blush.

'You could draw your parents,' Mags goes on, and it's all I can do to keep my eyes on the paper.

'Have you had any word from them?' I ask, gathering up the charcoal pencils I stole from the art shop down the road a few weeks ago and stuffing them into my canvas bag.

'Not yet, pet,' Mags says.

I'm not surprised, but a lump forms in my throat.

She doesn't bother suggesting I draw Granny or Granda. She knows the grief is still too raw.

'Here,' Mags says roughly as I get up from my little stool. 'Go hide that in the basement, would you?' She dumps the huge tin canister in my arms and turns me by the shoulders towards the stairs.

Mags makes poteen: old Irish moonshine. She distils it in her garage and sometimes sells it in her pub – to those in the know – when she's sure the local police are turning a blind eye. The rumours say it makes you blind, but behind closed lids you'll see the future. The rumours say it'll rot your teeth, but that's probably just all the sugar. I haul the canister down the stairs into the basement and hide it behind a bunch of old kegs and crates.

Back upstairs, the others have arrived. They come in the side door by the kitchen and right away I can hear Mags order Rowan out again to chase up a missing order. Good thing, too. I'm not sure I could look at my brother just yet. I don't know for sure that he was with Ivy last night, but until he tells me any different that's what I'm going to assume.

Ivy's our only friend right now, except for Mags, and she's our boss so she doesn't count. Ivy's the only person who knows our whole sorry story. She's the only one who called us after our granny died and our granda stopped recognizing us. She's the only one who worried when she heard we'd been sent back to live with our messed-up parents again. When we ran away from home, she's the only person we told. So she packed her bags and ran away to join us. Her own mother hardly batted an eyelid. Ivy says her mum thinks of it as a rite of passage, like it's perfectly normal for her seventeen-year-old daughter to run away from home to hole up with two teenage alcoholics in a ghost estate. But then there's nothing really mainstream about Ivy and her mum.

I've only just thought of Ivy when I see her. She must've come in with Rowan. She's sitting by the window. Her eyes are ringed with shadows and she hasn't gelled her hair. It's all soft blue tufts around her face, blonde roots just about showing through. But even when Ivy's tired and her hair's a mess, she's the brightest point in the room. She's all floaty dresses and big boots and eyes that match her bright blue hair and can probably see right through you. She glows so strongly that everything around her looks prettier just 'cos she's there.

Rowan and I have known Ivy since we were kids. She lives with her mum in Sligo, and Rowan and I lived with our grandparents in Dublin for most of our lives. But every once in a while our mother – the drunk, the train wreck, the one who abandoned her children – would get in another fight with Dad – and then she'd want her kids back and her oldest friend for support. So she'd come and fetch me and Rowan and drag us halfway across the country, and Granny and Granda wouldn't be able to do anything about it.

She'd turn up on Ivy's mum's doorstep with us in tow and tears on her cheeks. Ivy's mum would try to help, but pretty soon Mum would be off again, chasing after our father for the millionth time, and we'd be back in Dublin with Granny and Granda and we wouldn't see Ivy – or our mother – again for, like, another year.

I can't pinpoint exactly when it was I fell in love with Ivy, but I remember vividly the day two years ago when I realized that Rowan felt the same. Probably it was because he had his tongue inside her mouth.

'What are you doing here?' I say to Ivy. She doesn't work at Maguire's, like me and Rowan.

'We're out of tea,' she says in her soft voice. It's hard to hear over Alicja carrying a crate full of glasses, over Mags dumping a pile of logs in the fireplace. 'And I came for the paper, too.'

Mags grabs a Sunday paper from one of the tables and throws it to Ivy. It flutters like a giant black-and-white-winged bird. Ivy catches the paper neatly and opens it to the crossword page.

Mags is related to Ivy in a way that none of us, including Ivy, can really figure out. She's some kind of great-aunt or third cousin twice removed, on Ivy's mother's side (Ivy never knew her father). Mags has lived in this town for ever.

Granny and Granda used to live here, too, just down the road from Maguire's. After they moved to Dublin, they'd bring us back here sometimes to visit.

When Rowan and I ran away, this is where we ended up. It felt right. We couldn't go back to Dublin; this was the only other place that ever felt like home. We asked Mags if we could crash with her for a bit, but she just grunted and said, 'I don't take in strays,' like we were a couple of lost dogs. But then Ivy turned up, and she was the one who led us to Oak Road, to the house we're now squatting in. I still don't know how she knew about it, but I'm glad she did.

I dig under the coffee machine for the fancy loose-leaf tea that Ivy likes. Ivy always wakes up first. Every morning I come downstairs to find her sitting at the rickety old fold-out table with the morning paper and a cup of tea.

Except this morning, because she was still at the party. With Rowan.

I lost them somewhere between the end of the bar-becue and the third beer that I nicked from the cooler behind the deflated bouncy castle. A bunch of girls with straightened hair and short dresses had cake, so I went up and asked for a piece and they gave me a slice off the second layer – there were seven and each was topped with a different colour icing. One of the girls was cute – shoulder-length hair that went blonder at the edges, and shiny pink gloss on her lips. But by the time I'd licked the last of the green icing from my fingers she was wrapped round some guy like a noose. My problem is I fall in love too easily.

The pub's pretty empty for a Sunday; most of the town must still be nursing its hangover. When my first break comes around, I make myself a cup of coffee and join Ivy at her table. She's sitting right beside the fire now and her cheeks are flushed. The crossword in front of her is almost filled in – just two clues left to find. I know without looking that they're the same clues written on the Post-it note beside Ivy's teacup.

Every day Mags leaves the paper rolled round a packet of chocolate digestives – Ivy's favourite – on our porch. On top of the paper she sticks a Post-it with a clue number or two written on it.

'Twelve across.' Ivy shows me. 'And two down.'

The answers to those clues are always a sign of something that'll happen that day, or some truth about the three of us. They'll say something like *breakdown* the morning before our generator runs out of diesel. Or *abundance* on a particularly good tip day. It's pretty weird, but we've all come to accept it.

'So,' I say to Ivy quickly, before I can chicken out. 'How come you and Rowan got home so—'

But Ivy looks down at the clues on the crossword and jumps up suddenly from her stool, as if she's just been kicked. Her teacup smashes on the tiles in front of the fireplace.

I jump up, too, slopping coffee all over myself, and I ask, 'What? What does it say?' A few of the people around us look up and stare.

Ivy says something under her breath. It sounds kinda like, 'It didn't work.'

'What didn't work?' I ask, still flustered and covered in coffee.

'What?'

'You just said—'

'What? Oh, no, nothing,' Ivy says quickly. She sits back down and swivels slightly in her seat. It creaks under her. Back and forth, back, forth. 'I'm sorry about the cup,' she adds vaguely, eyes still on the paper.

Mags appears at our table with a dustpan and a mop. She hands them to me and raises two thick eyebrows in Ivy's direction.

'Is there a reason you're destroying my crockery today?' she asks.

Ivy reaches across the table and takes a sip of my coffee. She makes a face. 'Twelve across, two down?' she asks.

'Hmph,' says Mags.

I turn the crossword towards me and scan the page, hoping the answers'll make sense even if Ivy doesn't. I'm worried about what they might say.

Twelve across: *Pain of a hidden French breakfast (5).* Two down: *A beetle saint (4).*

'Did you lose something last night?' Ivy asks me suddenly.

'Yeah, my denim jacket.' Then I narrow my eyes and say, 'And you mean *besides* you and Rowan?'

Ivy doesn't meet my gaze. 'You didn't lose us,' she says. 'You went home early, remember?'

'And you didn't come home at all.'

'We were just by the bonfire,' Ivy says, but there's

some colour creeping over her cheeks. She clears her throat. 'And I've just realized I lost one of my necklaces. It fell off at the party. And Rowan came back without his cap.'

'Thank Christ,' I mutter. That hat was an eyesore. 'So you *did* come home with Rowan.'

Ivy sighs. 'And Mags said a bunch of beers kept going missing, too,' she says like she didn't hear me.

'So, what, there's some kind of town thief?' I don't mention with Mags right there that I know exactly where those beers went.

'I don't know,' Ivy says.

My gaze goes back to the two blank spaces in the crossword. Twelve across, two down.

Pain of a hidden French breakfast.

There are plasters wrapped round two of Ivy's fingers. She holds her pen in a bandaged hand.

'What happened?' I ask, nodding at her hand as I try to work out the clue.

What's a French breakfast? *Crêpe*? Bread?

'Cut them on a broken glass last night,' Ivy says.

Then I get it. *'Perdu,'* I say, and I point at the newspaper. *Pain of a hidden French breakfast. Pain* is bread, and *pain perdu* is French toast, an old way to use up stale crusts. It translates, literally, as *lost bread*.

On the floor the tea leaves gleam.

Ivy nods at me meaningfully. She's already figured it out.

I've always been good at crosswords, but Ivy's like lightning. She can crack a clue in thirty seconds flat. '*Perdu*. Lost.'

'So some things at the party got lost,' I say, and I shrug again even though Mags says it'll make me a hunchback when I'm old. 'It's no big deal. I can't get the other clue, though,' I add. 'Two down. *A beetle saint*. Four letters. I don't get it.'

Mags says, 'Hmph,' again, and Ivy says, 'Jude.'

It takes me a second. 'Hey Jude'. A beetle means the band, the Beatles, and the saint is—

Ivy's voice is very small. 'The patron saint of lost causes. St Jude.'

'So what – we're a lost cause?' I say.

'I've been saying that for years,' Mags grunts, but her eyes twinkle.

'I'm starting to take that crossword of yours personally,' I tell her.

'Oh,' says Ivy, and she looks worried. 'I'm sure it's not about you.'

But I don't believe her. Every morning since Rowan and I got here I've been waiting for her to find me out. For the crossword clues to spell my name and tell her what I've done. The problem is I've too many secrets and sometimes it's hard to keep up with your own lies.

I can guess what she thinks today's clues mean. Rowan and I have lost our granny already. We've lost our granda, too, in a different way. He doesn't know us. He can hardly speak. When we call him, it's always the hospice nurse that answers.

But Ivy also knows we're expecting our mum to come find us, apologize, try to make things right. Ivy knows we haven't heard from her in over a month. I've tried calling, but her number's been disconnected.

Ivy probably thinks the crossword means we've now lost our parents, too.

The thing is, even though she and Rowan don't know it, I'm pretty sure she's right.

Olive

Monday 8th May

Lost: Half an hour's sleep; concentration;
delicate gold bracelet with tiny charms

Rose sneaked into my bedroom on Monday morning somewhere close to 2 a.m. My mum must have left the back door unlocked. Rose clambered over me and nestled down between me and the wall, all elbows and knees and hair snaking across my face. I grunted and shoved her, hard, my own elbow sinking into her side. She smelled like she hadn't been home since before the party.

Waking slowly, I rolled over on to my back and stared at the ceiling. Rose continued to make herself comfortable, like a dog in a new blanket. Shifting, sighing, tugging the covers. I wanted to ask her where she'd been, but sleep was like a spell pulling me back under.

'I'm sorry,' she whispered, or maybe that's what she whispered – my hearing aid was sitting useless on the bedside table and she was facing my deaf ear.

'Whatever,' I said back, not unkindly. 'It's not like I thought I had lost you for good.'

Rose made a *hmm* sound that I thought might have been a smile or a sigh.

By the time my door bursts open to the sound of Dad reciting Thomas Moore, Rose is gone. She has left a flower – her namesake – on the pillow beside me. Thoughtfully, she's had the foresight to remove the thorns.

Downstairs, the others are up already. Emily is glued to her phone as always and my mum is making a mashed-banana clown face for Max's breakfast.

'*So soon may I follow, / When friendships decay, / And from Love's shining circle / The gems drop away.*' Dad quotes his way through the poem, following me into the kitchen.

'Want some?' Max asks me as Mum pops a raspberry in the middle of the foul-looking mush as a nose. The raisin mouth grins ominously.

'No thanks.' I make a face and opt for toast and the coffee that's been brewing since my mum got up. It's dark as night and smells like a sharp slap.

'*When true hearts lie wither'd, / And fond ones are flown,*' Dad insists on finishing the poem even though we are all awake and de-bedded. He amps up his performance for the last few lines, doing a mock swoon to the words, '*Oh! who would inhabit / This bleak world alone?*'

'Nice,' I mutter.

'Can I go to Chloe's later?' Emily asks, ignoring our dad's antics as usual. Chloe is her best friend but could be her identical twin. They buy the same pastel skinny jeans and Topshop crop tops that Dad is dutifully scandalized over, and one is not usually found without the other. Rose and I share jewellery and spend all our time together, too, but I'd have a hard time being a carbon copy of Rose. Also her clothes would never fit me, seeing as how she's eight inches taller and three dress sizes smaller than I am.

Mum tells Emily she can go to Chloe's after school and I try my luck by asking, offhand, 'Can I go to Rose's, too?' but she sees right through me.

'You're grounded, as I'm sure you'll remember. You can come straight home,' she tells me. 'And, much as I enjoy Rose's company, she'd do well to go straight home, too.'

I put Rose's rose up on the bookshelf above my bed before I leave and wonder again where she went yesterday after the party.

Emily and I cycle to school single file on the twisty road, our uniform jumpers round our waists, the backs flapping like big blue swan wings behind us. My shirtsleeves are pushed as far up my arm as I can get them. All that is left of the words written there is *you'll never be found* – the word *never* fading grey in the crook of my elbow; *be found* bleeding black into my wrist.

I only realize my bracelet is gone when the school bell rings and I am hurrying down the corridor to my first lesson. It must have slipped from my wrist as I cycled to school. I've been wearing its absence on my arm since I lost it. A ghost bracelet singing with invisible charms.

While all the other girls have their Pandoras heavy with round silver beads shaped like birthday cakes and teacups, I have a tiny, linked gold chain from which dangle miniature stars and cats and mountains, and – my favourite – a delicate little olive tree, light as air and sounding like musical notes when they tinkle together. It was my mum's when she was a girl. She gave it to me for my sixteenth birthday and I haven't taken it off since.

I slide into my seat and drag my school bag on to my lap. I take out my school books and pencil case, my dad's copy of the collected poems of Sylvia Plath, the loose pens and packets of tissues and used hearing-aid batteries and hairpins and crumpled-up pieces of paper at the bottom of the bag. I open every pocket. I turn out the linings. The class fills up in dribs and drabs, the bell long since rung. My searching becomes more frantic. I roll up the sleeves of my jumper; I roll down my socks; I check through each pleat of my skirt until Cathal Murdock turns round and asks loudly, 'How much for the striptease, hot stuff?' He waggles his tongue suggestively.

Fortunately Ms Walsh, who has heard Cathal's delightful question, intervenes before I can dump the jumbled contents of my school bag over his head.

'Mr Murdock, please take a seat at the front of the class,' she says. 'I will not tolerate sexual harassment in my classroom.'

Muttering darkly, Cathal takes his seat right in front of the teacher, to applause from most of my female class-mates. I take advantage of the distraction to continue my search.

Rose slouches late into class and sits down beside me. 'What's wrong with you?' she asks. 'Does Weetabix have fleas again?'

I shoot her an evil look and check under my desk to see if I've dropped the bracelet in all the searching. 'I've lost my bracelet.'

'Your mum's one?'

'Yeah.'

'Shit.'

'Yeah.' I start to scoop the detritus back into my school bag. Amid the mess, I've managed to find my globe-shaped pencil sharpener, a wrinkled fiver and a silver, star-shaped hair clip from the same set as the one I was wearing and then lost at the party. I'm glad I still have one left at least.

Rose is immaculately made-up as always, her black hair gleaming and her uniform skirt stapled three inches above the required hemline. She's the photo negative of last night's mess.

'Ooh, cute.' Rose seizes the hair clip and uses it to pin back her waterfall of hair. It works about as well as trying to hold back an actual waterfall.

Ms Walsh has started the class, but I lean towards Rose and quietly say, 'Are you going to tell me where you went after the party?'

Her gaze goes blank for a second and she says, 'Are you?'

'Am I what?'

'Going to tell me where you went?'

'Home,' I tell her. 'At, like, six a.m. Without you.'

'*I* went home,' she says. 'At, like, six a.m. Without *you*.'

I scrunch up my mouth with suspicion. It's possible, I suppose, that we missed each other. That she woke up minutes before me and went to pee behind the trees. That I was up searching for her when she came back to get me.

'It didn't look like you'd been home when you came to mine last night,' I say, and I poke her shoulder playfully. 'Where were you really? Did you go somewhere with a guy?' I say *guy* because it's unlikely she found a girl to go somewhere with. We live in Balmallen, County Mayo, population 2,400. There's only one secondary school; if there were any eligible girls around, we'd know it. Last year Rose and I drunkenly decided that, as the only two openly bisexual girls our age in town, we should probably give it a go. Turns out some people really are just meant to be friends.

'I don't know what you're talking about,' says Rose.

'You must still have been seriously wasted,' I observe.

Rose laughs. 'I wasn't the only one.'

Can I've another kiss before you go?

'You're not wrong,' I concede.

After English, Rose and I retrace my steps through the school and out across the yard to the bike rack, but my bracelet isn't there. I hope it's at home and not lying in a ditch somewhere.

All day, I keep catching myself rubbing the words on my skin – the ball of my right thumb bumping over the tiny bones of my wrist, the blue and purple veins, the *never be found*. Like the blood on Lady Macbeth, it doesn't want to come off.

'*Olive*,' Mr O'Neill says sharply for the second time in the first ten minutes of geography class.

'Sorry, sir.' I grab my pen, although I have no idea what I'm supposed to be writing. Rose shrugs infinitesimally beside me.

Mr O'Neill, in an uncanny fit of telepathy, says, 'You're supposed to be writing about the three Fs of primary economic activities in this specific peripheral region.'

I stare at him blankly. 'Um.'

'Anyone? The three Fs?' Mr O'Neill opens the question up to the rest of the class. Rose scribbles three words on the textbook between us: *Frolicking, flying, fucking.* I cover the paper quickly with my hand before he can see.

I lean over and whisper, 'I don't want to think about Mr O'Neill doing *any* of those things.'

Rose's ensuing 'HA!' is so loud that it gets both of us kicked out of geography. We decide to take this as a sign from the universe that we're not meant to be in a hot, airless school building on a beautiful warm day and that instead we should spend the rest of our morning beside the lake. We have two free classes before lunch and neither our teachers nor my parents will ever know I've defied their grounding if I'm back in school by maths class.

We unchain our bikes in the silence of the schoolyard and set off out to the edge of town. There isn't much to Balmallen, and there isn't much to the edge of it either. We cycle past the supermarket and the industrial park and we take a sharp right just after the main road. I glance back behind us for a glimpse of the field where the summer party was held. I don't know what I'm looking for. Maybe the boy with the glasses and the dark curly hair who I haven't been able to stop thinking about. Rose cycles straight ahead, leading us right down to the forest by the lake, and the ghost estate that sits there. Oak Road.

It was built in the boom years: a nice, modern development, all mod cons, identical houses with identical gardens in a neat little semicircle of Celtic Tiger satisfaction. But then the recession hit and the economy crashed and for the last few years all these perfect little patches of pastoral suburbia have been left sitting empty, the rooms never furnished, the grass never cut.

The city council boarded up the windows and put up signs with half-hearted warnings like TRESPASSERS WILL BE PROSECUTED, but we trespass all the time and no one has yet come to prosecute us. We can't actually get into the houses – we're not about to break down the boarded-up doors just for kicks – but on weekend nights we drink in the storm-drain tunnel and on weekdays, when our classes are boring and stressful, we like to hang out on the overgrown lawns, smoking, reading magazines, listening to music on our phones with tinny speakers, painting our nails. Nobody ever comes looking for us.

We haven't been here in a few months and already the weeds – killed by frost over winter – have grown up past our knees. 'This is kind of like Neverland,' I say as we lay out our jumpers on the tangled grass to sit on.

'So, what, does that make us the Lost Boys?' Rose asks.

If there is anybody in the world who looks least like a Lost Boy, it's Rose. Chewing gum aggressively – the only way Rose knows how to do anything, apart from dramatically – she's busy pulling off her knee socks and balling them up in the long grass beside her, hitching up her skirt and unbuttoning her top three shirt buttons.

My best friend is the daughter of a stout, ruddy Corkman whose accent I can never decipher, and a beautiful, willowy, half-Indian Dubliner. She is her mother from the tips of her painted toenails to the ends of her long black hair. From her father, she only inherited her impressive vocabulary of curses. Her eyes are always smoky, her eyebrows perfectly arched and her nails painted. Rose was made for fashion magazines, not children's books.

'I get what you mean, though,' she says. 'No teachers or parents to tell us not to smoke—'

'I've never smoked,' I remind her. 'And you don't any more either, remember?'

'Or drink, or keep the music down.'

'*Second star to the right*,' I say with relish, opening a packet of crisps. *'And straight on till morning.'*

Looks-wise, Oak Road is as far from an enchanted island as you can get. The houses are an ugly, faded mustard like the wall surrounding them and the grass is dotted with daisies and dandelions. The road through the estate is unfinished, ending in a heap of rubble on one side and an exposed storm-drain tunnel on the other. It's completely incongruous with the forest beside it, the lake shining blue just beyond.

'Who'd even ever live here?' Rose asked the first time we came, watching with a sort of rapt horror as two rats fought in the rubble at the back of the estate.

'Lots of people,' I told her. 'I mean, apart from the paint job, they'd've been nice houses. Big. Modern.' In my own house, the windows are single-glazed and let in every molecule of cold air. The plumbing is archaic and if any-one runs a tap while you're showering the hot water disappears completely. My parents wanted the Authentic Country Life, and they've got it, bad wiring and every-thing. Also the deer eat all their fuchsias.

Rose and I sit sunning our legs in the long grass, our skirts hitched up so high our knickers are visible, not that there's anyone around to see them. (Not that we would care if there was; if I am prone to embarrassment by myself, my shyness is generally eclipsed by Rose's constant ease.)

I roll my eyes when Rose takes out a little yellow bottle. She quit smoking three months ago and after several weeks spent chewing the ends of the wooden sticks used to stir paper-cup coffee, or plastic straws, or raw spaghetti, she has now taken to carrying a bottle of bubbles everywhere she goes. She blows them out like exhaling smoke, the wand held between two fingers like a cigarette. Soap bubbles pop on car seats and kitchen windows, leave wet rings on footpaths and wooden school desks.

She sits with her elbow on the knee of one long leg and I am always surprised at how she can take such an innocent act and make it look lascivious. It's a disturbing talent.

'You're in great danger of becoming a parody of yourself, you know,' I say.

'It's helping my craving,' she replies blithely.

'So would a nicotine patch.'

Rose blows a whole batch of bubbles straight in my face. 'Tell me about the saint thing again,' she says.

The saint thing. I root through my school bag for the little metal medal I found with the bubblegum in the denim jacket I wore home from the party. 'St Anthony,' I say, showing her. 'The patron saint of lost objects.'

Rose rubs the medal between two fingers as if it's a genie lamp she could wish on. She brings it up to her myopic eyes (she refuses to wear glasses even though she owns a pair of those thick-rimmed vintage kind that makes her look like a secretary in a porn film). She scratches a thumbnail over a stain that looks like brown rust. Then she brings it to her mouth and bites down on the edge of it, like a pirate.

'Fool's gold,' I mutter.

'It's tin.' She tosses the medal into the air with a flick of her thumb that sends it spinning, then catches it and slaps it on the back of her hand. 'Heads or tails?'

I take the bubble wand and blow. 'Tails.'

'Heads,' she says. She scrutinizes the medal again. Then she takes the bubble wand back from me in exchange for the saint.

'My nana says a prayer to St Anthony every time she can't find her car keys.'

'Don't your aunts hide them from her?' Rose says.

'That's probably why she can never find them.'

My grandmother is ancient and cantankerous, and drives like it. I doubt St Anthony ever helps her with her keys, unless he is also the patron saint of finding things that well-meaning relatives have hidden from you.

Rose leans towards me and takes the medal again. 'Who's the baby?'

St Anthony, crowned with tin stars, appears to be holding a slightly rusted child in his arms. I shrug. 'Jesus?' I guess. 'Peter Pan? Who knows?'

Rose stretches out languorously on her back. 'Lost Boys,' she says, pocketing the medal. 'I get it.' A flurry of bubbles rises into the air.

Rose's phone pings. It has done this about twelve times in the last half-hour. She ignores it. She's ignored the last eleven, too. My self-restraint is wearing thin.

'Are you ignoring your messages?'

'Nobody messages me,' she replies breezily. 'Except you, and you're right here.'

'Yeah, I'm right here. So I can hear your phone playing the world's most monotonous song all by itself over there.'

'Oh, they're just reminders.' She waves a metallic-green-nailed hand dismissively.

'Reminders for what – to stop your best friend murdering you over the incessant pinging?' I throw a crisp at her. 'I give up. I need to pee.'

The problem with hanging out in a ghost estate is that when you need to pee there's nowhere to go but the forest.

I keep an eye out for rats in the rubble and hunker down behind the wall on the forest side, uniform skirt bunched up in my arms. Back in the centre of the estate I think I can make out Rose's raised voice, but it might just be a video or the music she's playing.

When I've hopped back over the wall, I notice something strange: just up ahead, in the cracks between the slats of the boarded-up windows of the next house, there is a light. It's a sliver in the chink between one board and the next where there should be darkness. It flickers like a candle, or the reflection of a TV screen. I edge quietly towards the house.

It's the furthest from the road and the closest to the lake. The nearer I move to it, the less I can hear whatever Rose is doing. Instead, I hear voices.

I flick the tiny boost switch on my hearing aid with my thumbnail, but the voices are still only whispers so I creep round the back of the house to the wooden boards hiding the veranda doors. One of them is hinged slightly open.

That's when I realize that I'm probably not in an extremely safe situation. The chances of squatters in a ghost estate being up to anything wholesome and law-abiding are pretty slim. Heart suddenly beating a little harder than before, I turn to hurry away – but something at the edge of the rubble to my right catches my eye. A grey-brown flat cap. It's lying at a jaunty angle like it just flew off someone's head. Like someone lost it heading home from a party in the early hours of the morning and never thought to pick it up.

I can hear Rose calling my name. I check the time on my phone. We have less than twenty minutes to cycle back to school before the start of maths. I give the house one final glance and I run as quietly as I can back to the grass.

Laurel

Monday 8th May

Found: A boy

There have always been three of us: a coven, a crowd, a three-headed dog. We have names that our parents gave us, names our teachers call in class, names the girls in school shout nastily in the hallways, names written in our textbooks and sewn into our PE shorts, but they're not the names we give ourselves. Laurel, Ash and Holly. If there had to be a collective noun for us, it would be a forest. A forest of teenage girls.

There's nothing two of us know that the other doesn't. There's nowhere two of us go that the other doesn't follow. Although some of what Holly wrote in her diary was news to Ash. Holly has so much watery sadness. Ash has so much rage and fire. It's a good thing I'm there to ground them. But then who grounds me? Maybe that's the problem with being three.

There have always been three of us, but then yesterday Jude appeared, and now there are four.

It's funny how you can completely understand somebody after having known them for a day. It's funny how soon you come to realize somebody is going to change your life.

After school, we went to Ash's house on the other side of town. They're cutting down trees there to build on the land, so we stood on her wall and watched them. Ash whooped when the first tree fell.

'TIMBERRRR!'

But it wasn't like that at all. No slow-motion trunk falling with a thud to the ground. Just chunks of dying trees, like when Mam cuts the carrots for stew, hacked off bit by groaning bit.

Ash crowed some more. 'Ha-HAAAA!' She loves most forms of destruction; you can tell by how she tears her nails off in strips with her teeth.

Ash's dad came out into the garden with a tray of chocolate digestives and tea. Ash's mam was on the phone in the hall, standing by the open front door. I like Ash's parents because every time Holly and I come over they ask us what we're reading, and the next time we visit they'll be halfway through the same book.

'How are you liking *The Sound and the Fury*?' I asked Ash's dad as he put the tray down on the wall beside us. Holly grinned. We'd decided to recommend something a little racier than usual, just to see how Ash's parents would take it.

Ash scowled. She wasn't interested in Faulkner. Or in talking to her parents about books. Holly and I have always been the readers, the daydreamers, the thinkers. Ash has always been the wildfire of movement that keeps us both awake.

'Look at them go!' she shouted at the trees.

Ash's mam, still on the phone in the hall, shushed her and her dad smiled. 'Beautiful language,' he said. 'Beautiful, meaty masterpiece.'

'*Meaty?*' Ash sneered. 'It's a big old book written two hundred years ago.'

'It was written in the twenties,' Holly said, surprised.

Ash rolled her eyes.

'Don't worry, Caroline,' Ash's mam was saying. 'He's eighteen – he's probably just sleeping off one too many pints over the weekend. He'll be back before you know it.'

She said goodbye and put down the phone, brows furrowed. She stepped into the garden to join us and said to Ash's dad, 'Caroline's boy didn't come home after the party on Saturday. You haven't seen him around?'

Ash's dad shook his head and Ash's mam sighed, then smiled over at me and Holly. 'Have either of you read James Joyce?' she asked. 'Faulkner's stream of consciousness reminds me of that. It's beautiful and confusing.'

Ash's dad nodded. 'I'm definitely not smart enough for Joyce,' he said. 'But you two sure would be.'

'Let's go for a walk,' Ash said suddenly, loudly. She slammed the front gate open and left. Holly and I waved goodbye to her parents and thanked them for the biscuits.

Ash walked ahead of us, as always, a trail of cigarette smoke behind her like a speed-cloud in a cartoon. It made it look like her bright red curls were on fire. I walked close to Holly, touched the back of her hand with mine. She'd been quieter than usual since the party, unsettled. I thought she'd be relieved to have her diary back, but something still seemed to be worrying her.

'Are you OK?' I asked her, not for the first time.

Holly shrugged. She leaned in towards me. 'Was it real?' she whispered so Ash couldn't hear.

'Was what real?'

'The spell,' Holly said. 'The pages from our diaries came back. We called for them and they were found. Because of the spell.'

'Maybe we just had them in our bags all along. Maybe whoever took them put them back there.' I paused. 'I do wonder where the spellbook came from, though.'

'It looks ancient.' Holly nodded.

'Old-fashioned handwriting,' I said.

'I don't know.' Holly frowned. 'I told you, I thought I recognized it from somewhere.'

'I doubt it.' I shook my head. 'Unless you know a lot of old people with spectacular penmanship.'

Holly paused for a moment, then said, 'Whoever wrote it thought it was real.'

'Whoever wrote it was wrong,' I told her patiently.

'But the pages from our diaries,' Holly whispered. The back of her hand disappeared from beside mine. Ahead of us, Ash had reached the tree.

That was when we found Jude. Or he found us.

He came down from the giant oak tree like he'd been living there. He said to our wide eyes, our open mouths, 'Did you know that in Greek mythology dryads are the spirits of trees? The word *drys* actually means oak, so originally dryads were the spirits of oak trees.' He pressed his palm to the trunk of the tree he'd been sitting in. 'Sorry,' he said. 'I despise small talk. I'd rather know if you believe in God than talk about the weather. So do you?'

'Do we what?' said Ash.

'Do you believe in God?'

'I thought you were talking about dryads,' I said.

'Do you believe in dryads then?' he asked.

'Yes,' Holly whispered. 'Oh, yes.'

The boys in school only care about football and rumours, sex and games and films. Jude has long hair and makes wooden beaded bracelets that he gave to us and also wears himself. He reads books that are banned at our school and that we can't find in the library, but that he says he nicked from bookshops in the city. He doesn't play football, but can climb trees better than a squirrel. He's not from around here. He's not like anyone we know. Already Holly is in love with him and maybe Ash is, too, although she'll probably scratch this out if she sees it. Maybe we are all a little bit in love with Jude. I should scratch this out myself.

We spent the evening together and we talked about everything that could ever be important in the world. We showed him the spellbook and it was like an offering: *Look, we know about magic, too. Look, we also despise small talk; we are different and interesting; we are just like you.*

Jude knows all about lost things. And magic. He says there is a balance between goodness and evil, environment and consumerism, light and dark, lost and found. Love and death. I'm not really sure why we listened to him, but I suspect it had something to do with his light eyes, his long hair, his lips.

Lust. I wonder what balances that one out.

Olive

Monday 8th May

Lost: Make-up bag (large, red, gold zip)

Just before our second-to-last class I get a text from Rose to meet her in the girls' toilets by the science rooms. We got back from Oak Road just in time for maths class, but I haven't seen Rose in over an hour and clearly something's happened.

MEET ME IN TOILETS ASAP STOP, her message says. HAVE CRIED ALL MY MAKE-UP OFF STOP LOST MY MAKE-UP BAG STOP CAN'T BE SEEN LIKE THIS STOP BRING EYELINER STOP ROSE.

Rose and I went through a *Sound of Music* phase a few years ago and since then have sent all our text messages in telegram format. I grab my make-up bag (which is paltry in the extreme compared to Rose's) and make my way up the stairs, wondering what could have happened to make Rose cry.

I shoulder past a crowd of our classmates loitering outside the bathrooms. 'And I swear it was in my pocket at the barbecue,' Chrissy Jones is saying. 'But then in the morning it was gone and I haven't seen it since.'

'Maybe there's, like, some secret klepto in town,' says Julia Mullochney.

'Maybe it's someone in school,' says Shannon Ryan.

All three of them hush and look around as if they'll suddenly catch a thief red-handed. Julia catches my eye.

'What did *you* lose at the party on Saturday?' she asks me.

'It's the hot question on everybody's lips,' says Chrissy.

I shrug my shoulders. 'I didn't lose anything,' I say. I don't mention my shoe, or my jacket, or my silver, star-shaped hair clip. I don't mention the fact that I woke up without Rose. My hand circles my left wrist. I assumed I'd lost my bracelet on the way to school this morning, but have I seen it since Saturday night?

Rose clearly hears us from behind the bathroom door. 'I'm losing my patience,' she growls from inside, and the girls let me through. They reconverge behind me, continuing their speculation about lost items and town thieves. I let the door swing shut with a clack.

Rose is sitting on the floor between two sinks, her back to the dirty tiles of the bathroom wall. Her hair, which was wavy and gleaming a couple of hours ago at Oak Road, is tangled and frizzy and her skin is blotchy from tears. I sit on the floor in front of her and hand her my make-up bag.

'Lifesaver,' Rose mutters, and she rifles through it for anything she can use. 'I had my make-up bag with me this morning, but it's gone missing, which is perfect fucking timing,' she says, and swears again, softly but eloquently, at my bag's meagre offerings.

There are certain things that Rose can be counted on to do in moments of minor crisis (a break-up, a D in a test, an argument with her mother): dramatic door-slamming, vigorous eye-rolling, frustrated screams accompanying wild gesticulating and the occasional plate-smashing. She is not the type to hole up quietly in the school toilets and cry off all her painstakingly applied make-up. I'm at a loss as to what to say.

'What's wrong?'

Rose forgoes my too-pale powder and goes straight for the eyes. Her breath still comes in jumps and she mascaras her lashes with rather more vehemence than usual. The bell signals the start of the next class, but we don't move.

When Rose finally speaks, her voice is angry, which I'm used to, but also small, which I'm not. 'I lost it,' she croaks, then clears her throat and looks annoyed at herself for having said anything.

'Lost what?'

She huffs out a breath. 'Your stupid saint medal,' she says. 'I put it in my pocket at Oak Road, but it must have fallen out on the way back to school.'

'*That's* why you're crying? It wasn't even mine to begin with. I just found it in that old jacket.'

'Yeah, but what if it was protecting you and now it's lost?'

I can't tell if she's being serious. 'Rose, it's a bit of metal. It wasn't protecting anyone. Besides, I thought you didn't believe in that stuff.'

'I don't,' she says, pouting at her reflection in the mirror of my powder compact. 'But it's kind of true what Chrissy and the others were saying.'

'You lost something at the party?' I ask.

'No. Well, memory of it, I guess,' she says. 'Like you.' The smallest corner of her mouth curls. I can't tell if it's a smile or a snarl.

I cross my legs and lean my elbows on my knees. 'Where did you go?' I ask. 'On Saturday night. Sunday morning, I mean. After the party.'

I looked all over that field. I'm not buying that she was there and we just missed each other. Rose has been my best friend since we were twelve and her abandoning me at a party and then climbing into my bed at 2 a.m. hardly raises a red flag any more – but I've never seen Rose quite like this before.

She shrugs. 'I was at the party.'

'You weren't. I checked. I saw some things I probably *shouldn't* have seen, but I checked.'

Something flashes in her eyes. 'What did you see?'

'I dunno, some nudity, casual substance abuse, nothing special.'

'Whose nudity?' she asks. 'Male or female?'

I frown. 'Who cares? It's not like I was trying to look too closely. Just enough to know none of the bodies were you.'

'*Bodies*,' she repeats, making it sound like I meant dead bodies.

'You know what I mean,' I say. 'Rose.' I press my hands down on to my knees. 'Seriously. What happened at the party?'

Rose tilts her head back against the tiles beneath the sink behind her, the ends of her hair skimming the grimy ground.

'I can't remember,' she says finally.

'That'd be the half-bottle of vodka,' I say.

'Yeah. Well.'

'What can't you remember?' I purse my lips. It's a stupid question.

Rose understands, though. 'We were dancing,' she says, inviting me to join her in filling in the blanks.

'The music was woeful, but we sang along anyway.'

'We hung out by the bonfire.'

'There was a blond guy.'

'I don't remember a blond guy.'

'Kind of scruffy? Eyebrow piercing? He remembers you.' I don't mention what he said to me about another kiss.

'I remember crying.' Rose takes out her bubbles and unscrews the lid.

'That was our plan for the evening,' I remind her.

'I remember that, too.'

The word *remember* is beginning to lose all meaning. Rose isn't Rose-like at all; she's too quiet, almost hesitant. She hasn't even asked what was with the blond guy.

We trade memories of the party until there are none left to tell. We drank, we danced, we sang, Rose cried, I woke up alone. Yet something's still missing.

Rose screws the lid back on the bubbles and puts the bottle in her pocket. Smoky-lidded and cat-lined, Rose's eyes look more like her eyes, although they are still ringed with red. She stands up and swipes her hands over her skirt a few times to dry them, then she bends down and gives a quick kiss to the top of my head. 'Thanks for the make-up, Olive,' she says. She slings her school bag over one shoulder and it's like she's putting Rose back on with it – one cocked dark eyebrow, a quirk of her mouth that is not quite a smile.

'I need to get out of this place,' she tells me. 'Tell Mr Murphy I'm going home sick.'

She stomps out of the toilets like she owns the place, nearly ploughing down a bunch of First Years just outside the door. They turn and stare in awe until she's disappeared round the corner. The hurricane that is Rose often has that effect. I pick up my make-up bag and slink out of the toilets, unnoticed, to slip into my last class without her.

Hazel

Monday 8th May

Lost: One wallet; one phone; one temper;
pack of cigarettes (only two left)

I don't have to look up St Jude from the crossword. I've kept yesterday's paper like it's some kind of proof, sitting stark on the kitchen camping table in front of me. *Perdu*, lost. St Jude.

When you've been to an Irish convent school, you know all about the saints. There are two for lost things. St Anthony of Padua is the one on Mass cards and medals. He helps little old ladies find their keys and kids find their lost dogs. Mags had a St Anthony medal stuck to the side of the till in Maguire's until I nicked it to keep in the pocket of my denim jacket. It's kinda fitting that I can't find it now.

St Jude's another story. He lost his head to an axe and now he's the champion of lost causes. Like me and Rowan, I suppose.

This morning is the twenty-third since we got here, and the fourth Monday. Twenty-six days since I last saw my parents. Twenty-six days since I knew that number was just gonna keep on getting bigger for ever.

I still haven't got used to not having to go to school, even though I hated school the whole time I was there. Ivy's at the table, having finished with today's crossword. I didn't have to explain the saint thing to her yesterday, even though she's home-schooled and knows more about constellations, plant reproduction and the Fibonacci sequence than she does about the church.

Rowan's in the empty front room, plucking his guitar. Because there's no furniture anywhere but the kitchen (except for our mattresses upstairs), the rest of the house has pretty great acoustics. We never spend too long anywhere but the kitchen, though, because it's the only room with any natural light; the windows of the rest of the house are all boarded up.

I put the tin coffee pot on the little double-burner camping stove in the corner of the kitchen and wait for my coffee to brew. Ivy puts the kettle on for tea. The smell of coffee fills the house, calls Rowan out of the other room and into the kitchen with us. This coffee's the good kind, the organic Fair Trade Italian kind our mum only ever drinks – when she isn't drinking anything else, that is. I have a flowy top that fits a packet of this coffee and a packet of Ivy's fancy tea inside each sleeve. If I pretend to be tying up my hair when I leave the shop, the security guy doesn't notice a thing.

'We're out of milk,' I say, withdrawing my head from the cool of the fridge.

Rowan sighs and runs his hands through his hair. 'We're out of everything,' he says.

We're always out of everything.

'Out of luck, time, our minds,' Ivy supplies.

'I was thinking more like toilet paper,' I say. 'Tea bags. Pasta sauce.'

Ivy gives a little laugh. 'Those, too,' she says.

'OK,' says Rowan. 'Only one way to settle this.' He rolls up the right sleeve of his old knitted jumper and puts his bare elbow on the table with determination. With his other hand, he jams his stupid flat cap back on his head. I'd hoped he'd lost it for good, but Ivy found it on the rubble behind the house this morning.

'Nope,' I say, and I lean back against the counter. 'No way. It's your turn to do the shopping.'

Ivy, grinning, wanders over to the wind-up camp radio Mags brought over one day.

'Come on, Hazel,' says Rowan. He braces his elbow on the table and invites me over with a cocked eyebrow. 'May the best man win.'

'You haven't got a chance.'

Ivy finds a radio station in a burst of static. 'Ride of the Valkyries' fills the house. It builds and swoops, and Ivy and Rowan look at each other and laugh, and they look at me and invite me to laugh along, too, but suddenly all I can see are their faces pressed together, laughing over the same song, their faces pressed together, reflecting the flames of the bonfire, their faces pressed together, kissing as I stumbled home alone.

Rowan swore blind last night that he wasn't with Ivy at the party, that he spent the night hanging out with some local kids in the next field, but why should I believe him? We're all thieves and liars here. I grab a handful of shopping bags from the pile by the sink and throw the change jar into my canvas bag. 'I'll go,' I say to my brother. 'But if I'm late to work because of this it'll be your fault.'

My head's a mess of moving pictures like a slideshow. Ivy and Rowan laughing. Rowan and Ivy dancing round a bonfire. Ivy and Rowan kissing with green icing on their tongues. I'm walking through Tesco with the security guy's eye on me, slipping tea and biscuits up the sleeves of my top when I'm out of his line of sight.

More slideshow images: Granny, still and waxy in her coffin. Weeks of Granda slipping away. His vacant eyes the last time we saw him.

My mum's face, jaw slack and eyes closed, passed out drunk on the couch.

The old lady behind me in the checkout queue digs a sharp finger into my back. 'Move on up there,' she says. 'It's your turn at the till. We don't have all day here.'

'You can fuck right off, lady,' I say to her loudly. She makes a shocked face and moves to the next till.

I could head to work early, but my veins are live wires and I really need a drink. This is what thinking about my mum does to me. Ivy – who's no teetotaller herself – says me and Rowan drink too much. Well, she said it once, and she was pretty stoned at the time, which is kinda ironic if you ask me. But I heard between the words. I know what it looks like. It looks like I'm just turning into my mum, and I'm not gonna think about that. Except to say that there are a whole lot of ways someone can mess up another person. Even though she isn't here, she's still in my head. I'm not gonna think about her.

I take out her credit card and pay for the shopping I haven't stuffed into my clothes. When I get out of the shop, I look at the card again, the letters of her name raised against the plastic. Instead of going into work, I head for the tattoo place down the road.

Later that afternoon I walk into work with new ink on my skin. In the pub kitchen, I hear raised voices. I stow my groceries in the little closet where we hang our bags and I rub my thumb over my older tattoos, the ones on my forearms. The new one stings too much to touch. In films, girls' wrists are so little that men's hands can circle them thumb to middle finger, all the way around. My wrists aren't little. *Big boned*, my granny always said, but it isn't just the bones. Big bones, big meat, I'm a meal of a girl. Tall, too. A mass of curly brown hair to top the whole thing off. But I've got a sailor's mouth and skin inked black over freckles, and I know I've got legs that go on for days. A meal of a girl and you wouldn't go hungry.

The tattoo artist was smug. The kind who sees a teenage girl and takes her money even though it's illegal to tattoo anyone under eighteen, smirking the whole time because he's imagining Chinese symbols for love or purple swirls on the small of her back, a butterfly on her ankle.

I rolled up my sleeves and he eyed up the keyhole I already have tattooed on one arm, and the key to fit it on the other.

The guy narrowed his eyes. He probably expected me to be coming in for my first tattoo after some kind of fight with my parents. A tattoo, a piercing, a way to rebel. I could tell he was trying to calculate how old I am.

'I'm seventeen,' I said. 'But if anyone asks I'm twenty.'

Then I took my top off. His expression was priceless.

'I want these words,' I told him, handing him a piece of paper. 'Here.'

I ran my hand along my ribs. The very top, just under my bra line. His Adam's apple bobbed and I scowled. In the end, he undercharged me.

Rowan's voice carries through from the kitchen. 'I *said* I didn't see the damn thing, Cian. You must have lost it.'

Cian mutters something in reply.

'If he says he didn't see it, he didn't see it, Cian,' says Alicja peaceably.

I root through my shopping bags for my cigarettes.

'I don't see you asking Alicja if she's seen your phone,' Rowan's voice cuts accusingly through the air. Cian's reply is covered by the clattering of dishes in the sink.

'Because what?' Rowan's almost shouting now. 'I'm not from around here so automatically I'm a thief?'

'That's not what I'm saying.'

'It certainly sounds like that's what you're saying,' Rowan says to Cian, who mutters something in reply.

I was sure there was a packet with a couple of cigarettes left in this bag.

'Turn round and say that to my face.' Rowan's voice is dangerous.

It sounds like Rowan's taking a leaf out of my book. He's never really been the fighting type. He's got an easy grin that brushes away insults and tends to shrug things off. Unlike me. *Just like your mother*, Granny'd say when she was particularly disappointed in me. She didn't really mean it, though. She knew it was the only thing that ever worked – hearing those words'd make me calm down pretty fast. I miss her so much it's like a burning. Her and Granda both. My veins fizz up again, beat in time with the shouts from the pub kitchen. I guess my brother's veins can get to feeling like live wires, too.

I quickly step into the kitchen to stop Rowan from doing something stupid. Inside, the air is like a sauna, if saunas smelled of pub grub and were full of guys about to fight. I grab my brother by the elbow and pull him away from Cian. Rowan shakes me off, but he doesn't move forward again.

'Might want to think about getting a muzzle for that brother of yours,' Cian says with a sneer.

I arch an eyebrow. 'Whatever you're into, man, it's none of my business.' And I steer Rowan out of the kitchen.

'What's *up* with you?' I say through my teeth.

'He's an asshole,' Rowan starts to say, but cuts himself off when Mags suddenly appears, heading outside for, like, her twelfth smoke break of the day.

'We need a new thing of Coke,' she says as she goes outside. 'They're in the basement. And make sure that canister you carried down yesterday is still out of sight.'

The canister of poteen. Not on the inventory.

The kind of thing no one will notice if some of it goes missing.

I step into the storeroom and dig through a couple of boxes while Rowan continues muttering darkly about Cian by the door.

'Here,' I say, and I thrust an empty lemonade bottle at him, the kind with the cork that swings into place over the lip. 'Mags has a fresh can of poteen behind last week's Guinness kegs. I don't think she'll miss a few drops.'

Rowan gives me a weird look. 'Poteen?' he says.

'It's like ninety per cent alcohol,' I tell him. 'It probably tastes like shit, but I've heard it gives you visions. I think we should try it.'

His eyes are still narrowed.

'What?' I say.

He shrugs. 'I've heard it rots your teeth and makes you go blind.'

'Yeah, well.' I hand him the bottle. 'That's a risk I'm willing to take.'

By the end of the night, Rowan and Cian have almost come to blows five times and Mags is starting to get bristly. I wait for Cian to leave before rounding on my brother.

'Take it easy, OK?' I tell him. 'Can you at least *try* to keep out of trouble?' He doesn't remind me that I'm usually the one causing it. 'We want to stay here as long as we can.'

Rowan gives me a look. 'I know,' he says.

'Seriously, if the Guards find out we're—'

'I *know*, Hazel.'

'And if you want to keep up this whatever-it-is with Ivy, then we can't be starting fights—'

'I said I *know. Jesus.*' He clatters down the hall, thumping the doorjamb on the way out.

He didn't say there wasn't a thing with Ivy.

He didn't say there was either.

When we messaged her to tell her we'd be coming to town, we made a pact together, him and me. If we got here and we were both still in love with her, neither of us could make a move. If something happened between them at the party, he's broken the pact. He's lost my trust.

After my shift, I search through my bags for my cigarettes. Groceries, wallet, sketchbook, phone, box of charcoal pencils, half a bar of Dairy Milk, no cigarettes. Maybe Cian's right: maybe there is a thief about. Or maybe I just dropped them on the way across town.

I bum a cigarette off Mags and sit on the back doorstep, facing the car park, to smoke it. My phone rings, vibrating shrilly in my back pocket against the concrete I'm sitting on. It's Ivy.

'Did Mags say anything to you about today's cross-word?' she asks the second I answer.

'Huh? Oh. No, nothing. Why? Is the generator gonna break down again?' I say it lightly, but really I'm worried the second she says it. Worried the clues Mags points out – the ones she somehow knows can predict our immediate future – have finally said *police* or *Hazel* or *monster.* Have finally told Ivy what I've done.

'No,' Ivy says, and her voice is kinda worried. 'I was just hoping she could clarify something for me.'

'Like Mags ever clarifies anything.' Mags refuses to even acknowledge that she sends the fortune-telling clues. 'What's it say?'

I can hear paper rustle.

'Someone's coming,' Ivy says. 'The clues were *expect* and *guests*.'

My heart starts to hammer in my throat. 'You think it means the Guards?'

'They wouldn't be guests, though,' she says uncertainly. 'Would they?'

Something rises in me. Something scared and twisted and hopeful. 'Ivy,' I say. 'Have you had news of my parents?'

'Oh. No. But it might be them. I mean, who else could it be?'

'I dunno. Your mum maybe. Did you tell her where we're staying?'

'Oh, no,' Ivy says. 'It's best if she doesn't know.'

'You're probably right.' Even Ivy's mum might draw the line at us staying in a boarded-up house on a ghost estate.

'So it might be them,' Ivy says again. 'That wouldn't be such a bad thing, would it?'

It wouldn't, but I don't say that to Ivy. I take a deep drag of my cigarette. 'Ivy, you know my parents,' I say, and I'm surprised my voice is steady. 'And I thought you were sure the crossword said we'd lost them.'

'If someone's lost,' Ivy replies softly, 'it means they can be found.'

Not always, I think to myself, and hang up at Ivy's quiet goodbye.

I lied – my veins aren't live wires. They're liquid lava. They're fire. I don't know what I'd do if my mum showed up at the door of the house in Oak Road. Hope and fear bubble up in my body like a physical thing. It's like oil on the flames in my veins until I remember the real flames. The real fire. The real reason I don't think my mum is going to show up at our door. Ivy and Rowan don't know it, but there's a reason why I don't think my mum's going to show up anywhere any more.

Olive

Monday 8th May, Tuesday 9th May

Lost: Purse
(purple, embroidered with mirrors)

I'm lost without Rose, and without my bracelet. I walk my bike all the way home from school, keeping my eyes on the road. It takes two hours and by the time I get home I'm cranky and starving and still braceletless.

I search the whole house. Between bedsheets, in the shower drain, under couches, at the back of the fridge. The dogs follow me, sniffing around as if they know what I'm looking for.

My dad is in the study, marking essays, listening to tuneless modern jazz. He takes his role as a stereotypical, eccentric poetry professor very seriously.

There are boxes full of my mum's old things stacked up around the desk. They'd been in my nana's attic since Mum left home at nineteen. Nana begrudgingly kept them the whole time we lived in Dublin, but has been trying to get Mum to move them into our own attic since we moved to Balmallen five years ago. Nana must finally have got her way. I take a quick look inside the open ones, but my bracelet hasn't fallen in there either. A couple of old photographs and a bunch of loose papers flutter out.

'Weren't you supposed to be back from school two hours ago?' Dad asks.

'I walked home; that's why I was late.'

Dad raises his eyebrows.

'I *swear*. I was looking for my bracelet. I was worried I'd dropped it on the way to school this morning.'

'And now you think it might be in a box that's been in your nana's attic for the past twenty years?'

'I'm just covering all my bases,' I say.

'Have you tried the last place you put it?' Dad asks serenely.

I smack the palm of my hand against my forehead. 'Of course!' I exclaim sarcastically. 'I would never have thought to look there!'

The thing is, I still amn't sure where *there* is. Where *is* the last place I had it? Increasingly, I'm beginning to wonder if the girls in school are right.

What did you lose at the party on Saturday?
Everybody lost something.

The next morning I cycle slowly to school – partly because I spend half the journey texting Rose, and partly because I'm still hoping to catch sight of my bracelet on the way – and I'm almost late for my first class. I take my seat in chemistry behind Julia and Chrissy, and when the teacher isn't looking I tap gently on their shoulders.

'Did you have any luck with your missing things?' I ask when they turn round. 'The stuff you lost at the party.'

Chrissy shakes her head. 'Why? Didn't you say you *didn't* lose anything?'

'I did,' I admit. 'A bracelet. It was my mum's. A charm bracelet.'

Julia makes a sympathetic face. 'If we see it, we'll tell you,' she says.

Rose doesn't come to our next class, which we usually have together. Or to any of our classes for the rest of the day. She doesn't ask me to tell our teachers she's going home sick. She doesn't ask me anything at all. She just fires off a quick text after the start of our next class to tell me she's going home early.

I message her updates periodically even though she doesn't reply to any of them.

NOT MISSING MUCH STOP
CHRISSY J AND CATHAL M
HAVE HAD PHONES
CONFISCATED TWICE
ALREADY STOP CHRISSY FOR
CRIME OF IN-CLASS SELFIES
STOP CATHAL MOST LIKELY
WATCHING PORN STOP IF I
AM CAUGHT TEXTING
AVENGE MY DEATH STOP
OLIVE

I only hear what happened at the end of the day. Rose got kicked out of German class this morning.

Mr Fallon comes up to me in the corridor after my last class and asks where she is. 'I sent her to the principal's office this morning, but that doesn't mean I gave her a pass to skip her next class, too.'

I give Mr Fallon a helpless shrug and an excuse I've heard Rose use before, word for word. 'She had to go home sick, sir. Really bad period cramps. Couldn't stand up straight. I get them myself sometimes when my flow's particularly heavy. It's basically hell.' I hardly even blush.

'Right,' Mr Fallon says, looking a bit uncomfortable. 'That might explain – But look, Olive, tell Rose that I won't tolerate that kind of behaviour in my class again, whether or not she's having . . . woman trouble.'

Woman trouble indeed. I promise to keep an eye on her and Mr Fallon goes on his way.

HEARD YOU WERE REBELLING WITHOUT ME STOP, I text Rose.

Rose doesn't answer to elaborate on her behaviour so I have to assume she just drew rude pictures on her textbook or something again. But then I end up walking behind Chrissy, Julia and Shannon on the way to the car park and I hear them say Rose's name.

'I heard she punched someone,' Chrissy's saying in a Chrissy-undertone that probably the whole corridor can hear. Julia replies in a low voice that I can't make out.

Sean Moran, who is one of their boyfriends, but I can never remember which – possibly because they rotate boyfriends to keep the rest of us guessing – says, 'I heard she started screaming and swearing in the middle of class and, like, tore up a book and threw it in some guy's face.'

I speed up a little to stay within earshot.

'I heard she ripped up her homework and *ate* it,' Shannon says with relish, and Julia rolls her eyes.

'Oh, come on.'

That's when they see me. 'Olive,' Chrissy says, looking a bit uncomfortable. 'You'll know. What *did* Rose do to get kicked out of Mr Fallon's class?'

'I heard she's been expelled,' Shannon adds helpfully, to which Julia snorts.

'Bullshit – it was just one class.'

I hurry past them and unlock my bike.

This doesn't sound right. I thought I knew Rose as well as I know myself, but ever since the party something's been different. It feels like I'm losing her. I send her a message before I cycle home.

> SERIOUS QUESTION STOP
> ARE YOU OK STOP PLEASE
> TALK TO ME STOP OLIVE

My phone finally pings just as I cycle in the gate.

> UNDER HOUSE ARREST STOP
> PHONE USE DISCOURAGED
> STOP MUM INSISTING ON
> BONDING TIME STOP BEING
> FORCE-FED SCONES AND
> MEDICAL TV SHOWS STOP
> KILL ME NOW STOP ROSE

I prop my bike against our overflowing recycling bin and reply, leaving the letters and bills and receipts that have fallen out of the bin to skitter across the garden.

> THAT DOESN'T EXPLAIN
> YOUR ABSENCE ALL DAY

STOP WAITING TO HEAR
WHAT HAPPENED IN
FALLON'S CLASS STOP KEEP
ME A SCONE OR OUR
FRIENDSHIP IS OVER STOP
OLIVE

Emily and Chloe are doing their homework at the table when I get home. Dad is washing the dishes. They don't notice me. If they had, maybe Chloe would have stopped talking about Rose.

'. . . heard about Rose Driscoll going crazy this morning?' she is saying to Emily. I stop on the threshold. Emily looks over at my dad and leans towards Chloe to answer in a voice too low for me to make out.

'I *know*, right?' Chloe says loudly. 'And then she, like, flipped out,' she goes on. 'Tore up the money and' – a slight pause for effect – 'like, stuffed it in her *mouth*.'

'Well, *maybe* if she had a mouth as big as *yours* she'd be able to fit more in there.' I speak before I realize I'm speaking.

Chloe freezes, an expression of shock on her face. Emily has the courtesy to look ashamed.

'Don't you have any other vapid rumours to be spreading?' I ask, my tone scathing.

'I'm just saying what I heard,' Chloe says. 'It sounds like she seriously lost it. I'd be worried if I were you. I heard she stuffed a tenner in her mouth and chewed it all up and spat it out again *right on the teacher's desk*.'

Dad, ostensibly not eavesdropping, turns from the sink with an exaggerated gasp and cries, 'Lock the back door!'

Chloe starts, obviously having forgotten my dad was there at all. She shoots Emily a look that clearly communicates, *Your dad is a weirdo.* Emily studiously avoids my eye.

'The phrase you're looking for,' I tell my dad calmly, 'is *shut the front door*.'

'Ah,' Dad says. 'Right. That's the one.' He winks at me almost imperceptibly as he turns back to the dishes. Emily and Chloe flee the kitchen, as if his embarrassing nature is contagious.

My dad is sneakily good at defusing situations.

When Dad's finished with the dishes, he places a wet, sudsy hand on the top of my head. '*Water, water, everywhere, / Nor any drop to drink*,' he says solemnly.

I wave his hand away and shake my head to dislodge the drops. 'Coleridge,' I say. 'Samuel Taylor. Born in 1772. Credited with several important idioms, contemporary of William Wordsworth, probably never frizzed up his daughter's hair after she'd managed to keep it perfectly straight all day.'

Dad nods with approval. 'I could never live up to such a man.'

'Coleridge abandoned his family after his daughter was born,' Mum says, having come into the kitchen without me hearing. 'He was also addicted to opium and was horrible to his wife. There's not much to live up to there.'

Some manner of enthusiastic pop music blasts in through the kitchen door from Emily's bedroom upstairs. I click the battery out of my hearing aid and the world's volume mercifully turns down. Sometimes, being deaf in one ear can be a serious asset. I can still feel the bass reverberating in the ceiling.

'Can we abandon Emily?' I mumble. Neither of my parents hears me.

Mum looks around the kitchen. 'Where's Rose?' she asks.

'I'm grounded, remember?'

'Well, yes, but I didn't think Rose would actually stay away.'

'There's a first time for everything,' Dad says cheerfully, and he disappears into the hall. Seconds later we can hear him loudly and enthusiastically singing along to Emily's music on the landing. Emily turns it off mid-song.

Mum sighs in relief. I click the battery back into my hearing aid just in time to hear her mutter, 'She'll probably never listen to that song again.'

'Her life'll be the better for it.'

'As will mine.' Mum closes her eyes. 'I'm dropping your grandmother down to Dr Driscoll's for a check-up. Back in an hour or so.'

I stop at the kitchen door. 'I thought Rose's mum wasn't working today,' I say.

'No, she is. Nana's got an appointment with her in half an hour.'

Rose is lying to me. She's not home bonding with her mother, being force-fed scones. Why is Rose lying?

'It's only going to get worse,' Mum says softly. The hairs on my arms stand up.

'What?'

'I said, have you seen my purse?' Mum says, snapping out of it. 'I swear I'm getting as bad as your nana – I can't seem to find anything any more.'

But there's something – a little twist to her mouth, a little crinkle to her eyes – that gives me shivers. *I can't seem to find anything any more.*

Hazel

Wednesday 10th May

Lost: Black-and-white kitten; two bruised mandarins

I'm cycling home from work late on Wednesday with some groceries Mags has given us when I come across a wishing tree, hung with ribbon and trinket offerings. These trees are said to spring from holy wells. The roots drink the water and bless the branches. When the offerings blow away, the wishes are granted.

I have so many wishes I wouldn't know where to start. I'd stop and make one, but it's lashing rain and I want to get home, be dry, drink the whiskey I stuffed into my boot at the off-licence this morning. Those are my only real wishes right now. Apart from Ivy. And maybe Ivy already sees through me.

I have secrets. I tell lies. I drink too much and I steal things sometimes. One day my freckled skin will go scaly and everyone will see what a monster I can be.

This rain is heavy and my glasses are blurred by raindrops. I make out something skittering across the bumpy road in front of me, scurrying in the mud. Then my tyres are slipping, and I have to brake by slamming both my feet on the ground. In the middle of the road, a small cat cowers.

I drop my bike where I stand and go to pet the tiny creature, but an enormous clap of thunder strikes and the kitten darts away under a fence and into the field at the other side of the road.

I swear under my breath and check out my bike for damage from the skid. That's when I notice something caught between the spokes of my back wheel. I pull it out. It's a shoe – flat, thin and silver; one of those cheap ballet pumps that you can crumple in your hand like a slipper. It's scuffed at the toes. I drew it a few days ago in charcoal on the page as if I knew it. This makes no sense. *Did you lose something last night?* Ivy asked that day. It looks like lots of people have lost something. I stick the shoe in one of my shopping bags so I can show it to Ivy, or maybe ask Mags if she thinks there might be something kinda weird going on.

A few of the groceries have exploded out of the bags and I have to slop through the mud to find them. A tin of baked beans, two rolling mandarins, a now-soggy loaf of bread. They lead me like a trail of crumbs to the gate at the edge of the next field.

I pick up the bread and hop over the gate to see if I can find the kitten. I make little kissy kitten noises with my mouth. The rain pours. The wind blows. If I was a cat, I'd be holed up in the middle of a bush right now, sheltered and licking myself dry. Three magpies on a nearby tree watch me. I caw loudly to warn them off, but I close my mouth when I see the girl.

She's shadowy, standing by the biggest tree beside the fence at the edge of the field. I can't see her face because she's turned slightly away from me. She's wearing a tight little sundress whose colours – purple, maybe, or bloody red – have faded to grey by the dim light of a rainy evening. Her hair is long, red and tangled, curlier than mine. She's holding a cigarette. Something about the way she's standing makes me think that she doesn't want to be disturbed.

Without noticing me staring, she turns and walks away. She follows the fence to the edge of the field and disappears round the bend in the road ahead.

When I'm sure she's gone, I walk to the spot where she was standing. The muddy grass is covered in her footprints and when I look down I notice something half buried there. When I tug on it, I unearth a notebook. It's small and red, covered in mud, damp and dripping. It's kept shut by a thick black elastic band and bulges as if there are things stuck between the pages. The ribbon lolls like a tongue through the middle of it, marking a page.

I snap off the elastic band and pull at the ribbon to open the notebook and something falls out. I pick it up out of the mud and place it on the fence post with trembling fingers.

It's a big bronze key. I recognize it right away and my heart skips three beats while I hold my breath. I see this key eighty times a day. It's been inked on my skin for the last three years.

I roll up the sleeve of my jumper and line up my wrist with the key on the fence post. It's rusty-looking but not rusted; the handle you grasp between finger and thumb large and round, almost heart-shaped if you look close enough, the gap filled with curls and circles. I trace the shapes with my finger hovering just above the key. I know the design by heart.

I haven't seen the real key in three years. I thought I never would again.

When I pick up the key, I almost believe something'll happen. A thunderclap, an earthquake, an omen. But it's just a key, and I'm alone in an empty field.

Olive

Wednesday 10th May

Lost: Phone signal

Rose doesn't come to school on Wednesday. She messages vaguely in telegram-speak about exam stress, but everyone's worrying about exams, and not coming to school certainly isn't going to help. I know that's not what's wrong. I just don't know what is.

After school, I tell Emily to go home without me so that I can head over to Rose's.

'Mum's going to kill you,' Emily says as I'm about to pedal away. 'You're still supposed to be grounded, you know.'

'If you knew your best friend was so stressed she couldn't come to school, you'd go to her, too. Even if you were grounded.'

Emily gives me a measured look. Finally she rolls her eyes and says, 'Fine. I'll tell Mum you're doing an extra maths class this evening. Just remember to stick to the story tonight or I'll get in trouble, too.'

'You're a star.' I give my sister a relieved grin.

At Rose's, nobody answers the door. She doesn't answer her phone either. I stick a note in her letter box that says: *HOPE YOU'RE OK STOP CALL ME STOP OLIVE.*

Since I've already got an alibi, I decide to look for my bracelet on the way home, starting with the field where the bonfire was built. I must have lost my bracelet there; it hasn't shown up anywhere else. But there's nothing in the pile of soot and charred wood or the crumbling hay bales or the grass where I woke up, where the scruffy blond boy was sleeping.

The clouds get darker overhead and it starts to drizzle.

My search takes me on a slow loop all around the field, from the small copse of trees where I saw the beautiful curly-haired boy to the fence at the opposite edge of the field along which I searched for Rose that morning.

At the furthest corner, I nearly walk into a rose bush I'm certain wasn't there before. I stop and stare at it. No roses were growing in this field on Saturday night. I tug at a branch, but the bush is rooted in place. Not for the first time this week I wonder if I might be losing my mind just a little bit.

Mostly, though, my mind is occupied with Rose and her sudden silence. Maybe that's why I'm misremembering rose bushes. I'm beginning to wonder if I've done something wrong. Maybe I said something to Rose at the party, the memory of it lost like the rest of that night. Maybe I did something stupid and she's only pretending she can't remember because she doesn't want to tell me. I almost lost her friendship once over some ill-thought-out kisses and we vowed never to let that happen again, but it turns out there are plenty of other ways you can lose a friend.

When the rain intensifies, I grab my bike and begin to cycle home. I've just kicked off when my tyres bump over something sharp on the road and I lose control, swerving into the fence between the field and the road. I jump off the saddle and swear. My back tyre is punctured. To add insult to injury, the sky above me opens and the rain becomes a downpour. I button up the denim jacket I sort-of stole after the party and shiver.

The rain pours down in fat, cold drops. I take out my phone. It says, *Check connection. Network signal lost.*

Something catches my eye from across the road and while I wait for my phone signal to reappear I cross over to look closer. It's a wishing tree. It's more a shrub than a tree actually, but there are rags and ribbons and rosaries wound round the branches, and coins and Mass cards wedged in among the leaves. There are other things, too: a tiny bronze Buddha statue, a plastic-beaded bracelet, a child's shoe, a faded photograph. The rain tinkles on the trinkets, makes eerie music on the empty road. I don't know why anyone would think tying an offering to the branch of a tree could ever make a wish come true.

I check my phone again. Still no signal. I just need shelter until the rain eases off. Oak Road is close by. There'd be plenty of shelter behind the boiler houses or in the storm-drain tunnel at the edge of the estate. I check my phone one last time and hurry in the opposite direction.

Five minutes later I'm leaning my bike against the flat-topped wall that rings Oak Road when I see a boy. He's standing in the weed-tangled driveway of the house right in front of me, staring at me like a deer in the headlights. Not just any boy. Frayed jumper, skinny jeans, black-framed glasses, curly brown hair under a flat cap. It's the boy I saw the morning after the party.

The wind picks up, snatches leaves and stones and sends them skittering along the ground between us. The rain lashes. Somewhere in the not-so-distant distance thunder growls. The boy looks up at the darkening sky. I raise my head to the rain and look up, too, and there's a fork of lightning – a trident, thin and brilliant, above us. Automatically, I start counting. Me and this boy alone in the middle of a ghost estate in the oncoming storm, silent countdown in my head.

When the thunder sounds again – is it closer this time? – I finally say something. 'Is it supposed to be a mile for every second between the thunder and the lightning?' I ask. 'Although that hardly sounds scientific.'

The boy laughs, but his reply is drowned out by yet more thunder. At this point, the world is more water than air. I cover my left ear with a cupped hand so my hearing aid won't get wet.

'What are you looking for?' he asks.

How does he know I was looking for something? 'My bike got a flat tyre,' I tell him, shouting over the noise of the weather. 'And then the sky decided to turn into Niagara Falls. I'm not having the best day ever.'

The boy gives me an appraising look.

'I was going to shelter in the storm-drain tunnel,' I go on. 'To wait out the rain. What are *you* doing here?'

'I live here,' the boy says.

'You *what*?'

He shrugs and says with a smile, 'Unorthodox, I know.'

I blink. I know which house he lives in. It was his voice I must have heard on Monday, his light I saw in the cracks between the wooden boards.

'D'you wanna come in for a bit?' He gestures behind him. 'Wait out the rain? I promise I'm not an axe-murderer or anything.'

'That's exactly the kind of thing an axe-murderer would say.'

'My sister lives here, too,' he says. 'And our friend. Who is also a girl. You don't have to come in. I mean, you can shelter in the tunnel like you said, if you prefer. I won't take it personally.'

I purse my lips at the concrete tunnel. The wind whips my hair around my face. 'OK,' I tell him. 'I'll take my chances with you. But no funny business.'

He gives a surprised laugh and I blush to the soles of my feet.

'I mean no axe-murdering,' I clarify quickly. 'Or murdering of any sort.'

He beckons for me to follow him. 'You're perfectly safe with me,' he says, and for some reason my mum's face flashes into my mind. Her blank eyes at the breakfast table when I came home from the party. *He's trouble. He's lost a lot and so will you. Stay away from him, or you'll lose everything.*

I shake my head to dispel the thought and I follow the boy across the mud and sodden weeds of the ghost estate. I can't remember the last time I did something like this without Rose. I can't remember the last time I met someone new on my own.

'I'm Olive, by the way,' I tell the boy.

He grins and says, 'Olive. Like the tree.'

'That's right,' I say, even though most people would think of the fruit first.

'I'm Rowan,' he says then.

I grin right back at him. 'Like the tree.'

'Exactly.'

I follow Rowan to the empty house that has a rusty number five on it. He moves the planks of wood to one side and shoulders open the door.

Inside the house the radio is on, or maybe a television, but I can't see evidence of either in the dim light. The floor is dirty, mud-tracked, and our footsteps echo. Above us, it sounds like someone might be singing. I twist my head to try and see up the stairs. The banister is thick and gleaming, the steps bare wood. Everything empty and echoey and old-new.

I follow Rowan into the kitchen, which is slightly brighter than the hall because the windows are unboarded and the sliding French-style doors let in whatever light is left in the storm. Which, admittedly, isn't much.

Rowan goes around the kitchen lighting the candles and torches on every surface. I suppose there wouldn't be electricity in an estate full of empty houses. The music I'm hearing is coming from a little wind-up radio, the kind you take on camping trips when you're a kid.

And it must be a bit like camping, living here. The fitted marble counters lining three of the room's four walls are covered with tins and packets of food, and a few plates and bowls and mismatched mugs – all of them chipped, some clearly only held together by glue and good luck. A tiny fridge of the kind you see in films of college dorm rooms stands in the empty space designed to fit a proper fridge. It's attached by a cable to a small generator.

A gas camping stove sits on one of the counters. On it is a huge, heavy, cast-iron kettle that stands out starkly from its surroundings. The sink beside the back door is filled with dirty dishes.

In the middle of the room there is a big old camping table surrounded by chairs in various states of disrepair. An open box of chocolates sits in the middle of the table with empty wrappers scattered all around it. Nothing is left inside the box but the orange ones and the red ones.

Rowan leans against the kitchen door, watching me stare at his unconventional home. He has a silver Zippo lighter in his right hand and is flicking it open and shut, open, shut, in a movement so practised he must do it several hundred times a day. He's wearing an expression that looks something like recognition.

'I know you from somewhere, don't I?' he says.

'Oh,' I say, and I blush for some reason. 'Yeah. No, not really. I saw you at the party on Saturday. Or Sunday morning rather. Just briefly. I was looking for my friend and you were over at the edge of the field.' I obviously don't mention how much I've been thinking about that brief encounter since.

'No,' he says thoughtfully. 'That's not it. You sure we haven't met before?'

I laugh and look around the candle-and-torchlit kitchen again. 'No way,' I tell him. 'I'd definitely remember you.'

Then I shut my mouth and blush again because, of all the ridiculous things to do, of course I'd tell a boy I've just met he's memorable. Why not just throw myself right at him while I'm at it?

'No, I could swear—' Rowan starts to say, but is interrupted by the front door opening with a bang.

Because he didn't close the kitchen door behind us when we came in, I can see straight down the hall to the tall, curly-haired girl who storms inside, completely drenched by the rain. She slams the door behind her and dumps her heavy-looking shopping bags unceremoniously by the stairs. Then she kicks off her shoes, peels off her dripping jumper and her sopping socks, followed by her damp black shirt and her trousers that are wet and muddy to the knees, leaving the lot in a heap on the floor in front of the door. She shakes her hair out of her face, picks up the shopping bags and tramps down into the kitchen in her underwear. I have to pinch myself so I'll stop staring.

Rowan nearly chokes.

'Jesus, Hazel, put some clothes on,' he says. 'That's not a sight I need to see at any hour of the day.'

Hazel casually drops her shopping bags on the kitchen table and gives Rowan the finger before tying her wet hair out of her face with an elastic band from around her wrist. She wipes her glasses dry with a dirty tea towel. 'It's raining,' she says, somewhat unnecessarily.

'Yeah. And most people generally opt to put *more* clothes on when that's the case.'

Hazel turns and sees me.

'Who's this?' she asks.

'I found her,' says Rowan. 'Just by the gate.'

'I just wanted to get out of the rain,' I tell them.

I am standing in my own little puddle. The ends of my hair drip on to my shoulders, *pat-pat-pat*. I keep my eyes on the puddle to avoid staring at the tattoo Hazel has just under the cup of her bra.

Hazel looks from me to Rowan and back again. 'You're wearing my jacket,' she says.

I look down at the rain-drenched denim. 'This is yours?' Weird coincidence. 'I found it the morning after the town party.' I shrug it off and hand it to her. 'I ate all your gum,' I add. 'Sorry.'

Hazel laughs. 'That's OK.'

Rowan is still staring at me like he's trying to figure me out. 'I'm *sure* the party isn't where I know you from, though,' he says.

He's taken off his cap and is pulling his jumper up over his head, attempting to dry his hair on the wet wool. His T-shirt slips up slightly and I catch a glimpse of something that looks like a tattoo above his hip before he lowers his arms and the T-shirt covers it again.

Tattooed teenagers living in a ghost estate. I'm not sure I could live with myself if I didn't find out more about these two. I can't wait to tell Rose. It occurs to me that if I'd been with Rose this afternoon in the first place, I never would have ended up in this situation.

'Do you want to borrow some dry clothes?' offers Hazel.

'OK,' I say, and she takes me by the elbow and leads me into the hall and up the stairs. The house smells like candlewax and cigarette smoke.

'So,' I ask as we go up in the near-dark, 'what are you guys doing living here?'

The light is slightly brighter on the landing, even though it seems to be getting progressively greyer outside. Although the two large windows at each end of the hall are boarded up like those downstairs, there's a skylight at the top of the stairs above us.

Hazel doesn't answer my question. Instead, she calls into one of the bedrooms. 'Ivy, you were right. We do have a guest. This is . . .'

'Olive,' I say to the girl who steps out on to the landing. She's striking – and not just because of her hair, which is short, spiky and bright blue. She's small and very slim – beautiful in a fairy princess kind of a way – and her eyes are the kind you notice, which is unusual, because nobody notices people's eyes outside of fiction. They're a very light blue, like some kind of crystal. She's wearing a motley collection of woollen layers that make her look like a punky nineteenth-century farm girl. She is strange and lovely.

To my surprise, she comes over and hugs me, tight and quick, as if we know each other. She says, 'Hi, Olive,' as if she isn't in the least surprised to see a stranger in her weird, empty house. Then she says to Hazel, 'Why aren't you wearing any clothes?'

'I'm wearing underwear.' Hazel hooks a thumb under her left bra strap and coquettishly lowers it over her shoulder.

Ivy doesn't even bat an eyelid. 'That's true.'

Hazel authoritatively leads me into another one of the bedrooms. Like the rest of the house, it's blank and dark and almost empty. A sagging mattress pushed up against the far wall serves as a bed. Hazel clicks on a torch and roots through one of the Tesco bags piled under the boarded-up window. She pulls a bunch of clothes and toiletries and other random things out on to the floor.

'Everything's such a – dammit – mess. Here, take these – they're mostly clean.'

She hands me a white satiny dress that looks more like a slip than actual clothes, and a large Aran jumper. Then she wriggles into a very tight pair of cut-off denim shorts and an oversized T-shirt. She is all curves of pale, freckled skin and long, strong legs. She has a tattoo of a skeleton key on one arm, and on the other there's a keyhole that looks like it's been shaded in with galaxies – no negative space, only tiny white dots like clusters of stars. The other tattoo – the one I've been avoiding staring at all this time, the one across her ribs, right under her breasts – is new, covered in a clear plastic bandage. It's a line of words, but, while I'm curious to know what it says, I'm too embarrassed to look more closely.

I realize I've been staring when Hazel turns to look back at me. I peel my damp jumper and school shirt over my head and put on Hazel's clothes instead. I try hard not to appear self-conscious, fighting the urge to turn my back or cross my arms around my middle. The clothes fit even though I'm about half a foot shorter than she is. *Rose would love this girl*, I find myself thinking. Rose never mastered the art of shimmying her bra off under her top and instead strips flamboyantly, just daring you to look. Hazel seems to be of a similar disposition.

When I look back up at Hazel, she is fully clothed and considering me appreciatively. She comes over to stand in front of me and pulls my hair out from under the collar of her jumper. 'Cute,' she says.

'Thanks.' I pluck at the hem of the dress. 'For the clothes.' My legs are muddy and my hair is still wet, but I'm warming up considerably. 'And for the compliment.'

Hazel has a wicked smile. 'I've got more where that came from.' I don't know if she means the clothes or the compliment.

Hazel leads me back into the hall, where Ivy is waiting. She turns and says, as if she's read my mind, 'Both.'

Hazel

Wednesday 10th May

Lost: Two tarnished teaspoons;
one small candle

Olive goes into the hall to call her sister and I text Mags to ask if she'll give her a lift home. After I press send, since Olive's out of earshot, I turn to Rowan.

'So we're bringing girls home now?' I ask. 'Funny, I didn't get the memo.'

Rowan's cheeks go pink. 'It's not like that. She just showed up in the middle of the storm – what was I supposed to do?'

'The crossword said to expect guests,' Ivy says quietly. 'And this girl just got lost in the storm.'

Rowan's mouth opens slightly.

'She's important,' says Ivy. 'She must be.'

'Important how?' Rowan asks.

'I don't know,' Ivy answers. 'I just think she is.'

Then it hits me. The crossword wasn't talking about my mum.

There's ash in my mouth and I can't swallow. Ivy said *Who else could it be?* and I let myself believe it. It's been nearly four weeks since we've heard from our mother. What if she's really gone? When I close my eyes, I see flames.

When Olive comes back in, she has tea and biscuits with us and asks a whole bunch of questions about how long we've been living here and why and how come Ivy's here, too, and even though I like Olive – she's funny and kinda sarcastic, easy to talk to – I'm finding it hard to breathe. Smoke and flames. My mum not coming home again. Rowan's chatting and laughing with Olive and he doesn't know and I don't know how to tell him. And I don't want it to be true. But I've known it since the day we left. The day we ran away. I knew we'd never see her again.

I only tune back in to what's going on around me when Ivy spots the shoe I found stuck to my bike when I cycled home from work, sitting in the shopping bag where I stuffed it. I'd forgotten all about it.

'Did you meet Cinderella at work?' Ivy asks me, holding the scuffed ballet flat by the heel between her thumb and forefinger.

Immediately, Olive snatches it off her. 'Where did you get this?' she asks.

'I found it,' I tell her. 'When I was cycling home. It was stuck to my bike wheel.'

'Let me guess,' Ivy says to Olive in her lilting voice, the words like a song. 'You lost it at the party.' She cocks her head to one side like a blue-haired bird.

'You had my jacket,' I say slowly. 'And I had your shoe.'

'That's really weird,' Olive says, but then she shrugs and stuffs the shoe into her school bag. 'I suppose we're even then.'

It *is* kinda weird. 'I guess we are.'

I reach into my own bag and pull out the notebook. 'I found this, too.' I hold it up in a beam of torchlight and stolen candles. 'It was in the field where the party was last Saturday. Someone must have dropped it there.'

I don't mention the key that fell out of it. It's still in the pocket of the work trousers that I took off by the door. I also don't mention the red-haired girl. I'm not sure why.

Then I open the notebook and it's like the answer to my prayers.

It says: *Spellbook of the Lost and Found.*

'What is it?' Rowan asks from across the table.

'It's a spellbook,' I tell him as I peel off the elastic band and turn the pages carefully. It doesn't look like a spellbook from the outside. Not really. When I picked it up, I thought it was maybe a diary. It's red leather and pretty small, like the Moleskines poets carry around in films. But inside it the paper looks old. Yellow. The pages are water-logged and some of them are falling apart. On some the ink has run so much they're illegible.

But the page the spell is on is clear. I can read it perfectly.

'A *spell* book?' Olive asks.

'Spells and saints,' Ivy whispers. 'A list of gods and offerings.' I hadn't noticed her reading over my shoulder.

For every page that's written on, there's one with things stuck to the paper. As I turn the pages, a feather, bent backwards by the book, unfolds. An autumn leaf covered in strange symbols. An old coin shines in the light of the kitchen.

'What a weird thing to find,' Olive says.

There's something familiar about the handwriting.

'I wonder who wrote it,' Ivy says like she's read my mind.

I go back to the page with the spell on it and read it again. And again. And again.

Calling for the Lost to be Found.

You will need: A charm or talisman . . . A glass bottle filled with the waters of Lethe, the underground river in Hades that makes the drinker forget . . . A length of silver string. Red ink. Olive oil. A handful of rowan berries. A hazel branch. A vine of ivy. As many rose thorns as you have losses. Moss gathered from under an oak tree. Human blood.

Rowan and I have lost our parents. In my hand, there's a spell to call back what's been lost.

Olive comes up behind me and reads over my other shoulder. She reaches across me and turns the pages. She says 'Weird' and 'Wow' and 'How old do you think this thing is?'

But that's not what I'm wondering right now. 'Who does it belong to?' I think out loud. 'Who'd lose a spellbook?'

Olive laughs. 'Who'd bring a book of spells to a party?' she says.

'What?' Rowan asks.

Olive looks at me. 'You said you found it in the field the party was in last Saturday,' she says.

The party. My jacket, Rowan's cap, Ivy's necklace, Olive's shoe. Everybody lost something.

'Somebody cast this spell at the party,' I say slowly. I don't know how I know it's true, but it's like Ivy's crossword. Right every time. 'Everybody seems to have lost something since then.'

'Oh, don't be silly,' says Olive, then she backtracks. 'Sorry. I just mean people lose shit at parties all the time. I doubt it's the first time any of us lost something after a few drinks.'

But Ivy's nodding, flipping to the end of the spell. '*Be careful what you bargain with: every lost thing requires a sacrifice — a new loss for every called thing found.*' She closes her eyes.

'That's why we've all been losing things. Somebody cast this spell to find something, but they didn't sacrifice something as well. So everyone who was at the party is losing things to make up for that.'

'Seriously?' Olive laughs a bit. 'You really believe all that?' She looks at Rowan, who just kinda shrugs.

'I mean,' he says, 'it does explain a lot.'

'A lot of what? I lost a shoe. Hazel lost a jacket. That all sounds pretty normal to me.' But then Olive stops, and the look on her face changes. It's like she's just thought of something. Something she's lost. Something more than a scuffed silver shoe.

'A hazel branch,' I read aloud. 'Olive oil. Rowan berries and a vine of ivy. Hazel, Olive, Rowan and Ivy. There's an ingredient for each of us.'

Olive leans closer. 'And rose thorns,' she adds quietly.

Ivy takes the book from me and says with something a bit like wonder, 'You're right – there's a part for each of us to play.'

Olive's phone buzzes suddenly in the silence. She checks the message and stands up fast. 'Shit,' she says. 'That's my sister. My parents are looking for me. I have to go.'

As if on cue, we hear the crunch of tyres outside. Mags. Olive leaves, holding her school bag over her head against the rain.

We watch her go, sitting silently round a table we found at a garage sale, on chairs we salvaged from the side of the road, drinking from mugs that we stole. Rowan doesn't know this isn't temporary. He doesn't know our mum's not coming home. That she probably died in that fire. But he looks like he knows something. His face is drawn and he stares out of the kitchen door where Olive left, but he's not looking at anything at all. Ivy's frowning, her bottom lip between her teeth. *There's a part for each of us to play*, she said. A spell to make lost things found again.

The only problem is, how do I get them to cast it with me without ever telling them why?

Olive

Wednesday 10th May

Lost: Train of thought;
small umbrella (red, white dots)

Mags Maguire drives me home. Rowan told me she's
related to Ivy somehow, and that's why she keeps an eye
on them. I watch her covertly, trying to see a family
resemblance between her broad, lined face and Ivy's
delicate features, without much success. Although they
do both have those very pale blue eyes.

Pressed uncomfortably against my feet is a big old
brown Labrador with rheumy eyes. (*Lucky. That's her seat,
so if you don't want to sit in the back you're sharing the passenger
seat with her.*) I would have sat in the back except that the
entire seat is taken up by a row of big metal canisters that

clank ominously as we drive. They are belted in tighter than I am. The whole car smells like cigarette smoke and wet dog. Still, it's good to be out of the rain.

'So, how long have you known the twins?' I ask conversationally. I see why she would want to watch over her great-grand-niece or whatever Ivy is to her, but I'm still a little fuzzy on her connection to Hazel and Rowan and why they seem to trust only her with the knowledge of their current living situation.

Mags looks across at me. 'I've known the twins' mam all her life. I'm the closest thing to family they have right now.'

'And,' I say, hoping it's not too indiscreet, 'you're OK with them staying at Oak Road? How come they aren't staying with you?'

'I don't take in strays,' Mags says bluntly.

'Right.'

When I nod, she finally looks back at the road, but before I can allow myself to relax she has folded over to root around under her seat for something. I brace myself for what seems like inevitable death, but when I open my eyes Mags is calmly lighting a cigarette, one hand back on the wheel.

'And, um,' I say when I've caught my breath, 'what about Ivy?' Rowan described her as *our friend, who is also a girl*. I'm half hoping Mags will clarify if that means *girl-friend*. I secretly cross my fingers.

'She's keeping an eye on them.'

'So she's not . . . with . . . either of them?'

Mags squints her eagle eyes at me. 'That's something you should ask her, not me,' she says curtly.

'Right.' The rain lashes across the window. At my request, Mags stops the car far enough down the road from my house that nobody will see me even if they do happen to be looking out of the window. I thank her and untie my bike from her roof.

'They're OK, you know,' she says with a brisk nod. She turns the wheel like she's throwing a discus at the Olympics and I wince at the loud squeal of tyres on the wet road. It's only when she's gone that I realize I never gave Rowan or Hazel my number. And now it's too late to ask Mags to pass mine on.

Emily texts me the all-clear and I climb up on to the kitchen roof and in through her window. When I get inside, she greets me with a Cheshire-cat grin. 'I *told* you to get back quickly. But don't worry. I just said to Mum that you came in fifteen minutes ago. The shower's running because I told her you're in it. So what do I get for covering for you this time?'

I stand on her folded-out desk chair to get down from the window.

'Watch my stuff!' she shouts, putting out her hands as if to shield her desk from my wet clothes.

'I'll give you a tenner?' I try.

'Twenty.'

'Look,' I reason, 'I needed to find my bracelet. I'm pretty sure I lost it at the party on Saturday so I went back to the field to try to find it.'

'Oh, maybe that's what Rose was looking for when I saw her at the party,' says Emily.

'Looking where?' I ask.

She shrugs. 'She was talking to Chloe's brother and looking around, I don't know. Maybe she was looking for your bracelet.'

'Actually,' I tell her, 'loads of people lost stuff at the party. Or had stuff stolen.' I speak in the kind of hushed voice I know will appeal to my sister's dramatic streak. 'The girls in school think there's some kind of klepto-maniac in town.'

'Oh my God, really?' Emily's eyes open wide. 'I have to tell Chloe.' She grabs her phone and begins to text furiously.

I drip across her bedroom and she wrinkles her nose at the lingering smell of smoke and wet dog that I can detect still clinging to me.

'One more thing,' she says, jumping off her bed and blocking my way out of her bedroom door, mostly with her elbows. On a girl as skinny as she is, they're basically weapons.

'What?'

'I'll have that twenty,' she says, palm out.

I slap a twenty-euro note into her hand and make to go past her, but her elbows are still in my way.

'What *now*?' I ask.

'Who were you with tonight?' she says.

I manage to shoulder past her. 'Rose,' I say. 'Who else?'

Emily follows me out of her bedroom and on to the landing. 'What are you even wearing anyway?'

'I got wet. Rose lent me some clothes.'

'That's not Rose's jumper,' she says. 'And Rose quit smoking. You smell of smoke.'

'Look, I have revision to do.' I shut my bedroom door and leave Emily pursing her lips outside.

At dinner, I keep surreptitiously looking at my mum's eyes, replaying what she said the morning after the party. *He's lost a lot and so will you.* My shoe in Hazel's bag. Ivy's sharp face. Lost things. Findings.

Rose comes over after dinner. We sit on my bed and I plug in the fairy lights that hang above it. They twinkle on the pictures of me and Rose, the pressed flowers, the concert tickets, the collection of tiny porcelain cats I've been keeping since I was a kid.

Rose lies back on my pillows and when she speaks I smell the alcohol on her breath. 'Did you find your mum's bracelet?'

I shake my head. 'I even went back to the field where

the party was in case I'd dropped it there, but if I did it's long gone. Speaking of which, where have you been and why haven't you answered any of my calls?'

'I'm sorry. I just needed to take a mental-health day.'

Usually, we take our mental-health days together. 'And replying to any one of my messages would have been detrimental to your mental health?' I ask.

'My mum kept confiscating my phone.'

'Your mum was at work all day, Rose. And yesterday, too. Is this about what happened in German yesterday?'

Rose sighs. 'I dunno.'

'Are you going to tell me what happened?'

Rose tries to say, 'Nothing,' but I make a face in warning and she says, 'I just lost it a bit,' instead.

I *ack* in frustration. '*Rose*,' I say.

'*Olive*.' She imitates my tone. 'Some of the guys were being particularly annoying so I tore up their notes.'

'With your teeth?'

Rose grins. 'You shouldn't listen to rumours, Olive,' she says.

She leans over to tousle my hair, but I move out of her reach and say, 'Maybe I wouldn't have to if you'd actually, you know, talk to me. Or answer my calls.'

Rose sighs and twists her mouth to one side. Finally she says, 'Sorry. I just needed to be alone for a bit.'

'Did I . . .' I line up the words in my head before saying them. *Why are you mad at me?* is too needy. *What did I do wrong?* screams of guilt. 'Did I do something stupid at the party?' is what I end up asking.

'Olive, we drank a bottle and a half of vodka between us, passed out against a hay bale and only got home at six in the morning,' Rose says. 'Stupid's *one* word we could use.'

Maybe I'm reading too much into this.

'You promise we're OK?' I say.

'I promise we are always OK.'

I clink my mug of tea against hers and set aside my worries. I can't ask for much more than a promise.

'Well,' I say to change the subject, 'wait till you hear where I've been all afternoon.'

Rose listens intently as I tell her about Rowan, Hazel and Ivy.

'And they've been *living* there? At Oak Road?' she says when I've explained the entire surreal encounter. '*Why?*'

'Family stuff, I guess.'

'I've heard those houses are full of asbestos. And ghosts. Totally full of ghosts,' she says. 'And Hazel had your *shoe?* That's some fairy-tale shit right there.'

'Ivy said that. I half expected Rowan to try it on me to see if it fitted.'

Rose smirks. 'Trust you to fall in love at first sight with some dodgy squatter,' she says.

'I'm not in love with anyone,' I protest. 'He's just really very pretty.'

When Rose finally rolls off my bed and heads home, I lie underneath the fairy lights for a long time, listening to the rain. It hammers on the roof and against the window I cracked open earlier to air out the room. I get up to close it and nearly trip over my school bag. It topples over and vomits a pile of books on to the carpet.

I start to shove it all back in with my foot, but I stop short when I see something that doesn't belong to me. A slim red notebook, leather-bound and fastened with a black elastic band. *Spellbook of the Lost and Found.*

Laurel

Wednesday 10th May, Thursday 11th May

Found: TV remote (grey, broken); wallet (black, leather); make-up bag (large, red, gold zip); set of car keys (dog-charm key ring); reading glasses (purple); football (white and green); hairpins (approx. fifteen); blue plastic lighter; two tarnished teaspoons; one sock (multicoloured, stripy); silver, star-shaped hair clip; delicate gold bracelet with tiny charms

On the way to the woods on Wednesday I rolled over a TV remote in the middle of the road. It crunched under my tyres, and I spun to a halt, Ash and Holly hot on my heels. I kicked it into a ditch, not thinking that a small rectangle of plastic could be the start of something.

We cut class to be with Jude. We sat in the shade of silver birches and studied for our summer exams. Jude snorted at our textbooks, our homework journals. He made us his own list of required reading: Keats and Coleridge, Kerouac and Vonnegut. He took his own tattered paperbacks out of his satchel and read passages aloud.

His voice is like music – did I mention that before? He doesn't have our accent; this town is etched on each of our vowels. His voice is almost accentless, like a TV presenter, like he's never stayed in one place long enough to speak like a local. Like he's only ever been a local of our dreams.

Or at least that's what he wants us to think. Ash and Holly listened raptly, but I found myself sighing impatiently at his beautiful voice. He only ever wants to talk about 'things that matter', but everything about him seems increasingly like a careful front. When he took a breath to rest, I asked him where he lived, where his parents were.

'Small talk,' he said, brushing my questions aside with a wave of his beaded wrist. 'I can't abide small talk. Let me tell you the myth of Icarus. Let me tell you how he almost flew into the sun.'

I didn't tell him that I knew the myth of Icarus, that I'd already read Kerouac and found it all pretty boring, that sometimes small talk is a good way to get to know somebody better. But I'm beginning to suspect that Jude doesn't want us to know him at all.

'*The only people for me are the mad ones*,' Jude was reading. '*The ones who never yawn or say a commonplace thing, but burn, burn, burn like fabulous yellow roman candles exploding like spiders across the stars.*'

Ash was nodding furiously. 'Yeah,' she said. '*Yeah.*'

Holly's eyes were closed. Frustrated, I scratched out the equation I was working on and started over. *Burn, burn, burn.*

Ash wandered into the trees to pee. We heard her feet rustling leaves and small twigs and it reminded me of the spell for some reason, the moss we foraged, the penknife we used to cut the tips of our fingers. I can still feel the seam of the cut, tidy and white. It is right over the whorls of my fingerprints, marking them, changing my identity. I am not the person I used to be.

When Ash came back, she was holding a wallet.

'I found it,' she said. 'Sitting on a rock like it'd been rained there. With twenty quid inside, no ID.'

We left Jude with our things and cycled into town. We waited until one of my sisters was on her break from the bakery, smoking outside, and beckoned her over.

'Shouldn't you be in school?' she asked.

'We skipped class. We're studying in the forest.' Then I gave her the money and asked her to buy us a couple of six-packs.

'You little rebel,' she said to me with admiration. '*Finally.*'

We cycled back to the woods with the beer in our school bags, the bottles clinking every time we hit a pothole on the bumpy road. If we hadn't been watching the road for stones and holes, we wouldn't have found the next thing.

A powder compact, red and shiny, the powder several shades darker than any of our skins. It was sticking out of a big red make-up bag sitting on the ground just at the edge of the forest, after the road turns away. We brought it with us. We stowed the beers in the hollow between the branches of the old oak tree at the fork of the road, where Holly had found the spellbook. It seems so long ago now that we first read the spell to get our diaries back.

We sat among our schoolbooks and took turns admiring ourselves in the compact's mirror, drawing pictures on our hands with the eyeliner, trying on the lipstick. I went back and found the TV remote I'd kicked into the ditch and we put them together: the make-up, the wallet, the broken remote. We set them up like a shrine.

'The spell is working,' Jude said. 'Look: the lost things are coming home to be found.'

Ash and Holly nodded, but I knew this wasn't what we wanted. We'd written only two words each on the branches of the oak tree when we cast the spell. *My diary.* Three times.

'Why would we be finding this stuff now,' I asked, 'when we've already found what we'd lost?'

'The power of the magic,' Jude replied, but Holly bit her lip. I knew Holly believed in all this, even if I didn't quite. I knew she'd learned the spell by heart. The part about balance. The part about sacrifice. If it *was* real, and we were finding so much more than we'd lost, did that mean others were losing things because of us? Or were our findings just coincidental?

We started on the beers that afternoon in the branches of the tree, and when we got tipsy we stumbled down to the lake and waded in the water. It started to rain and we sang and laughed under the drizzle, drops collecting on our hair. In the shallows, Jude and Holly kissed. Ash and I clapped and whistled, but I thought I saw a look of pain flash across Ash's face. We fell over each other and the rocks on the shore. I stepped on something sharp and looked down to see a set of car keys poking between my toes. I pocketed them and drank some more.

The rain became a storm: thundery showers blurring the world around us. Since we were wet already, we all took off our clothes and swam in deeper. Holly averted her eyes as we undressed, and Ash and I pretended not to watch, but we caught each other looking and reluctantly grinned. Holly is thin and very white, blue veins showing under the translucent skin of her chest, veins like lightning strikes connecting her hipbones and rivering down to the soft blonde hair underneath. She looked like she might disappear into the water and never come out again. Ash is more like me: our thighs touch and our breasts are round; the hair between our legs is coarse and wiry – mine black and hers as red as her fiery curls.

Jude stood naked on the largest rock under the rain, beer bottle held aloft. Boys' bodies are strange to me, not quite human. But maybe that's because I've seen so few. I am used to the way I look, to girls' bodies in changing rooms, to the hairs and lumps and curves and colours, but boys are different. They are something entirely other. My breath caught in my throat, but I tried not to make it obvious. I think we all breathed easier when Jude joined us in the water.

We giggled and shivered, keeping our beer bottles just above water, gulping from them as we went. Splash, splash, ducking each other and drinking lake water. Kiss, kiss, Holly and Jude wrapped round each other and me and Ash watching. A pair of reading glasses floated by and Ash grabbed them. When we came dripping out of the lake, a football rolled down the hill towards us. Hairpins twinkled in the rainy trees. I reached up and picked one like a silver, star-shaped fruit.

We cycled home late and shaking, wobbly on the flooding road. I was lucky; my sisters covered for me. They smuggled me upstairs and stood me in a hot shower fully clothed until I was warm and sober. They told Mam I'd eaten something funny and they tucked me into bed. Holly's parents were less forgiving. She spent the evening crying in her room, grounded until after the exams. Ash's parents tried the same trick, but only got a screaming match. Ash is not the crying type.

'Mam and Dad are worried,' Holly whispered over the phone to us the next day. Ash's legs were crossed over mine on my bedroom floor, her ear pressed to the house phone. 'Haven't you heard? A boy from town has been missing since the party.'

'Who?' I asked.

'D'you mean whatshisname in Sixth Year?' Ash said. 'I heard my mam talking about it to her friend Caroline again this morning.'

'Whatshisname?' I asked. I vaguely remember Ash's mam saying something about a boy who hadn't come home when she was talking on the phone the other day. *He's probably just sleeping off one too many pints over the weekend. He'll be back before you know it.*

Ash shrugged. 'You'd know him if you saw him. He's scruffy and blond and he's got his eyebrow pierced.'

'He hasn't been seen since Saturday night,' Holly said, her voice coming so softly through the phone. 'I'm scared that we . . . That it was because of us.'

Be careful what you bargain with:
Every lost thing requires a sacrifice —
A new loss for every called thing found.

It couldn't be. I shook my head and heard Holly take a nervous breath.

'It wasn't us,' I tried to reassure her. 'We didn't do anything, Holly. Spells and magic aren't real.' But I wasn't so sure any more. 'Anyway, nobody's saying this boy is really lost. Like Ash's mum said, he's probably just still out partying or hung over somewhere.'

That afternoon, Ash and I skipped class and sat under the trees and tried to study to keep our minds off our guilt about the missing boy. We didn't tell Jude about him and he didn't seem to know. Maybe he doesn't listen to town gossip; maybe it's too close to small talk. Maybe he just doesn't care.

And all day long we found things in the forest. We brought some of them home to Holly, afterwards, holed up in her bedroom. We laid them out on her covers like an offering. Two tarnished teaspoons, a blue plastic lighter, a stripy sock and – my favourite – a bracelet full of delicate little golden charms: cats and stars and trees so detailed each branch is individually etched in. Holly flicked the charms with a nail to hear them tinkle.

'Too bad it's not a laurel tree,' she said.

'What kind of tree is it?' I asked. I didn't recognize it from any of the trees in the forest or around here.

Holly looked closer. 'It's an olive tree, I think,' she said. 'Look at these tiny gold pinpricks. They must be the fruit.'

We sat on her bed until her mam asked us to leave, talking about Jude, about magic, about findings and lost things. The blond boy was still missing, but we didn't talk about that.

'Jude is the greatest thing we've found,' Ash said.

Holly nodded and her smile was so wide. 'My heart's the greatest thing I've lost.'

I avoided Ash's eyes. I shouldn't even write this, but I'm careful now to carry my diary everywhere; I'm careful not to let it out of my sight.

So there's this: Jude's arm round Ash in the tree while Holly isn't there to see it. Jude and Ash wandering away from me. Laughter dappled through the leaves.

Olive

Thursday 11th May

Lost: Reading glasses (purple);
pink faux-leather handbag (gold clasps)

On Thursday morning I am awoken by my door being thrown open and Seamus Heaney boomed by my father from the top of the stairs. I suffer through 'A Hazel Stick for Catherine Ann' until the bit about cows before shutting my door and thunking my half-asleep head against it.

'At least he's moved on from dirges,' Mum observes when I have shuffled downstairs for breakfast. She's on her second coffee of the morning (I can tell by the ring stains on today's paper) and is sorting through a towering pile of notebooks and old papers on the kitchen counter.

Her hands are tanned and calloused, the fingers covered in large silver rings: Celtic swirls and thick leaf patterns, big turquoise stones. A Claddagh with a tiny sapphire in the centre serves as a wedding ring.

'Small mercies,' I mutter.

She disappears into the study and comes out with another pile of papers that she spills on to the table to sort through next. She has moved a bunch of the boxes of her old stuff out of the study and they are currently stacked by the table, threatening to topple on to the dogs. I push Coco Pops's head away from my plate.

Dad comes into the kitchen with a sleepy Max in his arms and doesn't even put him down before kissing Mum.

'Ew,' Max whispers. Dad drops him on to a chair and kisses Mum harder.

'Take it outside, lads,' I say. Max makes his own kissy noises at the dogs and sneakily feeds them toast under the table. Dad and Mum pretend not to notice. I worry about my parents being a bad influence on a five-year-old child.

'No, *you* take it outside,' Dad says. 'And you can put the recycling out while you're at it.'

I roll my eyes at his joke and haul the recycling out to the green bin beside the garage. My bike is leaning against the wall of the house by the back door, beside Emily's. I don't know what makes me glance into my bike basket, but I find some loose pieces of paper stuck inside.

They're mushed up against the mesh of the basket, which has left diamond-shaped dents in the paper. They rustle when I pull them out. I expect them to be worksheets from school, or notes that fell out of my folder at some point.

I scan the first page quickly. It looks like a page from a diary, in delicate handwriting I half recognize but can't quite place. The top right corner says *Sunday 7th May*. Four days ago. I slip the pages into my pocket and go back inside.

Emily stops me as I pass by the bathroom. 'Have you seen my lucky socks?' she asks me.

'Your what?'

'My lucky socks.' She has something like defiance in her face, but when she realizes I won't make fun of her she goes on. 'The paisley ones. My exams start tomorrow and I want to wear them.'

'What?' I make a face. 'You're in Second Year – summer exams don't count for anything.'

Emily gives me her best *You're an idiot* look. 'Listen,' she says then, unexpectedly. 'I'm sorry for what Chloe said about Rose the other day.'

My eyes narrow. 'You should know better than to listen to Chloe's vapid rumours.'

'I'm *trying* to apologize here, *God*.'

'Sorry,' I say. 'Go on.'

'That was it,' Emily says, still sounding slightly annoyed. 'I'm sorry I didn't say anything to Chloe, but in fairness she was just saying that stuff because Rose was, like, leading her brother on at the party or something.'

'Rose leading *him* on? Hardly likely.'

'I *know*, OK?' says Emily. 'I said that to her. Chloe knows it's not true.'

'OK,' I say. 'Thanks.' I stop at my bedroom door. 'And I haven't seen your socks,' I add. 'But I have the exact same pair. You can have them, if you want.'

'Really?' Emily seems surprised at my suggestion. 'Thank you.'

I find Emily outside her room once I've retrieved the socks. 'Here you go, Dobby,' I tell her. 'You're free.'

Emily puts them on right there on the landing.

'I thought your exams started tomorrow?' I ask.

'I need all the help I can get.'

I can still make out my dad's voice booming from our parents' room. He is reciting another poem in the same way that normal dads sing in the shower. Emily shakes her head when she hears him. 'Have you noticed that he really likes old men?' she asks.

'What?'

'Like, when was the last time we were woken up with Sylvia Plath or Emily Dickinson? Or, like, Adrienne Rich or Margaret Atwood,' she says.

'You know Adrienne Rich?'

Emily gives me another one of those chin-tilted looks of defiance.

'Sorry,' I say quickly. 'You're right. I hadn't really thought about it before, but his choices do tend towards the masculine.' Our dad is overly fond of Shakespeare's sonnets, anything of Blake's with animals in it and Keats. I can't remember the last time he woke us with a female poet.

I also can't remember the last time I spoke to my sister about anything like this. Maybe I shouldn't be surprised she reads the same poetry as I do. Maybe I shouldn't be surprised she has a critical mind. I spend so much time with Rose that I usually bypass Emily completely. But with Rose pulling away for some reason at the moment, I'm beginning to understand that I might have been under-estimating my little sister all this time.

Emily shrugs and stomps down the stairs in my socks. 'Oh, have you seen Mum's reading glasses?' she calls up to me as an afterthought. 'She was looking for them earlier.'

I shake my head.

When I come downstairs – dressed and made-up and ready for school – the back door is open and a warm breeze rustles the herbs hanging over the stove. Mum is still waging war with her letters and bills.

'Did you by any chance find—' Mum says.

'Your glasses? No, sorry. Emily said they were missing.'

'A lot of things are going missing,' says Mum.

'Am I still grounded?' I ask her as I put on my shoes.

'Hmm?' She looks up from the papers and her eyes are a little unfocused.

It's quite unlike my mother to be distracted, but it may well work in my favour. 'Can I go to Rose's tonight?'

My mum rubs a wrist wrapped with leather bracelets over her forehead. 'It's Thursday. You have an exam tomorrow,' she says to me. 'And we said you were grounded for a week. You can go to Rose's on Saturday.' *Dammit. I was sure that would work.* 'Keep an eye out for my glasses, would you?' Mum asks. 'Hopefully, I put them down somewhere in the house.'

'Loads of things are going missing,' Emily says as we cycle to school. 'Like Mum's glasses? And Chloe lost her bag the other day. It's kind of weird.'

I think of the spellbook Hazel found. The spell for calling up lost things. Ivy talking about sacrifice and findings. I shake my head. It's all nonsense, I tell myself. It's all just coincidence.

'I guess things go missing all the time,' I tell Emily. 'But you only really notice when you're keeping an eye out for them. Like when you learn a new word you'd never heard before and suddenly it's everywhere.'

'Yeah, maybe. Anyway, Chloe's brother probably nicked her bag just to screw with her.'

'Ugh.' I shudder. 'I can't imagine having Cathal Murdock as a brother.' We hop off our bikes and chain them next to each other on the rack.

'She hates him,' Emily says matter-of-factly. 'He calls her ugly all the time. One time he called their mum a fat bitch.'

I whistle low. 'Charming.'

'He's really sexist, too,' Emily goes on. 'Not, like, quoting-men-poets-all-the-time sexist. But, like, rating girls' bodies out of ten and stuff.'

'Ugh,' I say again, because it's the most appropriate sound for the likes of Cathal Murdock. 'He's an absolute waste of space. You stay away from him.'

Two thoughts come in two flashes of lightning, almost instantaneous.

One: I sound like my mother. *Stay away from him.*

Two: Emily said Chloe saw Rose with Cathal.

Something must show on my face because Emily says, 'What?'

Rose and Cathal? It doesn't even begin to make sense. Probably what Chloe saw was Rose blazing drunken fury at him for having whistled at a First Year, or attempted to grope her while she danced. Little blue sparks of worry flit around in my peripheral vision, but I don't quite know what to make of them yet. I want to ask Rose about it, but don't think I could fit those sparks of worry into one telegram-speak text message, so I let them buzz about by themselves and go to my first class, planning to talk to Rose about it in person.

Rose doesn't show and my worry builds. I message her halfway through economics.

WOULD APPRECIATE NOT BEING
ABANDONED IN EVERY CLASS
STOP GET YOUR LAZY ARSE OUT
OF BED STOP OLIVE

My phone lights up on my lap under the desk.

WILL BE IN FOR GERMAN EXAM
TOMORROW STOP, DID YOU
KNOW THE GERMAN FOR NIPPLE
TRANSLATES AS BREAST WARTS
STOP ROSE

DARE YOU TO USE IT IN THE
EXAM STOP OLIVE

I slip my phone back into the pocket of my skirt and take out the diary pages I found in my bike basket. I unfold them quietly in my lap.

Sunday 7th May, it says. The day after the summer party.

We went to the party because our diaries went missing, it starts.

These pages are from a diary, but it reads like a story. A story about three girls called Laurel, Ash and Holly. Three girls who seem to be as close as Rose and me. Three girls who lose their diaries, who are bullied by the class-mates who find them, who vow to get them back. I read like my gaze is glued to the page.

And then there is a line that I have to read back twice.

Then we found the spellbook – the day before the summer party.

The spellbook Hazel found days later in the field.

I stop reading and look around. The classroom is full of bowed heads and scratching pens. I don't know anyone called Laurel, Ash or Holly, but there's only one school in this town. They must go here.

I keep reading. The girls find the spellbook in an oak tree. They bring it to the party. They sneak away from the bonfire and cast the spell.

Ivy was right. I can hardly believe it, but Ivy was right.

The girls pass out – most likely from the poteen – and when they wake up their diaries have been found.

Their spell worked.

And, if Ivy is to be believed, because of these girls, everybody else at the party lost something. My bracelet. My shoe. My memories of the night.

Rose.

Laurel, Ash and Holly. I wonder who they are, where they are now, if they know what they've done. Laurel mentions knowing Mags Maguire. Maybe Mags can tell me.

I chide myself momentarily for allowing myself to believe in this nonsense. And yet. Questions and secrets and girls with tree names and Rose talking with Cathal Murdock at the party. It all comes back to Saturday night.

It all comes back to that spellbook.

Hazel

Thursday 11th May

Lost: A heart (again)

The spellbook is missing. I found it, I need it, and now it's lost. It was on the table when Olive went home yesterday. We looked through it again, me and Rowan and Ivy. We read all the lists of offerings, the prayers to St Anthony and St Jude, we touched all the trinkets stuck to the pages. Then we got up to make dinner and it's like it disappeared. Ivy and Rowan say they didn't take it, but one of them must have. It couldn't have just vanished by itself.

It's all I can think about and I nearly smash, like, five glasses at work. Mags snaps at me and sends me on my break early. I grab my cigarettes and help myself to a bottle of beer on the way out. No one'll ever know.

When I get outside, there's somebody crying at the corner of the car park, their back to the fence where I chain my bike. At first I keep my distance. Crying makes me kinda uncomfortable. Especially crying girls. And it is a girl – I can see that as I come closer. She's hunched over and doing that crying-into-the-knees thing. Her hair's long, wild and black. The ends of it trail on the concrete. She's wearing a blue school uniform with the skirt stapled at least three inches shorter than would've been allowed in my old school, but that makes sense because of the weird stuffy heat and the fact that she has great legs. Her shirtsleeves are rolled up and as she moves to rub her eyes I see that there's something written in marker on her arm.

That's what makes me stop and talk to her. I stand awkwardly in front of the girl and say, 'Are you OK?' Then I change it to, 'Obviously, you're not, because otherwise you wouldn't be crying, but it's just not socially acceptable to go up to a complete stranger and say, *Hey, tell me why you're crying*, you know?'

To my relief, the girl laughs at that, head still in her arms on her knees. Then she looks up and I realize like a kick in the teeth that she's really, really beautiful.

'Fuck what's socially acceptable,' she says, and that's it – I'm in love.

Uninvited, I sit on the kerb beside her and take out my cigarettes. I offer her one, but she waves it away so I put the packet back in my pocket.

'So, hey,' I say. 'Tell me why you're crying.'

She takes a breath and swipes the tears away with the palm of her hand. Watery black streaks her cheeks. 'Waterproof eyeliner,' she says. 'My kingdom for waterproof eyeliner.'

'You're crying because you don't have waterproof eyeliner?' I say, just to hear her laugh again. 'Seems like a bit of a contradiction.'

Her laugh is addictive. Like I'll straight-up die if I don't hear it again.

'Well, if I don't cry every eyeliner off, how will I know which one's waterproof?'

'Good point,' I say. 'So this is all just a make-up test?'

'Basically, yes. I'm pretty passionate about my beauty products.'

'Well, I admire your dedication.'

She reaches into her skirt pocket for a plastic bottle. She unscrews the lid, lifts out a little wand and blows a bunch of bubbles over the car park. When she exhales, her shoulders drop slightly, like she's relieved.

'I quit smoking,' she explains when she notices me looking. 'This helps my craving.'

'Right.'

'You go ahead, though, if you're having one. I like the smell.'

I light a cigarette while she blows her nose. She takes out a little mirror and rubs at the make-up under her eyes.

When I cry, I look like shit. My skin looks like it's been scrubbed with a stone and I get red blotches around my nostrils. This girl manages to look the way crying girls do in films: red eyes and puffed lips and no blotches.

'What's your name?'

The question comes out more intimate than I meant it to.

'Rose.' She closes her mirror and glances at the tattoos on my arms. 'You're Hazel.'

'I am,' I say, and I try not to sound taken aback.

Rose smiles mischievously. She says, 'Your brother's called Rowan, you ran away from home, you're living in a boarded-up house in a ghost estate with a blue-haired girl.'

'How do you—'

'It's like something out of a film. Tattooed teenage runaways squatting in a ghost estate. Olive told me. She's my best friend.'

'Oh,' I say. 'OK.'

'We won't tell,' Rose says. 'I mean, Olive told me, but we won't tell anyone else.'

'Thanks.' I tap ash on to the concrete. Rose blows bubbles into the air.

'So why did you run away from home?' Rose asks.

'I'm testing out the waterproof-ness of ghost estates,' I tell her.

Rose nods. 'OK, I guess I deserve that.' Then she looks at me, right in the eyes. It's something people don't do a whole lot, and it feels weird, and good, and weird. I clear my throat. Her eyes are a soft dark brown, lined with smudged make-up like a photo shoot in a hotel bed. Her eyelashes go on for miles.

'OK,' Rose says again, seeming to steel herself. 'I lost my virginity at the town summer party, so that's why I'm crying. Mostly.'

I'm not sure what to say to that. 'Mostly?'

'Well.' She taps the wand like an ashy cigarette. 'I don't actually remember it. Mostly.' She dips the wand back into the bottle, takes it out and shakes it viciously. 'And I didn't realize that's what'd happened at first. But the guy who . . . was there, too . . . remembers it.' Her wrist makes a snapping motion, fast and violent. A bunch of bubbles appear and *pop-pop-pop-pop* like a spray of bullets all around us. 'And he keeps.' *Flick*. 'Sending me.' *Flick*. 'Fucking.' *Flick*. 'Messages.'

I reach out carefully and take the wand from her hand. It keeps shaking.

'OK,' I whisper. 'OK.' I put the wand on the ground. 'Do you know the guy?' I ask.

'He's in, like, half my classes.' It sounds as if she's trying to speak through a whole apple stuck in her throat.

'What kind of messages?'

She doesn't answer, but she hands me her phone. I scroll quickly through her messages, but she doesn't watch me. She picks the wand up from beside her foot and blows a bunch of bubbles across the car park instead.

The first few messages are from Sunday – the day after the party.

> Hi Rose did u get my friend
> request. Had fun last nite kind
> of thing. Do u want 2 go out
> sumtime.

'Who writes like that any more?' I mutter and Rose gives a weak smile.

> Ur beautiful. Do u want 2 get
> 2getr again.

I snort. Rose makes a face and waits for me to read on. It's a long string of messages sent over the last week. Most of them were sent on Sunday and on Monday morning, pretty much every half-hour.

> This is rose rite????

> Hope u had fun haha lets do it
> again

> Hi rose how r u

> Hows it goin

Sent u friend request dont no if
u got it

U want 2 go out nxt wknd

Rose never answers, but the guy doesn't get the hint. Then, on Monday afternoon, the messages suddenly switch gears.

Ur an ugly bitch

Ugly lesbo dike

Bet u loved ur pity fuck id never
go out with a hoor like u

How much 4 u to blow my
mates ill give u ten quid

U love 2 do it 4 free dirty slut

And it goes on. Some of the messages have pictures. I give Rose back her phone, holding it like there's something rotten in there. 'Why don't you just block him?'

'I did. He sends texts from his friends' phones now.'

'Jesus.'

'I told him I wasn't interested,' Rose says. 'That I didn't remember it and I didn't mean to—' She breaks off and shakes her head. 'He didn't take it well.'

'Let me guess, this was some time on Monday?' I point at the first of the awful messages.

Rose manages another weak smile. 'Full marks.' She nudges the bottle of bubbles with her foot and it tips over, spills on the ground. The stain spreads over the concrete. I reach out and drag my shoe through the soapy water. I draw a flower. Rose stretches her leg out and writes *Fuck this*.

'What are you going to do?' I ask her. She shakes her head.

'Drink too much,' she says. 'Not go back to school until September when it'll all have blown over. Keep telling my parents it's PMS.'

'Sounds familiar,' I say in an undertone. Rose gives me kind of a knowing look.

'My dad was never really around when I was little,' I say quickly. 'But when he was, my mum was different. He was always . . . kind of like that.' I gesture at her phone. 'Hot and cold, but always blaming her for it. I'd tell you to go to the Guards except I know first hand they can't do shit. Even if they're nice about it, they'll just say there's no proof.'

I kind of expect Rose to get upset, but instead she nods like that's something she already knows. 'Is that why you ran away?'

I sigh. 'No. She did. My mum. Ran away, I mean.' Rose raises her eyebrows in question. 'She left us with our grandparents and went off to be with our dad. Crazy, right – that she still wanted to be with him, despite the way he treated her? My grandparents raised us until my granny died a few months ago. Granda's in a hospice now, 'cos he's not doing so good. So. My parents came to get us. It didn't work out. Me and Rowan are kinda better off alone.'

Rose nods again. 'I'm sorry,' she says. 'About your grandparents.'

'Thanks,' I say. 'I'm sorry about . . .' I gesture at her phone again, at her smudged, non-waterproof eye make-up. 'All this.'

We stare out across the car park together. After about a minute Rose takes my hand.

'You're the only person I've told,' she says.

I kind of laugh and say, 'Same.' I don't tell her there's a lot more I amn't telling. 'I'm probably a shitty first person to tell,' I admit. 'I'm a complete stranger and I have literally no advice for you.'

'You know my best friend; you're not a complete stranger. Although you *are* pretty strange.'

I properly laugh this time, and say, 'You have no idea.'

Then she says, 'I like strange,' and I wonder if she might be flirting with me. I look down at her hand in mine. She's upset. Fuck upset – she's in bits. She's probably just looking for somebody to listen. For advice. For a solution.

I can still just about see a few letters of a word written in marker on her wrist. Like Olive had on her arms yesterday. Does everybody write on their arms in this town?

I look up at her suddenly.

'I don't have a solution for you,' I say. 'But I do have a spell.'

'A spell?'

'Yeah. There was a book. A spellbook. I found it yesterday on my way home, in the same field the party was in last weekend. Someone must have lost it there. *Spellbook of the Lost and Found*, it's called. It's got a spell to call up lost things. I guess if your virginity is a thing you can lose, maybe it's a thing you can find again.'

I don't tell her I don't have the spellbook any more. It doesn't matter. I read that spell so many times I know it off by heart.

Then, quick as a flash, I remember something. Something Olive muttered when she read it. There was an ingredient for each of us. And rose thorns. There's an ingredient for Rose.

Another flash of memory: the spell calls for poteen. It was something about the waters of Lethe, which Ivy said was a river in Greek mythology, but it said you could use poteen instead. It all lines up.

We're going to have guests, Ivy said she saw in the cross-word. When Olive showed up yesterday, we all figured that's what it meant. But what if it meant two guests?

She's important, Ivy said. Maybe Rose is important, too. Olive and Rose, the spellbook, the poteen. I know already that Rose and Olive will drink it with us. I know already that they will help us cast the spell.

Mags appears at the back door of the pub. She shades her eyes and scans the car park. I'm late back from my break.

'Olive told me about the spell,' Rose says, her eyebrows drawn together. 'But I didn't think it was actually . . . *real*.'

I shrug. 'I live with a girl who believes in magic and work for a woman who's probably a witch. *Real* is a kinda fuzzy concept.'

'I can imagine,' says Rose. Her smile is seven kinds of sunlight.

I stand up and dust off the back of my trousers. 'Come by the estate this weekend,' I say, stamping my cigarette out on the ground. My belly's a cage full of butterflies. 'Real or not, it can't do any harm to try.'

Olive

Friday 12th May

Lost: Faith in the world

On Friday morning, unexpectedly, it's my mum's voice that wakes me. It cuts through dreams of thorns piercing skin. I am glad to be woken up.

Without my hearing aid in, I can't make out what Mum is saying. I raise my good ear up off the pillow and her voice comes slightly into focus.

She's saying something about raking through rubble for her past. It takes me a second before I recognize the words: it's the first few lines of 'Delta' by Adrienne Rich. My mum's the one quoting poetry this morning.

I think I can make out my dad's voice laughing from the other side of my bedroom door. 'Usurper!' he cries in mock-horror, but he throws open my door anyway, as if he was the one reciting. I hear Emily's door bang open, then Max's.

I put in my hearing aid and meet Emily on the landing.

'Are our parents having a poem-off?' I ask her, brows furrowed.

'Sounds like it,' she says cheerfully. 'I guess she must have heard us talking about Adrienne Rich.' She yells down the stairs after Mum. 'Go feminism!'

I give my sister a baffled look and am not nearly discreet enough to hide it. It's one thing to find out she reads poetry; it's another to discover she identifies as a feminist. Maybe I have more in common with my little sister than I thought.

Max appears behind me, clutching Bunny in both hands. 'If you don't close your mouth, a fly will fly in,' he observes. I close my mouth. He makes his way past me and down the stairs, almost tripping over the ends of his Batman pyjamas. 'And then you'll have to swallow a spider to catch the fly, and then a cat to catch the spider, and then a dog to catch the cat . . .'

I shake my head. I am growing up in a madhouse.

'. . . And then a horse to catch the cow, and then a lost soul to catch the horse . . .'

'Wait, what?' I call down to him, but Max has reached the bottom of the stairs and is running into the kitchen for his breakfast. I make a mental note to change my hearing-aid battery before I go out, and I grab a towel and run into the shower before anybody else can.

Rose only comes to school halfway through lunch break, before our first exam. At this point, it's not like I've been expecting her in class. We sit in the spiky midday shadows of the bike rack and I hand her a stick of liquorice from my school bag.

'Emily said something to me yesterday that I wanted to ask you about,' I say, but Rose cuts me off.

'I met Hazel last night,' she tells me.

That distracts me for a second. 'You did? Where?'

'Just bumped into her. I recognized her from your description,' she says. 'Although she was wearing significantly more clothes.'

'And?' I say.

Rose looks a little wistful. 'She's kind of larger than life, isn't she? Confident, gorgeous, flirts with anything that moves.'

I give a little laugh, remembering her clothes and her compliments. *I've got more where that came from.* 'Yeah,' I say. 'So I was talking to Emily about the party last Saturday—'

'Oh, that reminds me.' Rose talks over me again, grabs some paper from out of her bag and waves it in my face.

'I found these,' she says. 'They were in my school bag this morning, like I grabbed them by accident when I stuffed my books in.'

I take the pages out of her hand. 'They're from someone's diary,' she says, but the moment I see the handwriting I know that. I know it's the same girl. Laurel.

Monday 8th May, it says.

'Shit,' I whisper. 'This is really weird.'

'Just read it,' Rose says with an intense look on her face. 'You have no idea.'

I read it. Laurel, Ash and Holly. Those aren't their real names, I learn. I look around me, at the uniformed kids everywhere. Now they could be anyone.

The three girls watch trees fall; they talk about Faulkner; they worry about the spell. They find a boy. They fall in love with the boy. *It's funny how you can completely understand somebody after having known them for a day. It's funny how soon you come to realize somebody is going to change your life.*

I look up at Rose.

'Have you finished?' she says. 'It's freaky, right?'

'It is freaky,' I tell her, zipping open my bag. 'Because I found some of her diary yesterday. That's what I thought was so weird about it. It's from the day before she wrote this one.'

'What?'

I take out the diary pages. Rose grabs them and reads quickly, mouth half open. I look at the people milling around the yard, eating lunch on the steps of the school building, smoking behind the cars parked outside. Laurel, Ash and Holly. They could be right here and we'd never know. How weird is it that we were at the same party, that we seem to be so linked, but we have no idea who they are?

The party. *Everybody lost something.* Rose is exclaiming something about the weirdness of it all and I've figured something out. About what Emily said earlier. About what Rose is clearly avoiding discussing. Little details click into place. Skin and thorns. 'You never did tell me what you lost,' I say to Rose. '*Did* you lose something at the party?'

'Not really,' Rose says. 'Can I see the pages I gave you again?'

I hand them to Rose and, finally, I ask her, 'Did something happen with Cathal Murdock at the party?'

Rose reads Laurel's words again and ignores mine.

'I wish she'd used their real names,' Rose says. 'How can we find out who they are?'

'I dunno, but back to the party—'

Rose props her legs up on the bike rack in front of us and stabs her liquorice strip towards me. 'Don't interrupt me, I'm reading.'

I don't allow myself to be sidetracked. 'Allow me to summarize,' I tell her. 'All we know about them is that they went to the party so they must live in this town, there's a Trina McEown in their class and that Ash wears red nail varnish. Did something happen with Cathal at the party?'

'*Everyone* wears red nail varnish,' Rose says. 'We're hardly going to go around to every girl in Balmallen wearing red nail varnish and ask if her friends call her Ash.'

'You make a valid point,' I say. 'Did something happen with Cathal at the party?'

Rose takes out her phone and starts to search for Trina McEown. 'There are like a billion,' she says. 'What about Jude? Does he have a surname?'

I shake my head impatiently. 'I don't think so. About Cathal—'

'He sounds like trouble,' Rose says.

'We know he's trouble. He rates our classmates' bodies out of ten and gropes girls in the canteen.'

'Jude, I mean.'

'Oh. Well. Him, too, I guess.'

Rose hands me the diary pages and I fold them up and put them back into the poetry book I was keeping them in, along with the pages Rose found.

'Yes,' she says finally. 'Something happened. At the party.'

'With Cathal?'

'No, with Santa Claus,' Rose says sarcastically.

'Well, I always thought his omniscience was a little suspect. Also who wears red to climb down a chimney?' I tear at the liquorice with my teeth. 'What happened?'

Rose purses her lips.

'I lost my virginity,' she says.

My mind is blank. 'You lost your *what*?'

She does a weird flailing-hand shrug thing. 'There you have it,' she says.

'Wait. Start again. Explain.'

More hand gestures. 'I . . . I don't really remember, I was pretty wasted. I think I fell asleep? Or passed out, more likely, because of all the drinking you already mentioned.' She traps her hands under her legs. 'And then, apparently, some girls cast a spell and everyone started losing things, and I lost my virginity and—'

My mind catches up with my ears like a train. There is an epic crash. Brakes scream, locomotives derail, carriages pile up in a mess of metal.

'*Rose.*'

'Olive.'

'Did Cathal . . . Was this . . .' I try to get my words in order so they don't come out jumbled. Or insulting. Or upsetting. Or plain wrong. Or maybe right. 'Consensual?'

Rose is quiet for so long that every single one of those options overlap and intertwine, crawling and clawing over each other to get free of the wreckage. Does she *like* Cathal? Has she *always* liked Cathal? Is what I'm suggesting completely insulting to her? Or does she think he's an idiot like I always thought we both did? Did she sleep with him drunkenly anyway? Rose's tear-streaked face in the bathroom, my unanswered calls, her absence from school. No. I'm right. I have to be. (I don't want to be.)

(Oh God, I don't want to be.)

'I don't . . . really remember,' Rose says finally. 'I mean, I thought I was out cold, but I have these vague memories. So I guess maybe it . . . wasn't *not*.'

I stare at her.

'I know what you're thinking,' she says, like it's something she's rehearsed. 'I've read all your feminist websites and listened to your weekly rants and I know what you're thinking, but it wasn't like that. I was really drunk but so was he. He probably just thought I was playing hard to get. And even if he didn't – even if he didn't care that I didn't . . . want to – there's nothing I can . . . I mean, it's done, it's done, right? It's not that big a deal.'

Not that big a deal.

'You said you didn't want to. You said you'd passed out.'

'Yeah, but like so did he afterwards.'

'Rose.' I want to cry. I don't understand why she isn't.

'It's fine,' she says. 'It happened. I just want to forget about it and move on.'

She takes out her phone and opens up a message conversation. She hands the phone to me and waits in silence while I read. I start to feel sick.

I can't believe I didn't understand sooner, or ask better, or listen at all. I am the worst friend.

'Let's go to the Guards,' I say.

Rose looks annoyed. 'And tell them what? Some guy I drunkenly got with didn't get the hint? There's literally no use, there's no proof. I'm not even sure that's even what happened and also he was texting nice things for a while before he realized I was ignoring him . . . I don't know. I just know I never want to see him again.'

I drop the last of my liquorice on the ground. I don't know what else to say.

Rose wraps her arms round her knees and rests her forehead over the words markered there.

Everybody's lost something.

As if she's heard my thought, Rose says, 'Your virginity is something you can lose.'

'I really . . . I really don't think this is about those girls and their spell.'

'But—'

'No *really*,' I say, trying to keep calm for Rose's sake, but probably failing spectacularly. 'What happened that night has nothing to do with any spell and everything to do with Cathal Murdock. So the girls who cast that spell – *if* it was even real, which I'm not saying it was – are not to blame for what happened. Neither are you. That was one person, and one person only. And I will ruin his fucking life for what he did to you.'

That's when Rose bursts into tears.

'Oh, shit,' I say. 'Oh, shit, I'm sorry.'

Her shoulders shake. Her breath shudders. I wrap my arms round her like I can shield her from what happened, from what she's lost, from the train-crash wreck of her feelings.

When her sobs have quietened down, I say softly, 'I really, really think it would help to talk to my Aunt Gillian.'

Gillian's my mother's sister. She's also one of the local Guards. She'll know what to do.

Rose sniffs and shakes her head. 'There's literally no use,' she says. 'There's nothing she can do.'

'But—'

'I told you, Olive, I've read all those feminist blogs you link to. I've read all those articles and news stories. I know there's nothing she can do.'

My face feels heavy. My all of me feels heavy. 'I hate the world,' I whisper so low I know no one can hear.

I stroke Rose's hair. We are silent for a long, long time. Then Rose speaks from underneath her own arms. 'Hazel said we should try the spell.' It comes out only slightly louder than a mumble.

'What?'

'Hazel?' Rose raises her head. 'She said we should try the spell.'

'For what?' I ask.

'For . . . what happened. For bringing back what I've lost.'

I want to tell her again that we should talk to Aunt Gillian, but there are mascara tear stains all down my best friend's face and her eyes have brightened at this ridiculous suggestion. 'OK,' I say. 'I have the spellbook. They – it's in my room. It got put into my bag somehow the other day. We can try the spell.'

'You *have* it?' Rose's eyebrows shoot up, then she gives me a meaningful look. 'Olive, I think this was meant to be.'

If it was any other time, I'd question her sudden belief in fate, but for now I close my eyes quickly against the tears still building behind them and give Rose my bravest smile. 'Maybe,' I say. Meanwhile I think hard about how I would go about asking Aunt Gillian some hypothetical questions about a hypothetical friend over our family lunch on Sunday.

'So we'll do it,' she says, and she stands up. 'Let's go.'

'Rose.' I gesture towards the school building. 'You have your German oral in like . . . five minutes.' The very idea of having to sit an exam after all this is ludicrous. But the idea of letting Rose fail an exam because of Cathal bloody Murdock is unthinkable. My stomach twists painfully into knots.

'Afterwards then,' says Rose. 'Let's go to Oak Road tonight.'

Rowan's face flashes in front of my eyes.

'I can't, Rose, I'm still grounded.'

'Olive, *please.*'

'My parents will kill me—'

'When are you *not* grounded?' Rose cuts me off. 'I need to cast that spell.'

I shake my head. Our summer exams are starting and I've spent fewer hours studying than I have daydreaming about the trio at Oak Road. I need to study. I need to not be grounded any more. I need to help my best friend.

Also, and I'm not sure why, there's something about the idea of the spell that I find discomfiting. I think back to when I read it through at Oak Road. The part about human blood maybe. The part about sacrifice. The part about being careful what you wish for. Because right now, more than anything, I wish Cathal Murdock had never been born.

I reach out for Rose's hand and my resolve strengthens. 'Tomorrow. We'll go tomorrow.'

Hazel

Friday 12th May

Lost: Blue plastic lighter; mug (brown, chipped)

It's very early morning when the wind blows the boards off my window and they shudder to the ground below. I'm in the last phase of that light sleep that's kinda like an acid trip and the world's not really real. I see my dad at the window. I'm on the first floor. Maybe he's hovering like in those vintage vampire films where you can practically see the strings. Levitating. I go to the window and the floor slopes. There's something wrong with the walls. Probably I'm still dreaming. Probably I'm sleeping through all this.

By the time I reach the window I'm mostly awake. The walls are normal. My dad's not levitating outside my bedroom window. Of course. I start to close the windows and I see a shadow move by the wall of one of the other houses. I freeze. The shadow detaches itself from the blocky black of the space between two houses and walks – *shit* – it walks like the shadow of a person across the front of the house opposite ours, just a few metres from where I'm standing. My window's open and the boards are gone. It's obvious now that this house isn't empty.

The only light outside is from the moon and the stars and you wouldn't think that would be enough to see by but it is. The shape in the darkness turns into a boy. He steps out from the shadow of the house and grins up at me. He's my age maybe. His hair is long and there are beads that look like teeth strung around his neck.

I duck back against the wall, pulse thudding in my throat. I think I can hear a snatch of musical notes coming through the open window at me. A little refrain. Like the boy's whistling through his teeth, loud enough for me to hear clearly. Darkness and shivers. When I chance a glance back out of the window seconds later, the boy is gone. I close the window by wedging my thickest clothes into the cracks to make curtains. I don't fall asleep for a long time.

In the morning I call Mags to tell her I want a ladder.

'I'll drop by with it later,' she grumbles. 'You could have told me your boards'd broken before I came by this morning with the paper.'

I frown. 'I didn't tell you the boards broke.'

'Didn't have to,' Mags says. 'I may be old but I amn't blind.'

'Right.'

'Your mam—' she starts to say, but someone calls for her, a voice I can only just hear over the crackle of crappy reception.

'What about my mum?'

'One sec,' Mags says, to me or to the person she's with. 'I'll call you back, pet.' She disconnects the call.

It was probably nothing. It's not like she could possibly have heard from my parents. But I feel the nerves bunch up round my throat anyway. *Someone's coming*, Ivy said. *Expect guests*. I still think the crossword meant Olive and Rose – to cast the spell, to bring back what we've lost.

I part the clothes covering the window and look out. It's bright and calm. The estate is empty. The boy is gone. My dad was never there. I keep the clothes over the window anyway.

There are flowers on the table when I come downstairs. Like we've got company. The kitchen putting on its best dress, fresh lipstick. Someone has even cleaned the counters. The flowers are roses, thorny and beautiful, maybe snipped out of someone else's garden. Probably Ivy put them there. Rowan and I can't afford to buy flowers now, with our parents' credit card not working any more.

I really should tell him about that. It's been three days already.

I slip out of the back door with my tea and walk to the edge of the estate that borders the forest. Rowan is sitting up on top of the pile of rubble with his guitar. I can hear a few notes of the song he's singing float towards me on the breeze.

I climb up carefully, all hands and knees, my mug clinking on the cement and stone, and join him. We're far enough from the first trees of the forest for the sun to shine straight down on us and I turn to face it and close my eyes. Rowan stops singing and puts down his guitar.

Eyes closed, everything orange, I can smell the smoke from a cigarette. I open my eyes to slits and squint sideways at my brother.

'Since when do you smoke?' I ask, then I close my eyes again in the glare of the sun. 'Don't tell me you're taking up cigarettes to go with your alcohol problem.'

'Says you,' Rowan retorts. 'Thanks for the heart-warming concern, but I'm fine. I found a packet with two cigarettes left in it right here.' He flicks open his lighter, clicks it shut again. 'Figured it was my fate to smoke one of them. They were completely dry and everything.'

'So you're saying you had no choice.'

'Exactly.'

I side-eye Rowan again, but he looks pretty cheerful this morning, basking sober in the sunshine with his guitar and a found cigarette, cap at a jaunty angle, king of the rubble heap. It makes me want to draw him. Maybe Mags was right. Maybe sometimes people are more interesting than things.

'You said there were two cigarettes?' I say, remembering that I lost my last two cigarettes the other day. 'Weird. I think they might be mine.'

He hands me one and his lighter. Its silver reflects the sunlight on to my glasses, nearly blinding me. It's heavy in my hand.

'The credit card was declined the other day,' I say quickly, so I won't be able to take the words back.

Rowan goes very still. 'Faulty machine,' he says.

'I tried every shop on the street.' I blow on my tea and send the steam wafting away from me like dandelion clocks. 'It's gone.'

Rowan takes a deep drag of his cigarette and coughs.

'Well,' he says. 'It was only a matter of time before they'd cop we took it. I'll bet that's why they've cancelled it. They're trying to get us to come back.'

I shake my head.

'Do you think maybe we should?' Rowan says slowly.

'Should what?'

'Go back.'

I can hear my heart in my ears and it's not beating a rhythm I recognize.

'We can't stay here for ever,' Rowan goes on.

'We don't *need* to stay here for ever. Just until we turn eighteen. Then Mags can employ us legally and we can rent out a room somewhere and—'

'And what, never see Granda again? Never see Mum again?' He doesn't even mention Dad.

Thud goes my heart. *Thud-thud.*

'What if . . .' I say really, really slowly. 'What if that's not why the card's been cancelled?'

'What do you mean?'

'I mean, what if something's happened? To Mum and Dad?'

Thud. Thud-thud. Thud.

'Oh, come on,' he says. 'Somebody would have told us if they'd been found mangled in a car crash or something.'

Unless, a small voice in the back of my mind says, *nobody could find us to tell us because we've been off-grid for almost a month.*

'People go missing all the time,' I say softly. 'People get lost.'

I remember Rose crying into her knees, blowing bubbles across the pub car park. 'Ivy's right, I think,' I say. 'Someone must've cast that spell. At the party last week.'

Rowan nods – we've talked this over a few times since I found the spellbook. Found it, then lost it again. We've looked everywhere. It's gone.

'I met someone on Thursday,' I tell him. 'Someone who needs that spell.' I don't say that I need it, too. That I need it just as much as she does. I didn't tell her either. 'She's a friend of Olive's,' I add, and Rowan perks up a bit. He probably doesn't even notice it. But I do. So I tell him all about Rose. I tell him that I think what the crossword said last week, about expecting guests, meant Rose as well as Olive. I tell him I think this means we need to cast the spell.

He looks at his hands for a long time. I know my brother. I know what he looks like when there's something he's not sure he wants to say.

'What?' I ask him. 'Is it that you don't believe in it? Because you said it yourself – everybody's lost something since Saturday. You can't believe Mags can predict the future with the morning crossword and not believe in a spell.'

'It's not that,' he says. 'It's just . . . You did read it, right? The whole spellbook? You remember.' I nod. I remember it all. 'It's just that there's a lot of . . . darkness to it, I guess. All this talk of regret and sacrifice and blood. I'm just . . . not sure it's such a great idea to put our trust in something that could very well be evil.'

'Evil?'

'You don't know – *we* don't know – what kind of magic it is. What kind of things you have to lose so you can find something else.'

'Rowan,' I say. 'Rose needs that spell.'

I need that spell. And so does he. He just doesn't know it.

I put my cigarette out in the dregs of my now-cold tea. Just below us, beyond the low stone wall that borders the estate and the woods, something white catches my eye.

I clamber quickly down off the rubble and hop over the wall.

'What's wrong?' Rowan calls after me.

It's paper, tangled up in leaves. There's a date at the top. *Wednesday 10th May.* Two days ago.

'Hazel?' Rowan asks from the rubble behind me.

'I found something,' I call. 'I think it's out of someone's diary.'

I've never kept a diary. Too many things I don't want anyone to know. They're supposed to be secret, but here I am, clutching a whole bunch of someone's private thoughts in my hand right now. It's too easy to lose things once they're written down.

I come back over the wall and Rowan stands and holds out a hand to help me up. 'Is it Ivy's?' he asks, and his voice is kinda funny. Probably he's worried she's written about whatever's going on between them in her diary. Whatever happened at the party. He's probably worried I'd read it and find out. But it's weird: my stomach doesn't twist with familiar jealousy at the thought of it. For some reason, instead, I think of Rose.

'It's not Ivy's,' I tell him, checking the handwriting. 'And I wouldn't read it if it was.'

'Me neither,' he says defensively.

Then I remember waking up in the middle of the night. The whistling boy. His grin. His long hair. The teeth around his neck.

'I thought I saw someone,' I say to Rowan. 'Last night. In the estate.'

Rowan looks at me. 'Shit,' he whispers, his face stricken.

'I thought I might have been dreaming,' I say. 'It looked like a guy our age. I guess he must have dropped these here.' I don't mention how my skin crawls thinking about him. 'Just keep an eye out, yeah?' I say instead. Rowan nods. 'We can't afford to have people nosing around or telling the Guards.'

Ivy's in the kitchen when we come back inside. The kettle is singing. The paper is open on the table and the crossword stares blankly at the ceiling. Ivy has the end of a half-melted biro in her mouth and she grins round it when she sees us.

'Look what I found,' I say, joining Ivy at the table. I show her the diary pages and start to read the words aloud.

'*On the way to the woods on Wednesday, I rolled over a TV remote in the middle of the road. It crunched under my tyres, and I spun to a halt, Ash and Holly hot on my heels. I kicked it into a ditch, not thinking that a small rectangle of plastic could be the start of something.*'

'Sounds like a story,' Rowan says. He nods at me to read on.

Like any teenager's diary, it's mostly about being in love. Or lust, I guess. I smirk a little as I read bits out. '*His voice is like music – did I mention that before?* This girl's got it bad.'

'Seriously?' Rowan says. 'You're reading out someone's most intimate thoughts and you're just going to poke fun at them?'

'You're listening,' I huff at him. But I stop my slagging and read on. There's something kinda compelling about this girl's story, even if it's just about being in love with some pretentious guy.

Rowan eats half the chocolates in the tin on the table and Ivy absent-mindedly fills in the crossword as she listens. Then the diary mentions the spellbook.

'*It reminded me of the spell for some reason, the moss we foraged, the penknife we used to cut the tips of our fingers.*'

Rowan and Ivy sit up straight.

'Give me that,' Rowan says, trying to grab the paper so he can read it faster.

'Stop it.' I keep my fingers tight round the page and read on.

'*We stowed the beers in the hollow between the branches of the old oak tree at the fork of the road, where Holly had found the spellbook. It seems so long ago now that we first read the spell to get our diaries back.*'

'They found the spellbook,' Ivy whispers.

'They're the ones who cast the spell,' I say.

' *"The spell is working," Jude said. "Look: the lost things are coming home to be found."'*

Ivy's mouth is open, her crossword forgotten. 'Jude,' she says.

'What?' Rowan asks.

Ivy looks down at the crossword. 'The patron saint of lost causes. Remember?'

I remember. And I remember something else. The whistling I heard last night. The song's been stuck in my head all morning, but I've only just now copped what it is. 'Hey Jude'.

'*Shiiiit*,' I say through my teeth. 'This is really fucking weird.'

Rowan tugs on the paper again and this time I let him take it. He turns the page and keeps reading. The girls ask an older sister to buy them beers. They go skinny-dipping in the lake.

It's got to be our lake – just over the estate wall, down the slope of the forest and across the rocks.

Rowan reads on. He blushes at the descriptions of the girls' naked bodies. He shakes his head at the list of lost things they find.

Reading glasses, make-up bag, hairpins. A charm bracelet.

'Two tarnished teaspoons,' he reads. He gets up and

opens the drawer we keep our cutlery in and he takes out a single rusty spoon.

'We had three,' he says.

Ivy lets out a little breath.

I read on and we learn that a boy in town has gone missing.

I remember the words of warning in the spellbook. *Be careful what you bargain with: every lost thing requires a sacrifice – a new loss for every called thing found. Consider carefully before you cast the calling: it may not be for you to choose.*

Ivy's face is white. Rowan looks a little shocked. I don't know what to think.

I wonder, in a crazy kind of way, if the spellbook was left there for me to find. My head hurts with all of it.

'We have to cast the spell,' I say. 'I mean, if we're all losing shit because these girls cast it last Saturday, we need to do it ourselves to get our things back.'

'Hazel,' Rowan says like a warning.

'What? I told you – Rose needs it. And it looks like maybe we do, too. Or do you want more of your things to go missing because of these girls? It's not like we've got a lot we can afford to lose.'

'Who's Rose?' Ivy asks, so I tell her how I think she's one of the guests we were told to expect. I tell her how I think she and Olive are meant to help us cast the spell.

'I'm really not sure about this,' says Rowan.

'What do you think?' I turn to Ivy.

Ivy looks from my brother to me. 'I think . . . you're right. I don't want to lose what I've got. If we can undo what these girls' spell did, I think it's worth a shot.'

'It's decided then,' I say firmly, and this time Rowan doesn't argue. 'Now we just need to find Olive and Rose.'

Laurel

Friday 12th May, Saturday 13th May

Found: Five lost dogs; twelve Scrabble tiles;
a scattering of baby teeth

Holly was only grounded for a couple of days. When she came into the forest with us on Friday, Jude stood at the top of our shrine of lost things and spread his arms wide. He said grandly, 'Look at this. Look at us! We are the finders, we are the keepers, we are the guardians of the lost and found!'

Holly clapped and Ash crowed. Jude stared at me and waited for my applause, but I just stood and watched him. Did the others not realize how pretentious he sounded? Did they not understand that we weren't the guardians of anything, and that if it was because of us that these lost things were appearing then we'd clearly done something very wrong?

I think we all believed it now, that this was happening because of the spell. As if our sudden belief in magic was another found thing. Every time we walked into the forest, we'd find something new. We'd started to gather them in jars. Vases of jigsaw-puzzle pieces. Baskets of odd socks. Pint glasses full of hairpins. Jude had started finding things, too. He stood in the forest; the found things we'd gathered surrounded him like a dragon's hoard and he was the beast in the middle. We were wood nymphs circling him. It's like we'd forgotten that we were the ones who cast the spell, not him.

I kept asking where his parents were. I kept asking where he lived. He said, 'Small talk, small talk,' and he waved my words away. He said, 'Why don't you ask the real questions, Laurel? The questions with fire. The questions that matter.'

So I asked him, 'Where do you go with Ash when she sneaks out to see you in the middle of the night? What do you do?'

Ash's cheeks flamed the colour of her hair. Holly's eyes were huge in the shade of the forest. They turned on me with so much reproach, but I only asked the question.

Jude, for his part, laughed. 'That's more like it,' he said with relish. 'That's the fire I'm looking for.' But he didn't answer and I didn't ask again.

I wanted to say something to Holly, and even to Ash. I wanted to apologize, or maybe warn them against him, maybe tell them that they deserved so much more, and better. Maybe they also deserved a better friend than me. But we are so rarely without him now. Even alone in Holly's bedroom, her patchwork covers pulled up to our chins, it's like he is there with us. We bend our heads together in class, but somehow he's there, too. Our hair doesn't tangle together any more. The only strands I brush out at night are my own.

We were a coven; we were a crowd. We were a forest; we were a three-headed dog. Now all I want is a minute alone with the two of them, without feeling his breath hot on my neck.

Holly's been losing weight. I can tell by the bones of her wrists and shoulders, even though she never knots her shirt any more, doesn't take off her knee socks or tuck her skirt into her knickers when she climbs. She wears her scarf all the time now, wrapped so many times round her white throat it's like a blanket. I don't know how she stands the heat.

Holly's been losing her voice. Her words have lowered to a whisper.

Holly has lost her heart, but haven't we all? Ash's hand in the back pocket of Jude's jeans, her laugh loud every time he speaks. And even me. It's like my eyes always know where he'll be. I argue and I roll my eyes at his pretentious words, but I want him to think highly of me. I want him to see my straight spine, my sharp teeth, and I want him to fear my bite but desire it.

I should tear this page out. I'm going to. Crumple it, bury it, make sure it stays lost.

Ash and Holly can't know this: last night I waited until all my sisters had gone to bed and I snuck out – the youngest dancing princess alone without a ball. I tied a torch to my handlebars and I cycled to the oak tree. The rain had washed out the world and the wind had swept the clouds in under the rug and the sky was all speckles of stars and the moon, glowing. I didn't need the torch after all.

Jude was there, waiting for me.

Down in the deeper forest he kissed me, pressed up against the body of a tree. I dug my fingers into the trunk so as not to claw his clothes off. My hands came away filled with Scrabble tiles. I opened my palms to show them to him and he picked out two letters: L and J. He stuck them on to the soft bark of the tree and took my wrists in his hands, turned them so that the rest of the letters rained onto the mossy ground. If they spelled anything, the words were lost in the darkness.

My hands, now empty, ached to be filled. They clutched his T-shirt of their own accord and pulled it over his head. He kissed me harder. My hands grabbed at his hair, clawed their way down his back, hooked at the waistband of his jeans and pulled him fast against me. I could feel every pulse point in his body as my own. Burn, burn, burn.

Then somehow my T-shirt was off, my bra unclasped, my back against the tree and pressing so hard against the bark I'm marked by it still. His hands holding my face, his palms either side of my neck, his thumbs making paths down my breastbone, his fingers splayed over my breasts. His lips left mine and followed his hands, down, down, a chain of kisses, kisses like pearls, like tears. My mouth was open, my eyes closed, my breath heavy in the silence.

I only opened my eyes when I felt his hands at the buttons of my jeans, and when I looked down I saw that he was naked. It wasn't like when we swam in the lake, laughing, eyes averted but also drawn to each other's bodies, beer bottles in hand and water all around. It wasn't like that at all. It was dark but I saw everything, felt everything. The moonlight shone through the leaves and lit up our skin and the Scrabble tiles on the ground around us. As he took off the rest of my clothes, I could see the letters: the L that fell from where he stuck it on the tree, an A, an H. He took my hand and guided it down to where he was hard against me, and I looked up into the tree to see if the J was still there, stuck on with sap. He started to pull me away from the tree, to lay me down on the letters and the leaves, but my friends' initials stared up at me and all at once I wanted to be anywhere but there, anywhere but there with him.

Suddenly I was cold, and the forest felt dirty. Suddenly I didn't want to be naked any more. I pulled my clothes back on without saying anything and still he kissed me. He ran his hands over me even over my clothes. He left bite marks on my T-shirt. I kissed him until I had the courage to turn away. I cycled home shakily. He stayed in the forest. I realize now I've never seen him out of it.

It was on the road home that I noticed the dogs. Big brown Labradors, one every few miles, walking towards the forest. They were old and slow. Something about them made me shiver.

Then, today, after her Saturday morning bridge club, Mam told me that people have been finding things all over town. The lost things aren't staying within the boundaries of the forest any more. They spill into the lake water, trinkets tinkling on rocks and hairpins trapping frogs' legs together. Anglers catch brown trout heavy with more than their bones; when they gut them, they find car keys and small change in their bellies. In the nearby fields, horses rip up rings and earring backs with tufts of grass. Odd socks and the glass bulbs of Christmas lights are resurfacing in cowpats.

Then, this morning, a scattering of baby teeth appeared in a clearing. Jude and Ash laughed when they saw them, talked about the tooth fairy and coins under pillows, but Holly and I shivered. We buried the teeth. Hands deep in the soil of the forest, we decided to stay away from the woods.

I knew it then. I knew this was what we'd done. We hadn't made a sacrifice. We hadn't traded something we didn't want to lose for something we wanted found. We got our diaries back because of other people's sacrifices. Things they didn't want lost. Things they didn't realize would go missing. Trinkets, treasures, memories, beliefs. We stole them without knowing and now they were showing up all around us.

In town, people are wondering about thieves at the party, about something in the beer, about pollution in the lake and rubbish washing into fields with the rain. But it was us. It was the spell. It was three girls messing with something we didn't understand.

I keep replaying the last words of the spell in my head. *Be careful what you wish for: not all lost things should be found.*

I can't stop making lists of lost things that shouldn't be found again. Lost hair. Lost blood.

Lost souls.

I remember how Jude just appeared in that tree after we cast the spell. *No*, I tell myself. *Don't be silly. He couldn't possibly be.*

Olive

Saturday 13th May

Lost: Three earring backs; one friendship

On Saturday morning Dad wakes us up with a poem I don't know. The first few stanzas are drowned out by Emily yelling, 'It's BEFORE SEVEN on a SATURDAY for God's sake! LET US SLEEP!' at the top of her voice.

Dad opens my door and I blink in the light of the landing.

'*Lose something every day,*' Dad's voice booms through the house. '*Accept the fluster / of lost door keys, the hour badly spent.*'

'THIS IS CHILD ABUSE!' Emily screams, but a little screaming has never deterred our father from quoting poetry.

'*The art of losing isn't hard to master.*' He throws his voice louder, his lungs large from decades of broadcasting words from the bottom of lecture theatres to sleepy students.

'YOU ARE EMOTIONALLY UNHINGED!' Emily shrieks.

'*THEN PRACTISE LOSING FARTHER, LOSING FASTER,*' Dad bellows.

I lock eyes with Mum on the landing. Everything gets kind of quiet despite the noise. 'You think you know him,' she says softly, suddenly beside me. 'You don't know him at all.'

'What?' I have a moment of confusion where I think she's talking about Dad, and then a longer moment of even greater confusion when I realize she's not.

'We're leaving early this morning,' Mum says, like she's repeating herself. 'Emily's got dance and Max has his football.'

I look right into her face, her laughter-lined eyes, her short hair curling round the seven silver hoops in each ear, and I almost don't recognize her. Maybe I am losing my mind a little.

After all, I have planned to go see a group of tattooed teenage runaways in a ghost estate so I can cast a spell with my best friend. I'm weirdly nervous about it. Maybe because I feel as if Rose and I should be going to the police about Cathal, not casting spells. Maybe because spells aren't actually going to help. And also maybe because this all means seeing Rowan again.

With that in mind, it takes a while for me to get ready. I pick out a summer dress that's long enough to not look too attention-seeking, loose enough to hide my belly and low-cut enough to draw the eye. I try to find a pair of earrings that still has its backs and put on my silver ballet flats.

When I come downstairs, Emily is bent over her phone at the kitchen table, eating thick chunks of my nana's homemade bread while Mum reads the paper. Max is eating cereal messily.

'You look nice,' Mum comments, glancing up from her paper.

'Thanks. I'm going to Rose's. You said I could, remember? I'm not grounded any more?'

'Sure,' Mum says, eyes glued back to the paper. 'Just don't jump in the lake.'

'What?'

'Don't be home too late,' Mum says.

I nearly trip over Emily's dance bag on the way to the fridge and realize that Chloe, her partner in crime and jazz hands, is not at her usual spot beside her, waiting for my mum to drive them to class.

'Where's Chloe?' I ask Emily.

Emily tears off a bit of bread with her teeth and scowls. 'Up her own ass,' she says with her mouth full.

'Emily!' Mum puts the paper down on the table with a slap. Max breaks into uncontrollable giggles, smacking the table so hard in his glee that he spills half his Honey Nut Loops on to the floor. The dogs descend upon the mess he's made.

'Sorry, Mum,' says Emily. 'She's up her own posterior.'

Mum gives Emily a measured look, then shrugs and picks her paper back up. 'Slightly better,' she says. 'Although that sounds uncomfortable.'

Emily manages a grin. I make myself a cup of tea and take a packet of biscuits out of the cupboard. Max wanders off in search of Dad and Emily scowls at her phone.

'I take it you had a fight?' I ask, offering her a biscuit.

Emily rolls her eyes, but to my astonishment she actually answers. 'She's being unreasonable,' she says.

'Unreasonable about what?'

Emily takes the biscuit and asks me, mouth full of crumbs, 'If I told you that someone close to you had done something bad, would you want to know?'

In Emily's world, *something bad* is more than likely one of her friends buying the same top as another, or tagging an unflattering photo, or considering kissing a boy another friend liked. 'Sure,' I answer.

'Even if you could never un-know it after?'

'Of course.'

'And you wouldn't, like, shoot the messenger?'

'I'm guessing Chloe shot the messenger,' I say.

'Bullet wound. Straight to the heart.' Emily nods solemnly and clutches her chest. 'I thought she was my best friend,' she says with an angry shrug.

'Sometimes best friends screw up,' I tell her. 'Give her time. I'm sure she'll come round.'

Rose appears at the back door right at that moment, flushed from the heat and breathless from the cycle. The dogs bound over to her. My mum, who was probably monitoring our conversation for signs of sisterly bonding while pretending to be absorbed in this morning's news, looks up at Rose carefully. How is it that mums always seem to instinctively know when something's wrong? It's almost as if Emily does, too; she quickly begins to chat animatedly – and uncharacteristically – with Rose, who for her part looks a little unsettled by Emily's attention.

'And then I was just saying to Chloe, like, you are *the* best example of not having to straighten your hair all the time, but, like, if I tried to have hair like yours, it'd just be a big ball of frizz, you know?' Emily is saying.

Rose gives me a look. I shrug and grab my bag from the chair beside me.

Emily is still chattering. 'And, like, I was saying to Chloe, because I was reading all about it online, but isn't it, like, just really racist that we think straight hair is the best hair? Because forcing black women and, like, Indian women to straighten their hair, like, invalidates their heritage?'

'Um, I guess?' says Rose.

'We're going now,' I announce.

'Oh, OK, cool, well, um, if you have any tips for frizzy hair . . .'

I tune Emily out and grab Rose's hand. '*Okaaay* then,' I say. 'We're off now.' I give a little wave and usher Rose out of the door.

She stops just outside the kitchen, though, and turns back to Emily. 'Coconut oil,' she says. 'On damp hair after the shower. Don't brush it or blow-dry it. If you wear it in plaits at night, it'll be wavy in the morning and the oil will keep the frizz away.'

'Thanks!' Emily chirps, and I shut the back door before the dogs can follow us or the rest of my family can do or say any more strange things.

'What was that all about?' I say to Rose as we cycle out on to the road.

'Don't ask me,' she says. 'She's your sister.'

Before last week I would've said something about how Emily and I are polar opposites, but after learning that she has actual opinions on racist beauty standards, I just shrug and say, 'Ah, she's all right, as sisters go.'

At Rose's suggestion, we take a slightly longer route out of town that takes us past Maguire's, so that we can check if Rowan and Hazel are working today, which would slightly scupper our spell-casting plans. We pull into the car park by the back door of the pub.

'You go in,' Rose says. 'I'll watch the bikes.' She takes out her bubbles and blows a few as I get off my bike.

Just then the back door opens. We both look up, but it isn't one of the twins who emerges from the steamy belly of the pub; it's Mags herself. She's accompanied by Lucky who, more wobbly on her legs than when she was happily drooling all over me on Wednesday, drops heavily on to the step and unrolls her long tongue.

Mags nods to me in greeting (Lucky's tail beats feebly on the step as a hello), takes out a cigarette, and gestures to Rose after she lights it. 'Should have started on the bubbles when I was your age,' she says gruffly. 'But it's far too late for me now.'

Imagining Mags Maguire at seventeen is an exercise in the suspension of disbelief. Some people look like they were born sixty-five.

Rose laughs and offers Mags her bubble wand. 'Come on,' she says. 'You're never too old for bubbles.'

Mags cocks her eyebrows, but accepts the wand and blows a flurry of bubbles back into the dingy, cobweb-hung hallway of the pub.

Rose leans nonchalantly on the door frame and says, 'So, um, we were wondering—'

'Day off,' Mags cuts in.

'Sorry?'

'The twins. It's their day off. That's what you were going to ask about, yes?'

'Oh,' Rose says, looking about as taken aback as I feel. 'Well, yeah.'

'Actually,' I say, 'we were wondering about something else, too.'

'Of course you were.' Mags hands the bubbles back to Rose and takes a deep drag of her cigarette.

'We were?' Rose asks.

'Laurel?' I remind her. I ask Mags, 'You wouldn't, by any chance, know of three teenage girls with tree nicknames who might have taken some of your poteen before the town party last week?'

Rose gives me a look. Probably I could have phrased it better.

Mags looks a little put out (although that may be her face's default setting) and gives us nothing more than an 'I don't stick my nose into other people's business' for our pains. She stamps out her cigarette on the back step and retreats into the pub with Lucky limping behind her.

'So much for that,' says Rose, and we hop back on our bikes and head in the direction of Oak Road.

As we pass the supermarket close to the edge of town, we slow down. Rowan is arguing with someone in front of the main doors. There's a lot of gesturing and aggressive body language, and a small crowd of onlookers is beginning to gather. I raise myself up on my pedals so I can see better.

'What are they saying?' I ask.

'I can't make it out,' says Rose. Without discussing it, we drift over to that side of the road.

The guy with Rowan breaks away and comes striding purposefully towards us. He's a man in his twenties, sandy-haired and broad-shouldered. When he's only a few metres away, he turns back and shouts something I can't quite hear – and suddenly Rowan runs towards him and punches him in the stomach.

Fights in films are all choreography, but this looks more like an embrace. Within seconds, they're locked together, struggling and grabbing, legs circling the concrete, and the store security guard runs up and separates them.

'Take it easy, Cian, take it easy,' the security guard is saying to the other man, and he holds Rowan's arm in a grip so tight I can almost feel the pinch.

Rowan is breathing hard, his freckles standing out starkly from his flushed cheeks. Just watching him makes my own face warm up.

'He jumped me,' says Cian. 'You saw that – I hit him in self-defence.'

Rowan's jaw is red and swelling. His chest rises fast.

Out of the supermarket walks my Aunt Gillian, who's clearly just finished her weekly shop. She sees the fight, then frowns as she spots me and Rose.

'What's going on here?' she says in her official Garda voice.

'Cian says this young lad was shoplifting,' says the security guard.

'He's been stealing from work—' Cian starts to say. 'I mean, from people I work with.' Cian knows that admitting he works with Rowan will get Mags in trouble; she's not legally allowed to employ anyone under eighteen and, if the rumours about her poteen are true, that's not the only illegal thing happening on her premises. 'I wouldn't trust him as far as I could throw him.'

'Well, I don't know,' Rose surprises me by saying. 'You're a big guy. And he's a minor. You provoked him – we saw it.'

'What the hell are you talking about, Pocahontas?' says Cian, and I have to hold Rose back so she won't swing at him herself.

'*What* did you call me?' Her eyes are all fury.

The security guard looks uncomfortable. 'Ah, here now,' he says.

Aunt Gillian gives Cian a disapproving look. 'Is this boy a friend of yours?' she asks us, gesturing to Rowan. By way of answer, I wriggle myself between Rowan and the security guard.

'We were just leaving actually,' I say. 'Is that OK?'

Aunt Gillian looks like she'd love nothing better than to get back to her shopping trolley.

'Fine,' she says, then she points at Rowan. 'Turn out your pockets first.'

Rowan reddens again. 'I didn't steal—' he says heatedly.

'Unless you want me to arrest you both for assault, I

suggest you turn out your pockets,' Aunt Gillian says. I can see Cian puff up at the *you both*, but he doesn't say anything and Rowan takes a stick of gum out of the breast pocket of his T-shirt. He holds it out: exhibit A. He unwraps it and puts it in his mouth before taking exhibit B: his phone and his wallet out of the back pockets of his jeans, and exhibit C: a set of keys and his silver lighter out of his front pockets. If judged by the contents of his pockets, Rowan seems like an exemplary citizen.

'See?' he says, arms spread, hands full of his possessions, chin tilted in defiance and mouth chewing his gum loudly. 'You want to pat me down now, too?'

If judged by his attitude, he's trouble.

'Right!' I say quickly, and I take Rowan by the crook of his arm and turn him to face the road. 'We're just going to go now! See you tomorrow, Aunt Gill!'

I propel Rowan towards the road, Rose following behind with both our bikes. When we're out of sight, she starts to cackle.

'I like you,' she tells Rowan. 'And as always I'm glad that *you*' – she bumps my hip with hers – 'have Gardaí connections.'

I turn to Rowan. 'So what was all that about?' I ask conversationally. We wait on our bikes while he unchains his from a lamppost down the road.

'Nothing,' he says, tossing his hair out of his eyes. 'He's

an asshole. He's been looking for a reason to start a fight since we got here.'

'So you thought you'd give him one by punching him first?'

Rowan grins. 'Something like that.'

We cycle single file up the main road, skirting the town thronged with Saturday traffic and picking up the pace when the road widens again. When we turn off on to the smaller bumpy roads, we let ourselves slow down, breathing hard in the heavy heat. Rowan glides back to cycle beside us.

'Thanks for helping me out back there,' he says. 'I appreciate it.'

'No problem, Rowan,' says Rose. 'We figured you probably didn't want Gillian poking around, asking for your address or where your parents are.'

Rowan grins again, not looking in the slightest taken aback. 'You must be Rose. Or do you prefer to go by Pocahontas?'

Rose growls. 'I'd have preferred to get a punch in myself,' she says.

'Funny story,' Rowan says. 'I was actually coming to find you when I got into my latest brush with the police.'

Latest? 'Oh, yeah?' I ask. 'Wait, how were you going to find us? You don't know where we live.'

Rowan shrugs. 'It's a small town, figured I'd bump into

you eventually. I only realized after you'd left that I'd forgotten to ask for your number.'

I blush. Rose notices and gives me a look.

'Why were you trying to find us?' she asks Rowan.

'Hazel wanted – I mean, we wanted to ask you to help us cast the spell.'

Rose's mouth opens slightly. She looks at me, then says to Rowan, 'That's why we were coming to see you.'

'Well,' Rowan says with a look that's more resignation than surprise. 'Then it looks like it was meant to be.'

We swing on to the small and bumpy road that leads to the forest. Rabbits skitter across fields and we surprise four fallow deer just up ahead, who bound away over a fence and into the trees, the white undersides of their tails bobbing in the shadows.

'We found the people who owned the spellbook before us,' says Rowan. 'Three girls. Well, we didn't find the girls themselves – we found some pages from one of their diaries. We were hoping you'd tell us who they are, seeing as you know more people in town than we do. And where the spellbook is, too, I guess – we haven't been able to find it since you came over.'

'I found it in my bag, the day after. I thought it must have fallen in there by accident,' I tell him, before what he's just said about the spellbook girls sinks in. 'Wait, you found pages from Laurel's diary, too?'

'Too?' he repeats.

I exchange a glance with Rose.

'Rose and I found pages too. Mine were in my bike basket, and Rose found hers on the way to school,' I explain.

'That's a weird coincidence,' Rose says.

'So do you know the girls?' he asks. Rose and I both shake our heads.

'Isn't there, like, just one school in Balmallen?' Rowan says.

'Yeah,' I admit. 'But we don't know their real names, do we? So they could be in our class, but we wouldn't know them as Laurel, Ash and Holly. Or they could go to a school in the next town maybe. They mention a Mr Murphy, but there's probably a Mr Murphy in every school in the country.'

'There was one in mine.' Rowan nods.

'And they mention a girl called Trina McEown, but we haven't been able to find anything about her either. We don't even know how old they are – they could be Fifth Years like us, but they could be Sixth Years, or Fourth Years even. It's basically an unsolved mystery.'

When we get to the estate, Rose and I drop our bikes behind the wall closest to the road, where we usually leave them, but Rowan wheels his into the house.

'Can't risk anyone recognizing it,' he says.

'Nobody comes here,' Rose argues. 'Like, ever. It's like Neverland or something.'

'You guys did, though.'

'That's different,' Rose starts to say, but I speak over her.

'Who exactly,' I ask, 'are you hiding from?'

Rowan only blanks for half a second, but I notice it. His smile then is so easy it's like he doesn't have a care in the world, and if I didn't know better I'd think I'd just imagined his moment of hesitation.

'Captain Hook,' he says easily, opening the door of the boarded-up house. He looks back at Rose and says cheekily, 'Maybe Cian should've called you Tiger Lily instead.'

Rose rolls her eyes. 'Don't make me change my mind about liking you,' she says.

Hazel appears in the doorway to the kitchen, once again not looking in the least surprised to see us. 'You like Rowan?' she says to Rose in mock-horror. 'Nobody likes Rowan.'

Rowan gives his sister the finger and we all crowd in through the kitchen door. It's light in here today; with the wooden boards off, the French doors have been thrown open. It's refreshingly cool inside; the sun slants in on the tiles, but, because the rest of the house is dark and empty, the heat hasn't had time to settle.

Ivy, sitting on the back step, looks up in surprise and says, '*I* like Rowan,' as if Hazel was being serious.

There is a small awkward moment that I don't quite know how to interpret. *Does* Ivy like Rowan? Are they together? Rowan's reddening cheeks, Hazel's averted gaze, Ivy biting her lip like maybe she shouldn't have said that. Beside me, Rose watches each of their faces. Her eyes narrow and I'm sure she's wondering, like me, if Rowan and Hazel are both in love with Ivy.

It's something about the way they move around her, like they're aware of her at every moment. When I think back to the last time I was here, it fits in, too. Rowan's blush fades slowly and my heart sinks a little. I turn away and catch sight of Rose's expression as she watches Hazel: she looks a little like I feel. I remember her describing Hazel to me. *Confident, gorgeous.* Infatuation is a terrible thing.

'Yeah, well,' Hazel says boisterously to Ivy, as if to smooth things over. 'You've always had shit taste in friends.' She turns to her brother and says, 'Speaking of which, what happened to your face?'

Rowan rubs at his jaw thoughtfully. The red is slowly turning purple and it's still swollen. 'I got punched a bit,' he admits.

'Just a bit?' Ivy asks. She sounds slightly confused.

'Did you deserve it?' Hazel asks. She sounds like she knows exactly what's going on.

'Probably,' Rowan says at the same time as I say, 'Definitely.'

When he laughs, his eyes crease at the corners. 'OK,' he says. 'Definitely.'

'Your brother's got quite the temper on him,' Rose declares. 'Hence why I decided I like him.'

'They have that in common,' I explain to Hazel.

Hazel smiles right into Rose's eyes. 'I'll bet,' she says.

'A temper is a thing you can lose,' Ivy says softly from the back door, to nobody in particular.

'Besides,' I say, 'that Cian guy isn't exactly the friendliest.'

'Or the least racist,' Rose adds.

Hazel isn't smiling any more.

'*Cian* punched you?' she says to Rowan.

'It's fine,' he says. He takes a cheap bottle of beer from the tiny fridge and opens it on the side of the counter.

'Cian, who we work with almost every day, punched you?' Hazel says, her voice rising.

Rowan shrugs and hands round the rest of the bottles of the six-pack sitting in the fridge. 'I said it's fine, Hazel – just drop it.'

Hazel sits down at the table and shakes her head. 'I knew it was a bad idea for us to work there,' she says angrily.

'It's fine,' Rowan says again. He looks at me and Rose like this is a conversation we're not supposed to be present for. 'It's not a problem.'

'It is if Cian decides to go sniffing around,' Hazel argues.

'Sniffing into what?' I start to ask, but Ivy jumps up from the back step and cries out, 'Look!'

I run to the open door with the others despite myself. The light little wind that's been rustling the trees must have shaken up a rubbish bin somewhere, because a small swirl of sweet wrappers and receipts, of crisp packets and pieces of paper blows in across the weeds.

Ivy darts outside and grabs at the paper. It couldn't be. It couldn't possibly. But she comes back in holding another page of Laurel's diary.

It's torn across the bottom. It doesn't say much. They find random items in the forest. It looks like Laurel's beginning to believe in the spell. When I mention this, Hazel shows me the diary pages she found yesterday. Skinny-dipping and found things. A missing boy.

Rose, reading over my shoulder, says, 'I haven't heard anything about that. Have you?'

I shake my head. 'No. Which is weird, 'cos my nana's the biggest gossip in town.'

Rowan reads out Ash's description of the boy. *'You'd know him if you saw him. He's scruffy and blond and he's got his eyebrow pierced.'*

'Nope.' Rose shakes her head. 'Doesn't ring a bell.'

But he does ring a bell for me. Loud and clear, a great gong. *Can I've another kiss before you go?*

My thoughts must show in my expression, because Hazel asks, 'Do you know him?'

'Not exactly,' I answer. 'But I think I saw him. At the summer party. I think we were dancing with him at some point. I dunno, I was pretty drunk. He was blond and I guess kinda scruffy. He had an eyebrow piercing. I don't know. It might not even be the same guy.'

Rose gives me a funny look.

Laurel isn't the only one who's beginning to believe in the spell.

Hazel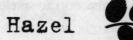

Saturday 13th May

Lost: A couple of beer bottles (discount brand);
a good few taste buds

We have everyone we need to cast the spell. I sent Rowan
to find Olive and Rose, but they were already on their way
here themselves. That has to mean something.

I open the spellbook and look down the list of
ingredients. Olive had it all along, she explains. Like it just
slipped itself into her bag.

'What do we have?' Rose asks. 'And what do we need?'

We lock eyes. My belly fills with nervous bees. We're in
this together. We need this – both of us. I almost wish I
could tell her why.

I take the roses on the table out of their vase. 'Rose

thorns,' I say. Rose smiles. Ivy, over at the cupboard, grabs a bottle of olive oil. Then she reaches in under the sink to grab the lemonade bottle full of poteen, stolen from Mags.

Rowan opens the bottle, smells the stuff inside and coughs. 'Jesus,' he mutters. 'Smells like paint thinner.'

'What else?' says Rose.

Red ink, silver string. I run upstairs and root through my art supplies until I find some red markers. Downstairs, Ivy's got a roll of silver string. The kind you wrap round birthday presents.

'We need a hazel branch,' I say. 'Rowan berries, a vine of ivy. We need moss from under an oak tree. And we need a talisman.'

I pass around some beers and Ivy grabs a little jar and Rose empties out her bag for us to put the spell ingredients in. Rowan shakes his head. 'I'm telling you,' he says for like the hundredth time, 'I don't think this is a good idea.'

We tramp through the forest, looking for the plants we need. Phone reception's too low for us to look up which trees are which, but Ivy has a little book of Irish native plants and trees she brought with her from home for some reason. Laurel said in her diary that this was like kids making mud pies, but I'm deadly serious. Rose tries to joke around with Olive and Rowan, but I know she's serious about this, too.

We end up on the pockmarked rocks by the lake, Rose's

bag bulging. We've got almost everything we need. We sit for a minute and catch our breath and drink our beers. We talk about Laurel, Ash and Holly and their lost things.

'It's probably just stuff blowing off the wishing tree,' Olive says. She puts her empty beer bottle down on the rock beside her with a clink and Rowan offers her another. 'Or rubbish washing over from the caravan park on the other side of the lake.'

'Speaking of which,' Rose says, and she points to the water. Not far from us, by a half-submerged rock, is a bottle, bobbing.

Olive takes off her shoes. 'We should get that,' she says. 'Rubbish in the lake kills the fish, you know, to say nothing of the poor ducks and swans.' Then she stops, a funny look on her face. 'My mum said not to jump in the lake,' she says slowly. 'Maybe I misheard her – or it was a slip of the tongue and she meant not to come home too late, but . . .' She trails off, eyes on the water.

'Well then,' Rowan says. He downs the rest of his beer and leaves the empty bottle by the full ones on the ground. 'Disobeying parents has always been our forte, right, Hazel?' He kicks off his shoes and takes off his jeans and jumps into the water in his T-shirt and boxers. Olive tries not to stare.

Rowan brings the bottle back to the shore, shivering. 'Fuck, it's cold,' he says. 'Here.' He hands it to Olive. 'Looks like there's something inside it.'

'Really?' I lean closer.

There *is* something inside it. Something that looks like a note. A message in a bottle.

'That's kinda cool,' Rose says.

Olive tries to get the paper out, but only Ivy's littlest finger is small enough to grab it.

The page is torn twice: across the top and across the bottom. It's a snippet, a snapshot, an afterthought.

It's Laurel's.

We read a couple of sentences each, our voices lowering as we go.

'I should tear this page out. I'm going to. Crumple it, bury it, make sure it stays lost.'

Laurel and Jude up against a tree. Diary pages and Scrabble tiles. A line of dogs all walking towards the forest.

'I knew this was what we'd done. We hadn't made a sacrifice. We hadn't traded something we didn't want to lose for something we wanted found. We got our diaries back because of other people's sacrifices. Things they didn't want lost. Things they didn't realize would go missing. Trinkets, treasures, memories, beliefs. We stole them without knowing and now they were showing up all around us.'

Rowan's frowning, like this is exactly what he's been afraid of. Olive's cheeks are red. Ivy stares quizzically at the beer bottle. Then she picks it up again and turns it upside down. A few drops of beer mixed with lake water spill into her hand, then something else falls out of the bottle with a small clink. Ivy picks it up with her thumb and forefinger.

It's a St Anthony medal.

'Hazel, it's your medal,' Olive says to me.

'*My* medal?' I look at it more closely. There's a rusty red stain on the corner that looks like dried blood. It *is* the same medal.

Olive frowns. 'I found it in the pocket of your denim jacket,' she explains. 'After the party.'

'It fell off the till in Maguire's last week when I was cleaning,' I tell her, and feel a bit of a shiver. 'It just keeps showing up.'

Rose's mouth is wide open. 'I *lost* that,' she tells Olive. 'I had it in my pocket on Monday after you showed it to me. It must have fallen out on the way back to school . . .'

'Finders keepers,' Rowan says like he's joking, but his eyebrows are drawn and he looks kinda creeped out.

'Hang on,' Rose says. 'The medal.' She looks at me excitedly. 'It's the talisman. A St Anthony medal. It's the only thing we didn't have yet for the spell.'

'We have everything,' I breathe. 'We can do it.'

Rowan's face darkens. Olive looks unsure. She takes the medal and flips it like a coin. It spins through the air, singing. 'Heads or tails?'

It stays in the air longer than is possible. 'Heads, we cast the spell,' Rowan says slowly, nervously. 'Tails, we forget about it. We just drink our beer and swim in the lake and don't mess around with things we don't understand. Things that could be dangerous.'

The water's clear and twinkling before us, reflecting the clouds that are starting to blow in overhead. We watch the medal spin. It's weird that it just keeps doing that. Heads to tails, tails, heads. Finally Rose reaches up and catches it, slaps it on the back of her hand.

'Heads,' she says.

Heads, we cast the spell.

The medal glints on Rose's hand, and all of a sudden the clouds are coming in fast and the wind's picking up and the rain's starting to fall.

'No!' Rose says. 'It was gorgeous a minute ago!'

'It's still gorgeous from where I'm standing,' I say under my breath. I know Rose's heard me 'cos she gives a little grin.

By the time we've climbed over the rocks to the forest, the rain's become a full-on storm.

'We can't stay outside in this weather,' Olive shouts.

'We should go inside,' Rowan agrees. The rainstorm makes his voice sound small. 'We can do this again another time.'

'No way,' I say, and Rose takes my hand.

'It's OK,' Ivy says suddenly. 'I know where we can go. And it'll be out of the rain.'

Laurel

Saturday 13th May

*Found: Tin medal (St Anthony); fingernails
(rainbow-coloured, acrylic); human hair; puddles of blood*

Something was building and it wasn't the storm.

The morning started cloudy. I went to Holly's before school. We had a two-hour optional revision class on Saturday afternoon and although we were all behind on our study she didn't cycle down with me.

'I'll meet you there,' she said.

I wanted to tell her what happened last night with Jude, to confess. Maybe I wanted to warn her about him. But I lost my nerve.

She was sitting in the middle of her bed, surrounded by some of the things we'd found in the forest. Christmas lights, reading glasses, odd socks. Hairpins lined up like picket fences. And bottles of red nail varnish, half-empty cans of hairspray, photographs of the three of us. There were no photographs of Jude.

'He talks about Icarus,' she whispered through the ever-present scarf around her neck. 'But he's more like Orpheus. I think his voice could bring me back from the dead.'

I wanted to shake her. 'You're not dead,' I said. 'You're just infatuated. He's only a boy, for God's sake.'

'Oh, no.' She clutched her scarf tighter to her throat. 'He's so much more than that.'

If I was the kind of girl who believed in vampires, I would have torn the scarf off her, but Holly has always been that pale and, no matter what either of them say, Jude is just a boy like any of the other boys in school, in town, in our families. He's no different from the three of us.

The very first time I asked Holly what she thought of him, before he'd kissed her, or Ash, or me, before he tore our friendship apart like the pages of a diary, she said, 'I think I love him.'

I wanted to be mean, wanted to say, *You thought you loved John Calhoun in Fourth Year, you thought you loved Seamus from Salthill, you thought you loved your aunt's new boyfriend. You're always falling in love with somebody.*

I wanted to be cruelly truthful, wanted to say, *I think I do, too. And so does Ash. We just don't have the guts to tell you.*

I wanted to tell her what I've been thinking all along: *And he knows it, our beautiful Jude – he knows very well how we feel about him. Can't you tell? Don't you see the way he looks at each of us in turn, how he eats up our affection and leaves only the pips spat out on to the forest floor?*

Instead, I left her to her bed full of found things, and I cycled to school.

There was a storm coming. The radio in the staff room next door was staticky; the forecast crackled. *West by south-west, twelve knots, falling slowly.* The newspaper my sisters read that morning was less poetic: *Highs of twenty to twenty-three degrees. Winds will reach gale force on all Irish coastal waters and on the Irish Sea.* Halfway through the revision class the wind began to blow and Holly still hadn't come.

'She'll show up,' Ash said, but I didn't think so.

'I'd say she's running through the forest with Jude.'

'Well, I wouldn't come back either.'

My clothes felt itchy, sticky around the collar of my shirt where my sweat had seeped. The wind outside the school sounded funny.

'Did you hear that?' I whispered to Ash. Mr Murphy kept talking up at the blackboard, writing out equations in staccato bursts of clicking chalk.

'Hear what?'

'Like a dog?' But I wasn't sure.

Lorraine Donnoghue behind us was eavesdropping. 'Bet it's just your little friend panting,' she said nastily.

'What was it she wrote in that diary? *After those kinds of dreams, I stroke with two fingers down between my legs and it's all I can do not to bite the pillow.* That's just *disgusting.*'

'Well, *I* can hardly hear anything over that cow shiteing on behind us,' Ash said to me as loudly as she dared. Lorraine went to say something else, but every time she opened her mouth Ash mooed.

I laughed, but I could have sworn I heard howling. And something else, like a child's spinning top.

Ash smacked her hand on to something on the desk in front of her and the noise stopped.

'What's that?'

She lifted her palm to show me: a holy medal. My mam has dozens.

'I found it on the side of the road this morning,' Ash said. She set it spinning again. 'Must be something about being so close to the pilgrimage site in Knock. People losing Miraculous Medals left, right and centre.'

'It's not a Miraculous Medal,' I told her. 'Those've got Marys on them. This one's St Anthony.' There was a stain on the medal, crusted across the rose on the back. I flicked a bit of it off with my thumbnail. It was the exact rustybrown colour of dried blood.

'Can I have it?' I asked Ash. I didn't tell her I was sure this was the medal we used for the spell. I recognized the stain. There was no reason for it to be there; we'd left the spellbook in the hollow of the oak tree where we found it, in part so that if whoever wrote it came back for it they wouldn't find it gone, and in part because none of us wanted to be the one to keep it.

'If you want.'

I attached it to the gold charm bracelet, right next to the little gold olive tree.

Something was about to fall and it wasn't the trees.

I didn't want to go near the forest after what had happened the night before with Jude – as if the trees would somehow spill our secrets, tell Holly I'd been with him – but Ash insisted, and I knew that's where we'd find Holly. The clouds blew in quickly, threatening rain. The sound of the wind was so much like howling.

Holly and Jude were in the oak tree, kissing. Long hair and wooden beads that, in the right light, almost looked like teeth; Holly's clothes covered in leaves. They were like something in a children's book and Ash and I stared up from our bicycles hungrily. A few tentative drops of rain came through the branches on to the ground and in several puddles small change glistened. I stood beside a sprinkling of acrylic fingernails painted in every colour of the rainbow.

Ash shivered in her little red sundress and Jude threw down his shirt for her to wear. When they climbed down, I pulled myself up into the oak to find the spellbook. I wanted to make sure the St Anthony medal was still there, stuck into it with the prayer for lost objects. I wanted to make sure the one I had on my wrist wasn't the one we used for the spell, stained with our blood, following us. But when I reached into the hollow of the oak tree the notebook wasn't there. Just the last two beers we didn't drink the other night.

Holly paled. 'Do you think someone took it?' she asked. She said it just to me, softly, while Ash opened one of the beers and told Jude what Lorraine had said earlier.

'What a cow,' Jude agreed. 'Maybe there's a spell somewhere to turn her into one.'

'Who else would know to look for it there?' I whispered back.

'I don't know,' said Holly. 'What if it just disappeared?'

Jude, unconcerned, took a silver hip flask from his back pocket. He uncapped it and put it to his lips. I watched his Adam's apple as he swallowed. He passed the flask around.

'What is this?' I said before tasting it.

'Whatever you want it to be,' he replied.

The waters of Lethe, I thought, watching Ash and Holly drink it down. *Something to make us forget any of this ever happened.* I turned the St Anthony medal over and over in my fingers. When nobody was looking, I slipped it into one of the empty beer bottles. So none of us would try the spell again.

I followed the others down to the lake under a drizzle that would soon become heavy rain. Ash stepped over a rock covered in clumps of hair. Holly splashed through a puddle of blood. Out of the corner of my eye I thought I could make out shapes between the trees. Faces looking at me. That howling I was hearing couldn't have been the storm. One of the faces opened a wide red mouth and screamed. I ran to catch up with the others, but the faces were gathering closer. The howling was louder. The lost souls followed us down to the water.

Jude raised his arms and howled along with them.

Dogs in the woods, I reminded myself. *Deer that sound like screaming children. Foxes calling. That's all this is.*

Holly opened her mouth and joined in. Ash whooped and crowed like all the trees in the world were being felled around us.

Bang went the thunder. *Whimper* went the rain. *Burn, burn, burn* went the lightning. The sky was a rush of water with the lake rising to meet it, and in its choppy waves I saw more bodies, more red, open mouths, hands like claws wanting to pull us under. My heart was the backbeat to the thunder.

'Marry me,' Jude said to Holly. 'On this rock, this altar, under the rain.' She stepped up there with him, me and Ash on the shore below, shivering and soaked to the skin, but feeling nothing. He kissed her, he hit her, he snapped her skinny neck. She went back to the forest and climbed the tree one final time, only to throw herself down with a rope around her throat. She swung between the branches.

How do you know if you've lost your mind? I blinked and she was back there, standing smiling on a rock with the boy she loves. The image I'd just seen was like a flash of the future. I felt a sudden lick of fear.

Ash climbed on to the rock, too, her hand round Holly's ankles, then round her proffered wrist, and the three of them howled and laughed.

'Can you imagine?' Ash said manically, long, tangled red hair in her face and fire in her eyes. 'If I'd never taken your diaries, we never would have met Jude. None of this would ever have happened.'

I could hardly speak past the sudden jump in my throat. 'What?' I croaked.

'We'd still be sitting in each other's bedrooms, you and Holly reading your big books and keeping your little secrets, and me running to catch up.'

'Ash,' I whispered, my voice choking on that betrayal. 'You didn't.'

The wind whipped our hair and our clothes. The rain lashed our skin.

'We'd still be worrying about exams and schoolwork, about the boys who don't care about anything but wanking off and the next football match. We'd still be wishing we were like Trina McEown, but she won't ever be anything more than a stupid cow stuck inside this nothing town. She'll never leave and her children will hate her for it.'

Thunder. Lightning. I didn't understand. When I looked at Holly, her face was blank. Jude held her to his chest. She turned her face away from Ash. She turned her face away from me.

'Holly,' Ash said. 'Laurel. Come on.' She had to shout to be heard over the storm. 'They're nothing. They're insignificant and ordinary. We've become magic.'

I was afraid if I left I'd get lost in these woods. I was afraid I would never find my way back.

'All because of the diaries,' Ash shouted louder. I shook my head because I couldn't do anything else. 'All because of me.'

'How could you do that?' I asked her. 'Did you give the diaries to Trina? How could you do that to Holly, to me?'

Ash laughed so hard she coughed. 'How could *I*?' she shrieked. 'Tell your precious Holly what you did with Jude in the woods. Tell her all about it.'

Holly's face was still turned away, but I thought she was crying. Jude's arms strong and safe around her. Her hair darkened by the rain.

'That's different,' I whispered. 'I'm sorry. I didn't know what I was doing. I just lost my head.'

Heads rolling in the water, tongues lolling, eyes staring blankly out at me. I could feel the bile rise in my throat. The wind pulled at our hair, our clothes, our frail limbs and fragile hearts.

'Let's go,' I pleaded. 'Let's just go. Let's get out of this rain and back home.'

But Ash said, 'No.'

Jude stepped down off the rock with Holly in his arms. He walked off through the forest with her head resting on his shoulder and I turned to follow before I could lose them between the trees. I looked back at Ash.

'You can't hate me,' she said. 'Just imagine where we'd be if we'd never met Jude. If we'd never called up the lost things.'

I shrugged. Somewhere nearby another dog howled. Just a dog. 'It's only rubbish,' I told her. 'Overturned bins that blew in on the storm. And Jude is just a boy.'

'He loves me,' she said. 'He tells me that when Holly's not around.'

'*We* loved you. We were your best friends.'

Ash shook her head. I held out my hand – it was like touching the end of a waterfall – but Ash laughed me off. She turned round and ran away, up the slope and away from the lake, just a shadow moving between the trees.

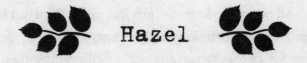

Hazel

Saturday 13th May

Lost: Blood

The second we step out of the forest the storm lashes our skin. Ivy says something, but none of us can hear her. Only the howling of the wind and the swish of the rain and the fat grey rolls of thunder in the distance.

Ivy gestures and we follow her to the edge of the estate. To the storm-drain tunnel.

We slip down into the ditch; we lose our footing in the mud. We could be a bunch of hungry trolls waiting for a traveller. Inside, the tunnel is short and dark. It smells of wet cement and stagnant water, but it's dry. We crouch on our heels and use our phones as torches.

Rowan passes the lemonade bottle of poteen around

and I take a burning sip that makes me cough and splutter. Ivy's eyes water. Rose utters a hoarse 'Fuck'.

Rowan wheezes and presses a fist to his chest. 'That'll curl your hair,' he says, and everybody laughs because his hair is all brown corkscrews, just like mine. With our hair, we might have drunk straight spirits since the age of twelve. Or else we're turning out just like our mother.

I push that thought away from my mind. I'm doing this to bring her back, even if she was a pretty shitty mum. I take a great gulp of the poteen and my throat's aflame.

Olive winces. 'I don't think I'll be able to taste anything ever again.'

Rowan laughs. It's not just the taste that's burning: the world's already feeling kinda soft around the edges.

Rose looks up from the spellbook she's been bent over. 'There's just one problem with this tunnel,' she says. 'No tree branches to write our words on.'

But I know how to make a tree. I jump up and grab a marker and I start to draw.

Big horse chestnuts, thin willows, silver birches. Wide hazels and tall rowans, prickled rose bushes and gnarled olive trunks and climbing ivy. They rise like a black forest on the pale grey tunnel walls. Silhouettes. Ghost trees on concrete. One time Granda told me that four hundred years ago Ireland was mostly forest. You could walk from coast to coast without leaving its shade. I wonder if the ghosts of lost trees stay on in towns and fields, in motorways and housing estates. Mags says this estate used to be trees. Oak Road. They named it for the trees they felled to build it and now nobody lives here except rats.

And us.

When I've drawn a whole forest, I sit down and I'm breathless. My heart's right up against my ribs.

'What do we do next?' Rose whispers.

'We write our losses on the branches,' I tell her. My eyes on her eyes. Dark and wide.

I give her a red marker and she moves to the other side of the tunnel, to the big rose bush I drew. The rest of us sit in silence and watch her. Olive doesn't say this is nonsense. Rowan doesn't warn us it might be dangerous. We just sit all lit up from the inside with Mags's poteen and we watch Rose uncap the marker and turn her back to us and write her losses on the branches of the rose bush. Her shoulders move and I think she might be crying, but when she turns round again she looks furious.

Behind her, scratched hard in red ink on the black branches of the grey concrete walls, are the words Rose wrote. *My virginity. My memory. My mind. My confidence. My happiness. Myself.*

'Oh, Rose,' Olive whispers, and she takes her best friend in her arms and starts to cry.

And just like that, I can tell, we're all decided. Olive, even though she doesn't really believe. Rowan, even though he thinks it's dangerous. Ivy, even though she didn't seem sure. Rose. Me.

I take my granda's old penknife out of my pocket and fold out the blade. Rose takes it.

'We need to bleed,' she whispers.

'What?' Olive says sharply. Either she didn't read the spell all the way through or she didn't think we'd really do the whole blood bit.

Ivy looks up at her and says, 'You can't have blood magic without a bit of blood.'

'Yeah, but—' Olive starts to say, but before she can do anything Rose has slashed the knife through the meaty part of her palm and is making a fist so that the blood drips down. Ivy holds out the jar of moss and Rose shakes her fist. The moss drinks the blood quickly.

I take the knife from Rose and cut my own hand to bleed on the moss. The slash stings. Ivy takes the knife after me. Then Rowan, even though he doesn't look happy about it. When he holds out the knife to Olive, she shakes her head.

'No offence,' she says, 'but that doesn't seem safe.'

'Oh, no,' says Ivy. 'Nothing about this is safe.'

But Olive looks at Rose, who's bunching the end of her dress up in her hand to stop the bleeding, and she squares her shoulders.

'Fine,' says Olive. 'Give it to me.' She flicks the blade across the palm of her own hand and adds her blood to the reddening moss.

Looking at it makes me woozy, even though I haven't lost that much blood. But the poteen's strong and the knife is sharp and the shadows are made in the branches of trees.

I remember why I'm doing this. For Rose, but also for me. So, while Rowan crushes the berries into the moss with his fingers, and Olive unscrews the lid of the oil and pours it over the bloody mess in the jar, and Rose snaps the hazel stick in two and presses the sticky, reddened moss into the centre, and Ivy wraps the ivy vine round it, I write my own words on the wall.

I write them small, so no one will notice, but Rowan comes over and sees. I don't know what to say to him. I don't know how to explain. On the hazel branch in front of me I've written her name. *Amy Aisling Kennedy.* Our mum.

'Not Dad?' Rowan asks. I don't say anything. I pick up the bottle of poteen and take a long, hard drink.

'What about you?' I say to my brother. I hold out the red marker for him to take. He goes over to the rowan tree and he looks right at me and he writes the same thing on his branches. He doesn't write Dad's name on the tunnel wall either.

Amy Aisling Kennedy.

He wants her back, too. Maybe he just wants the her we used to pretend existed sometimes. The real mum. The proper mum. The mum more like Ivy's, who kept her close, who taught her at home, who baked and built tree houses and picked fruit in the rain. Not the mum ours really was. The one who was never there. The one who was a mess. The one I'm turning into, bit by goddamn bit.

Maybe this was a bad idea.

But the words are written now, and Ivy's scratching things in red marker on her own tree branches. *My friends. This adventure.* And Olive is comforting Rose by making dry jokes about lost things and Rose is giving her a marker and she's writing things on the gnarly olive branches like she believes in all this. *My charm bracelet. My hair clip. My best friend.* And Rose looks like she's about to say something so Olive writes some words just to make her smile. *That drawing of a skunk Eoin Kavanagh gave Rose when we were eight years old. Several really great ideas for English essays. My first Barbie.*

Rose laughs despite herself. She says, 'Your mum probably just gave it to a charity shop.' And she takes another sip of poteen from the lemonade bottle.

'Still,' Olive says. 'It's lost and I want it found, so this spell had better work.'

But by the way she looks at Rose when she says it I know she's not joking around.

This spell had better work.

We get kinda frantic then, like this is our last chance, like we have to drum up the magic so we all believe, so it all comes true. We write more words along the branches of the trees. Things we've lost. Things we're afraid of losing. Trinkets, treasures, memories, beliefs. One of our phones goes out and we misspell words in the darkness. Spellings. Spells. The words become spells.

Home-made spirits slosh over the neck of the bottle, over our lips and our tongues. I drunkenly stumble against the side of the tunnel and graze my palm. The blood is red like the marker. Like our words on the walls. We've all lost blood tonight. Ivy unwinds the silver string that dangles from the hazel cross and makes spider's webs from each of the painted branches. She loops the string round the rose thorns she has stuck into the centre of each lost thing like a pin through paper, not a thorn on a concrete tunnel wall. I don't know how they even stay up.

Outside, another dog howls.

If the lights go out, you will know the lost are listening.
If you hear dogs barking, you will know the lost have
    heard your call.
If you hear the howling, you will know the lost have answered.

And, just like that, the storm is eerie. Blue metallic light on concrete walls covered in shadowy trees. The howl of the wind and the dogs. Silver threads like the webs of fat spiders. Rose petals – where did we get rose petals? – by the entrance to the tunnel. Our blood on a clump of moss. We've all stopped writing on the walls. We breathe deep.

None of us say anything for a long time. The rain falls on the roof of the tunnel outside; the wind stirs the dead leaves and the crisp packets. Our phones go dark and we don't turn them on again.

Then we hear a noise. The unmistakable sound of footsteps on the tunnel roof. Our eyes are wide in the darkness. The footsteps cross the roof above us and stop just at the edge where the entrance is. Our five heads swivel round together. We stare at the opening, but no one appears.

Before I know what I'm doing, I grab the glass lemonade bottle by the neck and dive for the tunnel mouth in a half-crouched run. I hear Ivy shout out behind me.

Outside, there's the grey and the rain. My glasses blur with water and I give them a swipe with my free hand. I look around slowly. There's nothing. No one. I crouch back down in the entrance to the tunnel and shake my head.

'There's no one there.'

Olive

Saturday 13th May

Lost: Shoe (white canvas, muddy and torn);
sight of someone through the trees

Without deciding anything out loud, we walk quickly back to the house. We close the boarded-up door and drip in the dark hall.

'Well, that was creepy,' I say, because I feel like someone has to.

Rowan goes upstairs and comes back with a couple of threadbare towels that we pass around until they're half soaked and we're merely damp. Then Hazel gets me and Rose a pair of her pyjamas and we all sit round the rickety old camping table in the only habitable room of the house. Ivy gives us plasters that we press over the cuts on our hands.

Rowan pulls the heavy wooden boards back over the sliding doors so we can't see out. The wood mutes the sound of the storm. Inside, the generator hums, charging our phones, making the fridge cold, lighting the three ugly desk lamps on the kitchen counters. The light flickers. Our eyes are wild. It's like the storm's in our bones.

'Who is she?' I ask to break the silence. 'Amy Aisling Kennedy.'

I'm fairly sure I know the answer, but Rowan tells me anyway.

'She's our mum.'

It's at exactly that moment that we all hear a knock on the door.

Hazel's face pales.

The knocking grows louder. Nobody has moved to answer.

'Aren't any of you going to get that?' I ask.

Ivy fidgets with the sleeves of her top. 'Bad luck to open the door in a storm,' she says. Her voice is slurred. I imagine that drinking straight spirits will affect you more if you weigh approximately the same as a small teapot. I, on the other hand, have a more robust constitution. I stand – swaying only ever so slightly – and open the kitchen door.

In the hall, the knocking's louder. I can almost make out a little 'Wait' from behind me, but I open the front door and pull the boards away from in front of it anyway.

At the beginning of *The Princess and the Pea*, a mysterious girl shows up at the prince's palace one night during a storm. She is half drowned and soaked to the skin and says she is a princess, but her hair is tangled and her dress is worn and her coat is several sizes too big. If I was Cinderella, hopping on one silver shoe after the summer party, the girl on the doorstep is the princess and the pea.

Behind me, the others step out of the doorway to the kitchen. The light from inside spills into the hall, and although it's still murky I can see her.

She's as pale as the lightning – ashen and freckled – with thick, curly red hair twisted round her head by the storm. She's wearing a man's shirt over a red sundress. Her feet are bare and muddy. Her eyes are wild and wide.

We stare at each other for several long seconds before my mouth can move. I've never seen her before, but I feel like I know her. Red hair, bare legs.

I whisper, 'Ash?'

'You're not Laurel,' she says – I think she says it; everything's howling in my head and the doorway is spinning. Maybe my constitution's not so robust after all. I flail an arm out to steady myself and she jolts away from me. Before I can say anything to reassure her, she turns and runs into the forest, scurrying over the rubble like a rat.

'Hey, wait!' Hazel pushes me aside and runs into the rain, her feet as bare as Ash's. Her pyjamas are soaked in seconds.

'What's she doing?' Rowan asks from behind me. I don't know if he means Hazel or Ash.

Ash turns round to us once she's over the wall, her face all in shadows, and thunder shakes the world. Then she takes off again and is swallowed by the forest.

'Stop!' Hazel calls, scrambling over the rubble to the wall.

'Hazel, come back!'

But all we can see is the rain and the trees. Beside me, Rowan pulls on his soaking wet shoes. I grab mine from beside his and Rose and Ivy follow suit. Laces lolling, Rowan runs out into the storm. Rose and I follow, unsteady on our feet, the backs of my shoes bent down under my heels and the soles slapping in the puddles. We put our phones in torch mode, train the beams on the rubble beneath us. We scramble over the wall, palms slick on brick. A mush of leaves and mud underfoot.

Lightning. More thunder. I've never seen a storm like this. I've never been out in such rain. Showers of it. Rivers. Lakes and seas of it.

In the next flash of lightning, I see two girls running. In the next flash of dark, I can see faces between the trees. I skid to a stop and hold on to the trunk of a silver birch for balance. Further ahead, Hazel shouts, 'She's gone down the slope to the deeper forest.'

Behind me, Rose yells, 'Where the fuck does she think she's going?'

Rowan calls, 'We'll break our necks going down the slope in this,' and he's right.

'She could be anywhere.' Ivy's quiet voice is right behind my good ear.

'Fuck.' I crane my neck to stare down the slope, but everything is darkness.

Hazel reappears. 'I lost her,' she says, then she realizes her wording and looks grim.

'She knows where we are,' says Rose, and Hazel nods.

Hazel leads us back to the house and we all trek muddy footprints through the dirty hall.

Hazel

Saturday 13th May

Lost: Some skin off the soles of my feet

I don't remember falling asleep.

The rain's bashing at my bedroom window. That's probably what woke me up. The wind sounds like howling.

I don't remember going to bed. Last thing I can picture is Rose putting plasters on my feet. It takes me a minute to remember how I cut them. Running through the woods after Ash. I sit up and the world sloshes. The wind howls inside my skull.

I reach out blindly to find my phone to give me some light, but I left it charging downstairs. I've no idea what time it is. I light a couple of candles and an answering light appears under the crack of my bedroom door.

'Who is it?' My voice is a croak.

The door creaks open and Rose steps in. I put my glasses on and watch her walk over, watch her fold her long legs underneath her and sit on the end of my mattress in one fluid movement. The shadows under her eyes are black in the candlelight.

'Did I pass out downstairs?' she asks me. 'I don't remember coming up.'

I shake my head. 'I don't remember either.'

Rose's hands twist together in her lap. 'It's what happened to Laurel and the others. Ash and Holly. In the diary, when they cast the spell. She said they were beside the oak tree and must've passed out, and when they woke up their diary pages were all around them.'

I nod my head slowly. It's heavy. 'You think the same thing happened to us,' I say. 'You think this means the spell has worked.' Because it's not a question, she doesn't answer.

'Do you feel different?' she asks.

'A bit, yeah.' My head's swimming and my throat is tight, but that fire I've been feeling in my veins is cooler, calmer. I don't feel so much like I'm going to explode. 'Do you?'

'Definitely different.'

A howl again. This time it sounds further away.

'It's not a dog, is it?' Rose asks. I can feel pinpricks down the back of my neck. 'I heard it at the party,' she says. 'Like tonight. The spellbook says you'll know the magic's worked if you hear the howling, but it doesn't say what howls. It sounds like a human, doesn't it?'

It sounds like a ghost. Lost lives, lost souls. For a second, I wonder if maybe Rowan's right and we should've stayed away from the spell, but then I look at Rose and I'm glad we didn't.

'Are you OK?' I ask her.

Her face is tight but she nods.

'At the party last Saturday,' she says. 'When I – when it happened. I didn't remember it the day after, but since then bits have come back. I remember I was, like, half asleep. I couldn't move. I wanted to get up and run away, but he was too heavy. I was too tired. I couldn't make myself get up. All I could focus on was, like, this hedge behind me. Right behind my head. And I remember thinking that . . . that if I turned into a rose I wouldn't be there.'

She's staring straight into my eyes and I can't look away.

'I wished it so hard. I wished I could become a rose bush so he couldn't hold me. Because my thorns would stick in his skin.'

'Rose—'

'I didn't come here because I believe in magic, because I thought the spell could really work. I figured if magic was real I'd've turned into that rose bush. I wished it *so hard.*' Her voice breaks. 'Your mind's another thing you can lose,' she says. 'You know? He came up to me in class the other day. He threw some money at me and said some stuff to make his friends laugh. I got so mad I just stuffed the note in my mouth. Maybe I wanted to scare him. Maybe I'm just losing it.'

'You're not losing it, Rose,' I whisper, and I put my hand on the back of one of hers.

'D'you think it's going to work?'

'The spell? You believe in it now.' That's not a question either.

'If it is, do you think your mum'll come find you? That's why you wrote her name, isn't it?'

Our hands, close together, sharing warmth. 'I dunno,' I say slowly. 'My mum, she's . . . She's dead. I think she's dead.'

'What?'

I take a shaky breath. 'There was a fire. I think I saw a fire. When we left. When we ran away. Rowan went on ahead with our bags to get a bus ticket, and when I left I saw a spark. A flame. Smoke under the door. I thought it was just her cigarette, you know, so I didn't think too much of it. But then we didn't hear from her for weeks.'

Rose's voice is low. 'So you think . . . there was a fire?'

Flames behind my closed lids. 'I don't know. At first I thought, *Hey, I was right, we ran away and she still hasn't contacted us and it's not like she doesn't have our numbers.*

She's just gone off with Dad again, like always. Rowan was the one who let himself believe it could be different. I kept telling him that she's been like this all our lives – why change now?'

'Because you're all alone now,' Rose whispers. 'Because you've got no one else.'

My throat closes. It usen't to matter so much. We had Granny, we had Granda. It usen't to matter.

'I'm sorry,' Rose says softly. 'I'm so sorry.'

Two tears come out of my eyes and I've no idea how they even got there. 'At first I thought: *So what? So what if they're dead? It's not like it's that big a loss anyway.*'

'Oh, Hazel.'

'But then the crossword – I dunno – it said that we were gonna have guests. And I thought: *Maybe. Just maybe.* What if it was her? And if she was here. And if she actually cared.'

Rose's fingers make little circles on my palm.

'But then it wasn't. You know?'

'I know,' she whispers. 'I know.'

The room's spinning like a fast carousel and I haven't eaten since morning and I haven't been sober a full day since we got here. Not twelve hours. Not ten. I'm just as messed up as my mother.

I need to not think about this. I need to believe I'm different. That I'm not a monster.

'Maybe she had her reasons,' Rose says.

I've never told anybody all this before, and here's this beautiful, messed-up girl in my messed-up life like she's meant to be here.

She's a lot closer to me than she was before. Her shoulder by my shoulder. Her hair a black ink stain down the length of my arm.

I ask Rose, 'Why *did* you come here? If it wasn't to cast the spell.'

'Mostly,' she says, 'it was to see you.'

I put my hand over hers and she turns her palm and interlaces her fingers with mine. She traces the keyhole on my arm with the tip of her other thumb. It tingles. I tilt my head to read the words written on her arm in what looks like permanent marker: *Everybody's lost something*.

'It's something everyone was saying,' Rose explains. 'And it was in Laurel's diary, too. Me and Olive, we have this thing where we write, like, our notes to self on our skin. I don't know. I guess getting a tattoo is like an extreme version of that.'

I laugh.

'How many do you have?' Rose asks.

'Tattoos?'

'Yeah.'

'Just three.'

Rose snorts. '*Just* three,' she says. 'What's the third one?'

I grin and pull my T-shirt up over my head. I let it drop to the floor. I lean back on the mattress so she can read it.

She runs a finger just underneath the words and my whole body lights up with her touch. Shivery tingles from scalp to toes.

'*Kill your darlings*?' she says. 'Dark.'

'Not really,' I say. 'It's William Faulkner. He wrote *The Sound and the Fury*?'

Rose just shrugs.

'My granda liked his books,' I say. 'Anyway, he said that when you're writing you have to kill your darlings. Get rid of anything you're just holding on to for the sake of it, because it's safe, because it's your favourite.'

'So you drop everything and run away to live in a ghost estate in the middle of nowhere?'

'Ha.' The bedroom is echoey, candlelit. The bed's unsteady underneath me. 'I guess it's advice I'm still working on taking.'

Rose takes her hand away, even though all I want right now is for her to keep it there for ever. But then she takes my face in her hands and she kisses me.

Her kiss is soft, then fierce, then kinda breathless, her hands at the back of my neck. She grabs handfuls of my curls and presses herself against me, and it's her lips on my lips, it's her hands in my hair, it's my hands at her back under her T-shirt, then her hands running the length of my bare legs. It's our eyes closed and our bodies close, it's the taste of her tongue, it's her electric hair like a curtain to shield us both from the rest of the world, it's her electric skin setting off sparks everywhere she touches me.

'Can I sleep in here tonight?' she asks, and my whole body lights up like a goddamn Christmas tree.

'Yes,' I say simply, and then her hands are at my pyjama shorts, mine pulling off the T-shirt I lent her. It tangles in her hair and we lose our balance – me tipping backwards on to the bedclothes and her pulled forward, falling on top of me. She shakes her head to free her hair and her face is just above mine; she's leaning on her elbows and her body is just a hair's breadth above me. Half an inch of thin air between our skin. She laughs low and I raise my head to kiss her, and finally she lowers her body down, her knees either side of my legs, her hips against my hips, her back under my hands arching up, our chests pressed tight together so that I lose all the breath in my body for the wanting coursing through me.

Naked bodies have so much skin. I can feel every inch of her over every inch of me and I could bite down with how much I want her.

So I slow down. I feel like I should stop. I don't want to make her think of it again, but I have to ask.

'Is this OK?' I murmur it into her hair.

'This is good,' she whispers. 'And this.' Her thumb across my lips. 'And this.' Her palm on my breast. 'And this.' Her hand at my hips.

When she kisses me again, I turn over so she's under me and I run my hands the whole length of her body. I want to kiss every bit of her skin. So I start with her neck, her breasts, her belly. I kiss between her legs and her whole body shivers. She tangles her fingers in my curls. I tongue her until she's wet and gasping. I follow with my fingers until she shudders and grabs my hair hard. She pulls me back up to her and kisses me fiercely; she slips a hand between my legs and I kiss her neck until I forget everything but this feeling, and honestly it's a lot less like losing my heart and more like finally being found.

Olive

Saturday 13th May

Lost: A chance

I wake up in the middle of the night to howling that doesn't sound like the wind. For a moment I amn't sure where I am, but then the room focuses slowly around me. I'm in the third bedroom of the Oak Road house, lying on a mattress on the floor that usually serves as Ivy's bed. But Rose isn't on the mattress beside me any more. Her impression is left on the discarded sheets, but that side of the bed is cold.

All the doors that lead off the landing are closed, but I can hear music playing softly from downstairs so I pad down the bare steps of the stairs to the kitchen. When I see the flickering light of candles on the counters, I realize I'm not the only person awake in the storm.

Rowan is sitting alone at the head of the kitchen table like an ancient king in his dining hall. In front of him is an opened bottle of whiskey and a half-full glass. He is topless and his chest is pale and broad. He has a tattoo of some kind of mythological creature all along the left side of his ribcage, and another – a line of words I can't make out from here – on his right arm. No one I know my age has real tattoos, except these two.

A phoenix. The name of the creature comes to me in a flash of lightning. I stand in the draught of the door for maybe longer than I should, then quickly lower my eyes when I realize I've been staring. My cheeks burn.

Rowan raises his eyebrows and smiles. I wish I didn't blush so easily or so pink. I wish I could believe that I'm enough in shadow at this side of the kitchen for him not to notice. But he does notice. Of course he notices.

I throw my shoulders back. 'Came down for a glass of water,' I say, and another long, languid howl from outside cuts me off. My muscles seize up. Rowan kicks his chair back on to two legs and swings his own pyjama-clad legs up on to the table. He has hair on his bare toes. I take a shaky breath. Rowan seems entirely unconcerned by the noise, or at least it seems like he wants me to think that. But I can see his hand shake slightly as he reaches for his glass.

I gesture towards the whiskey with my chin. 'Can I have some?' The wind rushes at the house again. In the distance, thunder rumbles.

'Ten-year-old single malt,' says Rowan appreciatively, tilting the bottle of whiskey so I can see the label. He gestures to the chair beside him and pushes his glass across the table to me. 'Last thing we ever used our parents' credit card for. It's delicious. Tastes like peat-fire smoke.'

I sit down slowly. I'm not sure how alcohol can taste like chimney smoke, but I'm too embarrassed to ask. I'm more versed in cans of tasteless cider and discount vodka mixed with something sweet than I am in fancy whiskey. A small part of me resents that *I* am the one feeling awkward, when Rowan is wearing only threadbare flannel pyjama bottoms, but even like this, drinking alone in the empty kitchen, he is more self-possessed than I'll ever be. I imagine telling Rose about this in the morning. *Flannel pyjamas and single-malt whiskey?* she's bound to say. *What. A. Hipster.* But the problem is, Rowan never seems like he's trying too hard, or trying at all.

I take a small sip of the whiskey. I'm probably not sophisticated enough to detect notes of peat-fire smoke. 'Mmm,' I say anyway, smacking my lips earnestly. Inside, I'm grimacing. It doesn't taste much better than the poteen.

'Right?' Rowan says, almost excited. 'Nectar of the gods.' He gets up to fetch me my own glass. I sneakily take another sip to see if that'll help me get used to it. Some Diet Coke would help, maybe some cranberry juice.

But I'm certain this is the kind of drink that is meant to be taken neat. I bite back a cough.

After the fourth small sip, though, I start to feel that triangle of warmth spreading somewhere between my ribs. My body recognizes the feeling from earlier, although I think I drank less of Mags Maguire's moonshine than some of the others did. My limbs begin to loosen slightly. The only howling from outside now is the sound of the wind. It's in part the whiskey and in part the wind that makes me say, 'I've never met anyone like you guys before.'

'Anyone like us?' Rowan asks.

'You know.' Maybe the whiskey is loosening my tongue. 'Painfully cool? Slightly tragic? Sad-eyed, tattooed hipster kids with no parental supervision and a tolerance for strong alcohol? Right now you're alone in the kitchen of a ghost estate in the middle of the woods, drinking single-malt whiskey, shirtless, during a thunderstorm. Come on.'

Rowan looks a little surprised at all this, but he's still smiling. 'I'm not alone right now,' he points out.

'Touché.' I take another small sip. There is significantly less whiskey in the glass than when I started. 'You're more like people in a story than someone real.' My tone is dreamier than I'd intended, but I find that I don't really mind, and anyway I'm not sure Rowan has noticed this time. He almost looks a little sad.

'Not really,' he says.

'Yes really.'

Rowan and I sit in silence for a spell.

'So,' I say. 'Why are you down here?' I wonder if the howling woke him up, too. Lingering flashes of a red-haired girl running through the storm. I hope she found shelter. I hope she made it home.

'I'm . . .' Rowan clears his throat. 'I guess I'm waiting.'

'For what?' I look around the ill-lit kitchen.

'To see if the spell worked.'

'Oh.'

He's said it so matter-of-factly. He's said it like he believes it's true. I give my feelings a little prod. Do I believe it? Before last night I would have given a resounding no. But now I'm not so sure.

'You look . . .' I say tentatively. 'You look a little sad.'

Rowan's mouth twists. 'Not sad so much,' he says, but I'm sure he's lying. 'More . . . afraid.' He smiles drily, tries to laugh it off.

'Afraid of what?' I ask. The howling wind. The darkness of the empty estate. Footsteps on the tunnel roof.

'I don't know,' he answers. The whiskey swirls in his almost-empty glass. 'It just feels like we found Laurel's diary as a warning. You know? All these weird things started happening to them after they cast the spell. A boy going missing. Finding that Jude guy. Not knowing anything about him. Creepy lost dogs. Blood and baby teeth.'

'I guess they're just some of the things we lose during our lifetime?'

'You're telling me you don't find the idea of finding teeth in the forest creepy as fuck?'

I can't help a shiver. 'OK,' I say. 'I'll give you that.'

We both take a drink.

'I'm just worried,' he says slowly, deliberately, as if he's trying not to slur. 'That with all the things we wanted to find – big things, like everything Rose lost, like my mum, like, I don't even remember what Ivy wrote – we might have called up other things that shouldn't be found. And the bit about sacrifice, you know? That scares me. There's not a whole lot I can afford to lose right now.'

The candles drip wax. The flames flutter.

'All I've got is right here. All I've got is this roof over our heads, my pay cash in hand at Maguire's, and Hazel and Ivy. They're all I've got left.'

I want to say he's got me and Rose, too, but I know we're not the same thing.

I honestly do not realize I'm about to say it until it's halfway out of my mouth. I ask, 'Have you ever . . . you know . . . with Ivy?' I mean to say *been out with* or *dated* or *become involved with*, but because of the way I've said it I know it sounds like *had sex with*. I open my mouth to clarify, but Rowan gets there before me.

'Have I ever what? Sat shirtless in the kitchen with her at two in the morning and drunk whiskey?'

I try not to blush even redder than I'm currently blushing. 'That's – I didn't mean—'

Rowan goes on as if I haven't said anything. 'Kissed?' he says. 'Yes.'

'Oh.' My voice is short, catches at every syllable. 'I mean, I guess that makes sense. I mean, you really seem like there's . . . history there.' I curse myself as I keep talking. I can't say anything right. My cheeks feel like they're on fire.

'Not that kind of history really.' He's looking at his hands.

'Oh.' I push the empty whiskey glass away from me. On top of the poteen earlier, and the beers before that, I'm starting to feel like this was a bad idea.

'Have we had sex? No.' He says it as if he's talking to himself, to his freckled hands folded round his glass. I realize that he's a lot drunker than I thought. It makes me feel a bit better about how bumbling I've been acting.

'No?' is all I say.

'No.'

In a way – a small, strange way – this is like talking with Rose after a party. Confessions and secrets and head-ducking whispers. I'm suddenly on slightly more familiar territory and it thrills me. Because, really, he's not just some unfathomable, sophisticated person who drinks single-malt whiskey in the kitchen of a ghost estate squat. He's also a boy. And I'm a girl. And we can talk to each other.

'Have you ever?' I ask, once I reach the end of that train of thought. Rowan looks surprised to hear me ask that, and he smiles when he looks up at me. I'm so relieved I giggle a bit – *giggling, really, Olive?* – and say, 'It feels like we should be playing truth or dare or something.'

That makes him grin wider. 'Not really,' he says. I have a moment of slight confusion before he clarifies. 'Had sex, I mean.'

A funny feeling skitters across my tummy. I clear my throat before I say, 'Not really?'

'More than kissing, less than sex?' he offers as an explanation.

That sounds like a mathematical equation. *If $x = k^2$ but $k^2 < se(x)$, find the value of 'not really' se(x).*

And then it hits me. '*Oh.* You – Right.' More than kissing, less than sex. Why didn't I realize it earlier? It could have been with Ivy. I can feel the blush to end all blushes flooding my face. How am I going to look at her in the morning? How am I going to hear her soft voice talking about breakfast cereals when they might've done 'more than kissing'? What is 'more than kissing' anyway? Part of me wants – no, *needs* – to know every exact detail so that I can stop mentally filling in the blanks. *Was* it with Ivy? How much is 'less than sex' anyway? Just some groping? Have they seen each other naked? Have there been orgasms? Has he gone down on her? Has *she* gone down on *him*? *Why can't I stop thinking about this?*

'How about you?'

My train of thought comes to a screeching halt. 'Huh?'

Rowan pours more whiskey into my glass, then his own. 'How about you?' he says again.

'Oh. Right.' *More than kissing, less than sex.* 'Same. I suppose.'

Rowan tilts his glass so that the candlelight hits it, refracts into sunbeams on the rickety old camping table. With every sip, the whiskey tastes a little earthier, a little warmer, a little more like peat-fire smoke. *Nectar of the gods.*

'Virginity,' Rowan says suddenly, as if he's answering a question.

'Virginity?'

'Something you can lose.'

'*Ugh,*' I cry. 'Why does everyone keep saying that?'

'Saying what?'

But I'm getting riled up now. 'Why doesn't everyone understand that the very idea of virginity is a hetero-patriarchal concept invented to make women feel bad about sex?'

Rowan splutters. 'A hetero-what?'

I ignore him. 'As if a woman is somehow worth more when she hasn't had penetrative intercourse, because of course there's a double standard when it comes to men, and anyway who the hell gets to decide what the cut-off point for virginity is?'

Rowan nearly swallows his whiskey the wrong way. 'Do you want me to draw you a diagram?'

I glare at him. 'I understand the mechanics, thanks. But ask yourself this: what if you're a girl who has only ever dated girls? Who decides on the mechanics then?'

'The hetero-patriarchy,' Rowan answers with an almost-straight face.

So he was paying attention. 'Exactly.'

'OK,' he says. 'I'm with you. But don't you think you need *something*? Like, to mark the occasion? I mean, not you personally. One. One needs something.' He frowns at himself and drinks more whiskey.

I think about Rose. I try not to think about Rose. I think, instead, about all the glorious freckled skin Rowan's got on display right now.

'Maybe it's more about firsts,' I say slowly, still figuring this one out. 'Maybe every first is a loss.'

Rowan leans forward in his seat. Suddenly he's watching me with this incredibly intense look in his eyes, as if he's drinking me like whiskey. I wonder if I'd taste earthy, like peat-fire smoke. 'Every first is a loss,' he breathes. 'I like that.'

He picks up a marker and stands in front of me. He's really not wearing very much. I take the marker he's offering. He hunkers down on the tiles beside me and hands me his left arm, the one not already tattooed. Before uncapping the marker, I take his other arm and turn it so I can see the words inked there. They are written in a particularly perfect cursive, and they say *Not all those who wander are lost.*

'So you're a Tolkien fan?' I ask, and he looks pleasantly surprised. *'All that is gold does not glitter,'* I quote. *'Not all those who wander are lost.'*

'I got it as a reminder,' he says, 'that no matter how far away from home I get, I don't have to be lost; I can still be myself. Of course, it's got a lot more meaning now,' he says. 'Lost things everywhere.' His face is lower than mine, tilted up so he can see me. So many freckles. The candles on the table reflect at the very edges of his glasses. I want to touch his cheek. I want to run my hand through his hair. Really, I probably just want to kiss him.

Instead, I uncap the marker and take his bare arm in my other hand. I swivel in my chair so that I can write steadily. He rests his arm on my knees. I start at the crook of his elbow where I imagine his heart beats and I write *Every first is a loss* in the same careful writing that covers my own left forearm. I've never thought my handwriting was particularly pretty until now. Somehow, it complements the cursive of his tattoo.

'Does that mean that every first kiss with a new person is also a loss?' he asks in an almost-whisper, his arm on my knees, his face just below mine.

'I guess it must,' I tell him.

'Then not all losses are bad.'

'I guess not,' I say softly. His face is tilted up towards me. He raises himself up on his knees ever so slightly and our lips are aligned. His eyes are not quite closed; he's staring at my mouth. I'm staring at his. We inch forward and the kitchen door slams open. We spring apart. A couple of the candles blow out and a bowl full of something or other on the counter tips over, spilling little things all over the floor. When I turn round, I see Ivy.

'Oh,' she says in that tiniest voice. 'I'm sorry.' The wind howls through the house; it must have been a draught that blew the door open. I somehow can't imagine little, quiet Ivy banging doors. 'I just wanted some painkillers.' Her voice trails off at the end of every sentence. Even with my hearing aid in, I can only make out half her words.

'Whiskey?' Rowan offers, sitting back in his seat at the head of the table. 'Nectar of the gods.'

'Oh, no,' Ivy says sadly, shuffling towards the sink. 'I think I've had quite enough strong spirits for tonight.'

My lips tingle, unkissed. Ivy runs the tap and drinks water from it like a cat, swallows two painkillers and waves goodnight with a sad-eyed smile before disappearing upstairs. Her skin is so pale and she is so thin and her lips are so soft and her eyes are so big; she's like Little Red Goldilocks or Snow Beauty. I can imagine Rowan kissing her. I can imagine his hands round her tiny waist. I look down at my own decidedly untiny waist and the soft flesh of my belly and I fold my arms over myself and scrape back my chair.

'I should get some sleep,' I say to Rowan, who is still staring at the door to the kitchen, at the invisible imprint Ivy has left behind. 'I'm in for a fun time explaining all this to my parents tomorrow.'

'See you in the morning,' Rowan says, as if from far away. He tilts the whiskey bottle and refills his glass. The candles flicker, almost all melted, around him.

Laurel

Saturday 13th May

Found: Two lost friends

Ash reappeared in the middle of the night. I couldn't sleep. My sisters had sneaked me inside and hidden my wet clothes. They'd given me tea and blankets and left me curled on the couch with my diary, staring out of the sitting-room window at the storm.

I wrote down some of what we'd found and it was like a length of silver thread connecting us to the people for whom this was a list of lost things. Silver, star-shaped hair clip; make-up bag (large, red, gold zip); set of car keys (dog-charm key ring); reading glasses (purple); hairpins (approx. fifteen); delicate gold bracelet with tiny charms; two tarnished teaspoons; packet of cigarettes; blue plastic lighter; three earring backs; human blood.

We pulled these people into our spell. We made them give these things up so that we could find our diaries. And Jude. I can't forget that we found him, too. Inside the list I hid four hearts. Laurel, Ash, Holly, Jude. I don't always know whose heart is whose.

Just as the sky was raining itself out, Ash arrived. She threw stones at the sitting-room window like someone in a film and I let her in. She dripped rainwater on the carpet and joined me on the couch.

'I've seen the future,' she told me, her eyes wild. 'I knocked on its door and it opened for me and I saw what was going to be.'

I sighed. 'Did you take something, Ash? Did you drink more of that stuff he gave us?'

'I didn't realize,' she said. 'I was stupid. I thought I loved him, but he's not what we thought. I've seen the future. I know how it goes. And I'm going to stop it.'

Ash's knees bounced. She gripped them with her fists and her whole body trembled.

I almost shook my head. I almost told her I didn't believe her. Instead, I said, 'What was in that drink he gave us?'

'He's a lost soul, you know. We called him up, with the spell.'

I felt goosebumps springing up over my skin. 'He's just a boy, Ash.'

She shook her head like she shook her body. 'Mm-mm, no,' she said. 'He's so much more than that.'

It reminded me of Holly earlier that morning, comparing Jude to Orpheus. How could a mere boy have such an effect on my best friends?

'Forget about him,' I said. I shivered and shook my head. 'He's trouble. He's lost a lot and so will you. Stay away from him,' I added, 'or you'll lose everything.'

The scene in front of me flickered and changed. Like a dream. Like a vision. Ash lay there asleep on the couch with her lit cigarette and the house went up in flames. I blinked and she was sitting again, and of course there was no cigarette in her hand on my mam's overstuffed couch with the ugly embroidered pillows. *What was in that drink?*

'Laurel,' Ash said softly, and she stared into my eyes. 'Don't you realize? Don't you understand what he is?'

'Just a boy,' I said again, but some of my certainty was lost. I thought Ash might be slightly delusional – thinking she loved him, thinking he was magic. Earlier she was all glee at our having found him, and now she was – what – calling him a demon?

'It was him,' Ash said. 'It was always him. He turned us against each other; he enchanted us all; he whispered his lies and made us believe him.'

The last of the rain beat against the windows. The last of the wind howled from the forest. Ash came closer.

'And where did he come from?' she asked. 'Where does he live? Who is he really?'

I should have pointed out that it wasn't Jude who took our diaries. It wasn't Jude who gave them to people to read out in front of the whole class. It wasn't Jude who betrayed his best friends. But with Ash wild-eyed before me, I didn't say any of that. I said slowly, 'We've never seen him outside that forest.'

Ash sat back and sighed like she'd had the last sip of a long, cool drink. 'He's one of the lost,' she said. 'A lost soul we called up without knowing. How else would he know so much about lost things, about magic, about light and dark?' She sat forward again, her stare intense, and said, very fast, 'He's all darkness. We must protect Holly. He has too much power over us already. It's going to get worse. We have to make him stop.' It wasn't that I believed Ash. It wasn't that I had forgiven her for what she'd done. It was seeing Holly's body swinging from a tree like it was real. It was seeing Ash go up in flames as if it was happening right in front of me. It was knowing that somehow, in all this, Jude played a part, and we could not trust him.

We have to make him stop.

We threw stones at Holly's bedroom window until she appeared at her front door, her hair dishevelled and her eyes half closed. It didn't take long to convince her. We sat together on her bed and she shook and shook her head.

'I knew it,' she whispered. Her thin hands worried at the scarf around her throat. 'How could I have been so blind?'

Somewhere outside, a dog barked in the darkness.

We got our bikes and cycled to the forest.

Maybe he saw us coming. Maybe he has always existed in this forest. Maybe he needs us if he ever wants to leave the shade of the trees.

We led him into the deeper forest, down the slope and close to the lake. The sky was lightening slowly, a pink tinge to the horizon, a spread of blue above the trees.

We stopped together and we grabbed him. We tied him to a tree with silver string. Our veins were awash with spirits still, but we didn't forget; we remembered everything.

We danced around him like wood nymphs, like frenzies. We made sounds that weren't words but a calling: a calling for the found to stay lost.

At first he asked, 'What are you doing?' But Holly tied her scarf round his mouth and after that he didn't ask anything. No small talk, no Kerouac, no questions with fire.

We twirled like Furies; we skipped and jumped. We circled the tree on our hands and knees, clawing at the earth like wolves. We filled our fists with leaves and moss and we threw it all at him. Marbles and key rings, buttons and bracelets hit his skin.

Ash took out her silver lighter and flicked it open. The flame was the brightest thing, reflecting on the silver string. She let it lick against the leaves at his feet, and as the smoke curled up into the body of the tree he broke free.

He tore the scarf from round his mouth. The flames licked the leaves, but he kicked them aside. He came towards us with his arms outstretched. He lunged at our throats.

We three held hands and we turned and ran.

Olive

Sunday 14th May

Lost: All control; appetite for breakfast

It isn't quite morning when I wake up again. My mouth is a desert and my hair is stuck to my face and the room is still spinning. The other side of the mattress is empty.

Faint light shines through the cracks between the plywood boards and the windows. My phone says it's a quarter to five.

There's nobody downstairs. In the kitchen, the candles are puddles of wax on the camping table. Two chipped glasses still sit there, the last drops of whiskey pooled in the bottoms, the ghosts of our lips around the rims. The place is a mess of wet clothes and damp towels, bowls of crumbs and empty glasses. There isn't a soul but me around.

There isn't anyone in the upstairs bathroom either, which leaves two rooms to find four people. I quietly turn the handle of Hazel's first.

It looks like a bomb has hit it, long enough ago for the rubble of cans and cups and make-up bottles and dirty laundry to have fossilized into small, sharp mountains around the room. I would have thought that runaways travel light, but there is very little about these particular runaways that I ever expect.

For example: as the light from my phone spills into the room, I quickly realize that Rose is in Hazel's bed. They are curled together, naked and sleep-tousled, Rose's hair a long black river falling over Hazel's shoulder. I back out of the room and shut the door silently.

The landing is full of my breathing. My phone goes out and I try to let my eyes adjust to the darkness. Two more people somewhere in this house. One more room to look in. I shouldn't but I can't not.

When I crack open the door of Rowan's room, a shadow on a mattress raises its curly head out of the covers. I can just about make out Rowan's hand groping along the floor beside the mattress, searching among the black outlines of clothes and his guitar, and coming up with his glasses. He rubs his face with both palms and puts the glasses on. He smiles when he sees me.

Ivy isn't there.

'Can't sleep?' he says hoarsely. He clears his throat and

beckons me in. The door swings shut behind me and we're left in deeper darkness. He turns on a big camping torch on the floor beside the mattress and everything glows. Soft light, soft smile, soft swish of the mattress when I sit down facing Rowan and cross my legs over the covers. We're so close our knees touch, mine over the bedsheet and his under; I see his discarded flannel pyjama bottoms on the floor and realize he's been sleeping in his boxers. Or naked. I blush.

'Sorry I woke you,' I whisper. 'I was looking for Rose.'

Rowan straightens a strand of hair on my fringe and my whole skin tingles.

'She's with Hazel,' I add, and I can't help but wonder what it will mean for Rowan and Ivy that Hazel is no longer a sharp corner of their triangle.

Rowan grins. 'From what I've learned of Rose, this might mean that Hazel's finally met her match,' he says.

I raise an eyebrow. 'Rose is kind of a force of nature.'

'Good,' Rowan says, and he leans back against the wall. ''Cos Hazel tends to burn through girls. She falls in love every other week.'

I laugh. 'Rose, too.'

'They have a lot in common.'

'Tall, gorgeous, outspoken, take no shit from anyone . . .' I say, without mentioning another thing they have in common. They're each one of our whole worlds. A sister, a best friend. Then again, if Rose and I were still completely attached at the hip, I wouldn't be here now.

Rowan grins. 'Definitely,' he says. 'I like Rose.'

'She likes you, too.'

'Glad to hear it,' Rowan says. 'Do you?'

'Do I what?'

'Like me?'

I'm not sure how to answer that – certainly not with what I'm thinking, which is that with his lips soft and his chest bare in front of me I don't so much like him as want to throw myself right at him. My breath comes a little faster. When Rowan breathes, the phoenix on his chest seems to move in the low light of the torch on the floor.

I let my eyes linger on his tattoo. I was avoiding staring too closely earlier, but something about the darkness and the bedsheets between us makes me brave. And makes me notice something I wouldn't have before.

The skin under the ink is scarred. I see waves of it when I look closer – knots and bumps and hollows becoming the wings of the bird. I reach out to touch it, slowly, waiting for Rowan to move away, but he doesn't. I run my fingers over it and Rowan goes very still.

'What happened?' I ask, and my voice is barely a whisper.

'There was a fire,' he says, and he shakes his head. 'It's not a great story, to be honest.'

Yesterday I asked what he was hiding from, here in this house. I assumed it was just the police, but obviously it's more than that. I don't want to push him to tell me, but I've never been very good at not asking questions.

'When did it happen?' I ask. It has to have been years ago for the burn to heal enough to tattoo over.

'The fire happened when I was fourteen,' he tells me. 'But I got the tattoo last month. It was a . . . running-away present.'

'A phoenix from the flames? Very fitting.'

Rowan grins. 'I'm a pretty literal kinda guy.'

'Well, it's beautiful,' I say, then I blush. Again. I quickly ask another question. 'Did it hurt?'

His grin widens. 'The tattoo or the burn?'

'Oh. God. The tattoo, of course. Sorry.'

Rowan laughs. 'Oh, sure,' he says. 'I nearly passed out.'

'And,' I say hesitantly. 'How did the burn . . . ?'

'OK,' Rowan says. 'But don't say I didn't warn you.' He's wearing half a smile, untroubled, like he doesn't mind telling me. 'So. You know how me and Hazel said our parents were never around much?'

'Yeah?' I have a sudden sinking feeling about where this story's going.

'My mum . . . She's not a bad person, she's just kinda . . .' He searches for a word. 'Lost. I guess. My dad's pretty messed up and manipulative, and she just follows him around the whole time, which is why she left us with our grandparents. But every once in a while she'd come back to Dublin solo and cart the two of us off to Ivy's place, so her mum could, I dunno, help our mum stay away from Dad, I guess. Stay sober. Stay with us. It never worked for more than a week. My parents . . . well, they mostly just drink and disappear. That's kinda what they're good at.'

I make myself close my mouth. I can't imagine having parents like that.

'Anyway,' Rowan goes on, 'the last time, which was three years ago, Ivy and her mum were away somewhere, so we showed up at their door and they didn't answer. We ended up renting a flat in Easkey, close to where Ivy lives. And my dad found us. He tried to act like this was some kinda family holiday, but obviously it wasn't, and my parents spent the whole time fighting, which is something else they're really good at. Me and Hazel were getting sick of it so Hazel stormed off, but I got in a fight with my dad about it and he locked me in my room like I was a kid. Then they both went out. I think they forgot I was there at all.'

He keeps a careful eye on me as if to gauge my reaction. 'My mum'd left a lit cigarette on the couch. She did that, like, every night. Me and Hazel would come home and she'd be passed out drunk and my dad would be gone and my mum'd have a lit cigarette way too close to whatever it was she was drinking and we'd have to put it out so the place didn't go up in flames. But that time there was no one there to put it out.'

'Oh God.' My skin tingles with shock.

'Yeah,' Rowan says. 'I ended up breaking down the door, but not before my clothes had caught fire.'

'Oh God,' I say again. No wonder they ran away.

'Told you it wasn't a great story.'

His blood is beating under the palm of my hand. His eyes are dark in the lamplight. He licks his lips.

'But it's all healed over now,' he says lightly.

It's a big tattoo. A lot of scarred skin to cover.

And.

It's a lot of naked skin right there in front of me, my fingers pressed to his chest. Slowly, deliberately, I trace the outline of the tattoo from the phoenix beak along the top of his ribcage to the tail feathers just above his hipbone. He stops breathing.

'Yeah,' I say in answer to his earlier question, my eyes on his eyes, my hand spread out over the tattoo on his chest, the tip of my little finger just touching the waistband of his boxers. 'I like you.'

He leans forward and says in a whisper, 'I like you, too.'

It takes a fraction of a second for me to close the gap between our mouths and kiss him. He takes my face in his hands and deepens the kiss. I touch my tongue to his and tangle my fingers in his hair. We kiss hard and serious, every moment deeper, every second more urgent until I completely lose control and pull myself forward so I'm straddling his hips and I can feel him hard against me.

He throws off his glasses and his hands reach down to cup my breasts under my top so I pull it over my head, tossing aside my insecurities as quickly as I can think them. I press myself even harder against him and he lets out his breath in a rush.

We kiss like we'll lose our minds if we don't, and when he takes my bottom lip between his teeth my nails dig into his back of their own accord. He grins and lowers me backwards, hands running the length of my body and slipping off the shorts Hazel lent me after my borrowed pyjamas got soaked in the storm. I move my arms to lower his boxers and we get tangled in legs.

He laughs into my hair. 'I like you a lot,' he says. 'Olive, like the tree.'

I trace the freckles on his cheeks, the side of his neck, his shoulders, his chest, his stomach, and I trace the thin line of hair from his belly button all the way down. Eyes shut, he shudders. When I move my hand round him, he curses quietly and says my name.

When he touches me, I have a moment of worry – that I'm not as pretty as Ivy, that I'm not as thin, that I should be sucking in my tummy or hiding my thighs – but soon his hands are all over me, his tongue at my breasts, his fingers dipping down between my open legs, and there's nothing else I could possibly think about, probably ever again.

I'm woken several hours later – I can tell by the brighter light spilling in the gaps between the boards over the window – by Rose opening the bedroom door. She squints in at me. Rowan sleeps on. I disentangle myself from his arms and his bedsheets and I join Rose on the landing, pulling my clothes on as I go.

In the light of the skylight brightening the landing, Rose is all long brown legs in a short borrowed dress, tangled hair and yesterday's make-up. She looks me up and down.

'Well,' she says.

'Well.'

We both glance towards the doors of the separate rooms we slept in, then back at each other.

'You have a love bite on your neck,' I inform her.

A smile creeps over my best friend's face. 'I could really do with a cigarette.'

'You quit,' I remind her helpfully. 'You can blow some bubbles and have a cup of tea.'

Rose throws an arm round my shoulder. 'That sounds great,' she says, and we go downstairs together.

Ivy is in the kitchen, looking out of the French doors to the glimmering world outside. The overgrown grass and the weeds are wet from last night's storm, but the sun's beaming down, reflecting off the raindrops.

When she hears us come in, Ivy speaks without turning round. 'Were you . . . Did you go outside last night?'

'We all did,' I remind her. 'We chased after Ash. Remember?'

'After that,' Ivy says slowly, her eyes still on the garden. Rose and I exchange a look.

'No,' Rose says in the same careful voice as Ivy. 'Why?'

Ivy beckons. We approach the French doors. The boards are hanging off. I thought Ivy must have moved them, but they're lopsided, the edges scored like they've been clawed.

'What the . . .' Rose says.

There's mud trampled all up the back steps. A boot stain on the glass like someone tried to kick the door in.

'Ash?' I ask, uncertain. But the boot print is much too big.

'Not Ash,' Rose whispers. I shiver.

'Ivy,' I say. 'Are you sure it's safe for you guys to be staying here? It's awfully . . . secluded.'

'Maybe Rowan's right,' Ivy whispered. 'Maybe we should never have cast the spell.'

'This isn't about the spell,' I tell her softly. 'This is about you guys squatting in an empty estate. I mean, it's romantic and bohemian and all, but, well, maybe it's not the best idea any more?'

Rose's eyebrows are knitted. 'What about your mum's house?' she says. 'Hazel said they've stayed with you before.'

Ivy's eyes are on the ground beyond the window. Boot prints trampled in the mud. 'My mum's gone visiting a friend. She's not at home. I thought we'd be safe here. Like an adventure.'

'Does your mum know where you are?' Rose asks.

Ivy shakes her head. 'She thinks I'm staying with Mags.'

'Why don't you call her—' I suggest, but Ivy freezes suddenly and says, 'Do you smell smoke?'

'Smoke?'

There comes the sound of feet on the stairs. Hazel bursts into the kitchen and says, 'I thought I saw smoke from my bedroom window – is something burning?'

Rowan is right at her heels, pulls on his shoes in the doorway. 'It looked like it was coming from the forest,' he says.

Suddenly we are all standing. Going outside. A plume of grey smoke rises from the trees.

'Is it coming from down by the lake?' Rose asks, and I think of the red-headed girl's wet clothes last night, her bare feet.

The grass underfoot is all dewdrops on spider's webs and, as we run, frogs scatter. We slip down the mud of the slope and grab on to wet branches for balance, and when we reach the bottom we split up, each following where we were sure we saw the smoke.

I break out of the forest to the shore. The tide is high after the storm; the little beach we found the beer bottle on yesterday has disappeared, the water hiding our footprints. I stop for a moment to catch my breath.

There's mist hanging three hand-widths above the lake like a veil. I can hardly hear the others searching through the forest behind me. Only the occasional trout leaping out of the water disturbs the quiet. When the breeze blows, the fog rolls like I only thought it did in books. Maybe it was the fog we saw. A plume of it rising like smoke in the distance. Everything's so wet from last night's storm it'd be impossible for anything to catch fire. Unless somebody really wanted a flame to take.

I remember the phoenix on Rowan's chest pressed to my bare skin, burning. Kisses like little flames.

The lake is clear and shallow at my feet. Underneath my rippled reflection I see stones and grit, moss, and minnows darting between blades of sunken grass. Something splashes in the water and I startle, but it's just a frog jumping from rock to slimy rock on the shore a few metres away from me. It flies off the last rock and disappears into the water and something glints under the ripples left in its wake. I bend to pick it up.

It's a silver lighter. A Zippo, expensive-looking and engraved. The same one Rowan keeps flicking open and shut. I turn the lighter over to read the engraving, expecting to see Rowan's initials, but instead they're his sister's. *HK*. She must have dropped it yesterday. I shake the water off it and dry it on my top as best I can. I flick it open and give the flint wheel an experimental roll. The lighter sparks to life, a flame rising merrily as if it hadn't spent the whole night underwater.

'They don't make 'em like they used to,' I mutter to myself, and the others come through the forest towards me.

Rowan walks backwards, looking up at the tops of the trees. 'Where did the smoke go?' he asks. But there are only the misty clouds, breaking and re-forming against the glow of the sun.

'Did you find anyone?' I ask him. Rowan turns round and shakes his head slowly.

'There's no one there,' Rose says. 'There's no fire. There's just a whole bunch of rubbish scattered around the forest.'

'Rubbish?'

Ivy opens her clenched fists, and in the palms of her hands are three marbles, two hair clips, half a clothes peg, a big red button and a whole bunch of Scrabble tiles. 'There's more,' she says. 'There's so much more.'

'What is all this?' Hazel whispers.

'The lost things,' Ivy says, but it can't be. No matter what the rest of them seem to believe, there really isn't such a thing as magic.

'They must have come from the caravan park,' I say. 'Or the dump. Or things blowing in off the wishing tree.'

'Then where did the smoke go when we came looking for it?' Ivy says, with uncharacteristic force. 'What did we hear last night out in the storm? Remember the footsteps and the howling?'

I rub my eyes. 'A fox,' I say wearily. 'On the roof of the tunnel. A dog howling in the woods.' I look back at the forest and say, 'Chimney smoke from a cottage somewhere that looked like it came from the woods.' I point down at the things Ivy's brought down from the forest. 'A bunch of rubbish that fell into the water.'

'Just rubbish,' Rose repeats, but there's a question in her voice that trembles.

I hold the lighter out to Hazel. 'I found this,' I tell her. 'I think it must be yours.'

Beside me, Rowan goes very still.

Hazel doesn't move to take the lighter.

'It must have fallen out of your pocket,' I add.

'Where did you find that?' Hazel's voice is very strange.

'Right here.' I point. 'Just now.'

'No,' she says.

'Well,' I tell her, 'yes, actually.' I throw the lighter at Hazel, who catches it automatically and then looks at it like it's about to burn her.

Her hands shake. Her whole body shakes. She's breathing too quickly. Rose reaches out to her, but Hazel squeezes her fist round the lighter, turns abruptly and marches back up the slope into the woods as if she's looking for something. Or someone. The rest of us look at each other and follow, almost having to run to catch up.

When we've clambered over the rocks and up the slope, we stop so suddenly we leave skid marks in the mud.

There are things everywhere in the forest. Random objects on each leaf and in every tree. Marbles rolled under roots and winter gloves blown on to branches. Toys on the path. Jewellery in the bushes. What looks a lot like human hair tangled round the trunks of trees.

We don't move. We stare.

I bend down and pick up a piece of paper. On it is a crude drawing of a skunk, like the one Eoin Kavanagh gave to Rose on Valentine's Day when we were eight.

My thoughts race. Maybe this is all some elaborate hoax. Maybe someone came by with big black bags of lost things and scattered them around for us to find. But I have to admit that the idea is pretty far-fetched. Almost as far-fetched as the idea that our spell might have worked.

Our spell might have worked.

'But,' I say slowly, still not quite able to wrap my head around it, 'why this stuff? Why *this much* stuff?'

'Balance,' says Ivy, the end of the word tilted up like a question. 'Like it said in the spellbook. *Every lost thing requires a sacrifice – a new loss for every called thing found.*'

'No,' says Rowan, and his voice is dark. 'It's happening like it did to Laurel. Like she said in her diary. We didn't make a sacrifice. Not enough of one anyway. Not for all the things we needed found.'

Ivy's mouth makes an O like she's understood. I'm not sure I have, though, entirely.

'So, what, we've, like, magically stolen all these things?'

'More like we've magically forced other people to lose things,' Rowan says. 'So we could find things of our own.'

I show Rose the skunk drawing and her eyes go wide. She grabs it off me and turns it over and over, as if there'll be a clue written on it somewhere. She looks at the forest around us in wonder. 'So does this mean we won't have to lose something in exchange?' she asks.

'I don't know,' Ivy says. 'I don't know. Maybe it depends on the things we want found. Maybe it depends on the things we lose. The bigger the thing we ask for, the more we lose. The more other people lose.' She quotes the spellbook again. *'What will you let go of? What can you not afford to lose? Consider carefully before you cast the calling: it may not be for you to choose.'*

I can remember quotes easily, too. I remember the part that comes after. *Be careful what you wish for: not all lost things should be found.*

At what point do you stop questioning and start believing?

'We shouldn't leave all this here,' I say warily. 'Right? I mean, it's littering the forest.' But nobody wants to touch the lost things. Instead, we watch Hazel shake herself and march from tree to tree, searching.

'What are you looking for?' Rose asks, but Hazel doesn't answer, keeps going from rock to rock, from tree to tree, becoming increasingly frantic. We follow, sidestepping small toys and phone chargers, wrinkled cardigans and folded umbrellas, pens and keys and wallets.

Hazel's like a tempest, like a whirling storm. She breaks into a run, following – I can see it now – the scuffmarks of boot tracks in the mud. She leads us back up to the house, then over to the edge of the estate, to the tunnel.

The storm drain is still dry but brighter. We file in one by one. On the ground with the litter are the pens we left behind last night, and muddy footprints. It's impossible to tell if they are only our footprints, or if someone else has been here. The tunnel walls are all black trees and red words and silver string, but when I come closer I can see that there are words there we didn't write. I stop and look around quickly, even though I know it's only the five of us squeezed inside. I touch the back of Rose's hand.

'Look,' I whisper.

It's a list. A list like ours, but written out all together, the letters strung out like rope, like a length of silver string. It starts by the mouth of the tunnel and climbs the walls like a vine to reach the other side. I point at the words running along the spindly branches of the rose bush, the gnarled olive branches, the rowan berries, the stout hazel trunk, the vines of ivy circling all the other trees.

I read: '*Silver, star-shaped hair clip; make-up bag (large, red, gold zip); set of car keys (dog-charm key ring); reading glasses (purple); hairpins (approx. fifteen); delicate gold bracelet with tiny charms.*'

Rose's make-up bag. My nana's keys. My mum's glasses.

I rub my bare wrist, the weight of the ghost of my bracelet still heavy around it.

Hazel continues to read when I falter. '*Two tarnished teaspoons; packet of cigarettes; blue plastic lighter; three earring backs; human blood; four hearts.*'

The tunnel is bright but still we shiver. I know we all recognize these as things we have lost. Things we've sacrificed to find what we needed. But was it enough?

My eyes are drawn again to the last item that Hazel read out. *Four hearts.* Rose and Hazel, me and Rowan. Have I lost my heart? I wonder. *Not all losses are bad*, Rowan said last night. How big a sacrifice is a heart you lost willingly?

And then it occurs to me: in her diary, Laurel wrote about finding some of these things. Rose's red make-up bag. The two tarnished teaspoons from the house at Oak Road. My charm bracelet. It's written twice, once on the tunnel walls in my handwriting as something lost, once in the pages of a stranger's diary as something found. I wish I understood this – how we're linked with these three girls, with their spell and their losses and their findings. I wish I wasn't starting to believe all this.

Hazel stops for half a second just before reaching the end of the list of lost things, and when she reads on it's in a different voice, strained and frightened.

'*Jack Kyle*,' she reads, like she's having a hard time getting the words out of her throat.

'Who?' I ask.

'Oh,' Ivy says in a very small voice.

I look to Rowan, but there is no expression on his face. He stays still, staring at the words on the wall in front of him. 'That's our dad's name,' he says blankly.

'Hazel,' Ivy says as if in warning, but Hazel's face is all fury.

'Where is she?' she shouts. 'Ash. Where is she? Laurel and Holly. *Where are they?*' She flies to the mouth of the tunnel. 'How the fuck do they know his name?' She storms up the side of the ditch like a sea. 'Why are they doing this to us?' she shouts louder. 'WHERE IS SHE?'

She bursts out of the tunnel and calls at us to follow. 'She must be in one of these houses,' she says, her legs moving out of sight. 'Why didn't we think of that before?'

'Hazel, wait,' Rose calls, and she and Ivy hurry out of the tunnel after her.

In the silence of their absence, I turn to Rowan. His eyes haven't left the wall.

'What . . .' I gesture helplessly. 'What do you think this means? This list, your dad's name?'

'I don't know.' He barely blinks. 'Every found thing requires a sacrifice, isn't that what Ivy said?'

A list of things lost to balance out what we wanted to find. And his father's name at the end of it.

My eyes find the words he wrote last night. They're at eye level, red ink on black branches. *Amy Aisling Kennedy.* I didn't really understand, until he told me about the fire, why he would write her name, why he'd want to find her, when he and Hazel were the ones who ran away from her. Now I almost get it. *She isn't a bad person, she's just . . . lost.* He wants her to find herself – to be the person she was always meant to be.

'They fight a lot,' he says, his eyes still on the tunnel walls. 'I used to think love was just like that. I used to think they left us with our grandparents so they could go and be in love and not have these two needy children around ruining it for them. But sometimes I wonder if she didn't keep on the move like that just to keep him away from us.'

I don't know what to say.

Rowan sets his shoulders. He holds his head high. 'You asked what I think this means. His name on this list of lost things.'

I nod slowly. I think I know what he's going to say.

'I think this is a list of everything we've had to sacrifice. I think this means that, if we want our mum back, this is what we have to give up. An eye for an eye,' he says. 'I think this means our dad is dead.'

Hazel

Sunday 14th May

Lost: Track of the past

In Irish, the word *aisling* means a dream. Not the kind you have at night about showing up to work naked or your teeth falling out. An *aisling* is a vision, a fever dream. The kind that turns skin to cloth and back again, the kind that stirs up ghosts.

My lighter in the lake. My dad's name on the tunnel wall. Maybe my mum isn't lost after all.

And, if my mum's alive, that means maybe I'm not such a monster.

My heart's a hammer. My feet pound the weeds. I try to prise the boards off the doors of the other houses to see if any are loose, to see if there are other squatters in the estate. They're all nailed fast. At the last house, on the far side of the estate, I stop. I think I can see something moving on the ground in the field up ahead.

What looked at first like a cluster of rags becomes suddenly, heart-stoppingly clear.

It's a girl. Face down in the shallow, swampy water of the storm-flooded field, red curls scattered around her head. As I move closer, I see that her hair is scorched at the ends.

I don't know how long I stand there. It feels like I'm waiting for something. For a sign. For someone to tell me what to do. The others are back by the tunnel, hidden by houses. If I don't call out, no one'll come.

Her dress is as black as ashes and her skin is charred. There's no way she's alive.

I almost crash into Rose when I run back through the estate to find her.

'There's a girl lying face down in the field just over there,' I hear myself saying. Then I add, 'I think she's dead,' in case that hadn't been clear.

Rose pulls me back, retracing my running steps, but slows when we approach the wall.

'There.' I point.

Rose walks slowly along the wall, eyes on the ground. I can hear the squelch of each wet step she takes. I don't let my gaze wander any further than her face, waiting for her reaction, waiting for her to tell me who the dead girl is, why she died here, what to do.

Red hair, bare legs.

Rose keeps walking. When she hits the end of the wall, she turns to me, and she says, 'You're sure she was here?'

At first I don't understand. Then my eyes scan the marshy field. There is no dead girl. I practically run to the place I saw her, but there's only the mud and puddles, the grassy ground.

'She was,' I say. 'She was right there.' I want to say, *I'm not crazy.* I want to repeat, *She was there, she was right there*, until the words become solid matter and conjure up the dead girl, scorchmarks and all. But I can't. Because I amn't sure enough to swear on it. Because of the haze of last night and the nights before that. Because of the last vestiges of the magic moonshine making the space between the trees become the reflections of the trees.

There's an old plastic raincoat caught on one of the spindly branches of the trees bordering the field. It sounds like wings flapping in the wind. 'It must've been that,' I say to Rose, pointing at the empty raincoat. 'It must've blown there from the ground. Rags and sticks and raindrops. That's all I saw.'

Rose takes me in her arms and kisses my hair.

'It's OK, Hazel,' she says, but it isn't.

We hear a shout from the far end of the estate. Rowan, calling our names. When Rose and I run over, he's pointing at Mags's car pulling into Oak Road.

Mags gets out of her car, a brown Labrador puppy jumping at her heels. '*Down*, Lucky,' she says, and marches towards us. 'What trouble have you got yourselves into this time?'

'What?' I ask. I can hear my voice get all defensive.

'The Guards are coming,' she says. 'Go put those boards back over the French doors.'

'*Shit*,' Rowan says. He doesn't ask questions. He just runs to the house.

Mags grunts and picks up the puppy. *Where's the usual Lucky?* I wonder.

Olive must be wondering the same thing, because she asks Mags, 'Where's Lucky?'

Mags purses her lips. 'Ran away,' she says shortly. 'Maybe got run over. Maybe crawled under a bridge to hide in the storm. They do that.'

'Oh,' says Olive. 'I'm sorry.'

I bring the subject back to the Guards who're apparently about to come find us squatting in an abandoned estate. 'Mags? The Guards?'

Mags gives one nod. 'Some young lad's gone missing,' she says. 'From town. Probably drunk in a doorway in Galway, but they're searching the area anyway.'

'A boy's gone missing?' Olive says faintly. I guess they didn't find that boy Laurel was talking about.

'C'mon,' Mags barks when Rowan returns, guitar slung over his back just in case. 'Get in the car. If the Guards find you here, there'll be hell to pay.'

Rowan shoves the guitar into the boot, but there's a car pulling up to the estate.

'Ah, bollocks,' Mags says gruffly. A man steps out and walks towards us. He's middle-aged, dressed in jeans and a green checked shirt, with a green baseball cap on his head. He looks surprised when he sees us. He isn't the police. Rowan relaxes slightly beside me.

'Mags Maguire,' says the man as they shake hands. 'It's been a while. Jesus, you haven't aged a day.'

Rose barely suppresses a snort.

'Howareya, Dave,' Mags says brusquely.

'Grand, grand,' Dave says vaguely, but he doesn't look all right. He's pale and clammy-looking, fidgety and frantic. His eyes are all over the estate. 'You haven't seen my eldest, have you?' he asks Mags. 'He's missing, we think. The Guards are searching in town, but I thought I'd check around here, you know – kids come here to drink sometimes. Still hoping he's just sleeping off a few too many pints.'

'Haven't seen anybody around here,' says Mags. 'Just walking the dog.' The newest Lucky sticks out a little pink tongue. Rose shifts beside me and glances at Olive, who looks like she's seen a ghost. She's almost as pale as Dave is. When he notices her, she gives a little flinch.

'Olive,' Dave says.

Olive knows the missing boy's dad?

Olive forces a smile. 'Hi, Mr Murdock,' she says.

I can feel Rose freeze. It's like she's stopped breathing.

'You girls haven't seen Cathal around, have you?' Dave asks, and I get it. I pretty much stop breathing myself. My hand finds Rose's and I squeeze tight. I recognize his name from the messages she showed me. Cathal Murdock.

'No, not at all,' Olive says, with a pretty convincing innocent look. 'I mean, I'm sure you're right and he's just at a friend's house somewhere with his phone off. I get why you're worried, but I'm sure he's fine.'

Dave nods, distracted. 'I'll just have a quick look around, make sure. Enjoy your walk. Good to see you, Mags.' And he heads off towards the houses.

'We should get out of here,' Olive says in an undertone. 'In case he sticks around.'

'The house is completely shut up, right?' I ask Rowan.

'Like we were never there.'

'Right,' Mags says, and she bundles the puppy into her arms. 'Back to work. You lot keep out of trouble.'

Rowan, oblivious to Rose and Olive ashen-faced beside him, gives Mags a grin. 'Have you ever known us to get in trouble, Mags?'

Mags grunts. 'Maybe you wouldn't so much if you listened to me every once in a while. Call your granda. He says he heard from Amy.'

'What?'

I feel like someone's spun me round so the sky's the ground and I'm about to fall upwards. The words go in my ears, but they don't reach my brain.

'He can't have,' I say.

'Call him anyway,' Mags replies. 'Just because you're hurt doesn't mean he isn't hurting, too. She may be your mother, but she's his daughter.'

Rowan bristles. 'We called him yesterday, Mags. We call him like twice a week, but it's no use. He can hardly speak. He has no idea who we are any more.'

Mags looks at us with eagle eyes. 'Well, do *you*?' she asks. She climbs into her car with the puppy and they disappear in a puff of exhaust and a squelch of mud.

'Batty old witch,' Rowan says nastily.

She can't be right about Granda hearing from Mum. Or probably *Granda's* not right about it.

Hope rises like smoke from the forest. I can't let myself follow it yet.

When we're out of sight of the estate, Olive stops and touches Rose's shoulder gently.

'Are you OK?' she asks.

Rose is staring at her hands. 'It was us,' she says. 'Wasn't it? It was me.'

'What was you?' Rowan asks, but I know what Rose is thinking. Cathal. The spell. Balance and sacrifice.

'I lost my virginity,' Rose says slowly. 'I wrote it on the tunnel wall. But I never expected to get it back. It's something you can lose, but it's not something you can find again, like keys or a bracelet.'

'Rose,' says Olive.

'So what if, instead of giving me my virginity back, the spell got rid of Cathal?' Rose says. 'What if I wanted him to disappear so badly that's what happened?'

'That has nothing to do with this,' Olive says, always trying to be the voice of reason. 'And, like Dave said, he's probably just out somewhere without his phone and hasn't thought to call his parents.'

'I wanted him gone.' Rose is staring straight ahead. 'Maybe the spell knew that. Maybe it knows what you're thinking.'

'Spells don't know anything,' Olive insists. 'Let's call Aunt Gillian.'

Rose seems to snap out of it. 'We can't tell her *now*. Not when he's missing,' she says, and she looks kinda scared. 'What if the Guards think we've got something to do with it? What if they find out about the spell?'

'The spell isn't . . .' Olive hesitates. It's like she realizes she might actually think it's real after all. Real – and powerful.

'I have to get back home,' she says finally, regret etched on her face. 'So my parents don't ground me again. They think I'm staying at yours, remember? My mum's already not too happy about that.'

Rose nods, then looks at me. 'OK,' she says. 'But I might stick around here for a bit.'

Olive looks disappointed for like three seconds until Rowan says, 'I'll walk you home.' I snort and try to pass it off as a cough that fools no one. Rowan scowls at me and Rose manages a little laugh.

When Rowan and Olive cycle off, and we're sure Cathal's dad is gone and the Guards aren't coming, I take Rose's hand and we follow Ivy back to the house.

Just before we reach it, we hear a crack and a thud. The three of us run the rest of the way. In the weed-choked driveway at the front of the house is a flat wooden board, the nails still in it, sticking up into the air like thorns. I hammered those nails in myself, up on Mags's ladder yesterday morning. I mustn't have hammered them far enough in, or else the storm last night weakened the wood. I look up at my half-uncovered bedroom window and freeze.

There's someone in there.

A dark shadow at the window. Tall and broad. I grab Rose's arm hard, reach out for Ivy's sleeve. I say, 'Stop.' They look up and see him, too. It. Something.

Ivy backs up and Rose gives a strangled scream. I race round the back of the house without thinking. I rip the boards off the French doors and clatter up the stairs.

'WHO'S IN HERE?' I yell. I can hear Rose and Ivy calling after me from below.

I slam open my bedroom door.

It's light for once. The mattress looks dingy, the bags of my stuff overflowing on the floor.

The room is empty.

I spin round and burst into the other two bedrooms. The bathroom. The linen closet. I hurl myself down the stairs and check the front room. The dining room. The downstairs toilet. The cupboard under the stairs. Everything empty.

Rose and Ivy stand hesitantly at the kitchen door.

'You saw it, too, right?' I round on them. Their nods are slow, their faces tight.

'Do you . . .' Ivy says. 'Do you think it might be Ash again?'

I nod, but only so I don't scare her. That shadow wasn't in the shape of a girl. I try to picture the boy I saw on Friday night, the first time the boards came off the window. I remember his longish hair, his necklace that could've been beads or teeth. His whistled 'Hey Jude'. He might've been tall, but he was definitely around my age. The shadow upstairs looked more like a man.

I'm not sure why I think of my dad. Maybe because he's tall and broad. Maybe because he was in the flat with my mum when Rowan and I ran away. Maybe because if she died, he did, too.

Maybe we've managed to bring our mum back from the dead with our spell. But we didn't write our dad's name on that wall beside hers. When his name did appear, it was on a list of lost things. Maybe that means we've condemned him for ever.

Olive

Sunday 14th May

Lost: Set of car keys (dog-charm key ring); large brown teddy (tattered and well-worn, answers to Bunny)

We cycle out of the estate in silence. The roads are still soggy. The sun has cleared all the mist away and the day's getting bright, the light reflecting in the water and the glossy black of the wet road. Our tyres splash mud up the backs of our bare legs. The world is warming up.

'So,' I ask, after we glide past the border of the estate. 'What was with that lighter?'

'What lighter?' Rowan asks as if I'll believe he doesn't know what I'm talking about.

'Come on,' I say. 'Hazel completely freaked out when I found it. Did she throw it into the water on purpose?'

Rowan's cycling a bit behind me so I have to turn my head to look at him. I can't read his expression. 'I can't—' he starts to say, then stops and bites his lip. 'I dunno,' he answers finally. 'I thought she lost it ages ago. But maybe she had it all along.'

I slow down so we can talk. 'It's the same as yours.'

'They were gifts from our parents. They were theirs when they were young. They had our initials engraved on them when they gave them to us.' He *huh*s a dry laugh. 'Gifts, bribes, what's the difference? What was with the guy the Guards are looking for?'

'He's a – he's – he—' I swerve to avoid a puddle. 'He's in our year. He's been harassing Rose. He's a sad excuse for a human being.'

'And now he's missing.'

'He might be missing, he might not,' I say to Rowan.

'The police are out looking for him, Olive.'

'That doesn't mean anything,' I insist. I pull ahead round a bend.

Rowan speeds up and cycles beside me. 'Hazel told me what happened,' he says. 'To Rose. It's one hell of a coincidence if he's the one who . . . who caused her to cast the spell.'

'If you mean he's the one who sexually assaulted her, then yes.'

'Yeah. I just mean maybe she's right. Maybe we did do it. Maybe it was the spell.'

Anger flares up hot inside me. 'Yeah, well, I have to say, if he is missing, I won't be terribly broken up about it.' I don't even care if Rowan thinks I'm a horrible person for saying it. But he just gives me a serious look, and nods. I think back to his parents' names on the wall of the tunnel; his mother's name, written in the hope that she'd be found; and his father's, appearing somehow on a list of lost things. Would you sacrifice one person for another, if you could?

I stay silent until we get to my road. I badly want to change the unspoken subject, but I'm not sure how to go about it. Finally I think how lucky it was that Mags drove all the way to Oak Road to warn us people would be searching the estate.

'Did Mags really call that puppy Lucky?' I ask Rowan suddenly.

He looks surprised for a second, as if that's not where his thoughts were at all. 'Yeah,' he says, giving me a sympathetic look. 'Mags is actually really unlucky with pets. They have this tendency to die or disappear. Then she gets a new brown Labrador and calls it Lucky, too.'

'She's a really strange person.'

Rowan laughs. 'You can say that again.'

We stop a few houses down from mine. Rowan pulls his bike up level with me and leans over to give my lips a soft kiss. My brain shuts down.

'D'you want my number?' I ask. 'Since we both forgot last time?'

He takes down my number and calls it to give me his.

'Goodbye,' Rowan says before he cycles away, 'Olive, like the tree.'

I watch him go. Last week Rose told me it was typical that I'd fall for some dodgy squatter and I laughed it off, but now I realize she was right. Four hearts lost, and mine looks like it was one of them. Not so much to a dodgy squatter, but to someone strange, sad and slightly magical. Rowan, like the tree. I can't keep the smile from my face as I open the door to my house.

Inside, my dad is tidying the kitchen before our monthly whole-family Sunday lunch and trying unsuccessfully to hum along to the plinky-plonky jazz coming from the radio. I grab a chocolate bar from the cupboard and he gestures at me to give him one, too.

'You'll spoil your appetite,' he tells me, mouth full of chocolate.

Mum comes into the kitchen with her eyebrows knitted. I panic for a minute that Rose's mum called last night for whatever reason, but Mum pats me absent-mindedly on the shoulder.

'Where's Emily?' she asks.

'Her room probably. I just got home. From Rose's.'

'Can you call her?' Mum asks.

'Rose?'

'No, Emily. She's not in her room and I put my phone down somewhere and now I can't . . .' She looks vaguely around the kitchen and shakes her head.

I hold my phone to my ear with my shoulder and wait until it rings out. Emily's voicemail comes on.

'Emily, call Mum,' I say loudly. 'Or it looks like for once you'll be the one getting in trouble. On second thoughts, don't call, because that's a conversation I've been waiting on for years.'

Mum gives me a look, but then half smiles and rolls her eyes. 'What did I ever do to deserve two teenagers?' she mutters.

'Have you considered swapping experimental jazz for boy bands?' I ask my parents. 'Might act like a siren call.'

'Hmm,' says Mum. 'Could be worth a try.'

'In that case,' says Dad, 'I have essays to mark. Olive, these dishes are all yours.'

My nana and the aunts descend on the house for Sunday lunch around two. They spill inside in a cloud of perfume and cakes covered in cling film towering on trays and plates. 'Like a funeral,' Emily always says. 'Nobody should make that much food unless somebody's died.'

Usually Emily disappears into her room after lunch with the cousins her own age. They sit on her bed and watch stupid videos on the Internet and blast music to drown out the sound of the younger cousins, who, with Max as their leader, rampage around the house with the dogs until one of the aunts has the presence of mind to open the kitchen door and let them loose in the garden. But, even when everyone's finished their last helping of dessert, Emily's still not home. The cousins pile into the sitting room instead.

As the eldest, every Sunday after lunch I am forced to stay in the kitchen with my mum – 'You are my sanity shield,' she tells me, 'don't you leave my side' – and listen to Nana order everyone about and exchange gossip.

'I heard Pattie Murdock's boy's gone missing,' Nana opens with, throwing a questioning glance at Aunt Gill.

'It's not an official report,' Aunt Gill tells her. 'Teenage boys disappear for a couple of days all the time. We're just keeping an eye out.'

'Didn't another boy go missing last week?' I ask, thinking of Laurel's diary. 'Out of Sixth Year?'

Aunt Gill looks surprised. 'Not that I've heard of,' she says. 'You sure you're not thinking of Pattie's boy?'

'No, probably just some guy who broke his curfew one night and his parents got worried.'

Nana harrumphs. 'Most likely off doing God knows what,' she says in what is meant to be a mutter, but can probably be heard all the way into town. 'I've seen those lads around, no respect, won't even give you the time of day . . .'

'Didn't a boy go missing when we were in school?' Aunt Lucy asks under the sound of Nana's rant. She's the closest in age to my mum so would have known the same people. 'The kind of missing that doesn't come back.'

Mum nods. 'Terrible thing,' she says. 'I can't even remember his name.'

'. . . with their hippy hair and their drugs; at their age, I was married with two children . . .' says Nana. She finally runs out of steam, then adds, 'I'm just glad our Olive is a good girl.'

I look anywhere but at Mum and Nana. The aunts hide their smirks as best they can.

'Olive's an angel. She's just like her mother at that age,' Aunt Lucy says, barely keeping a straight face.

'Laura was better than you, Lucy.' Nana glowers at Aunt Lucy, then she gestures towards Mum with her cup of tea. 'No, it was her friend who was a bit of a trouble-maker. What was her name again, Laura? The one that ran off with a Protestant.'

'You're going to have to narrow that down for me, Mam,' says my mum while the aunts laugh. Nana thinks anybody whose surname doesn't start with 'O' or 'Mc' is Protestant. My dad, with his beard and his tweed and his PhD from Trinity, is definitely Protestant in her books. She would probably consider my bisexuality proof of Protestantism except she held me while I was being baptized, and anyway I'm not particularly comfortable discussing my sexual preferences with my grandmother.

'Oh, so it was Mum's *friend* who was the troublemaker,' I tease. '*Suuuure.*'

'None of *my* troublemaker friends ever vomited in my mother's car,' Mum replies serenely. Rose has ruined my reputation for ever.

'Oh, I'm pretty sure Amy Kennedy would have given Rose a run for her money,' Aunt Gill says to Mum, one eyebrow raised. Mum just shakes her head.

'What's Amy up to now?' Aunt Lucy asks. 'Apart from having run off with a Protestant,' she adds, side-eyeing Nana.

'Kyle, that was it,' mutters Nana. 'I knew it was a Protestant name.'

Mum says, 'I don't know—' but Nana interrupts to ask Gill something. My mouth drops open.

Amy Kennedy. I knew I recognized the name. I saw it this morning, written on the tunnel wall. *Amy Aisling Kennedy.* It could just be another person with the same name, but Nana said she ran off with a guy named Kyle.

Jack Kyle. Another name on the tunnel wall.

My mum knows the twins' mum.

'Mum,' I murmur so my nana won't hear. 'You know your friend from school? Amy Kennedy? Does she have twins my age?'

Mum narrows her eyes. 'How do you know that?'

'I've met them actually. They're . . . staying in town.'

'They are?'

'Yeah. I mean, I knew their grandparents used to live here, but I didn't know you knew their mum.'

If my mum's eyes narrow any further, she'll be squinting. 'I don't,' she says. 'Not really. Not any more. We went to school together, but we lost touch when I left town. I was travelling, then at university ... I haven't heard from her in years.'

'Oh. I was just wondering what she was like.'

'I can't believe she's back in town,' Mum says slowly.

'Oh, she's not,' I tell her. 'The twins, they're ... staying with some friends.'

'And where are their parents?' Mum asks. 'Maybe I should try to contact Amy ...'

'Um.' I consider lying but decide against it. 'They didn't say. They live with their grandparents actually. Hazel and Rowan, I mean. In Dublin.'

'Hazel and Rowan,' Mum says. 'That's right.' She stares off into the distance for a second, then snaps out of it and says, 'Can you ring your sister again, please, Olive? She's probably with Chloe after the news about her brother, but I would appreciate her calling before missing Sunday lunch.'

I go into the back garden, where it's blessedly quiet, to call Emily, who still isn't replying. I text her and send a quick message to Chloe saying Mum is looking for Emily. Then I message Rowan to tell him what I just found out from my mum.

I KNEW I recognized you, he replies immediately. There was a picture of my mum with her schoolfriends on our mantelpiece. You look just like your mum at seventeen.

I'm constantly told I look like my mother. It's funny to think that when I look at her I could be seeing exactly what I'll be like when I'm older.

When I get back inside, Nana is on one of her favourite rants – the Price of a Pint and how you can't get a good Guinness these days for love nor money and the Decline of Rural Pubs.

'And Maguire's,' she says. 'Whatshername who owned it back when I was a girl – Mags – she used to make poteen the old-fashioned way. Nobody makes good poteen any more.'

'No, Mam,' says Aunt Lucy. 'Mags couldn't be more than sixty – she can't have run the pub when you were a girl.'

Nana looks into my eyes and says, 'It's happened before and it will happen again.' It's like her eyes can see right through me. 'There's nothing you can do to stop it.'

'What?' I stare at my nana, then look around at Mum and the aunts. Nobody else seems to have heard her speak. 'Nana, are you OK? What did you just say?'

Nana blinks, then yawns and waves my words away. 'I said will someone else look through my coat pockets. I can never find my damn car keys.'

I shake my head. Now I'm really losing it. Nana starts

arguing with the aunts over who will drive her home. The car-key fight will last half an hour and will more than likely culminate in Nana finding out who's hidden her car keys and threatening to write that particular daughter out of her will. This happens every Sunday lunch without fail.

I stand up and prepare to make myself scarce. Mum notices and yanks on my arm.

'Do *not* leave me alone with these nutjobs,' she hisses out of the corner of her mouth.

'I just really need to pee,' I lie. Luckily, a distraction arrives in the form of my father, who comes into the house at that very minute with a very muddy Max. There are tear streaks down Max's cheeks and rips in the knees of his jeans.

'Anybody seen Bunny?' Dad asks the assemblage of aunts. Everybody shakes their head. Max sniffs.

'Here.' I hold out my hand to my brother. 'I'll help you look.' I give a quick whistle and the dogs congregate around us. 'What we need,' I tell Max, 'is a good hunting hound to find him.'

Max wipes his nose on his sleeve. 'Not Coco Pops,' he says. 'He can't even find his tail when he chases it.'

'An acute observation,' I say. 'Weetabix it is.'

By the time Max, Weetabix and I have combed the house for his missing teddy, the car-key fight is over and my nana and the aunts have gone home. Bunny is nowhere to be found.

'Let's try the garden,' I say to Max.

Back in the kitchen, my parents are both on their phones, identical worry lines running across their foreheads.

Mum waves at me to stop before I go outside. 'Can you try your sister's phone again?' she asks me. 'She's still not answering.'

'Try Chloe,' I say when Emily's voicemail clicks on again. 'They've probably gone to the cinema in Castlebar or something.'

Max and I decide to split up to cover more ground. He searches the flowerbeds and the trees on the opposite side of the house while I circle the chicken coop and the bike shed. The garage door is open and a couple of the boxes that line its walls have toppled over. I stuff a bunch of gardening tools and car accessories back into one of them and nearly step on a plastic doll that has obviously fallen out of another box. I hold the doll up to the light. It's a Barbie. An old one, with hacked-off hair and pen marks on her arms and fingers and round her neck. I remember vividly drawing them on. They were supposed to be jewellery, but after ten years in a garage they look creepy. They look more like scars.

My first Barbie. I was sure Mum had given it away.

Max comes up to the door of the garage, looking despondent.

'No Bunny?' I ask.

'No Bunny.'

I give my little brother a hug. 'He'll show up,' I assure him. 'He's probably just off having adventures and he'll tell you all about them when he gets back.' Max sniffs. 'Anyway,' I say, 'I'm pretty sure there's still some ice cream left in the freezer. I'll distract Mum and Dad while you grab it.'

That perks Max up a little. He raids the freezer while I try once again to reassure my parents that Emily's probably off doing normal if vaguely rebellious things with her best friend and will doubtless be home before tea.

I take my own bowl of ice cream into my bedroom and lean against the door for a minute. I make a mental list of missing things that starts with the twins' parents, going through to Cathal and Lucky the dog, Max's Bunny, Rose's make-up bag and my nana's car keys that actually were lost this time because one of the aunts ended up driving her home.

I call Emily again, but she doesn't answer. It's probably nothing. It's probably fine. I've probably been spending too much time with troubled runaways in disused housing estates and Emily'll be back before tea. She'll find a phone and message us. She'll borrow a phone and call. Any minute now.

At ten in the evening, my parents call the police.

Hazel

Sunday 14th May

Lost: Dog
(brown Labrador, answers to Lucky)

We search the estate again. For my dad, or the boy who whistled 'Hey Jude', or a lost soul, or whatever was doing the howling. I message Rowan to keep an eye out on the way home and he calls to tell me to get out of Oak Road.

'Let's just go to Maguire's,' he says. 'Lay low for a few hours.'

But I want to find him. Them. My dad, if it was him behind my window. My mum, if it was her who left the lighter. Ash, if she's the one who wrote the words on the tunnel walls.

Ivy cycles off to meet Rowan, to watch the roads for anyone who could've broken in. Rose comes with me in the direction of the forest. We climb the rubble to get to the wall.

'Hazel,' says Rose. 'Who are we looking for? What were you looking for after Olive found that lighter?'

'I thought maybe . . . I thought it might've been my mum. That the spell worked and she . . . showed up. That lighter. It's mine, but I didn't bring it here. To Oak Road. I left it with Mum back when me and Rowan ran away.'

Rose looks stunned. She looks all around us like my mum could just appear at the edge of the forest. When she suddenly points into the woods, I think for half a second that it could be true. But then Rose says, 'Hey, isn't that Mags's dog?' She's pointing towards a shape moving slowly through the trees.

'Lucky?' I call. I give a whistle. The dog turns her big brown head, but then walks on. 'Yeah,' I say to Rose, frowning. 'I think it is. I mean, it's the *old* Lucky. Mags was carrying a puppy this morning.'

We look at each other. We climb down from the rubble. We hop over the wall into the forest and we follow the dog.

Lucky leads us through the silver birches, the fat chestnuts and gnarly oaks, down the slope to where the trees are older, bigger, closer together. She's not far ahead, but we're always losing her in the trees.

When we're almost at the lake, Rose stops and grabs my arm.

'Hazel,' she says very slowly, the way you would to an animal you didn't want to scare. It makes me really not want to turn round.

'Yeah?'

'There wasn't anything on this path earlier,' she says in the same voice. 'Right? That stuff was all by the slope up to the estate?'

Toy parts and trinkets, socks and umbrellas, key rings and cables.

I nod. 'Yeah?'

'Look,' she says, and I have to turn round. The first thing I notice is the thread. Silver and shiny, the kind Ivy used to bind the lost words we wrote on the tunnel wall. It's everywhere. It's on the moss (sprinkled with a red something like blood); it's in the bushes; it's tangled round branches and between the trees. It's wrapped round a pair of men's black hiking boots with zips up the sides.

I close my eyes and feel my heart drop right down my chest, knocking off each rib like the rungs of a ladder, cartwheeling down inside my belly and landing with a splat in the cradle of my left hip. There are words Tipp-Exed on the backs of the boots – I know it without even looking. *Nothing behind me, everything ahead of me.* My dad's motto. I looked it up one time. It's Jack Kerouac. *Nothing behind me, everything ahead of me, as is ever so on the road.* I've always hated that quote.

I keep thinking that I see him, and now here are his boots in the middle of this stupid forest.

Further down the path I can just about see what looks a lot like a row of small teeth. A line of diary keys. Fingernails. Dog bones. Yellow eyes in a dog's face blink at me from between the trees, then disappear. On the other side of the path, another dog stands silently. Rose's hand tightens painfully round my arm.

'Hazel . . .'

But I've caught sight of Lucky again, just a few metres ahead of us. She's plodding slowly towards the lake shore. I get this crazy idea in my head that she's trying to lead me to my dad. His empty boots are ghosts behind my eyelids. I take a couple of steps towards the dog, but Rose holds me back.

'Hazel,' she says again.

'It's Lucky,' I say, and something in my expression must've convinced her because she follows me through the last of the trees to the water, her hand still tight round my arm.

Lucky leads us down to the lake, where she steps into the water and wades out. When she walks, her steps are lumbering, but once she starts to swim she glides right in. Then she puts her nose in the water and dives. Rose and I stand on the shore and we watch her go under. We wait for her to resurface, but she doesn't come up again.

The lake is ringed by trees. We can see every edge. She couldn't have climbed out without us noticing.

I don't stop to think – I just run across the rocks and splash into the lake. My shoes are heavy on my bandaged feet and the water's cold on my legs. I slip on submerged stones and flail my arms to keep my balance. I wade out and I curse the water for making me so slow, but even if I'd been as fast as a fish I know I'd never have found her. You can't find something that isn't there.

'Hazel,' Rose calls.

I turn in circles in the water. 'Lucky?'

'Hazel, come *back*.'

'She was *right here*.'

'She's *gone*, Hazel,' Rose says angrily. 'And this is fucking creepy and I want to go home.'

I whistle one last time, without much hope.

'If you think I'm getting into that water after you, you can dream the fuck on,' Rose warns. 'Come back or I'm leaving without you.'

I wade back. I stand dripping in front of her and she's shivering almost as much as I am. She's tall but I'm taller. We're almost eye to eye.

'I don't know what I'm doing here,' she whispers.

I sort of wave behind me in the direction of the lake. 'We followed the dog . . .'

'No, I mean I don't know what I'm doing. Here.' She points down at her feet which are right in front of mine. I'm dripping on the shore. I don't know what she means and then I kinda do.

'With me,' I say like a question.

Rose sighs. 'With all this,' she answers. She looks back at the forest with its lost things, its findings, its string. With its smell of smoke and its yellow eyes watching us quietly from between the trees. 'I don't know if it's still whatever we drank last night, or . . .' She trails off. 'It's all just kind of fucked.'

I drip lake water on the rocks and I tell her, 'I think I'm falling in love with you.'

Rose gives a helpless laugh. 'You hardly know me,' she says.

'Sure I do.'

'I hardly know *you*.'

'I want you to,' I say. 'Know me. But I'm afraid you won't like what you see.'

I want to tell her, *Being with you makes me feel like I deserve to be loved. Like I'm less of a monster. Like if you trust me that means I can trust myself.*

Rose shakes her head. I don't know how to convince her when I can't convince myself. Trust. Acceptance. I decide right then to tell her the truth. Cold dread sweeps through me. That feeling that's been building. I feel like it's been leading up to this. '*Nothing behind me, everything ahead of me*,' I say softly.

'No offence,' Rose says, 'but that's a really stupid way to live.'

'Not if you're a monster.'

Rose laughs drily. 'I've seen pretty much every bit of your body, Hazel,' she says. 'I think I'd've noticed the spikes and the scales.'

'I killed my parents,' I tell her. Four words. My voice is so thin it could fit through a needle. Shaky as a leaf. Colder than cold.

I can't feel anything. I can't feel my skin.

'What?' she says. I take my hands out of my pockets. Half the lake spills on to the rocks. The key looks like it's part of a shipwreck. The lighter still sparks fire. The words come out like they're spilling on the rocks themselves.

'After our granny died and our granda went into the hospice, Rowan and I had to go back to live with Mum and Dad. We were staying in a rental place just outside Wexford. My parents were fighting so I packed our stuff, only the things we couldn't bear to leave behind. My dad passed out in the bedroom – they'd both been drinking. His stuff was packed, too, but I don't think Mum knew that. She should have, though. He never stayed anywhere for very long.

'She was wasted. Asleep on the couch with a cigarette in her mouth. We'd been there three weeks and I'd lost track of how many times I'd had to take a lit cigarette out of her hand when she'd passed out pissed on the couch. It was like she'd forgotten all about what had happened to Rowan. She said she was sorry, but she never changed.'

A flicker of a question crosses Rose's face and I explain about the locked room, the lit cigarette, the burning flat, Rowan's scar. Rose's eyes are wide.

'I guess I just wanted to teach her a lesson,' I tell her. 'I guess I just wanted to show her what she'd done. Let her sit with her own fate. Rowan's scarred for ever because of her. Of them. Of Dad. I dunno. They'd locked the door and he'd got burned and here she was again and I was just so mad.

'I lit her cigarette. I took it off her and I lit it with my lighter and I left the lighter open and didn't kill the flame. There was a bottle of drink spilled on the table. There wasn't much, but I saw it. There was a magazine open beside her. The tassels of the cheap throw on the couch. It was all so close together. All it would've needed was a small spark.

'I lit the cigarette. I left the lighter. Rowan was already outside with our bags. I thought I saw a light. A spark. Hot ash falling. Bright enough to catch a flame. But I still left.

'And when I left I locked the door.'

Olive

Monday 15th May

Lost: A sister

None of us slept much last night. In the morning I wake up slowly and it takes me a moment to figure out why I haven't been called out of sleep by my dad's reciting voice. My mum has left a note on the kitchen table.

> *Gone to station with Gillian to help find Emily. Max is at Nana's. Call us when you're awake.*

I message to let her know I'm up and that Rose and I will comb the town for Emily. I slip her note into my pocket.

Rose comes over and hugs me tight. She looks like she didn't sleep well last night either, but when I ask if she's

OK she shrugs off the question and says she's here to help find Emily.

We call all Emily's friends. None of them have seen her, but we can't get through to Chloe, so I figure they're together, which is something at least. It means she can't have gone far. Or else that Chloe's still asleep, or out looking for her own missing brother. My heart twists.

We look through what we can find of Emily's online activity over the last couple of days. Pictures of her nail varnish, of her made-up eyes, of her shoes. Posts about hating exams and saccharine self-help quotes on floral backgrounds. We drop by any of the places we'd have hung out at her age. The car park of the old service station. The empty playground. The low walls around some of her friends' houses.

'It's nothing,' I keep saying, trying to make sure my voice doesn't shake. 'She's having an all-night marathon of crappy romantic comedies with some friends and hasn't charged her phone. Or she's just tried her first beer and is throwing up in a bathroom somewhere.' By saying it enough, I hope I'll come to believe it. I hope I'll manifest it into being. Conjure Emily up from wherever she's hiding. But, as the morning goes on, my panic intensifies.

The playground is deserted when we get to it so we stop for a minute and sit on the swings.

Rose wraps her arms round the chains of the swing and asks, 'Do you think we can trust them?'

I don't need to ask who she's referring to. Secrets on tunnel walls, inked skin, kisses over handlebars.

'What makes you say that?'

'Nothing really.' She leans her head on the chain and swings sideways, knocking gently into me. 'It's just, they're just so . . . mysterious, I guess. Like they're keeping secrets.'

'Yeah,' I say. 'But I think they're OK. Troubled, yeah, but I think they're working through a lot of stuff. Dead grandparents, neglectful parents.'

Rose looks at me sharply.

'What has Rowan told you?' she asks. 'About their parents.'

'Apart from what we already know about them abandoning their kids with the grandparents and generally being shit at parenting?' I say.

Rose nods. So I tell her what Rowan told me about the fire, about his burnt skin.

'Hazel said something about that,' Rose says quietly.

'But he doesn't think his mum's a bad person,' I go on. 'Just messed up because of her relationship. He said their dad is . . . controlling. Abusive maybe. He thinks that's why their mother drinks.'

I don't say, *I think that's why they drink, too.*

'My mum used to know her,' I say instead. 'Amy Kennedy. Their mum. Nana said she was a troublemaker.'

'What did your mum say?'

'They lost touch when my mum left on her world tour to find herself. She says they haven't spoken since.'

'When we first met,' Rose says, 'I showed Hazel the messages I'd been getting from Cathal, and she said her dad was kind of like that. With her mum. Controlling, like you said. Abusive. But Hazel seems to blame her mum most of all.' Rose's voice sounds strange, distant, like there's something she isn't telling me.

My mind drifts to my own parents: the poetry and the coffee smells, the groundings, the dogs. Max's and Emily's music blaring from opposite ends of the landing, vying for loudest.

I think softly, *Emily, where the hell are you?*

It's nearing noon when the twins and Ivy meet up with us.

'Still no sign?' Rowan asks as they pull up beside us on their bikes. Rose and I shake our heads.

'If she was over at a friend's house, she might not even be awake yet,' Hazel says. 'That's probably why she hasn't called.'

Rose puts a hand on my shoulder. 'That is probably it, you know,' she says. 'She's gonna wake up in a couple of hours with her first hangover and call your mum to come get her.'

'I know,' I say, my voice a little weak. I've done the exact same thing many a time since I was her age.

Rowan touches my hair gently before suggesting we split up to cover more ground. Rose, Hazel and Ivy head in one direction, Rowan and I go in the other.

We end up at Maguire's, where Mags is stacking glasses behind the bar.

'Have you seen my sister around at all?' I ask Mags. 'Her name's Emily? She's thirteen? Skinny, tallish, blonde shoulder-length hair?' I take out my phone and show her a picture.

'I don't serve minors,' says Mags, and I raise one disbelieving eyebrow right up into my fringe. She looks down at the picture. 'Sorry, pet,' she says. 'I haven't seen your sister. I'm sure she'll show up, though.'

'I know she will,' I tell her. 'I'd just rather it be *before* my parents each have a heart attack.'

'I'm sure she will, pet,' Mags says, in what I assume must be her softest voice, before turning to Rowan and saying in her usual abrasive tone, 'If you don't move that feckin' guitar out of my storeroom, I'll burn the damn thing.'

Rowan gives Mags an ironic salute and leads me down a narrow corridor beside the bar to the storeroom (which is barely a broom closet), where he grabs his guitar and shoves it into its case.

'Wait,' I say. 'Stop.'

I unzip the case and take the guitar back out. Stuck between the strings is a piece of paper. It's probably sheet music or chords or something, but I take it out anyway.

It isn't sheet music. It's a page from a notebook. A diary. I pick it up and hand it to Rowan. I recognize Laurel's handwriting well enough at this point. I don't know how it could possibly have got in here, but when Rowan reads it out to me I'm not even surprised.

'Something was building and it wasn't the storm.'

It's about Saturday night. Two days ago. The night we cast the calling, the night of the storm. The night Ash knocked at the door and we lost her in the woods.

As Rowan reads, my face clouds over. It's the lead-up to that night. The storm starts; Ash and Laurel go to the forest to find Holly kissing Jude in the tree. They drink something he gives them that sounds like it's spiked.

Ash tells Laurel she's the one who took their diaries. *That's* how they went missing.

Ash running through the forest in the rain. Ash with the torn pages of the diaries in her hands. Ash running over the rubble.

Rowan falls silent, staring at the paper. Then he grabs my hand.

'We have to tell Hazel,' he says.

'Tell her what?' I ask, but he breaks into a run and pulls me along behind him, across the street and down a side road to Emily's favourite café, where Rose told me she and the others were going to look next. Rose is just coming out of the café. Hazel is waiting outside with Ivy.

Rowan stamps right up to his sister and says, 'Our mother's middle name is Aisling. *Ash*-ling.'

'So?' says Hazel.

'So it's been staring us in the face all along.'

'What has?' Rose asks.

'She always said we'd've hated her if she'd stayed in this nothing town,' Rowan says. He thrusts the newest diary entry at Hazel. '*This nothing town.*'

Rose says, 'What do you mean? What's wrong?'

But I feel the penny drop. It slaps on to the back of my hand like a tiny tin medal. *Heads or tails?*

'That's why we don't know them.' I almost want to laugh. 'Ash and Laurel and Holly. They weren't at the town summer party – at least, not the town summer party that happened last Saturday. They didn't lose their diaries last week.'

Rowan nods. 'They lost those diaries years ago.'

'Of course.' Ivy's eyes are bright. 'Of course.'

'Well, fuck it all,' Hazel says eloquently, and she sits heavily on the café windowsill. 'Ash is our mother.'

Laurel

July 29th, 1997; July 30th, 1999; October 21st, 2006

Found: Three lost letters (the third unsent);
half a thought on a scrap of paper

July 29th, 1997

Dear Holly,

I thought that if I left town I could forget
everything, but travelling only makes the memories
sharper. Things come into focus. A few months
ago in Greece I went to a lecture on the muses, but
the speaker was more interested in talking about
their mother, the titan goddess Mnemosyne, who

gave her name to a river in Hades, the one next door to the River Lethe. Lost souls drank from the Mnemosyne to remember like they drank from the Lethe to forget. Do you remember her name in the spellbook? I could still recite the list of offerings. Even this far away, everything comes back to home.

Last month, in Paris, I stayed with some art students and drank absinthe that would make Mags Maguire green with envy. Is it the magic she distils with the sugar and barley that conjures up visions, or is it that we expect the visions to happen that makes it so? Either way, these days I feel as if I have been drinking from the river of the goddess of memory, not the waters of oblivion.

I think about Jude sometimes, trying to tell us the tale of Icarus as if he was teaching us something new.

I ramble a lot in these letters, don't I? It's only because I miss you. I won't be home again for a while, although I won't be as far as I am now – St Petersburg is beautiful, golden and cold, you would love it. Come October I'll be in Dublin, starting a degree in Classics. Wait until you meet Daniel, Holly. You'll love him more than St Petersburg. I already do.

My best to your mum, and if ever Ash happens by again, tell her I think of her often.

All my love,
Laurel

July 30th, 1999

Dear Laurel,

I found a letter you sent me two years ago today. Things keep going missing and turning up again, although I expect you will tell me it's because I'm scatty. Perhaps I am. Or maybe even, years later, the spell we cast lingers. In it – the letter – you wrote about the goddess Mnemosyne. I can still remember the list of offerings suggested in the spellbook. Lost eyelashes, swathes of silk, ripe acorns, small flames.

You were in St Petersburg after Paris, after Athens, after Marrakesh. I have hardly been out of the county. Sometimes I worry I might disappear. Things are so quiet now without Mum around. I find myself ghosting through the house.

You mentioned Ash in the letter, too. I can count on one hand the letters in which you mention Ash. She came back to town last month. Her and Jude.

She has changed so much in – could it be? – four years. And yet she hasn't changed a bit. I told her you think of her often, because I don't expect that that has changed. I told her you're pregnant. You have that in common. She's carrying twins. Already her belly is twice the size of yours.

Do you remember we all got our first periods together? It was the same week. We bled at the same time every month from that day forward. Now all three of them have stopped, for a time. My belly's swelling slowly. If I have a daughter, I'll call her Ivy. It's a hardy little climbing plant.

With love,
Holly

October 21st, 2006

Dear Holly and Laurel,

There is so much I want to write I can't bear it. It would be impossible to make you understand.

I told you one day that I saw the future. That I knocked on its door and it opened for me and I saw what was going to be. It was the night of the storm. When I ran from you, I lost my way. I came across a house that wasn't there. I thought I'd got turned around. The oak tree where we found the spellbook, where we found Jude, had disappeared. So had half the forest. Leading all the way to my house. Those trees they were felling to make the road – I know now that that road led straight to there.

There was no oak tree. Only these houses – a whole estate of them, big but abandoned. I heard voices inside one of them. I knocked on the door. I saw the future. I saw his children. Jude's. They looked exactly like him. Twins. A boy and a girl – tall, with curly brown hair and a million freckles. The same chin, the same nose. The boy so like him I almost believed it was Jude. But they were bruised and broken. Cuts on his face and mud on their skin.

I don't know how I knew that what I was seeing would come to be, but I did. I thought they were your children, Holly – yours and Jude's. I thought that if you stayed with him that's what would happen. I didn't see you. I just saw the abandoned house, the abandoned children, and I knew that he was trouble.

You said it once, Laurel, long ago. *He's trouble. Stay away from him, or you'll lose everything.*

I knew I had to warn you. I knew I had to stop him. It's only now, years later – five years after you've stopped talking to me, Laurel – that I've realized they were not Holly's children. They were mine. Mine and his. They look so like him already.

That's why I couldn't stay with them. That's why I left them with Mam and Dad. I knew you never understood, Laurel, but I have to keep him away from them. It's my fault he came into our lives. If I hadn't taken those diaries, we wouldn't have needed the spellbook. If we hadn't cast the spell, we wouldn't have called up the lost things. The lost souls. The evil-hearted boy. I don't regret the things I've done, but I regret the way I did them. Either way it's too late to go back now, and the twins are better off with Mam and Dad.

Do you remember that boy from school who went missing after the town summer party that year? I can't remember his name, but I remember his face. Blond hair, pierced eyebrow. He was never found again. Do you think we did that? With our magic? There are so many things to be lost. One of those things is a life.

Mam and Dad have put a payment on one of the houses for me and Jude. Can you imagine? Oak Road. Where our old oak tree used to be. Number 5. The one I knocked at. The one I saw well before it was built. Well before the forest was felled. Well before the oak tree was cut down. They stalled the building for almost twenty years – problems with planning permission, Mam says – and finally now they're building again. They'll be finished in a year.

Sometimes I let myself believe that our children could play together on the grass in the front, that they could swim in the lake in summer, that they could run through the forest like wolves. I know that that can never happen, but I just want you both to know that I wish it.

You were right, Laurel. He's trouble.

He's trouble – but so am I.

Love,
Ash

A scrap of paper with one sentence lightly scratched, slightly slanted. It says just this:

How old is Mags Maguire and how long has she had that pub?

Hazel

Monday 15th May

Lost: Blood; nerve; belief

Rowan holds out the last diary page and Rose and I read it, Ivy peering in over our shoulders.

'My charm bracelet,' Olive says, and she sits down suddenly beside Rowan. 'I lost it and I thought, when I read the bit in the diary when Laurel found it, that she'd just picked it up wherever I dropped it, but . . . It was my mum's when she was my age. Her name is Laura.' Olive's voice sounds kinda funny. 'She was friends with your parents when they were at school,' she says to me.

Rowan nods. 'You know the picture—' he starts to say.

'On the mantelpiece at home,' I finish. Mum with two of her schoolfriends. Noelle, Ivy's mum, and another that we didn't know. Another who looks almost exactly like Olive. I don't know how I missed it.

Rose whistles through her teeth. 'Your *mum* wrote this?' she says to Olive. She shakes her head in disbelief. 'That's . . . kind of mind-blowing.'

'Kind of,' Olive says faintly. 'I think I might be stunned. I think this is what being stunned feels like.'

'But,' Rose says, 'Ash came to the house the night before last. In the storm. She knocked on the door. We all saw her, right?'

Olive lets out a breath. 'A coincidence,' she says. 'Some red-haired girl from town out in the storm. Or else it was Mags's bloody poteen. Take your pick.'

'Or a ghost,' I say softly at the exact same time as Rowan.

Rose exhales. 'You two are really spooky when you want to be.'

I take the key out of my pocket and put it on the windowsill of the café. The handle is almost heart-shaped, the metal making twists and curls. Its teeth are sharp and shining. Rowan just looks at it.

'It was in the spellbook,' I tell him. 'The first time I found it. It was pressed between the pages like a butterfly's wing.'

Rowan stares down at the key.

'It's the same as your tattoo,' Rose says to me.

'Where's it from?' Olive asks. 'What door does it open?'

'More like what door does it shut,' Rowan says slowly.

'After Rowan got burned, I went to get the key tattooed. I didn't have it with me – the key to the bedroom door they locked him in – because we didn't go back to the flat after the fire. There wasn't anything left to go back for, and when Rowan got out of the hospital we went straight home to our grandparents' house. But I remembered it well enough. So I drew it out from memory and went to get it tattooed. As a reminder. As a promise.'

If they ever do anything like this again, I'm going to kill them. Set a fire and lock the door.

'A promise of what?' Olive starts to ask, but the sound of her phone ringing cuts her off.

'Is Emily back?' Rose asks Olive when she disconnects the call.

Olive shakes her head, her mouth a thin line. 'Mum's been with Pattie and Dave Murdock all morning,' she says. 'Chloe's missing, too.'

'Murdock?' I ask. 'Isn't that the name of—'

'Chloe is his sister,' Rose says, eyes tight. 'She's Emily's best friend.'

'They had a fight . . .' Olive mutters to herself. 'Where *are* they?'

'Well,' I say, 'we know exactly how to get her back. I dunno why no one else is suggesting it, but we still have everything we need for the spell.'

'Again?' says Rowan. 'I really don't think that's a—'

'The way I figure it,' I tell him, not even bothering to keep my voice down, 'this is all our fault. Mine and yours and Ivy's. We took Olive and Rose into that tunnel, we gave them the poteen, we cast the spell with them. We've got to help them fix it.'

'That's not—' says Rose.

But Ivy takes the spellbook out of her bag and says, 'Third time's a charm?'

Rowan frowns at her.

Third time's a charm? A memory pops into my brain. Shaky and blurred, from the town summer party last Saturday. Ivy disappearing halfway through the night. A little red notebook sticking out of her bag.

That doesn't make sense. I shake my head. I try to focus on what's happening right now. 'Maybe . . .' I say. 'Maybe we need a bigger sacrifice. Something found for someone lost?'

'We never got to decide what we lost last time,' Rose argues.

'We didn't really *believe* we were going to lose anything,' Olive says.

Ivy nods slowly. 'So much of magic is about belief,' she says. 'Maybe making an offering – a sacrifice we decide – maybe that will work.'

'How do we *know*, though?' Rose insists.

'Instinct?' Ivy suggests.

'Either way,' I say, 'isn't it worth a try?'

Rowan's still chewing on his lip. 'I think,' he says slowly, 'that's not the best idea. Maybe this hasn't been the best idea all along. We don't know who wrote those spells. We don't understand them. Maybe we're just messing with things that shouldn't be messed with.'

'All the more reason to make it right,' I say.

Olive rolls her eyes and sighs. 'I hate to say this, but I'm with Hazel. If there's even a chance all this spell stuff is even remotely real, it *is* worth a try.'

We go back to Oak Road. We grab the lemonade bottle with the last dregs of poteen from the house. Out in the estate it's a bright summer afternoon, but inside the tunnel it's night. Our words are on the walls. The silver string. The branches and berries, the markers and penknife, the bloody moss. Nobody talks; nobody laughs. Everybody's face is serious. We wet our lips with the last of the poteen and Olive takes the knife.

She slices the side of her other hand, hard. Blood comes pouring out. It soaks the moss in seconds. Instead of putting it in her mouth to stop the flow, she reaches out to the tunnel wall and writes her sister's name on it in blood. I shudder and my skin feels cold.

'You said it was all about reciprocity,' she says to Ivy. 'Give and take. Balance. Payment.'

'That's right,' Ivy whispers. 'That's what it says in the spellbook.'

Olive grabs one of our red markers and slashes lines

through every single word she wrote. It didn't say that in the spellbook, but she acts like her hands know exactly what they're doing. She takes the silver string tied to the jar of bloody moss and makes a circle round her sister's name. The St Anthony medal swings from the other end.

'OK,' Olive says, her breath short and her hair all a mess. 'OK.'

Rose takes the knife from where Olive left it and, even though Olive protests, she adds her blood to the moss. She writes Emily's name on the wall in marker. She bites her lip and runs a line through her words. *My virginity. My memory. My mind. My confidence. My happiness. Myself.*

'Rose, no,' Olive whispers.

In the distance, we hear a howl. It doesn't sound like a dog. I don't know why we ever thought it sounded like a dog.

When we come out of the tunnel, Rose holds me back. The others fetch their bikes from behind the wall to go back into town. Rose and I watch them.

'I don't know if I did it,' Rose says softly. 'With the spell. I don't know if Emily's with him. All I know is that I wanted him to go away. When we cast the spell, that's what I was thinking. All that stuff Ivy said about intent. That's what I was wishing. I wanted it all to go away so I wouldn't have to think about it again. As if it'd never happened.'

'Rose,' I say. 'It's not your fault Emily's missing.'

'I know that,' she says. 'But if there's a chance that this could help . . .' She shakes her head and we rejoin the others, moving slowly like we're asleep. 'And anyway,' she says, 'maybe I didn't lose my virginity that night. Maybe I lost it on Saturday, with you.'

I take her hand. I don't know what this all means, but I know I want to keep her, more than I've wanted anything else in a really long time.

'I'm glad I met you, you know,' Rose says.

'I'm glad I met you, too.'

We get our bikes and set off again.

'Maybe she'll be there,' Olive turns her head and says. 'Maybe we'll come home and they'll have found her. Like magic.'

We melt into single file to let a car pass by, then spread out again when we hit the bigger road. We move fast in the direction of Olive's house, like we're racing to find out if the magic's worked. We cycle so quickly that when Olive's bike flies over a pothole her bag gets thrown from the basket and lands by the wall alongside us.

'Ah, *shit*,' Olive says loudly, and she veers suddenly to the side of the road. We all clutch our brakes and follow her. We pull up in front of a roadside shrine.

Holy wells are a dime a dozen on Irish country roads, and this one's nothing special. It has a statue of Mary, a plaque with a prayer, some browning flowers still in the plastic wrapper with a yellow price sticker.

Suddenly Olive gives a mirthless kind of laugh. I understand why quickly: inside the wrapper, among the roses, there's an empty sweet packet and a diary page.

It's close enough to Olive's house for it to have blown out of her bin; after all, her mother did write it. Maybe that's all this is: a woman leafing through her old diaries that were lost and found long ago, throwing them out with the junk mail and the carrot peel after she's read them.

Olive slips the page out of the bouquet and she reads as we walk on, pushing our bikes by our sides.

It's about the night after the storm. Ash – our mother – shows up at Laurel's house, dripping wet, barefoot, just like she did at Oak Road. They talk about Jude – his power.

He's trouble, Laurel tells Ash. *He's lost a lot and so will you. Stay away from him, or you'll lose everything.*

Laurel sees Ash lying on a couch with a lit cigarette. She sees the room go up in flames. It's like she knows – knew, twenty-something years ago – what was going to happen. Visions of the future. *Stay away from him, or you'll lose everything.* My mother didn't stay away. And it looks like she did end up losing everything.

Olive, already pale with worry, looks even weirder. 'My mum,' she says. 'She told me that. Those exact words. It was like she was in a trance or something, not seeing me at all. I thought I wasn't hearing her right. I mean, my hearing aid acts up sometimes. I thought maybe I was

losing it a little. I was worried she was talking about you.'
Her eyes flick to Rowan. 'But that wasn't it at all. She was
talking about Jude.'

'He *attacked* them,' Rowan says, disgusted, but it was
Ash who brought her friends to the woods. It was Ash
who tied Jude to a tree and flicked open her silver lighter.

*As the smoke curled up into the body of the tree he broke free.
He tore the scarf from round his mouth. The flames licked the
leaves, but he kicked them aside. He came towards us with his arms
outstretched. He lunged at our throats.*

We three held hands and we turned and ran.

It's creepy, even with the birds singing and the cows
mooing and the cars driving past on the sunlit road. It's
even creepier knowing what we know.

'The book about trees we used to identify the leaves for
the spell,' Ivy says softly. 'It's my mum's. I thought that's
why she called me Ivy. She used to read it to me every
night. That's why I brought it with me. I know it almost
off by heart.'

Ivy's mum, small and blonde, delicate like her daughter,
obsessed with constellations and the names of trees.
Holly.

Ivy quotes, her eyes closed: *'Ash, the mighty, is the tallest
common tree in the forest. Its branches sprout seeds that look like
keys. There is no better firewood than a felled ash tree. It is a
close relation to the rowan, or mountain ash, whose name comes
from the Norse* raun, *which means charm or spell. It's said*

that drinking the distilled spirit of the blood-red berries of the
rowan tree can make you see the future. The ash, however, boasts
no such properties. Although it does have the power of resurrection:
after it has been felled, it can resprout. It can grow again.'

It can resprout; it can grow again; it can persuade two
gullible girls that a boy they love is some kind of monster.

'But what if he was?' Ivy whispers like she read the
words right out of my head. 'What if he was a monster?'

'The only monster in that story is my mother,' I tell her.
'And maybe it's always like monster like daughter.'

There is no better firewood than a felled ash tree.

'Your mother wasn't a monster,' Olive says scornfully.
'She stole her friends' diaries because she was insecure.
She tied up a boy with some silver string and flicked open
a lighter to scare him. It's worrying, sure, it's kind of
fucked up, but it's hardly monstrous.'

'And you're not a monster either,' says Rose. 'It wasn't
your fault. None of this was your fault.'

'You weren't there,' I say. 'It pretty much was. I
murdered my parents. Now who's the monster?'

'Wait,' says Olive. 'You *what*?'

We are standing by the side of the road, holding our
bikes up by the handlebars. Cars drive past. I look my
brother in the eye and I tell them all of it. He doesn't break
my gaze. He hardly blinks. He doesn't say a thing.

Olive whistles slowly into the silence. 'OK,' she says.
'OK. That's . . . that's – I'm sorry – but that's, well . . .'

'How do you know,' Rose says then, carefully. 'That they . . . died?'

Ivy looks up at her. I don't really know how to answer. I've been carrying this around for so long. 'I told you,' I said. 'I saw a spark. I saw . . . I saw the fire start. But I still left. I still locked the door.'

'I mean, they could have got out,' says Olive in a voice that's trying to sound calm. 'There was probably another key . . .'

Her face falls when I shake my head. My voice is this skinny old ghost. 'I didn't mean to kill them. Not really. I told you I swore I'd kill them if it happened again. But I just . . . I was just so mad. I wanted to teach them a lesson. Scare them a bit maybe. I didn't care if they got scars like Rowan's. I thought they woulda deserved it. I wasn't thinking straight. I swear I didn't mean for them to die.'

Everybody's very quiet. When I blink, I can see flames behind my eyelids. The flames of the fire that burned Rowan. The flames of the fire Ash set under Jude. The flames in the flat lit by my silver lighter. The past repeating itself, over and over.

'But,' Olive says, still trying to make sense of this, 'didn't Mags say your granda'd heard from Ash – I mean Amy? Ghosts don't make phone calls.'

'He's not . . . right, our granda. He doesn't know who we are any more.'

Rose reaches out and holds my hand. After everything I've told her, she holds my hand.

Then Rowan finally speaks. 'You didn't kill her, Hazel.' Something about the way he says it stops me short. He looks at Ivy, who nods at him to go on. 'At least, not any more.'

'Any more?'

'You didn't need to call her back with the spell the other night,' says Ivy. 'She wasn't a lost thing to be found. She'd been found already.'

'What?'

Ivy and Rowan look at each other.

'She'd been found already,' Ivy says again. 'Because we'd already cast the spell.'

'*What?*' I ask again.

'Oh God,' Rose says suddenly. 'It was *you*. It wasn't Laurel and Ash and Holly who cast the first spell at the party, because they did that, like, twenty-five years ago. But someone had to have cast it this time around.'

'You wanted to know what I was doing with Ivy at the party,' Rowan says to me. 'That's what we were doing. We wanted to get her back. Find her again. But then Mags's crossword kept saying things about loss and I – *we* were afraid it didn't work. We thought we'd done something wrong. But it must have worked. Granda *heard* from her, Hazel. It must have worked.'

'What?' I say again, because it's taking a long time for the facts to hit my brain. None of this makes sense. Mags said Granda'd heard from Mum after we all cast the spell in the tunnel. If anything, that could mean *our* spell worked, not theirs.

Their spell. '*You* cast the spell at the party.' I repeat Rose's words. But even saying it aloud doesn't make it sink in.

'Yes,' my brother says. He looks at Ivy. 'Mags had brought a small bottle of poteen to give to someone and we both took a couple of sips when she wasn't looking. There's a grove of trees two fields over. That's where we went. We thought . . . Ivy thought if – if we'd really lost our parents, then maybe the spell could help us find them again.'

'Wait. Wait. You *knew*? You knew what I did?' I've been coping and hiding and drinking and forgetting and fucking hallucinating and he knows what I did?

Rowan looks sad. 'You told me, a few days after we ran away. I know you don't remember. I've never seen you that drunk before. You kept talking about this secret you had and how it was about Mum—'

'Why didn't you say something the next morning, once I'd sobered up?' I ask, my voice faint.

Rowan shakes his head. 'I didn't know how,' he says. 'For the first few days. Then we got here and I told Ivy what you said, and Ivy said she'd found this spellbook in the rubble of an old housing estate. She said she'd found a spell. It was the only thing I could think to do. I didn't

337

imagine it would actually work. I didn't think it would make us lose anything in exchange. I didn't know how to tell you. I just wanted to be able to help. To do something. Anything.'

My mum's on the couch with my silver lighter and a lit cigarette. I leave and lock the door. The cigarette sparks in the spilled vodka my mum had been drinking. The carpet catches fire. It goes up fast. My dad sleeps through. By the time my mother wakes up and tries the door, it's too late. All that's left is charred hair and bare feet, piles of ash in empty rooms.

'We wanted to undo it,' Ivy whispers. 'Take that loss and change it. Find them again.'

My mum's on the couch with my silver lighter and a lit cigarette. I leave and lock the door. At the sound of that last click, my mother opens her eyes.

Laurel

April 7th, 2017; April 10th, 2017

Found: Two letters

April 7th, 2017

Dear Holly,

I fucked up. I know this won't surprise you. I've been fucking up since the day I was born.

Mam's dead and Dad's as good as gone and now so are the twins. They hate me. I don't blame them.

I can blame Jude all I want, but it won't make what I've done better. It won't change the fact that I always followed him. I've spent my whole life chasing him. Loving him, hating him. Keeping him away from you, from the twins. I'm ready to let him go.

There was a fire in the flat. It was like a wake-up call. I took Jude's boots and broke the window. I don't know if he was in the flat or not, but still it haunts me.

I've been wearing his boots ever since.

Holly, I need your help. I was never strong unless I was with the two of you. I know this is too much to ask, after all this time, after everything I've done. But I need you. I need you to keep me away from Jude, and Jude away from me. I need you to make me stay in this goddamn place until I'm better. Until I'm sober. Until I'm free of him.

Will you help me? Will you come?

All the love and hope in the world,
Ash

April 10th, 2017

Dear Ash,

   The twins are in Balmallen. They called Ivy to
meet them there. It's strange that they ended up in
our old hometown, where everything began. I've
asked Mags to watch over them all. She said she
won't interfere – you know how Mags is – but I
know we can trust her. You don't have to worry,
you just have to get well.

   I'm coming. I love you.

   Your friend, always,
   Holly

Olive

Monday 15th May

Lost: A brother

The spell didn't work. Emily isn't home.

My mum is at the table with her head in her hands. My dad has just poured her a glass of wine and his hands are shaking. They aren't saying anything. Even the dogs are silent. I've been trying to convince myself my sister's just off with friends somewhere for so long that the sight of my parents like this hits me like a brick.

The others stand awkwardly at the door until Rose drops herself into a chair next to my mum. Mum slides her wine glass over to her and Rose takes a sip.

'We reckon she's just nursing her first hangover,' Rose

says gently. 'And she'll come home late and stinking of vodka, taking after her big sister.'

I can't even find it in me to scowl.

Mum takes her wine glass back. 'In that case,' she says to me, her voice faint, 'I should ground you again for being a bad influence.' She drains the rest of her glass and Dad pours her another.

Hazel and Rowan move into the kitchen slowly; Hazel lowers herself into the chair next to Rose, and Rowan stands against the sink with me and slips an arm round my back. Ivy stays at the door.

Suddenly she looks behind her and says, 'Oh?' in her permanently surprised voice. She moves aside and the back door opens.

Emily walks in.

Everybody stands up at the same time.

Chloe follows my sister into the kitchen. They are both pale and shaking, their hair – usually shiny and in identically straight styles – a mess. Their clothes are torn and there are scratches on their arms that make me think of rose thorns. Behind them, Mags Maguire stands at the threshold, wide and stout and solid, her arms folded across her chest.

'*Emily!*' My mum flies over to my sister and wraps her in her arms. Dad comes over, too, and covers the top of Emily's head tenderly with the palm of his hand.

'It's OK, Mum,' Emily says. 'We're OK.'

Chloe doesn't say anything, her eyes downcast.

'Where *were* you?' I ask, worry and annoyance and love tumbling out of me in the form of words. 'We've been looking bloody everywhere for you! We've been asking everyone about you! We've been worried sick! We've tried everything! *I cut myself!*' I hold my hand up to show her.

Mags looks at me sharply, at the cut on my palm. Something tells me she knows exactly what that means.

Mum takes Emily's face in her hands. 'Are you OK?' she asks her.

'We're OK,' Emily says again. 'Really.'

Mum looks over Emily's shoulder at Chloe. 'Are *you* OK, Chloe?' she asks.

Chloe nods but doesn't lift her head.

'I'll get her home,' Mags says roughly, but the hand she places on Chloe's shoulder is kind.

'Wait,' Mum says, her palms still cupping Emily's face. 'Where were you?' She looks over at Mags. 'How did you find them?'

'Lucky coincidence,' Mags says, and she turns Chloe firmly towards the door.

When they've left, there's silence for a minute. It's Rose that breaks it.

She doesn't ask, *Where were you?* Instead, she says, 'What happened?'

'Not what you're thinking,' says Emily, her hands unconsciously going to the rips in her T-shirt, the scratches on her skin.

'You don't know what we're thinking,' I tell her, another little lick of anger spitting up from inside my chest. I'd pictured her hung over on a mattress in Chloe's room so many times I'd come to believe it. She does look OK, but her scratches are scaring me.

'Where were you, Emily?' Dad asks, leading her to the table.

'Gankilty,' Emily says in a small voice.

'What's in *Gankilty*?' I ask at the same time as Mum says, 'And what exactly were you doing in Gankilty?'

The village of Gankilty, population five hundred, on the other side of the lake to us, consists of a shop, a post office and a couple of pubs, neither of which are as lenient about the minimum drinking age as Maguire's. I can't think why Emily and Chloe could have been there at all.

'So,' Emily says quickly. 'Chloe said her mum was worried 'cos Cathal hadn't come home, right? Chloe knew where he was, but she was sworn to secrecy. She wanted to get him to come home 'cos her mum was freaking out, but he wasn't answering his phone, probably because of the party.'

Dad puts up his hands to slow Emily down. 'What party?'

'Oh. They – Cathal told Chloe he was going to have a party on the lake. There's a little pier in Gankilty that's super secluded so no one'd know.'

Then Emily goes very quiet and bites her lip. I steal a look at Rose. She isn't moving. Her eyes haven't left Emily's face.

'But?' Mum says. I remember, suddenly, for the first time since we got home, that Mum is Laurel. She wrote that diary. She cast that spell. It's difficult to believe, seeing her here, in our kitchen, with her short, greying hair and her ears full of tiny hoops, the big silver rings on her fingers, the sensible sandals on her feet. There is still so much I don't know about her.

'But,' Emily says, wincing slightly. 'When we got there . . . it was . . . strange. I don't really know how to explain.'

'Try,' says Dad.

'We got . . . lost,' Emily says slowly. 'It was stormy and we knew we were close to the lake, but there was all this smoke, or mist, and these noises—' She breaks off again, chews on her bottom lip some more.

'Howling,' Ivy says softly. 'Howling and screams.'

Emily continues as if she's half asleep, as if part of her is still back there, seeing it. 'We could hear the music from the road, but we couldn't find it. There was . . . stuff . . . on all the trees. Blood and . . . things. There were eyes, too. People maybe.' She tries to shake herself a little. 'People from the party probably, but they looked like . . .'

'Did you take anything, Emily?' Dad asks gently. 'Drink anything?'

Emily shakes her head. 'I told you, we never got to the party. We just got lost in the woods.'

Mum's eyes are narrowed. We're probably thinking the same thing: there are no woods on the other side of the lake. Just the fields and the shore and the houses outside the village, their boats tied to tiny wooden jetties and bobbing in the water.

'The people,' Emily says. 'The . . . I know this sounds crazy, but they didn't look real. But I told Chloe they were probably just her brother's friends, so we followed them down to the lake.'

She's quiet for so long then that Dad touches her wrist and says, 'Emily?' and my heart makes loud noises in my chest. Howling and smoke and faces between the trees.

'It's like the branches didn't want us to go down there,' Emily says, her fingers pulling at the tears in her clothes. 'But Chloe thought she saw her brother, so we pushed through and everything was loud and weird and we thought we saw . . . But it couldn't have been . . .'

'What?' Ivy whispers.

Emily blinks. 'We thought we saw him go into the water and not come back up again.' She shakes her head. 'But then we were just back on the road right where we'd been before and everything was normal except there was no one around.' Emily frowns. 'And it was . . . a lot later than we'd thought.'

'And Cathal?' Hazel asks.

Emily shakes her head. 'I don't think the party ever happened,' she says. 'Or maybe it did and then he went home.'

'He didn't go home,' I tell her. Emily pales.

'Do you think . . .'

'It sounds like you and Emily must have dozed off,' says Dad firmly. 'Or tripped and bumped your heads. We should bring you over to Dr Driscoll.'

Emily's expression clears a little, like she's relieved.

'Why didn't you call us to come get you?' Mum asks.

'Both our phones had died,' Emily says, her expression apologetic. 'And anyway Mags Maguire just showed up right then and took us home.'

Mum stares vaguely out of the window to where Mags's car disappeared from our driveway. 'Lucky coincidence indeed,' she murmurs.

'We didn't mean to worry anyone,' Emily says pleadingly. 'When I stay over at Chloe's, I don't always call, and I thought we'd be back by dinner last night, I swear.'

'It's OK,' Dad says, because Mum is still staring out of the window, her thoughts far away. 'Why don't you go upstairs and grab some clean clothes, and we'll nip down to Dr Driscoll and make sure you're all right.'

When Emily has gone upstairs to change, Dad goes over to Mum and strokes her hair. She doesn't even notice.

'There was a boy,' she says in a strange, distant voice. 'I don't remember his name. He was blond; he had a pierced eyebrow, I think. He drowned in that lake, maybe twenty-five years ago. Mags Maguire was the last to see him. She said it was by the lake.'

My skin prickles. *How old is Mags Maguire and how long has she had that pub?*

Where did that thought just come from?

'They thought it was suicide,' Mum half whispers. 'But no one ever knew for sure. I just know he went missing. Lost.'

'The girls must have fallen,' Dad says in the same gentle tone he used for Emily. 'They must have bumped their heads and seen a bunch of kids at a party messing about in the lake and thought it was something sinister. They're OK, Laura. They're OK.'

Mum nods. She seems to come back to herself under his touch.

'We found your diaries,' I find myself saying, loud in the silence. 'From when you were our age.'

Mum finally snaps out of her trance and turns to me.

'You found—' She still looks shocked. 'I was looking everywhere for those,' she says. 'That's why I agreed to move those boxes out of your nana's house. I've spent the last week looking through things from twenty years ago, trying to find them.'

She spent two entire mornings searching through papers on the countertop. Papers spilling on to the floor in the study. Papers fluttering out of the recycling bin. Who's to say those pages didn't just get lost? Thrown into the bin with the rest of the bills. Not really magic spells at all.

'It's always so surprising to teenagers,' Dad says with a slight twinkle in his eye, 'that their parents ever had lives as exciting as theirs.'

Rose and I exchange a look.

'So what happened in the end?' Hazel asks, her voice strange after everything we've heard. 'With my mum. And Holly.'

Mum allows herself a small smile, even though it looks like she's still processing the idea of us having read her old diaries. 'Holly's real name is Noelle,' she says, and Ivy nods. 'She picked her nickname because there's holly at Christmas. Holly and Ivy.' She nods towards Ivy. 'I hadn't even realized we'd given you all tree names.'

I decide not to mention that they also inadvertently named us after the ingredients in a spell.

'You actually named me Olivia,' I remind her. 'And ivy's a plant, not a tree.'

'Indeed.' Mum picks her wine glass back up again and raises it at me.

'But what happened to you all?' Hazel asks, and I know she's really asking what happened to Ash.

'After we finished school?' Mum says. 'I left town. I wanted to find myself, travel the world. Amy left, too, soon after, with Jude.'

Hazel closes her eyes like she's in pain.

'I mean Jack,' Mum says. 'Jack Kyle. Or *Caill*, I think he

said it was, although I don't know that that's a real surname. It's the Irish for *to lose*. He used to get people to call him Jude.' She shakes her head. 'The patron saint of lost souls and pretentious young men with big ideas and narrow minds.'

My mum shakes her head. 'We were so young,' she says. 'We knew he was . . .' She looks at Hazel and Rowan, then seems to choose her words carefully. 'We knew he was trouble, at the time. It was easy to get carried away. Amy said it was the only way – her leaving with him, I mean. Noelle seemed almost relieved.'

'Wait, what?' says Rose. 'You're saying the guy you all tied up and threatened to set on fire – the guy who went for your throats – ended up marrying Ash? *He's* Hazel and Rowan's dad?'

Mum shrugs. 'I never understood it myself,' she says, with the truthfulness of someone who has had three glasses of wine in quick succession. 'But love is love, in its myriad forms.'

'*Love, strong as Death, is dead*,' my dad quotes. '*Come, let us make his bed / Among the dying flowers.*'

Mum looks into her wine glass like a fortune-teller into tea leaves. She says softly, 'Who knows what would have happened if Noelle had stayed with him? She was so much frailer than Amy; so much more delicate . . .'

What was it she wrote in the diary? *He kissed her, he hit*

her, he snapped her skinny neck. She went back to the forest and climbed the tree one final time, only to throw herself down with a rope around her throat. She swung between the branches.

Stay away from him, or you'll lose everything.

I stare at my mother. *You knew what would have happened if he'd stayed with her*, I think at her.

And so did Ash.

'We must protect Holly,' Ash said.

Maybe by following him Ash was just saving Holly all along.

Hazel

Monday 15th May

Lost: Old red leather-bound notebook,
thin and worn, secured by a black elastic band

When we get back home from Olive's, the house is ransacked. Our stuff's all over the floor in the kitchen like somebody's thrown the boxes away from the counters to check behind them, not caring about the snapped spaghetti, the dented cans, the biscuits broken to crumbs, the bread smushed underfoot. There are boot marks up the stairs and in every room.

'Like Dad's,' Rowan says hoarsely, although he doesn't know about the ones I found in the forest.

'Like Dad's,' I murmur.

It's just the three of us again. Rose disappeared soon

after Olive's sister showed up, and we all figured Olive and her mum had some catching up to do. Olive and Laurel.

Nothing's been taken, or it doesn't look like it. Not that there's much here to take. We do a careful sweep anyway. When we go back outside, there are boot prints on the ground around all the houses. There are loose screws and bent nails from where all their boards have been torn off. It's a pretty thorough job.

'The Guards then, looking for Cathal,' says Rowan, like he's trying to convince himself. I shake my head and tell him about the boots I found with Rose.

'And you're sure they were his?' he asks me. I just look at him.

'Show me,' he says.

But when we get into the forest – down the slope and close to the lake, me leading and Rowan behind me and Ivy following with a frown – there's nothing there.

The boots are gone. The baby teeth. The diary keys. The bloodstains could be the shadows of the bark of trees.

'I hate that this keeps happening,' I say. 'I hate that I can't tell what's real and what's in my head. Like Olive's sister said. I hate that I don't know.'

Rowan sits heavily on a rock and rests his elbows on his knees, pressing his hands together in front of his mouth like he's about to pray. 'I know,' he says. 'Just – I hate not knowing whether Mum's alive or not. I hate all this.'

'*I* know,' Ivy says very softly from a few metres away. 'I know. About your mum.'

Rowan's voice is blade-sharp when he says, 'What? What do you know?'

Ivy looks like she really doesn't want to answer. She looks like she wishes she hadn't said anything at all.

'Ivy?' Rowan asks.

Ivy's shoulders droop and my heart drops with them.

'Did Mags tell you something?' he says. I still can't speak.

'It's not that,' whispers Ivy.

'Then *what*?'

I open and close my mouth like some silent song. My heart beats another irregular rhythm.

Ivy looks at the ground, then she looks at me. 'The spell worked,' she says. 'Both spells worked.'

Each word's loud in my ears.

Rowan asks, 'How do you know?'

'My mum's with her,' Ivy says then, and my heart's a whole drum kit. 'Your mum. She's in a treatment centre.'

'She's in *rehab*?' says Rowan, but I can hardly hear him over the beating of the drums.

'I didn't want to tell you in case it didn't – in case she doesn't – in case afterwards things are still the same.'

Heartbeat drumbeats getting so loud my whole body jumps with it. I can't stay in my skin.

'But Ivy, she's alive. She's getting help. That's *huge*. That's already different.' Rowan's eyes are bright, but I've heard through Ivy's words to what's hidden behind them.

'You knew all along,' I say to her when I can finally speak. 'You've known since the very beginning.'

Ivy looks like she's about to cry.

'Didn't you?' I say, my voice like sandpaper.

'I'm sorry,' she barely whispers.

'You *what*?' Rowan says, like he doesn't believe it. Like it hasn't sunk in yet.

'I didn't want you to leave me. It was only ever me and Mum. I was so lonely. I love you both so much.' Ivy's eyes fill with tears.

'But *why*, Ivy?' It's like I'm pleading with her to explain, because I don't understand how she could've kept this from us. When all this time I've been torturing myself.

Ivy says, 'When I got your message that you'd run away, that you were thinking of coming to Balmallen, I told my mum and she – she'd just heard from yours. I told her I'd keep an eye on you and she said to tell you your mum was trying to get better, that she couldn't contact you just yet, and I meant to, I really did. But we were here together and it was so wonderful. You have to understand: Mum keeps me so close. Like she needs to keep me safe from the world. But I love the world! I loved being here with you. It was this amazing adventure, and I felt like I had a proper family for once, not just me and Mum. I was going to tell you. I just . . . wanted this to last as long as it could. I was so afraid if you went back to your mum it'd be like every time you came to us when we were kids. Everything would be going so great, and then your parents would just whisk you away and I'd be alone. I couldn't lose you again.'

I shake my head. Rowan looks kinda shell-shocked.

'*That's* why you wanted to cast the spell again?' he asks. 'Not because you thought the one we cast at the party didn't work. You knew it had. You knew she was alive. You knew exactly where she was. *This* is why you did it? To keep us close? To stay living in this – this – *place*? This was not a cute camping trip, Ivy.'

Ivy's tears spill over. 'I know that,' she says. 'I know that. I swear that's not why I did it, not at first. I cast the spell just like I told you – because I didn't want you to have lost your mum for good. I did it so it would work. Treatment. Rehab. So she'd come back to herself. So she'd find her way.'

'But you lied to keep us here.'

Tears drip off her chin. 'Where would you have gone?' she says. 'This place is – it's yours. It's yours.'

'It's an abandoned estate, Ivy; it's nobody's,' Rowan says angrily.

'No, some of the houses were paid for before the work stopped,' she says. 'The one we've been staying in – number five – your grandparents bought it. For your mum and dad, when you were small, before it was built.'

Rowan and I look at each other and I know we've got the same look of disbelief on our faces.

'*Why*, Ivy?' I plead again. 'Why didn't you tell us all this? Why did you let us believe our mum was dead – that I'd *killed* her – that we had no place to go? Why would you do that?'

Now Ivy's really crying. 'I was going to,' she sobs. 'I really was. I just didn't want to give you false hope.'

'Ivy,' Rowan says. 'We could take it. If you'd told us. We'd've been okay. Even if Mum still doesn't – if she's still the same – we can take it.' He stands up and gestures towards me. I go to follow him up the path back to the estate.

'Will you forgive me?' Ivy asks softly behind us.

He doesn't say anything, but I know that we will.

I follow my brother up through the forest and Ivy stays by the rocks and the trees, but we're not far away when she says, 'But there *was* a fire.' Rowan and I stop and turn round. Ivy's eyes are red from all these truths she's finally telling. 'Those boots you found – your dad's ones – she was wearing them.'

'What?'

'Your mum said it to my mum in her letter. There was a fire. She used the boots to break the window. She's been wearing them ever since.'

Rowan and I both look around the forest like our mum will just appear out of thin air, new streaks of grey in her red hair, our dad's big boots on her feet.

'There's one last thing I didn't tell you,' Ivy says. 'Your dad didn't – I don't know if he—' She takes a little breath. 'I just mean my mum says they haven't heard from him since.'

Tonight I'm just waiting for my parents to appear. Outside my window in the darkness. Face down in a field. Deep in the forest, looking like the ghosts of their younger selves. I keep feeling like this is them coming back in pieces: a silver lighter, a pair of boots. *Nothing behind me, everything ahead of me.*

I watch the world darken from the cracks between the boards covering my bedroom window, my drawing pad loose on my lap, charcoal dust in the air. Tonight I've been drawing people, not things. Rose at the corner of a car park, her head on her knees. Rowan on the rubble heap. Ivy with her crossword. Olive on her bike. My mum as a girl.

There's a figure walking along the wall of the estate. I freeze and watch it, remembering the boot stains, the ransacked kitchen. When Ivy said that stuff about my mum earlier, I let myself believe that maybe it was her. Tearing the place apart with grief or guilt. Looking for us. But what if it wasn't her? Would she really wreck the place like this out of guilt? What if I'm just choosing to believe it was her so I can't think it was somebody else?

But what if it was my dad, with his hard hands, his angry voice? *They haven't heard from him since*, Ivy said. As if he just disappeared the same way he just showed up back when my mum called herself Ash. She thought she and her friends had called him up – found this lost soul in the middle of the forest and fell in love with him. In hate with him. Maybe both. If she thought he was a lost soul, did she think me and Rowan were always half lost?

Maybe we called him up, too, with our spell. Maybe it was him howling in the forest, burning. Maybe it was him ghosting the estate. If he did lose his life in that fire, maybe it's his lost soul we called up. And, if that's the case, I guess Ash was able to burn Jude after all.

I press my face closer to the crack in the boards to see the figure walking towards the house. It stops moving before I can make the person out clearly. I'm about to go call the others when, quietly into the dusk, a small stream of soap bubbles floats out into the estate.

I take the stairs two at a time and nearly fall flat on my face. I stop a few metres in front of Rose, who doesn't smile.

'I didn't know if you'd come back,' I say. She knows all my secrets now.

'I didn't either,' she tells me.

I want to touch the sides of her eyes where her make-up has smudged.

'I thought this was . . . kind of too much,' Rose says. 'The spell, the . . . crazy magic. Cathal disappearing. Because of us. It's . . . a lot. To know that we're responsible. That I'm responsible.'

I think, *Good riddance.* I think, *I'd do it again in a heartbeat.* But I'm not sure that's what she wants to hear. Instead, I say, 'You're not responsible. It's not your fault.'

'You should have seen Chloe.' Rose's hands shake when she sends another bunch of bubbles blowing through the estate. 'My mum's treating her for shock. You should have seen her and her parents come in. Eyes like they'd lost everything.'

'Rose,' I say. 'Even if we did make him disappear – which there's no proof of – I mean, he was at a party with some friends. Maybe he fell in the lake. Maybe he OD'd. Maybe he got on a bus to Dublin as a dare and will come back broke and hung over next week. But if we *did* do it, if it was the spell, he's the one who attacked you. He's the one who made you think you'd lost everything. *He* did that. Not you.'

Rose's eyes are wet. 'I wanted him gone, wanted to teach him a lesson, wanted to find something big in exchange.'

'So maybe we're both monsters. But they were worse monsters than us.'

'And that makes it OK?'

'We didn't know what would happen. Hell, we didn't know we could cast a magic spell. There's no way we could have *actually* wanted this, because we wouldn't have believed it possible in the first place.'

'I'm not sure I still completely believe in it now.'

I shrug. I'm pretty convinced. And I'll bet she is, too. 'What are you going to do,' I ask, 'if he comes back?'

Rose squares her shoulders. 'I talked to my mum,' she says. 'She called Olive's Aunt Gill right away. I figure . . .' She looks down at the bubble wand in her hand. 'There's more than magical ways to make somebody pay.'

Maybe it's the same for my dad. Maybe it's enough that we want to keep our mum away from him now, too. Maybe this kind of thing needs people to work together. To find each other.

I kinda laugh. 'It looks like the spell did work,' I say to her. ''Cos it sounds like you've found your strength.'

Rose laughs as if what I've said is totally cheesy. She sends a bunch of bubbles flying right at me. 'So what have you found?' she asks.

'My mum, I hope,' I tell her. I explain about what Ivy said. I tell her there was someone in the house. If it was my mum, she might still be here in town. She might just be waiting with Mags. Waiting for us for once. Then I smile at Rose and I add, 'And I found you.'

Rose laughs again. And I know that I fall in love too easily. I keep secrets and I tell lies. I drink too much and I steal things sometimes.

I've lost my heart. Not all losses are bad.

'If it *was* your mum who came here,' Rose says, 'if she's staying in town and was waiting for you to get back home, or for Mags to tell you where she is – I hope you'll stick around a while.'

'I'll stick around a while.' My lost heart glows.

Her kisses are serious. We're all lips and tongues and hands in hair and it's so easy to lose sight of the things we're not sure of. Both of us like monsters casting spells that destroy other people's lives because they've destroyed ours. It would be easy not to believe it. To say they'll both show up someday – Cathal and my dad. To tell ourselves there's no such thing as magic.

Except: I had the spellbook in my pocket. I felt it there the whole time we cycled home. It was there when we found the house broken into. It was there when we went down to the woods. It was there when I looked out of the window and saw Rose walking towards me and I put my hand into my pocket and touched it just to make sure. I felt the leather cover and the threadbare elastic band. I felt the crinkle of well-worn pages. My fingers were round it.

I felt it when it disappeared.

Olive

Monday 15th May

Lost: Ourselves, over and over

Mum walks around the kitchen while she waits for Emily to come back downstairs in clean clothes and dry shoes. She straightens the vases by the window, but her sleeve knocks some flowers on to the sill. She arranges all her spice jars in a row. She touches the dried herbs over the stove.

'She's OK, you know,' I tell her, even if it's not something I'm entirely sure of myself.

'When you're a parent,' Mum says, 'you're always worried for your children. Even if you don't let them see. When they ride a bike at night. When they stay out late. When they come home drunk.' I stare hard at the floor. 'Last night was any parent's worst nightmare.'

'But she's OK,' I say, even though I understand. This whole day was one long nightmare. 'We found her.'

Mum twitches at the word *found*. I wonder if she suspects we cast the spell, like she did long before we were born. If she does, she says nothing.

But I know the spellbook – or at least her old diary – is on her mind, because she says, 'I'm going to give Noelle a call later. Get Amy's number. She should be with her kids.'

I freeze. Hazel's words run round my brain. *I murdered my parents. Now who's the monster?* If the spell brought Emily back, does that mean it can bring Ash back, too? Or was Emily never really lost to begin with?

'Is she . . . Did she stay in touch with Ivy's mum?' I ask. 'Like, she'd have her number?'

Mum nods, her gaze still absent, her mind elsewhere. 'They stayed as close as anyone could be with Amy,' she tells me. 'Although there were always things Noelle shared with me that she didn't with Amy.'

I'm still finding it so hard to believe my mum is Laurel. That everything she wrote about in that diary happened to her.

'Like what?' I ask.

Mum stares out of the window into the garden. 'I don't think she ever told Amy who Ivy's father was.'

My mouth hinges open.

'She must have suspected,' Mum says. 'It was fairly obvious to the rest of us.'

'No,' I say. 'No way.'

'But Amy was always wilfully oblivious at times.'

I actually have to sit down. I lower myself on to a chair and the dogs come to nose at my lap.

Jude. Of course it was Jude. Ivy's father was Jude.

She's Rowan and Hazel's half-sister.

'She kept that kid locked up so tight,' my mum is saying. 'Like she wanted to keep her safe. I'll call them both tonight,' she adds. 'It's long overdue.'

I wince and consider telling her what Hazel said to us all about her mother and the fire, but at that moment my phone lights up on the table. It's a message from Rowan.

> Ivy lied. Her mum was with mine
> all along, and Ivy knew it. Mum
> was in rehab. The magic made her
> find her way.

A second message follows straight after.

> When we got back to the house
> today someone had been there,
> looking for us. We called Mags.
> Our mum is in town.

My jaw drops open. It can't have been the spell. But I can see why Hazel and Rowan would believe it was.

Emily appears at the door to the kitchen in clean clothes, her hair brushed and tied up in the kind of messy bun that usually takes me at least five hours to get right. 'Dr Driscoll thinks there was probably some kind of leak in the gas pipeline under the road,' she says. 'It's over that side of the lake. But she said to come in anyway.'

Dad follows her into the kitchen and Mum hands her a packet of biscuits – 'For the road.'

'I know what happened,' Emily says in an undertone as she passes by me to get to the door. 'To Rose.'

I can feel my brow furrow. 'You do? How?'

'I used my brain, Olive,' Emily says scornfully. 'It didn't make sense what Chloe was saying about seeing Rose with Cathal at the party. And then I was at her place and his phone was charging and I saw all these messages . . .'

'You looked through his *phone*?'

'And they were *horrible*,' she goes on. 'I don't know exactly what happened at the party, but I do know he's a dick.' She gives a furtive look in our mum's direction. 'I mean, a male reproductive organ.'

So she doesn't know exactly what happened. I decide to wait before telling my little sister. I decide to let Rose tell her, if that's what she wants to do.

'Anyway,' Emily says, 'tell Rose I'm sorry, OK? That I couldn't confront him about it.'

'*That's* why you agreed to go with Chloe?' I ask, a certain amount of wonder in my voice. 'That's what you two fought about. The whole kill-the-messenger thing.'

'She came around eventually,' Emily says. 'I mean, she agreed to come with me.'

'*You* wanted to go to Cathal's party?'

'I wanted him to admit to it,' she answers. 'To realize what he did. To say it with Chloe right there in front of him that if any guy did something like that to his little sister he'd want to kill him.'

Entirely unexpectedly, I feel myself tearing up. 'Oh, Emily.' I hug my sister tightly. 'I'm glad you're OK.'

When Emily leaves with my parents, my mum stops at the kitchen door and gives me a funny look. I think she might say something about sisterly bonding and how she and her sisters were always so close and that she's glad Emily and I are finally getting along, too, but what she says is, 'I expect your friends are waiting for you.'

'I can go?' I ask.

Mum nods. 'Don't be home too late,' she says, then she steps outside as the sound of Dad starting the car revs up from the driveway.

'I won't,' I tell her, and I give a little wave.

Mum looks back at me one last time and says, 'Olive?'

'Yeah?'

'Burn the spellbook.'

Night is already falling slowly when I get to the estate. *Don't be home too late* is a very vague instruction anyway. What's late, on a balmy evening, when your sister has been found and there's a beautiful boy waiting for you on a low wall with his guitar?

The first few notes float towards me when I reach the edge of the estate with the storm-drain tunnel. I stop suddenly, disorientated. The tunnel isn't there. Instead, there's an oak tree.

It takes me several minutes to realize what's wrong with what I'm seeing. There is no oak tree usually. There was once, before the estate was built. The tree Laurel, Ash and Holly found the spellbook in. Where they found Jude. Where they cast the spell and made everything happen. That was here. The estate is named for that very tree. A hint of weird wonder creeps over me.

But there it is. A big old oak at what used to be a fork in the road and is now an ugly old storm-drain tunnel on the border of an empty estate. For a moment I think I see something – someone – up there between the leaves, but when I stop my bike to look there's nothing there. No oak tree, no fork in the road. Just the empty estate, the packed earth under my feet and the tunnel beneath it. I must be in some kind of shock still. I tell myself to get a grip and I move on.

I make my way towards the wall around the estate on foot and nearly crash into Rose, who is staring at the storm-drain tunnel, just like I was a moment ago.

'Rose?'

She shakes herself. 'I thought I saw . . .' she says, then trails off.

'Yeah,' I tell her. 'Me, too.'

'I was just on my way to find you.' She gives me a quick hug hello, even though we saw each other only a couple of hours ago. It's been a long day.

'Well, you found me,' I tell her, and she turns so we can walk on together. I stop her by touching her elbow.

'What is it?'

'I just . . .' I'm having a hard time figuring out what to say. It's been a really, really long day. 'I thought I lost you for a while back there. I guess I'm trying to say that I hope you're OK.'

Rose takes my hand. 'I thought I lost myself,' she says. 'But I think . . . I think I'll be OK. Eventually. How's Emily?'

I tell Rose everything Emily told me. Rose's smile is sweet and sad at the same time.

'I'm starting to like your sister more and more,' she says.

'Me, too,' I tell her. I wonder how much of me now understanding Emily would have happened anyway, and how much is not having been around Rose so much over the last week or so. I'm a bit different without her. A bit more open to other people. Like Emily. Like Rowan. Maybe it's the same for Rose. Maybe, if we hadn't had that distance, she never would have met Hazel.

It's as if she reads my thoughts. 'Do you think we can trust them?' she asks, like this morning. But the question is softer this time, as if she's already figured out the answer.

'Can we ever trust anyone really?' I say, trying to keep my voice light. 'With our hearts?'

Rose looks a lot more serious than I'm used to her being, but I suppose that's what change does. 'I've always trusted *you*,' she says.

I wrap one arm round her waist and walk with her towards the estate.

'I don't count,' I tell her. 'I'm your best friend. We're each other's only constants.' I think back to my mum in the kitchen, Emily by the back door. 'Besides our families.'

Rose laughs. 'Oh, my little breast wart,' she says, one perfect eyebrow raised. 'You *are* my family. Now go talk to that boy who's been eyeballing you for the last ten minutes.'

She pushes me towards Rowan and walks off towards the entrance of the Oak Road estate.

'Forget what I said,' I call after her. 'I think we can trust them. I think you can trust that lost heart of yours.' She waves a hand behind her back in reply.

I hop up on the wall beside Rowan, who doesn't stop playing when he says, 'I've decided to stay.'

'Oh, yeah?' I try to sound casual, but my heart jumps around at his words.

'Yeah.' He nods towards the estate. 'Turns out we own this house. Or our mum does anyway.'

'For real?'

'Yeah. My grandparents bought it for her when we were babies.'

I stare into the estate. 'Really? How did you find out?'

'Ivy,' Rowan says shortly. There's a small pause before he continues. 'She never told us,' he says when he has explained everything to me. 'She knew all along and she never said.'

I take a moment to consider my next words. 'Is it wrong that I don't blame her?' I ask him. 'I mean, I get why she'd want to keep you.' I blush beetroot. 'The two of you, I mean. You're like . . . family to her.' I trust in my expression not to give my thoughts away. Not to reveal what my mum just told me. 'I just mean I understand why she'd want to stay here for as long as she could.'

'I suppose,' Rowan says.

'Love makes you do really stupid stuff sometimes,' I say gently. 'And if it was only ever her and her mum for pretty much her whole life, maybe she doesn't quite have the . . . social skills the rest of us have.'

'Hazel and I aren't exactly the most sociable either,' Rowan agrees.

We stare out into the estate for a while, Rowan's fingers still strumming softly.

'So you think your mum's back?' I ask. 'That she's in town?'

Rowan nods once. 'It's going to be really weird,' he says. 'Seeing her again.' I put a hand on his shoulder and he leans backwards slightly into my touch. 'I'm not – me and Hazel, we're not gonna let ourselves believe she's changed until we see it. It's not enough that she's here. If she's here. I mean, we'll be OK either way. We're almost eighteen so we won't have to hide out for ever. I hope . . .' He trails off. 'But we'll get by either way.' I keep my hand on his shoulder. 'I guess this whole thing with Hazel and the spell has made it easier to let people go.'

'Yeah.' I think of Rose. 'I know.'

Soon we are joined by Rose and Hazel, quickly followed by Ivy. We all sit in a line on the wall and Hazel and Rose both take out identical bottles of bubbles.

'What happened to your cigarettes?' Rowan asks his sister.

She gives an insouciant shrug. 'I decided to quit.' She sends a flurry of bubbles matching Rose's floating over the estate and into the forest.

A little breeze rustles through the trees. Dry leaves and rubbish skitter along the wall at our feet. A small scrap of paper blows up and I catch it without thinking.

I recognize the paper. I recognize the handwriting. It's

the tail end of a diary entry, torn off, windswept, scuffed and wrinkled.

It's just one sentence. *How old is Mags Maguire and how long has she had that pub?*

Rowan puts his guitar down against the wall.

'It's Laurel's diary again,' he says. 'Your mum's, I mean.'

I pull the note Mum left me this morning out of the back pocket of my jeans. I hold it up and we all compare the handwriting.

'It's changed since she was our age,' I say in my defence. 'It's similar but different enough that I didn't recognize it.'

'What does it mean?' Ivy asks. *'How old is Mags Maguire and how long has she had that pub?'*

'Well,' I say, 'how old *is* she? How long *has* she had that pub? My nana said yesterday that a woman named Mags owned it when she was a girl. That she made poteen the old-fashioned way.'

Ivy looks unsure.

'Did your mum ever say what kind of great-aunt-type relative she was?' Rowan asks Ivy.

'Or how many greats?' Rose mutters.

'I don't know.' Ivy shrugs. 'She's never been sure herself.'

'Huh,' says Hazel.

'Huh indeed,' I say.

'What if she *did* leave the poteen out on purpose?' Rowan asks. 'For us, for Laurel. What if she knew about the spellbook?'

How old is Mags Maguire and how long has she had that pub?

What was it my nana said? *It's happened before and it will happen again. There's nothing you can do to stop it.* A thought pops into my head and comes out of my mouth before I can stop and rationalize it.

'What if Mags *wrote* the spellbook?'

'Huh,' Rowan says. 'The handwriting did look familiar . . .'

Ivy hops off the wall and runs into the house. She returns with a yellow Post-it note. The writing on it is old-fashioned, slanted and scratched. It says, *Eighteen across, seven down.*

We all bend over the note.

'I don't know,' I say. 'Maybe? Show us the spellbook and we'll compare.'

'It's gone,' says Hazel.

'What do you mean it's gone?'

'I mean it's gone. Disappeared. Lost.'

'That makes no sense.'

'Right,' says Rose. ''Cos so much of this made perfect sense already.'

We all laugh a little.

'It is weird, though,' Rowan says then. 'How Mags showed up just when Emily and Chloe needed her.'

Or how she was coincidentally around for whatever happened to Cathal. The same way that my mum said Mags was coincidentally around after what happened to

SPELLBOOK OF THE LOST AND FOUND

the boy who disappeared when she was my age. It almost sounded like Mum was wondering if Mags had something to do with it.

It's only now that I'm linking what my mum said earlier to what she wrote as Laurel in her diary. I keep having to remind myself that they're the same person. My mum and Laurel. For a while back there, when we all thought what was happening in the diary was happening right now, I thought that the missing boy was the one I woke up next to after the party. But it couldn't be. That boy has been dead for twenty-five years. My skin prickles into goose-flesh. Lost lives, lost souls, howling in the storm.

I realize I've been staring into space when Rowan touches my knee softly. 'Olive?' he says. I shake myself.

'Mags was probably just out for a drive,' I tell him. 'It was lucky.'

'Yeah,' he says. 'Definitely lucky.' His hand is warm on my knee.

I know we're all thinking that luck probably has very little to do with it. Just Mags, whoever she really is.

'Is Emily going to be OK?' Rowan asks.

I nod. 'They went to Doctor Driscoll, but there's nothing wrong. Rose's mum – she's our GP – has her convinced it was some kind of gas leak. She's going to be fine.'

A gas leak, or visions of lost souls in a forest that wasn't there. A flame, or a spark that went out before it caught fire. A spell, or things that get lost and found every day without us realizing it, until we start to notice.

Maybe a mix of both.

Rowan picks up his guitar and begins to sing. *'Hey Jude . . . take a sad song and make it better.'*

Out in the estate, the houses stand silent. Over by the rubble there's a scurrying of rats. A small dark shape comes darting out towards us and we jump, then relax when we see that it's a kitten. It's tiny, black and white, with a nick in each ear. Ivy approaches the cat with caution, and it lets itself be picked up and petted.

'So the spellbook is really gone,' I say. 'That's the end of the magic.'

'What?' says Ivy. 'Don't be silly. It's not just the spellbook. We're all magic. Magic's all around us, all the time.'

'Oh, come on,' I say. 'You don't come across an ancient spellbook every day.'

'You don't need to,' Ivy replies. 'There are spells everywhere. You cast a hundred a week without realizing.'

'I assure you,' I tell her, 'I do no such thing.'

'Knock on wood,' says Ivy.

'Superstition,' I reply.

The others watch in bemusement, as if we were a spectator sport.

'It's a spell,' Ivy insists. 'You say *Bless you* when somebody sneezes. That's a spell.'

I roll my eyes. 'It's a common courtesy.'

'You drink ginger tea with lemon and honey before you even have a cold. You take baths when you feel tense.'

I say, 'Ivy—' but she's not done yet.

'Your parents are married, right? Saying *I do* is a magic spell. They're just words like every other word, but said in a ritual, with intent, it's a spell. *Something old, something new, something borrowed, something blue.* When they named you, it was a spell. When they let you pick flowers and keep dried leaves, it was a spell. Your dolls came to life because of your spells. Your invisible friend. Your dreams. The way you write your initials and somebody else's in hearts all over your notebooks. What is that if not a love spell?'

I don't even try to stop her now, but I can't help picturing my mum's Claddagh ring, the collection of things like talismans above my bed, the words written on our arms in marker.

'You cast spells every day. Your make-up is glamour magic. Hiding and highlighting. The clothes you pick out to make your legs look longer, your waist smaller. The red you wear for confidence; the black when you're sad, the blue for clarity. Your favourite bra. Your lucky socks. The way you take an hour on your hair. It's a ritual. It's never just about clothes, or make-up, or perfectly messy buns. It's about magic.'

I touch my hair self-consciously. All this cycling has downgraded my bun from perfectly messy to bird's nest.

I reach into my bag to find some pins to try and tame it and I come out with my charm bracelet. I stare.

What is that if it's not magic?

'Embrace the unexplained, Olive,' Rowan says to me with a grin.

Rose laughs low, her hand in Hazel's. 'Embrace the uncertain,' she adds. We share a secret smile.

'Embrace the magic,' Ivy breathes. Hazel produces a marker from who knows where and writes the words on our arms.

I click my charm bracelet into place on my other wrist, over the words that are faded now, almost illegible: *never be found*. Next to the little olive tree charm is one that wasn't there when I lost it: a medal of St Anthony.

Not all losses are bad, Rowan said to me the other night. Maybe we need to lose some things to make room for others. The everyday things we let go of so we can move on with a lighter load. Rose was right: if you don't get lost, you'll never be found.

It's like my mother said: everybody's lost something. They may not know it, but everyone's got their defining loss: a parent, a pet, a trinket, a treasure, a memory, a belief. Some people have more than one. And if you're not careful you can spend your whole life looking for what you've lost.

But the truth is we're always losing something. Every day stray hairs fall from our fringes; we discard fingernail clippings; we shed skin. We're all made up of all of it: of longing, of belonging, and of all the things we lose along the way.

What have I lost?

Beside me, Rowan flicks his lighter open, then clicks it shut again. When he catches me looking, he smiles.

What have I found?

Ivy perches on the wall like a little blue-haired bird, watching over us. Hazel threads her key on to a length of silver string. It hangs strange and pretty around her neck.

What have I kept?

Rose picks up her bottle of bubbles and blows a bunch up in the air.

They don't pop or float away. They just stay there, still and shining, right above our heads.

Cryptic Crossword of the
Lost and Found

CRYPTIC CROSSWORD OF THE LOST AND FOUND

Across

8 His partner was old one, cold and brave (6)

9 May a sign lead you to the training grounds (8)

10 Quick! You lose your case if this is shown up (4)

11 Strangely need credit to have been a go-between (10)

12 Sounds like a couple of sexist jokes (3,3)

14 A lost 24 across and one quiet ingenious type (8)

15 Mal seems to have lost his meaning in French (5,10)

18 You'd lose your life if you met two donkeys around Ulster (8)

20 Lessor could end up with nothing (6)

22 The organization demands the worker to be nasty (10)

24 Sounds like the only fish in the sea has the blues (4)

25 To slip on the boots that have been shaved around the garden tool (8)

26 You've lost control when the umpire takes back the Spanish cross (6)

Down

1 Lose the ties of bondage in a no-honey zone (2,4)

2 Left nothing on the street with 24 across, damned (4)

3 The accountant reversed your passport into a coin and crash! (8)

4 Start last Guinness before time is called an open society (1,1,1,1)

5 Proves Moïra drops a rose off the top of her head (6)

6 Confused stalker awe is lost down 14 down (5,5)

7 Strange silence to the east leads to one who sells alcohol (8)

13 Peels back up a loud Henry to start nodding off (4,6)

14 What a waste to raid a direction (5)

16 Sound like the alcohol was missing in the basin (8)

17 I lost Ray for a hard stretch (8)

19 Salt is fashionable in this (6)

21 Lose the way without this in crazy outer-space starter (6)

23 Tina isn't wrong (4)

24 It's OK to lose your jewellery if you crack this (4)

Acknowledgements

A hundred million thank-yous to:

Maman for the advice and the character psychology sessions; Dad for the crossword clues and the loan of books about Irish trees; Kevin and Thomas for the puns and quotes; Claire, *circa* 2003, for the teen-girl-bedroom aesthetic; Claire, *circa* 2016, for the first chapter read-throughs and critical feedback; my entire family for being the perfect sounding-board, and for never-ending lists of lost things; Trish, Barry and Lorraine for patron-saint medal consultations; pretty much all my friends for answering very specific questions on Facebook; Elsa and Luna for reminding me, with their collections of random objects, about the importance of trinkets and shrines; Trish and Barry, Maman and Dad, Claire, Kevin, Thomas and Erin, and of course Joan for minding the girls; and finally Alan for the bright ideas, the plot-hole excavations, the right wording, the slightly different paths for the story to take, the hearing-aid troubleshooting advice, the shoulder to cry on, the suggestions of takeaway, the cups of tea or glasses of whiskey depending on what he felt was needed – and for eight years of love.

Thanks also to Etta Monahan's father (presumably Mr Monahan), who woke his children by loudly reciting Thomas Gray's 'Elegy Written in a Country Churchyard' every morning before school – an anecdote Etta once shared with Alan that I then borrowed and adapted for Olive's dad.

Another hundred million thank-yous to:

Claire Wilson for the deadline peptalks, the lack-of-sleep commiseration, the fresh pair of eyes, the constant support; Rosie Price for answering a million questions and concerns; Natalie Doherty and Kathy Dawson for the amazing editorial feedback, the two-hour-long plot-detangling phone calls, the belief in this book, and mostly for taking the mess of a manuscript I sent them and, with great skill and careful magic, bringing out everything I meant to say all along; Harriet Venn for being the most wonderful train-platform-running, buggy-pushing, box-and-bag-hauling, book-tour-with-a-baby-embracing, unbelievably organized publicist the world has ever seen; Wendy Shakespeare and Jane Tait for the brilliant copy-editing and for accepting the inconsistency of Hiberno-English; Maeve Banham for sending my books all over the world; Claire Evans, Julia McCarthy and the ever-amazing team at Penguin Young Readers US; and the always-incredible team at Penguin Random House Children's UK for making a book out of a whole bunch of my words.

The poems, song and passages quoted and mentioned in this book are: 'The Stolen Child' by W. B. Yeats (pages 23 and 24); 'The Last Rose of Summer' by Thomas Moore (pages 42 and 43); 'The Rime of the Ancient Mariner' by Samuel Taylor Coleridge (page 88); 'A Hazel Stick for Catherine Ann' by Seamus Heaney (page 132); 'Delta' by Adrienne Rich (page 152); 'One Art' by Elisabeth Bishop (pages 184 and 185); 'All That Is Gold Does Not Glitter' by J. R. R. Tolkien (page 251); 'An End' by Christina Rossetti (page 351); 'Hey Jude' by the Beatles (page 377); and *On the Road* by Jack Kerouac (pages 125 and 305).

The spell to call up lost things was inspired by real spells found in *The Element Encyclopaedia of 5000 Spells* by Judika Illes. Tree names and folklore are all taken directly from two books: *Into the Forest: An Anthology of Tree Poems*, edited by Mandy Haggith, and *Irish Trees: Myths, Legends and Folklore* by Niall Mac Coitir. However, Ivy is mistaken when she says that ash trees are a close relation to the rowan (or mountain ash). Although they share a name, the two trees are not actually related at all. Also, Hazel is mistaken when she says that William Faulkner coined the phrase *kill your darlings*. It's a common misattribution and, although no one is quite sure whose quote it is, it's generally traced back to Sir Arthur Quiller-Couch, who gave a lecture in Cambridge in 1914 on writing style, in which he said to *murder your darlings*. Which would also have been a fitting tattoo.

The Cryptic Crossword of the Lost and Found was created by my dad, for which I am heart-warmed and so grateful – even if it's far too hard for me to solve. For crossword information and solutions, please visit www. moirafowleydoyle.com/spellbook/crossword.

An Interview
with Moïra Fowley-Doyle

How did the idea for *Spellbook of Lost and Found* come about?

The idea for this book didn't come all at once, neatly pre-packaged and delivered on my doorstep. Fittingly, it came in scraps of found thoughts, snippets of plans, sprinkles of salvaged suggestions. I knew I wanted to write about lost things and findings: a book built on the bones of that idea. I didn't really know anything else.

When I start to write I go in blind. I have a central thought, I have a couple of characters, and I have what I call my vignette: a small collection of unrelated ideas, snippets and snapshots, thoughts and miscellany, set up like a little shrine. If the idea is the bones, the characters are the heart, and the vignette makes up most of the major organs. After that, in theory, all I need's a bit of lightning and my story-creature lives.

When I set out to write *Spellbook*, this is what I had: poteen and patron saints; summer rain and flooded fields and the forest; a spellbook; a bonfire; tattoos and rusty keys. I had a list of lost things. I had Olive and Rose, Hazel, Rowan and Ivy, even though their names weren't the same. I had the idea that I wanted to write about longing, belonging, and all the things you lose along the way. I don't know how I had these lists and thoughts and snippets; I'm not sure where they came from. I suppose I just found them lying around inside my own personal lost and found.

Can you tell us about a significant lost or found from your own life?

I never met my maternal grandmother's grandmother, but by all accounts she was a formidable woman. The first female schoolteacher in her small, rural French town in the late 1800s, she was once insulted by the local priest who told her that women weren't fit to be teachers. In response, she smacked him across the face. Smarmily, the priest retorted that, just like Jesus, he would turn the other cheek.

'Oh, you do?' she said to him, and so she smacked his other cheek just as hard.

This particular family legend is just as infamous as my great-great-grandmother's large feet (which inspired her nickname, *Berthe aux Grands Pieds*, 'Bertha of the big feet') and the enormous rings she wore on every finger. When she died, these rings – huge semi-precious stones held in place by small silver claws – went to her daughter, my great-grandmother, who passed away when I was fifteen. She knew I always loved wearing big rings. She left me one of Berthe's. The smallest one, the amethyst one, the one Berthe wore on her pinkie, was a giant on my right ring finger.

For two years I wore my great-great grandmother's ring every day, until the day, somehow, I lost it.

I was heartbroken. I searched everywhere. I tore my room apart. I scoured the whole house. I emptied my school locker and retraced my steps, but it was gone. My grandmother, who had been left the rest of Berthe's rings when my great-grandmother died, knowing how upset I was, gave me another of the rings. I never took it off to wash my hands again; I kept it in a special box by my bed when I slept.

Every time I thought of lost things, I thought about that ring. When I moved out of my parents' house, I removed every bookshelf from the walls of my old bedroom, I tore off the skirting boards, I stuck knitting needles between the floorboards, to no avail. I took the last boxes of my teenage things into my new home and I mourned the ring I was still hoping to find.

A few years later, my husband, Alan, and I were clearing out our old things and decluttering the house after having our first baby. I'd filled boxes full of stuff I'd never really used or didn't need any more to bring to charity shops. Alan was about to take everything out to the car when he noticed that there was a tiny pocket inside an old picnic bag in the oldest of the boxes. He opened the pocket. The ring was inside. It had been there for ten years. If it hadn't been for a chance check, I would have lost it for ever.

I wear Berthe's rings every day and they remind me that I come from a long line of strong and formidable women. And that one in particular reminds me to trust in luck – and to always check the pockets.

Do you have any particular writing habits?

I can write anywhere, at any time, on anything. The first draft of this book was written in the notes app on my phone, scribbled on scrap paper, in notebooks, on napkins, on my skin. Bits and thoughts pinned down before they could melt away from memory. I wrote in bed and on my couch, in the car on long journeys, on buses and planes and trains. I wrote while my toddler napped, while I nursed my baby at 3 a.m. I wrote bits on my hands at the queue for the supermarket till and dictated whole chapters to my phone while pushing the pram in the park. Sometimes these are the only writing habits you can have as a parent.

Because I wrote so much of this book with two very small children, it took a while for me to settle enough to learn my own writing habits. I've learned that I can write anywhere, at any time, on anything. I've also learned that I'd often rather not.

These days I write on my laptop at a desk in my office, with coffee in the morning and tea in the afternoon. I stick notes to self around the screen for when I need them. I listen to the same quiet, wordless music on repeat, from playlists with names like 'Calm Down and Get Some Work Done, Moïra'. I burn lavender or tea-tree oil. I take breaks to stretch, to pull a couple of tarot cards, to pet the cat, to read a poem. My writing habits involve calm and space, because a lot of the time writing's about getting in so deep you've barely got your mouth above water. It's important to ground and centre. It's important to remember to breathe. You can swim a lot deeper that way.

Apart from your editors and agent, do you share your work with anyone else during the writing process?

Because my first drafts are always rough and rushed, I tend not to share them widely. They're the blueprints, the pencil sketches. When I wrote my first novel, *The Accident Season*, I shared the first draft with my sister, Claire. She read it on her phone on the Tube commuting to and from work and she re-read the whole thing in later drafts too. She read the first few chapters of *Spellbook* and gave me great critical feedback, but the only person who read this one the whole way through, from first to final draft, was my husband, Alan. He saw every change and transformation, he asked questions and made suggestions. I dedicated *The Accident Season* most especially to Claire. I dedicated *Spellbook* to Alan.

Which other authors have inspired you?

I've loved magic realism since before I knew what it was. I read everything by David Almond as a child and the way he melded fact and fantasy felt truer to life to me than ordinary contemporary fiction. I suppose I've never had the firmest grip on reality. Then as a teenager I read the Weetzie Bat books by Francesca Lia Block and they were like a glitzy mirror, little life-savers. Like Almond, Block takes the everyday and makes it magical, finds the spark of mystery in the mundane, makes the ordinary extraordinary. I've always thought that life's a little like that, and finding fiction that reflected this was a revelation. After that I read the pioneers of magic realism, which originated in South America: Gabriel Garcia Marquez, Isabelle Allende. I fell in love with their sprawling family sagas, their mystery, their folklore, their magic. I read books that balanced the dark and the dreamy, the beautiful and the disquieting, books by Neil Gaiman and Helen Oyeyemi, by Kate Atkinson and Jeanette Winterson. I read and still reread these authors and will never not be awed and inspired by their words.

Do you really believe in magic?
I believe in magic realism. I believe in the blurriness between reality and fantasy. Mostly, I believe in story. I read tarot cards not as divination, but as a way to check in with my subconscious, as a way to tell myself the stories I secretly need to hear. I light candles and burn oils and keep crystals in my pockets as reminders. Little notes to self to stay present, to focus, to direct my energy. I cast small spells because I believe in the power of ritual as grounding, as mindfulness, as a way to give meaning in small actions. As a way to connect to the world around me.

Maybe that isn't magic. Maybe it's only smoke and mirrors, maybe it's superstition, maybe it's just looking up at the moon too much. Maybe it's all just a story. But maybe that's all kind of the same thing. I believe in finding the magic in the mundane, the extraordinary in the ordinary, the little slivers of mystery stuck into the cracks of the world.

Read on
for an extract from
Moïra Fowley-Doyle's debut novel,

THE ACCIDENT SEAS•N

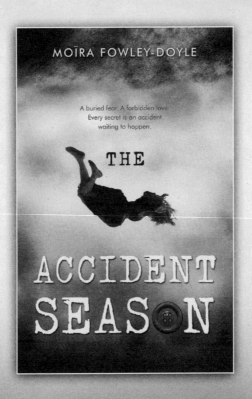

MOÏRA FOWLEY-DOYLE

A buried fear. A forbidden love.
Every secret is an accident
waiting to happen.

THE

ACCIDENT
SEAS•N

So let's raise our glasses to the accident season,
To the river beneath us where we sink our souls,
To the bruises and secrets, to the ghosts in the ceiling,
One more drink for the watery road.

When I heard Bea chant the words it was as if little insects were crawling in under my spine, ready to change it. I was going to crack and bend, become something other. Our temples were sweating under our masks but we didn't take them off. It felt like they had become part of our skins.

The fire broke and moaned in the middle of the room and the arches above the doors whispered. I don't know how I knew that Sam's eyes were closed or that Alice had a cramp in her side. I only knew that I was everyone. I was Alice with her mouth half open, maybe in excitement or fear; I was Sam with his hands in fists; I was Bea swaying in front of us all, her red dress soaked with sweat; and I was me, Cara, feeling like I was coming out of my skin. Bea's feet struck drum beats on the wooden floor. Her words grew louder. Soon we were all moving and the floorboards were shaking the ceiling downstairs. Wine flew from our glasses and dropped on the floor like blood.

When we stamped around the fire in the remains of the master bedroom we woke something up. Maybe it was something inside us; the mysterious something that connects every bone of our spines, or that keeps our teeth stuck to the insides of our mouths. Maybe it was something between us; something in the air or in the flames that wound around us. Or maybe it was the house itself; the ghosts between the walls or the memories clicked inside every lock, the stories between the cracks in the floorboards. We were going to break into pieces, we were going to be sawn in two and reappear whole again, we were going to dodge the magician's knife and swing on the highest ride. In the ghost house in the last days of the accident season, we were never going to die.

1.

Elsie is in all my pictures. I know this because I have looked through all the pictures of me and my family taken in the last seventeen years and she is in them all.

I only noticed this last night, clearing six months' worth of pictures off my phone. She is in the locker room at lunch time. She hovers at the corner of the frame on school tours. She is in every school play. I thought: *What a coincidence, Elsie's in all my photos.* Then, on a hunch, I looked through the rest of the photos on my computer. And the ones glued into my diaries. And in my family photo albums. Elsie is in them all.

She turns her back to the camera at birthday parties. She is on family holidays and walks along the coast. A hint of her even appears in windows and mirrors in the zoomed-in background of pictures taken at home: an elbow here, an ankle there, a lock of her hair.

Is there really such a thing as coincidence? *This* much of a coincidence?

Elsie is not my friend. Elsie is nobody's friend, really. She's just that girl who talks too softly and stands too close, who you used to be sort of friends with when you were eight and your father'd just died but who mostly got left behind with the rag dolls and tea sets and other relics of childhood.

I've put a representative sample of seventy-two pictures taken in the last few years onto my phone to show to Bea before class. I want to ask her if she thinks there's something really strange going on or if the world really *is* so small that someone can turn up in all of another person's photographs.

I haven't shown the photos to Sam yet. I don't know why.

In the older pictures, my house looks like a cartoon house: no cars in the driveway, coloured curtains framing the windows in hourglass shapes, a cloud of smoke attached to the chimney like white candyfloss or cotton wool. A seven-year-old me playing Snatch the Bacon with Alice on the road in front of it. And there, at the side of the frame, a leg, the hem of a tartan skirt and the heel of the type of sensible brown shoe that Elsie always wears.

Those pictures were taken a decade ago; this morning there is no cotton-wool smoke coming from the chimney, and the hourglass curtains of the sitting room frame the image of my mother hopping on one leg as she tries to wrestle a boot onto her other foot. Alice, outside, stamps her own feet impatiently. She stalks up to the window and raps on the glass, telling our mother to get a move on. Sam laughs from the hallway, invisible in the morning sun that casts everything past the front door in shadow. I push my fists deeper into my pockets and look up at the sky. There are a few wisps of cloud just hanging there mirroring me, leaning against the side of the car.

Alice is my sister. She is one year older and a million years wiser, or so she'd like to believe (and she may be right; how should I know? I am hardly wise). Sam is my ex-stepbrother, which is a mouthful to say, but as our parents are divorced he isn't technically my brother any more. His father was married to my mother until he disappeared four years ago. He ran off with a biological anthropologist and spends his time studying gibbons in the rainforests of Borneo. Sam has been living with us for seven years now so I suppose to all intents and purposes he is my brother, but mostly he's just Sam, standing tall in the shade of the hallway, dark hair falling in his eyes.

Knowing that getting everyone into the car will take some time, I take my hands out of my pockets and pull out my phone again. I flip through the photos for the third time this morning, playing Spot-the-Elsie like in those *Where's Wally?* books.

I'd never realized that Elsie always looks worried. Frown lines crease her forehead and her mouth makes a little pout. Even her hair looks worried, somehow, when her head is turned. That's quite an accomplishment. I wonder what my hair looks like when my head is turned. The back of my head is not something I see very often; unlike Elsie, I pose when a photo is being taken, and smile.

When Alice's head is turned (when, for example, she is

banging on the front-room window for the twentieth time to hurry my mother, who has forgotten something – her phone, her bag, her head – and has gone back upstairs to fetch it) her hair looks severe. It is dyed two shades lighter than her natural blonde, always right to the roots, perfectly straightened, tightly wound into one of those make-a-bun hair grips and stuck with two sticks. Alice has don't-mess-with-me hair.

My mother's hair is purple. It tumbles down her shoulders in unbrushed waves as she drives, and swings when she shakes her head. Strands of it stick to her lip gloss; she spits them out as she speaks. Today, she has painted her nails the same colour. If it were any other time of year on this drive to school she'd be reaching across to Alice in the passenger seat or fixing her hair, licking the tip of her finger to smooth the edges of her eye make-up or drinking from a flask of coffee like some people drag on a cigarette, but it's coming up to the end of October and Alice fell down the stairs last night, so my mother grips the steering wheel with white-knuckled, purple-nailed hands and doesn't take her eyes off the road. She wouldn't have driven us but she's convinced walking is more dangerous.

'How's your head feeling, honey?' she asks Alice. It's the thirty-second time she's asked that this morning (the eighty-ninth since coming home from the hospital last night). Sam marks another line on his hand in red biro. Every time my mother asks this question, Alice's mouth gets smaller and smaller.

Sam leans over and whispers in my ear. 'Bet you a tenner Alice screams before a hundred.' I hold my hand out to be shaken. Sam's grip is firm and warm. I silently urge Alice to hold on until we get to school.

'You all have your gloves, right?' my mother is saying. 'And, Sam, I'll write you a note for chemistry. Are you all warm enough? You did take your vitamins this morning, didn't you?'

'Sure, Melanie,' Sam says to my mother. He grins at me. Alice will never last under this onslaught. My mother chances the tiniest peek at her before hurriedly looking back at the road. Alice is carefully tying a silk scarf to hide the bandage around her head. She has darkened her eyes with kohl so the bruise on the side of her face seems less severe. She looks like a storybook fortune-teller in a school uniform.

We come to the intersection before the school. My mother's hair whips round as she frantically tries to look every way at once before crossing the light traffic. We crawl past at a snail's pace. The other drivers sound their horns.

When she has parked, my mother cracks her knuckles and shakes out her hands. She takes off her sunglasses and gives us each a packed lunch. 'Now, you will be careful, won't you?' She squeezes Alice's shoulder affectionately. 'How's your head feeling, honey?'

Alice's lips disappear. She gives a short, wordless scream without looking at our mother, and storms out of the car and into the main school building. I slump back in my seat.

'Cough it up, sister,' Sam cackles.

When we've got out of the car I reluctantly hand over a tenner. We wave my mother goodbye and she drives carefully away. 'I'm not your sister,' I remind him.

Sam drapes an arm over my shoulders. 'If you say so, *petite sœur*,' he says.

I sigh and shake my head. 'I know that means sister, Sam. We're in the same French class.'

When Sam heads for his locker to get the books for his first class, I go find my best friend in the main school building.

Bea is sitting at the back of the library, her tarot cards spread out on the desk in front of her. She likes to read the cards every morning, so she can know what kind of day she's getting into. Bea doesn't like surprises. It wouldn't surprise her to know that the small group of third years sitting a few desks away from her are snickering and whispering behind her back, so I don't draw her attention to them. Anyway, I'm half convinced Bea can give the evil eye to anyone who insults her.

I take one of my two pairs of gloves off my uncomfortably warm hands (it's not the weather for hats and gloves but my mother wouldn't let us out of the house without them) and pull up the chair behind me to face Bea across the little desk. I rest my chin on the chair back in front of me.

'Elsie is in all my pictures,' I tell her.

Bea and I automatically look across the library towards the window. Usually by this time in the morning Elsie will have opened up her secrets booth for the day. The youngest are always the first to come to her, before the bell rings for assembly, before the caretaker opens the locker rooms and the librarian comes out of her office to tell us to get to class. They come one at a time, type up their secrets on Elsie's antique typewriter and shuffle out of the library, heads bowed, pretending to be engrossed in the contents of their school bags. Elsie's box gets fuller and fuller with the things that can't be said. She isn't here this morning, though. Maybe she's running late.

Bea turns back to me. 'What do you mean?'

I take out my phone and show it to her. I point out the mousy hair, the sensible shoes, the worry lines on the brow of every Elsie in every photograph.

Bea takes a long time over the photos. Finally she looks up. Her eyebrows are drawn together and her mouth's a thin line. 'Cara, this is . . .' She shakes her head slightly.

'A little weirder than usual?' I rest the tips of my fingers against my forehead and close my eyes. Bea reads tarot cards and lights candles for ghosts. She talks about magic being all around us and laughs when our classmates call her a witch. But this is different.

Bea goes through the photos again, scrolling, stopping, tapping the screen and peering close.

'Do you think it's real?' I say to her from behind my hands. 'Or do you think I'm crazy? Please don't say both.'

Bea doesn't say anything. Instead, she shuffles her cards and lays them out slowly one by one on the desk between us. She looks down at the cards, and up at me, and back at the cards again. When she finally looks back at me she's wearing an expression I haven't seen in a long time.

She takes in my woolly hat, my remaining pair of gloves under the pair I just took off, the thick leggings I'm wearing as well as tights under my uniform skirt, the plaster on my finger, the sprain support around my wrist, the vague aroma of echinacea and anxiety following me around like a strange sad cloud.

Bea sighs and nods; she understands.

It's the accident season, the same time every year. Bones break, skin tears, bruises bloom. Years ago my mother tried to lock us all up, pad the hard edges of things with foam and gauze, cover us in layers of jumpers and gloves, ban sharp objects and open flames. We camped out together in the living room for eight days, until the carefully ordered takeaway food – delivered on the doorstep and furtively retrieved by my mother, who hadn't thought how she would cook meals without the help of our gas oven – gave us all food poisoning and we spent the next twenty-four hours in hospital. Now every autumn we stock up on bandages and painkillers; we buckle up, we batten down. We never leave the house without at least three protective layers. We're afraid of the accident season. We're afraid of how easily accidents turn into tragedies. We have had too many of those already.

'Alice fell down the stairs last night,' I tell her. 'All the way from the top. Her head cracked on the banister rail on the way down. She said it sounded like a gunshot in a film, only duller.'

'Oh God.'

'There was no one in the house. They said at the hospital that she had concussion so we had to keep her awake, walk her round and round.'

Bea's eyes are wide. 'Is she OK?'

'She's fine now. Mum didn't want us to come to school today but Alice insisted.' I take off my hat and shake out my hair, then try to smooth it down. Unlike Alice, I don't dye my hair (also unlike Alice, I amn't blonde), and it's too short to straighten, so my perpetually-growing-out pixie cut sticks up in fluffy brown spikes whenever I wear hats.

Bea covers my hands with hers. The pinkie of her right hand loops through the wool of the hat I'm holding. 'Why didn't you call me?' she asks; then, as if to answer her own question, she looks back down at the cards. She clears her throat, as if she's hesitating before she speaks. Then she says it. 'I think . . . It's going to be a bad one, Cara.' She tries to look me in the eye but I stare down at her cards instead. It takes a minute for me to answer.

'How bad?'

Bea touches my gloved hand gently. She says it softly. 'One of the worst.' She turns one of the cards to face me. On it there is a figure on a bed being pierced by swords. I shiver. My knee knocks into one of the desk's legs and I feel a sharp pain. When I look down I see that my leggings and tights have been ripped by a huge nail sticking out of the wood. A few drops of blood collect around the edges of the tear. I can feel my eyes start to fill.

Bea gets up and wraps her arms around me. She smells like cigarettes and incense. 'It'll be OK,' she whispers into my ear. 'We'll make sure nothing happens to you. I promise. We can change this. And I don't think you're going crazy. We'll talk to Elsie. It doesn't look like she's in school today, but we'll talk to her together tomorrow. It'll be OK.'

I squash down the panicky feeling rising in my throat and take a packet of pirate-print tissues out of my school bag. I blot the blood off my leggings, trying to move my wrist as little as possible. I don't remind Bea that something's already happened to me, even if it's just cut skin from a nail and a sprained wrist getting out of the car last night. It's always like this: things happen and things keep happening, and things get worse and worse. I look back across the library at where Elsie's secrets booth usually is. The empty desk is like a missing tooth.

Praise for *The Accident Season*

'A magical debut that you will devour'
Guardian

'Eerie and edgy, dark and intense . . .
You'll read it in a single breathless sitting'
Bookseller

'Months after reading Moïra Fowley-Doyle's stunning
debut, I am still blown away . . . One of the best books
I've read in years. An exquisite story – the kind to
win awards, top bestseller lists, and become the
obsession of book lovers everywhere'
Publishers Weekly

'Beautifully crafted and atmospheric . . .
Readers will be swept away'
Booklist

'*The Accident Season* is brilliant'
Holly Black, author of *The Spiderwick Chronicles*

'Compelling'
The Times